THE FIREMASTER'S LEGACY

The Kyprian Prophecy Series

Beginnings – An Origins Novella

The Earth King's Heir – Book 0

The Firemaster's Legacy – Book 1

The Water Catcher's Rise – Book 2

The Air King's Return – Book 3

The Ice Queen's Revenge – Book 4

Other Series

Fae of the Crystal Palace

Anthologies Featuring Kylie Fennell

Lighthouse

Forbidden Doors

Stories of Survival

First Peoples Shared Stories

THE FIREMASTER'S LEGACY

THE KYPRIAN PROPHECY BOOK 1

KYLIE FENNELL

Published by Lorikeet Ink, Brisbane (Yuggera and Turrbal Country), Australia. The publisher acknowledges the Aboriginal and Torres Strait Islander peoples – the Traditional Custodians of the lands on which we live and work.

www.lorikeetink.com

First published in Australia in 2021.

ISBN 978-0-6488769-2-2 (eBook)

ISBN 978-0-6488769-3-9 (paperback)

A catalogue record for this book is available from the National Library of Australia.

Cover design by Jo Edgar-Baker

Maps by Dewi Hargreaves

Author photo by Marissa Powell

Ornamental break icon by Freepik via Flaticon.com

For Nathan and Arty

Thank you for the magic and the mayhem x

NORTHEM
Arykyl
ISLAND OF KYPRIA
THE KYPRIAN SEA
KENGIA
Lochlen
LAMORE
Obira City
ETTE
IVANE
The Capital
Nadis
THE
KYPRIAN NATIONS

KYPRIAN SEA

LAMORE

KENGIA

NYMOI ALPS

Shizen Falls
Ulph Festival
Shizen Lake
Riverend Falls
Fisherman's Hut
King's Forest

LAKEFORD

Talbot

Lakelands Road

Lamore River

Dunhin Village

Iveness

LOWLANDS

King's Road

Calliope

King's School
Smuggler's Gate
City Gate
Lion's Den Tavern
Market
Apothecary

OBIRA CITY

Obira Port

Lamore Castle

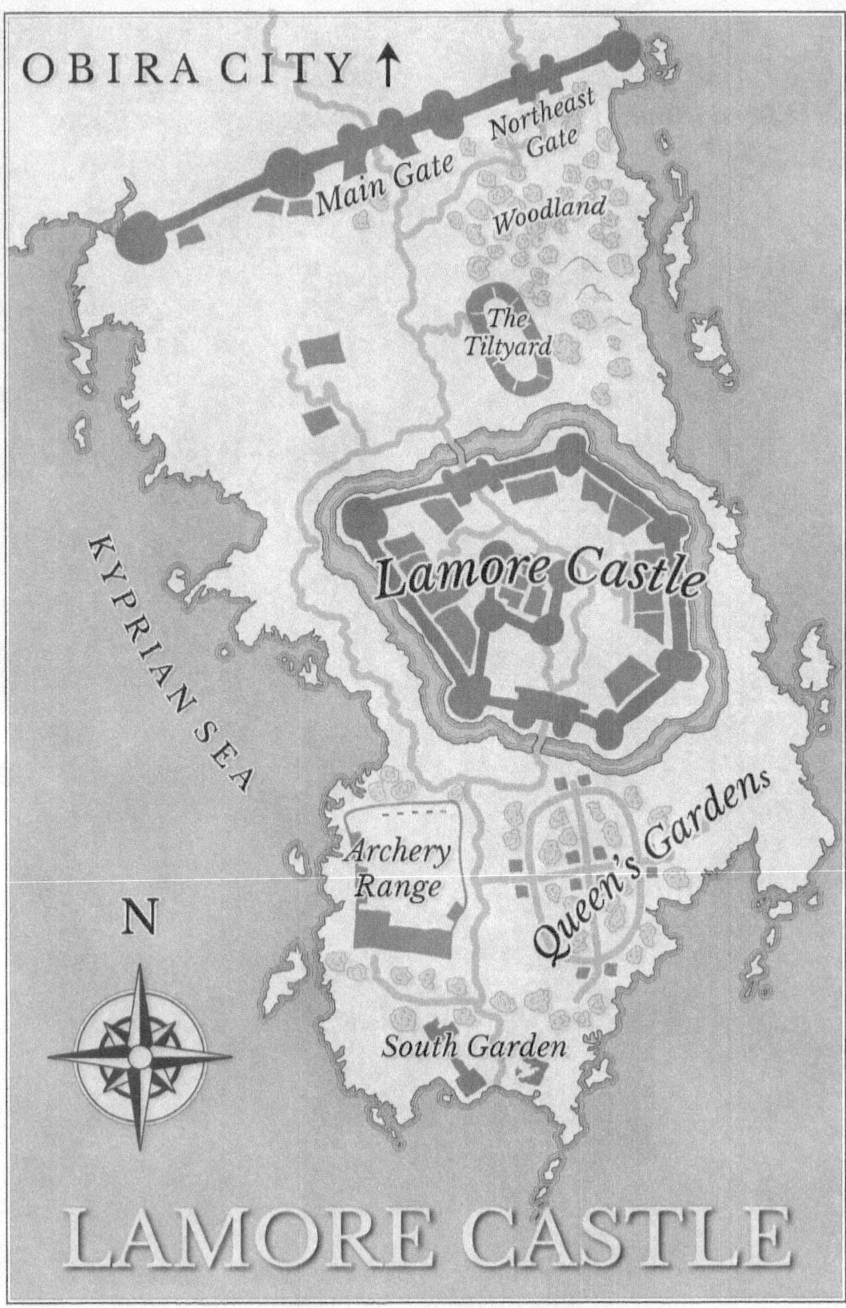

OBIRA CITY ↑
Main Gate
Northeast Gate
Woodland
The Tiltyard
KYPRIAN SEA
Lamore Castle
Archery Range
Queen's Gardens
South Garden
N
LAMORE CASTLE

Darkness and defeat, a King is to blame;
A regime must fall for everything to change.

Heed the three signs by looking to the skies:
The first will be seen in a blood moon's rise.

On the brink of war, the next is firesky:
Promises of destruction, many sure to die.

An empire's fate uncertain, until comes the third:
A catcher of water. Kengia's firstborn returned.

Hopes will be tested; some will be betrayed.
Fire or water — the choice must be made.

— Old Kyprian prophecy

PROLOGUE

Hope is for fools and the damned.

Arisa was eleven-and-three-quarters when she vowed she would be neither.

It was the first time they came for her. It was the day she learnt that being Kengian and one of the silver-eyes was the surest path to death. And it was the day she knew for sure that the Water Catcher would never come.

The silver sun was high in the sky casting welcome beams of shimmering light into the shadows made by the school's high stone walls. The cherry blossom tree sighed as it surrendered its last flower. Arisa watched with a dreamy smile as the white petals floated through the crisp wintry air and landed at her feet.

'Arisa.' Rea cast an accusatory glance at her. 'Are you watching?'

She turned to her friend, who was standing perfectly poised on one leg in the hopscotch square. 'I'm watching.'

Rea nodded and tossed her chestnut braids back over her

shoulders. She screwed up her mouth in concentration and threw the stone along the line of squares marked out in the playground dirt. It fell just outside a space three places ahead of where Rea stood. She pouted for a moment, before scrunching her eyes shut and reaching out with her left hand. Her fingers glowed, and with the tiniest flick of her wrist, she sent the stone catapulting until it came to rest neatly in the middle of the square.

'Ha!' Rea clapped her hands in delight and looked back at Arisa with a grin. 'Did you see that?'

Arisa should have smiled and said yes, but she couldn't share Rea's enthusiasm. It wasn't just the fact that she was nearly three years older, so had outgrown many of the games Rea liked to play. It was because a jolt of fear had coursed through her when Rea had used forbidden magic. She was scared for her friend – her only friend.

Their friendship had been instantaneous when Rea had arrived at the King's School. Arisa had been drawn to the girl with the glittering silver eyes. They were kindred spirits – each of them an outsider. Arisa was the lowborn orphan and ward of an eccentric healer, at a school reserved mainly for the nobility. Rea was a Kengian. Part of a people displaced from their homeland, only tolerated for their uncanny ability to nurture crops in the barren land of Lamore. Being a Kengian made Rea a pariah in Obira City, and a source of admiration for Arisa – especially given Arisa's guardian made her hide her identity.

Rea had left her farming family outside the city's gates and was boarding at the school, but she still embraced her Kengian heritage and beliefs. Arisa had never been beyond Obira City's walls. Her guardian, Erun, wanted to keep her close to him. He said it was the only way to keep her safe. So she had never met anyone who lived openly as a Kengian – until she'd met Rea.

The way Rea lived was admirable and terrifying at the same time. Arisa asked her hundreds of questions about her powers.

Rea shared her language, her traditions, her Kengian affinity with nature. Arisa was spellbound by tales of the nation cut off from Lamore, and of its people. Rea was her teacher, and Arisa was Rea's protector. But every time Rea used her powers in the schoolyard, Arisa's job got exponentially harder.

Rea tilted her head, as if trying to read her mind. 'Let's play something else. You can pick.'

'It's alright. You choose.'

Rea's dazzling smile returned. 'Let's chase each other. I'll be the Water Catcher and you can be the evil king and try and get me.'

A cold gust of wind manifested from nowhere, sending shivers up Arisa's spine. She could have sworn she heard the word *'shhh'* whispered on the breeze.

Kengians who defied the King's rule were routinely sent to the dungeons under Lamore Castle, never to be seen again, or else ended up hanging from the gallows. But something even more disturbing had been occurring in recent days. There had been stories of silver-eyes being taken from their homes in the night – permanently vanishing. It wasn't just silver-eyes, either. Kengians who hadn't defied the King's rule but openly practised traditional customs had also been targeted. And it was rumoured that anyone who openly sympathised with the Kengians would be next.

Erun had implored Arisa to temper her outspoken tendencies and not to publicly support the Kengian cause. He knew she would never distance herself from Rea, so he begged her to try to stop Rea from doing anything that would draw any extra attention to either of them.

Now, she hurried to Rea's side. 'You can't mention the Water Catcher, or anything to do with the prophecy.'

Rea crossed her arms and glared at Arisa. 'What's the matter? Don't you believe the Water Catcher will come?'

Arisa glanced around to ensure they couldn't be overheard. All the other students were well out of hearing range, but it didn't mean they would escape notice. She dropped her voice to a whisper. 'Erun says the prophecy will come to pass, but he also says we should be careful speaking about it. Especially now.'

Rea rolled her eyes. 'Everyone I know believes the Water Catcher will come.' Her tiny voice rose. 'And they aren't scared to say so.'

Arisa grasped her friend's wrists. 'But you *should* be scared. Speaking about the prophecy is the same as speaking out against the King, and he has spies everywhere. It is said Kengians are being kidnapped on his orders.'

'The King should be the one who is scared. The Water Catcher is coming to get him.'

'I don't know what it's like in the rest of Lamore, but here we can't talk about the prophecy and threaten the King. And you can't keep using your magic.'

Rea put her hands on her hips. 'Why not? What will they do to me?'

They will come for you. They will come for me, she thought, wondering desperately how to get Rea to see sense – but she was distracted by the sudden clattering of wheels and horses' hooves on the school's cobblestone driveway.

A lump caught in her throat as she took in the wagon with its barred windows. An impeccably dressed nobleman and a boy, each on horseback, preceded the wagon, and stopped to speak to the school's groundsman. Arisa couldn't make out the words, but could guess their meaning when the visitors looked in their direction.

She bent down to Rea's eye level. 'We have to go. Now.'

Rea stood frozen. All of her earlier brazenness and courage had slipped away.

'Rea!'

Arisa tried to shake her friend to life, but it was too late; the man on horseback had already ridden over and dismounted. He was now standing before them, examining each of the girls with cold eyes. She held Rea's hand tightly in hers as a groomsman wearing the King's livery leapt from the top of the wagon and ran to help the boy from his pony. Arisa noted that the boy wore an ermine-trimmed purple cloak – the colour reserved for royalty.

The boy scowled at them, his black eyes narrowed, as he joined the nobleman. He was a heavyset lad, a good half-head taller than Arisa, but slightly younger, judging by the boyish roundness of his face.

'That one.' The nobleman pointed at Rea.

The boy peered suspiciously at her. 'How do you know?'

The nobleman yanked Rea's arm, wrenching her away from Arisa. He grabbed her jaw and turned her to face the boy. 'Take a look yourself.'

The boy stepped forward hesitantly until he was close enough to properly examine Rea's face. He gasped. 'Silver eyes.'

Rea hissed in the boy's face, and he stumbled backwards. Arisa was torn between unspeakable fear and an urge to smile.

The boy recovered himself and shot an angry glance at Rea. 'I've never seen one before. Not one of the silver-eyes.'

'It's an anomaly. Silver eyes only appear in the most dangerous Kengians.' The nobleman then addressed Rea. 'We hear you've been telling tales about the prophecy.'

Rea lifted her chin and met the man's gaze defiantly. '*Mikret Tawreh elli tacusa.*'

'What did she say?' the boy demanded.

Arisa's lips thinned. She wasn't about to tell him what Rea had said in Kengian: *The Water Catcher will come.*

'Who cares?' The nobleman waved his hands. 'It's enough that she's Kengian, and one of the silver-eyes. The King wants them all out of the city. He feels safer if they're far away in the fields where they belong.' He paused to smile to himself. 'Or even further away.'

Arisa noticed a small crowd of their fellow students gathering around them. 'Get help,' she appealed to them, but they were silent and unmoving. Some smiled slyly, as if they had known this day would come.

'*Rhe sri.*' Rea projected her voice so everyone could hear. She focused her gaze on the boy; her eyes were burning silver-hot. '*Noy hno uebu tof rom, eo Mikret Tawreh.*' *The King's right. He's not safe from me, or the Water Catcher.*

The boy clamped his chubby hand around Rea's arms. She struggled hard against him, as Arisa pulled at the boy's wrists. 'You can't take her.'

The boy spun toward her, his face flushed red. 'What did you say?'

She stood a little taller, determined not to show the fear gurgling inside her stomach. 'I said, you can't take her.'

'What about this one?' The boy indicated Arisa as he called back to his companion.

The nobleman approached her and closed his hand around her chin. 'She was mentioned in the report. Doesn't have silver eyes, but doesn't mean she isn't Kengian. She could be one of the ones in hiding.' He released his grip and glanced down at her worn gown and battered boots. 'More likely she's just lowborn.'

The boy stepped menacingly toward Arisa and made a show of sniffing the air near her. 'Smells like a Kengian to me.'

She could hear in her mind Erun's warning to keep her head down, but she couldn't stop herself. Someone had to stand up to this bully. Someone had to stand up to *them*.

'*Noy farik noy, aodru-tec.*' She spat the words in the boy's smug face. *You're smelling yourself, turd-face.*

The boy flung his hands over his ears. 'Now she's speaking Kengian, too. She's trying to bewitch me, Sir Marcus!'

Sir Marcus? Arisa shivered. The nobleman was Lamore's High Sheriff, which didn't bode well for them.

Sir Marcus exhaled heavily. 'Kengian magic doesn't work like that. She's just baiting you.' He picked up Rea and headed toward the wagon.

'You can't take her!' Arisa cried. 'She's done nothing wrong.'

The boy poked her hard just below her shoulder blade. 'You can't tell me what to do. Do you know who I am?' he snarled, not waiting for a response. 'I'm Lord Guthrie, the Earl of Chisolm, and kin to King Delrik.'

She had heard of the belligerent boy, Guthrie, who was also the son of the King's closest adviser, Chancellor Horace, but his titles didn't scare her. They only made her angrier.

'So?'

'*So!*' Guthrie's face distorted and turned beet-red.

'So, you're no one to me.'

A smirk tugged at the corner of Guthrie's lips. 'But I *will* be someone to you. You were reported too. You're coming with us.'

Arisa's throat closed up and her palms dripped with sweat as Guthrie's arms went around her. He half yanked, half shoved her toward the wagon, where a burly-looking guard lifted her up and threw her roughly inside. She landed heavily against Rea. Her friend's normally carefree face was drawn with terror.

Arisa scrambled back toward the wagon's open door to see the Schoolmaster running toward them.

'Sir Marcus,' he panted, trying to catch his breath. He bowed hurriedly. 'These girls have done nothing to afford you taking them. They are innocents.'

Sir Marcus shook his head. 'You know the King's orders. No silver-eyes in the city. He will not abide anyone defying his laws, or threatening to disrupt his rule.'

The Schoolmaster pointed at Rea. 'But Rea has permission to be here. She's sponsored by the Duke of Lakeford and is the daughter of one of his most trusted tenants.'

Sir Marcus's brow furrowed. 'You can take it up with the Duke, but I'm afraid by the time you speak to him, it will be too late.'

'Too late?' the Schoolmaster and Arisa said in unison.

'We're taking them to Ette.' It was worse than Arisa had feared. There was little chance they could be saved if they were all the way across the Kyprian Sea. 'You're looking at Ette's new Governor.'

Guthrie puffed out his chest. 'And I'm to be his Lieutenant-Governor.'

Arisa thought she saw Sir Marcus wince slightly.

'Yes. Lord Guthrie will be under my tutelage. And these girls will serve in my household. We set sail at first light.'

More likely we'll be treated as slaves, she thought.

'The King has agreed to this?' The Schoolmaster's voice was impossibly high.

Sir Marcus nodded. 'We have need of a household befitting my and Lord Guthrie's positions, and the local servants are notoriously unreliable.'

'It was my idea to take the Kengians.' Guthrie thumped his chest. 'The silver-eyes' magic won't work in Ette.'

The Schoolmaster seemed to collect himself. 'Congratulations on your new post, Sir Marcus, and yours, Lord Guthrie. But only one of the girls you have apprehended is Kengian. Arisa' – the Schoolmaster pointed at her – 'is as Lamorian as you or I. I have known her since she was a babe.'

A bolt of relief shot through her, but it was just as quickly overcome with guilt. Being saved meant she would have to abandon Rea.

'She's a known sympathiser,' Sir Marcus said.

'And she tried to curse me with her filthy Kengian words,' Guthrie said.

The Schoolmaster shot a desperate look at Arisa that said, *Really?* She bit her lip, unable to deny it.

'I'm sure it was a misunderstanding, Lord Guthrie.'

Sir Marcus sighed. 'Both girls are coming with us.'

He mounted his horse as Guthrie was helped on top of his pony. Guthrie shot a triumphant smile at Arisa as the guard slammed the wagon door in her face.

The wagon lurched into action, leaving her to contemplate her fate. She hadn't heeded her guardian's many warnings. She hadn't protected Rea. And look what had happened. She couldn't put Guthrie's cruel smirk or his lifeless black eyes — the colour of death — from her mind.

Rea sat beside her. 'It's alright, Arisa. The Water Catcher will come.'

'Stop saying that,' she snapped. 'That's how you got us into this mess.'

Rea's face fell. 'I'm sorry.'

She immediately regretted her comment. Rea had done nothing but be proud of her heritage and who she was. 'It's not your fault,' Arisa said in a softened voice. 'You didn't do anything wrong.'

'I did. You told me to stop talking about the prophecy and not to practise my magic. But it's not proper magic; I can only do a few little tricks. I can't actually hurt anyone. I didn't think anyone would care.'

Arisa's gut churned with anger. Rea was in the right, but it didn't matter. Being right and just held no power in Lamore. 'Don't blame yourself. You can't help who you are. It's not fair that we can't say what we want.'

Rea nodded her head miserably. 'We'll be alright. They might not really take us away.'

Arisa took the girl's shaking hands in hers. 'Sure, they might not,' she lied.

THE WAGON JOSTLED its way through Obira's winding alleyways until it came to a stop at the port, where Arisa and Rea found themselves being pulled across the gangplank of a cargo ship. The King's peregrine falcon flag flew high on the mast.

They were shoved down three floors until they reached the ship's hold. Arisa shuffled forward in the dark, the guard pushing her further toward the sound of Kengian voices. He threw her to the floor. Her back thumped hard against a post.

She could feel a sea of limbs moving around her, and hear the clinking of chains as the prisoners made room for the newcomers.

'Sorry.'

Her apology went unanswered in the fetid hold. Straw scratched at her legs. The space reeked of human waste. Arisa shuddered at the coldness of the metal as manacles snapped closed around her wrists. She heard the click of a second pair next to her. She reached out for Rea's hand.

The guards left them, and her eyes adjusted to the darkness. Dozens of eyes peered back at her. Many of them were silver, but a few weren't. Some of the captives looked like they hadn't seen light or a good meal for years. She wondered if they had been freed from the dungeons, only to now be bound to a life of servitude.

A frail-looking man fixed a blank silver stare on her. His eyes were empty, as if he had long ago given up trying to make sense of what was happening.

'Arisa?' Rea squeaked.

'It's alright.' She squeezed Rea's hand. 'It will be alright,' she lied again.

'I'm never going to see Mother and Father again,' Rea cried.

'It will be hard. Trust me, I know. But at least we're together. We can survive, as long as we're together.'

'You promise you won't leave me?'

'I promise.' Arisa could feel Rea's warm tears as they dropped onto her hand. 'Don't cry.'

Never let them see you cry. Erun's words were etched in her mind. Words she'd never hear again.

'Don't cry,' she repeated, biting back her own tears.

Arisa wasn't sure how long they had been in the hold. She couldn't tell if it was day or night. She had managed to fall asleep at some point, despite the voices all around. A Kengian chorus repeated the same mantra over and over: *Mikret Tawreh elli tacusa* – the Water Catcher will come. Others just rocked themselves back and forth, moaning.

Arisa propped herself up against a barrel, being careful not to disturb the sleeping Rea snuggled up against her. On the deck above, she could hear the crew as they prepared to set sail. Supplies had been delivered periodically into the hull where they were being kept.

Rea's eyes opened with a start as the noises above them intensified. A guard appeared at the bottom of the ladder.

'This way.'

The guard led a man toward them. He was carrying a wooden case, and wore a uniform Arisa recognised from Smith & Son – the establishment of a merchant friend of Erun's. There was something familiar about the man's gait; the way his lanky limbs knocked together.

He lowered the case to the ground next to her. The bottles inside it chinked together, and the guard licked his lips greedily. 'The finest rum,' the man said.

Arisa bit her tongue as she recognised her guardian's voice.

'I don't suppose you'd like some?' Erun reached into his coat. 'I've got a little extra here.'

'Could I?'

'Of course – but you will *want* to do something for me in return.'

'Yes, I suppose so.' The guard's voice had turned flat and mechanical.

'You want to let one of these girls go.'

'No…' The guard shook his head slowly. 'No, I don't.'

Take it easy, Erun, Arisa thought. *He has to believe your words.*

'No one will notice one little girl gone. No one.'

The guard's face distorted in the dim light.

'And a little Lamorian girl at that. A Lamorian, just like you.'

After what seemed like an age, the guard nodded. 'A Lamorian girl.' He took the rum and shoved it in his coat, before unlocking Arisa's manacles.

She didn't budge.

'Come on,' Erun hissed in her ear.

'Not without Rea,' she whispered back, relief and guilt warring within.

Erun approached the guard again and pointed at Rea. 'That one too.'

The man shook his head, trance-like. 'Not that one. She's Kengian.' He was still under Erun's suggestive powers, but only just.

'She's a wee little thing.' Erun's voice was carefully measured. 'No one would notice if she was gone.'

The guard shook his head violently, as if he had a tic.

'It's no good,' Erun whispered. 'He will never agree to releasing Rea.'

'No!' Arisa cried, but Erun clasped his hand over her mouth and pried her away from her friend.

'The Schoolmaster is speaking to the Duke about Rea, but right now you have to come with me. Put this on.'

He handed her a uniform. She shook her head, refusing to leave – but Rea nodded her encouragement, as did some of the other prisoners present enough to realise what was happening.

'Rea, I – I'm going to get help.' She choked on her words. 'I promise.'

Rea smiled a little too brightly. 'I know.'

Arisa put on the uniform. It was large on her, but she could probably pass for a delivery boy. After a long hug with Rea, and more promises to be back soon, Erun led her up out of the hull, onto the upper deck, and across the gangway to the wharf.

Everyone on the ship was too busy with their own duties to notice the deliveryman and boy. But all the while, Arisa didn't dare to breathe. Erun led her wordlessly along the wharf and up the steep path leading back into the city. He didn't slow his pace until they made it back into the anonymity of Obira's bustling streets. They stopped in the shadows of a quiet laneway.

'Where's the Schoolmaster? We have to make sure…'

Erun's downcast eyes stopped Arisa in her tracks.

'We have to get help for Rea,' she finished.

'We can't.' Erun's voice broke. 'We can't help her.'

'What do you mean? You said—'

'The Schoolmaster went to the castle and tried to get an audience with the Duke, but he is away at Talbot. The Chancellor was hearing petitions on the King's behalf and laughed him from the room.'

The realisation washed over Arisa like a series of needles stabbing into her one by one. She tried to ignore the heartbreak she saw in Erun's eyes.

'We have to go back.' She clutched her guardian's arms. 'You have to use your powers.'

'You saw what happened. I could only get you out. They won't let a silver-eyes go.'

'No! No! No!' She thumped her fists against Erun's chest. 'We have to go back—'

Erun wrapped his arms around Arisa and held her to him. 'I'm sorry, little one, but you have to believe she'll be alright.'

She pulled away from her guardian. 'No! Believing in impossibilities is how Rea ended up on that ship. There's no hope. And there's no Water Catcher to save them.'

'The Water Catcher will come, Arisa. You have to believe that.'

'No. The Water Catcher can't be real. If they were, they would never let terrible things like this happen.'

Erun's brow crinkled. 'There's always hope,' he said with certainty.

'Not for Rea or people like us.'

'And that is why no one will ever know the *real* us, or we will end up like Rea. As you have seen, it's too dangerous.'

Arisa's next words were bitter in her mouth. 'Not as dangerous as waiting for a hero that will never arrive.'

Arisa didn't cry that day. She couldn't let anyone see her cry. But she did make a promise to herself. From that day on, she wouldn't rely on hope. She would do whatever she could to protect those who couldn't protect themselves. Maybe it might help wipe her conscience clean for not being able to save Rea, and for knowing her secrets were the only thing that had kept her safe.

At eleven-and-three-quarters, Arisa replaced stolen hope with a grim determination to never let anyone – to never let *them* – get the better of her again. They would pay for what they had done. And she would be ready the next time they came for her or anyone she loved.

1

———————

Six years later

r-risa walked alongside the towering wall of stone and wood that surrounded Obira City, separating it from the rest of Lamore. It was the same wall that divided Lamore's capital from the all-seeing castle on the headland above.

It was a wall she yearned to escape beyond.

She tried to force herself to forget the fact that she was trapped in this place. She let her thoughts wander to the Nymoi Alps and their snowy peaks in the distance, the glittering sun hovering above them. For the millionth time, Arisa imagined what it would be like to cross the mountain range and visit the long-lost land of Kengia that lay on the other side.

It was that fleeting time of day when dusk and twilight met. When the silvery hues of the afternoon sun gave way to pearly roses and purples, and the first evening stars pierced their way through the sky's blanket. When anything seemed possible and she could forget, if only for a few magical minutes, that everything she wished for was in fact impossible. At this time of day, she could forget the darkness; a darkness that only intensified with the coming of night – and right now was setting in fast. She must have stayed back at school much later than she thought.

Arisa quickened her pace along the cobblestone streets, jostling through the end-of-day crowds. She screwed up her nose as the city's stench came to her on the wind. She was overly familiar with the smell: a mixture of raw sewage and sickness. Obira's foul air was something you couldn't easily forget or become accustomed to, but tonight the odour was worse, amplified by the yowling wind tunnelling its way through the city. Arisa shuddered as the temperature dropped. She pulled the boy's cap further down over her ears and wrapped her cloak a little tighter. It was frightfully cool, even for a winter's night. The kind of cold that burrowed into the core of your bones.

Another blast of the unfamiliar wind came, howling as it startled a flock of pigeons. She shielded her face as they hurtled toward her. But just as abruptly, the birds turned skywards. The flock tracked across the sky, silhouetted by an immense full moon. The sight reminded her of Erun and his steadfast belief that the strangest things always occurred when the moon was full. She smiled at the thought of her guardian and his fantastical mind. But her smile faded as she registered again how quickly the light was disappearing around her.

She walked faster, striding easily in her boy's tunic and battered leather boots. Arisa was seventeen, but her slim build meant she could still easily pass as a boy. She need only tuck her long hair under a cap. It gave her a certain level of protection when travelling Obira's unpredictable streets at night, as she did all too often. She felt a little safer seeing the lamplighters move from one streetlight to the next, illuminating a path through the city's murk.

She passed a row of groaning stone townhouses, each as dirty and rundown as the last; shopfronts with their overhanging second stories, and lines of threadbare rags strung between the buildings. It was a sea of grey-and-brown sameness. Hollow-faced children looked out from doorways with wide eyes and outstretched hands, and scrawny women balanced screaming babies on their hips.

Arisa reached the city gates, watching enviously as lines of Lamorian citizens passed through, returning to their homes in the countryside for the night. Coming in the opposite direction were noblemen re-entering the city. A pair of Royal Guards stood outside the gatehouse, nodding deferentially to the richly dressed lords as they headed back to the safety of the castle after visiting their grand manors in the counties. Wordlessly, the nobles passed the fishermen, the villagers and the farmers whose blood, sweat and tears sustained their luxurious lifestyles.

Arisa and her lowborn compatriots stood aside as a liveried coach passed through the gates. Beside her, a merchant she recognised from a stall that sold mackerel pies struck up a conversation with another man.

'What news from your village?'

The man shook his head and sighed. 'Taxes have been raised again to make up for the shortfall in crops.'

'It's the same in ours,' the stallholder lamented. 'But it could be worse, I suppose.' He looked around surreptitiously and dropped his voice. Arisa leaned closer to hear. 'The Chancellor has enclosed the common lands near Calliope. He's dismissed his farmer reeve, Sergei, and evicted many of his tenant farmers.'

'Sheesh,' the other man muttered under his breath. 'I guess after they managed to get the silver-eyes and Kengians under control, it was only a matter of time before they came after us.'

It unsettled Arisa, how easily each man accepted this latest act of cruelty. She wanted to physically shake them, to urge them to stand up for their rights, but the pair had moved on, rejoining the queue to leave the city.

She would usually turn away from the gates now and head into the labyrinth of alleyways that weaved through the city, but a sudden darkness fell around her, swallowing everything in her path.

She looked up, a little hesitantly. The full moon, which had filled the sky just minutes before, was gone, completely obscured by clouds. The glowing line of lamplights that had stretched out ahead was now a series of dull, disconnected dots in the distance. Obira had been reduced to a mass of sinister shadows.

A heaviness formed in the pit of her stomach. Arisa was thankful when one of the guards lit extra torches outside the gatehouse and along the wall.

The remaining guard kept a watchful eye on the Lamorians leaving the city. 'Don't we know you lot?' he interrogated one family, a man and a woman who were attempting to lead an old workhorse and a rickety cart through the gates. A boy who looked to be seven or eight years old – it was hard to tell from his thin frame – was sitting in the cart among small piles of rejected vegetables. He caught Arisa's eye and gave a shy smile. She smiled back.

'We do. We do know them.' The other guard pointed a stubby finger at the family.

The father shook his head and gave an apologetic smile.

'They're some of those grubby Kengian farmers we booted off the Chancellor's land,' Stubby Fingers persisted.

His offsider gave a menacing smirk. 'I think you're right. A little hard to tell, though – Kengian filth all looks the same to me.'

Arisa watched nervously as the boy stood up, as if to challenge the two guards, but his mother reached out to still him.

The first guard picked up an undersized potato from the cart and examined it. 'Where did you grow this?'

'In a village near Iveness.' The mother spoke with downcast eyes.

'You wouldn't be sneaking back onto the Chancellor's lands and taking things that don't belong to you?'

'You accuse us of being thieves?' The father stepped forward, his shoulders squared.

Stubby Fingers surveyed the man with a sneer.

The woman grasped her husband's arm. 'Please be assured, we would never steal from the Chancellor. These were grown on a small allotment a villager was kind enough to share with us.'

There was a moment of silence while the guards stared at the family and their cart. Finally, Stubby Fingers grunted, 'I think I believe the Kengian wench. Take a look at this.' He picked up a spotty-looking squash. 'You'd never find produce like this on the Chancellor's lands.'

Stubby Fingers' friend wandered over. He took the squash with a smirk, before dropping it to the ground and smashing it under his foot. Arisa's face burned in anger.

'Not even fit for pigs.' The pair laughed heartily.

She heard the woman urge her husband in Kengian to forget about it. But Arisa couldn't. She bit her lip, trying to avoid drawing attention to herself.

In the years since Rea had been taken, she'd let the darkness grow inside her, fuelled by hatred of the injustices she saw every day, but she'd been careful not to speak out. She knew where speaking out in Lamore got you. But every inch of Arisa's being urged her to do something now; to stand up for what was right. She couldn't fail to protect these people, like she'd failed Rea.

She stepped toward the guards, not knowing what she would say – but she needn't have bothered, for the guards' attention was elsewhere. Their eyes were fixed on the sky above.

Arisa followed their gaze upwards, catching sight of the moon as the clouds parted. It transformed from darkness into grey, into shades of yellow and orange, before finally turning a bright, fiery red.

'It can't be,' she whispered to herself.

'A blood moon,' came the Kengian woman's unbelieving voice beside her.

The guards pointed at the moon, their mouths agape.

A buzz started around the gates as everyone stopped what they were doing. People came out of nearby houses to watch as the sky morphed from black all the way to crimson, until it matched the flaming red of the moon. The air was full of wonder for a few moments – before it thickened with fear.

'A blood moon…I haven't seen one of those since the year the Prince was born.' Stubby Fingers' voice was shaking. 'It's a bad omen, it is.'

Arisa shuddered at the truth in his words. The last blood moon had brought death to her doorstep, as well as many others.

'Mother, does this mean the Water Catcher is coming?' came the boy's small voice.

'Shush, Hyando.'

'It does!' He clapped his hands with glee. 'The blood moon is the first sign. It means the Water Catcher will come and save us. And defeat the mean King.'

'What's that?' Stubby Fingers spun around to face the boy.

The father stepped in front of the cart, waving his hands pleadingly. 'Nothing. The boy said nothing.'

'It didn't sound like nothing. It sounded like treason to me.'

The boy jumped up and down on the cart, and began shouting at the top of his lungs. 'The blood moon is here. The Water Catcher is coming. The Water Catcher is coming!'

His cries elicited a mixed chorus of whoops and hisses from the crowd.

'Listen here, brat—' Stubby Fingers manoeuvred his bulky frame up onto the cart and tried to grab the boy.

'Leave him. He's just a boy.' The mother struggled against the other guard as he pinned her arms behind her back, and the father tried futilely to pull Stubby Fingers away.

Arisa watched on, frozen, as the guard clambered toward the boy and slipped on a stack of hessian sacks. The cart wobbled heavily and the horse bolted forward. It happened so quickly, yet time seemed to slow as the sudden movement propelled the boy into the air, momentarily suspending him.

Then everything quickened again, and he plummeted to the ground.

His head connected with the cobblestones with a sickening crack. And then there was nothing but silence. Silence and blood. The ground, the sky, this night; they were all stained with blood.

And Arisa had done nothing to stop it.

2

———

$\mathcal{P}$rince Takai had been back at the castle for two days, and other than at supper in the Great Hall among all the other nobles, he still hadn't spoken to his father.

For the many years he had spent under the stewardship of the Duke of Lakeford at his property in Lamore's north, Takai had only seen his father a handful of times. He had seen his mother even less. They were practically strangers to him, but now that he was back, he expected things to be different. He was nearly eighteen, so it was time he took his rightful place at court, and become involved in ruling the kingdom that he would one day inherit – but he seemed invisible to the court's decision-makers.

He was intent on putting a stop to that.

Takai left his apartments and was heading toward his father's private rooms when the King's chief adviser, Chancellor Horace, emerged through the privy chamber doors. The Chancellor was one of the people – if not the only person – who had unchecked access to the King. His position was at odds with his humble origins; Horace had ascended to power far beyond someone of his lowly birth. He was elevated at court because he had been the King's childhood companion, and was now married to the King's distant cousin, Countess Datanya. Yet, from what Takai knew, Horace had his sights set even higher.

Judging by what the Duke of Lakeford had told Takai, being the King's chief adviser and strategist wasn't enough for Horace. These, after all, were just job titles. Positions that could be easily taken from him at the smallest slip-up or sign of the King's displeasure. Horace needed to shore up his and his family's power. He wanted the kinds of titles that could never be taken from them – and he would do anything to get closer to the crown.

'Your Highness.' The Chancellor greeted him with half a bow.

'Chancellor,' Takai grunted, and made to go around him, but Horace blocked his path. Takai gritted his teeth, knowing the Chancellor took his role as the 'voice' of the King seriously and wouldn't be in a hurry to allow anyone else access to the monarch. 'I'm just calling on my father.'

Horace clicked his jaw and grimaced. 'Apologies – the King has just retired for the evening. But please, come and speak to me a moment.' He indicated the way to his own rooms, and Takai resigned himself to another day without speaking to his father.

The Chancellor occupied the grandest rooms at the castle, second only to the King's apartments next door. It was a testament to his position and influence at court. There, Horace pontificated for some minutes about how glad he was to have the Prince back at court, and invited him to join the King's council at its next meeting. He went on to highlight his son Guthrie's achievements in Ette and how much Guthrie had impressed the Governor-General, Sir Marcus. Finally, he droned on about the virtues of his daughter, Theodora – a pretty enough girl whom Takai had gladly re-acquainted himself with; but he had no interest in discussing her with her scheming father.

As Horace's speech seemed about to draw to a close, Takai

nodded politely and was about to excuse himself when a howling sound outside silenced their conversation.

'That sounded like a—'

'A wolf,' Horace said, eyes wide as they both went to the window and opened the shutters.

Takai peered out into the darkness, convinced his ears had deceived him. He couldn't remember the last time a wolf had been sighted in the kingdom. But there it was again. An unmistakable howl – and it sounded close.

He tried to make out the animal in the darkness of the castle grounds. And that was when he saw it.

Not the wolf. The moon.

Takai rubbed his eyes and looked again to confirm his mind wasn't playing tricks on him. But the moon was undoubtedly blood-red.

Lamore had gone almost two hundred years without a blood moon – until around eighteen years ago, the year of his birth, when one had appeared. And now there was another.

Horace frowned. 'Two blood moons in as many decades – both in the King's reign. The King will see it as a bad sign.'

'Surely he doesn't still believe in the Water Catcher prophecy?' Takai said. 'I thought there was no way of it coming to pass. That the firstborn Kengian line no longer exists.'

'Yes, any hope of a Kengian with the power to catch water – whatever that means – died with the last blood moon. I made sure of it. But your father is superstitious. Especially after—'

Takai's hand curled into a fist. 'After the Kengian Prince tried to bewitch him. No wonder Lamore turned on all the Kengians and silver-eyes.'

Horace clicked his jaw again from side to side. His lower jaw was permanently misaligned. Takai had heard that the Kengian Prince himself had given the Chancellor the injury, not long before the Prince had been killed in a riot when the people of Obira rose up against the Kengians.

'That kind of magic doesn't have a place here,' Takai spat.

Horace raised a curious brow, but Takai wasn't about to divulge the reasons for his dislike of Kengians. It would bring back painful memories of his time in Lakeford. Even as a child, he had been singled out by the Kengian farmers, distrustful of the King's son. Some had been rude, some outright abusive – terrifying for a young boy far from home.

Takai looked out at the fiery moon with a new sense of satisfaction. Perhaps the blood moon *was* a sign – not of a prophecy coming to pass, but a sign that Lamore was on the rise, and that Kengians would soon learn their place in the kingdom he would rule...even if they had to be taught the same lesson all over again.

3

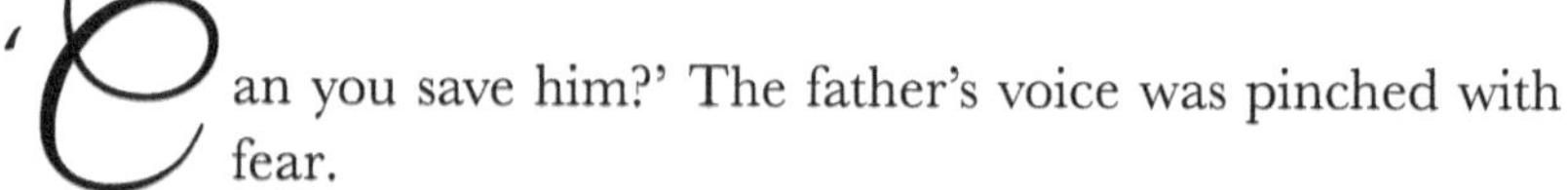

'Can you save him?' The father's voice was pinched with fear.

Arisa cast her eyes across the room to Hyando, the boy's broken body disturbingly small in the makeshift cot set up at the back of Erun's apothecary. Soft dawn light broke through the cracks in the shutters; the blood moon was long gone, but had left its devastating mark.

Hyando's mother, Lina, hovered over her son, murmuring words of comfort into his unhearing ears. Arisa stared at his mop of red curls – matted with blood, clumps sticking to his ashen forehead. She desperately wanted to assure Hyando's parents that their son would be fine, but something in Erun's manner told her otherwise. She watched as her guardian carefully applied gauze to Hyando's head. There was a nervous energy in his overly precise movements. Erun examined the boy's chest and stomach, his expert hands gauging the extent of the injuries beneath.

He pushed his eyeglasses up his nose and his lips thinned momentarily. A lump formed in Arisa's throat as Erun walked slowly back to his workstation.

'Can you? Can you save him?' the father repeated, more urgently.

Arisa turned to meet the man's intense gaze. *'Te elli wuru sou rotse,'* she replied in Kengian. *We will do our best.*

The father nodded and gave her a grateful smile. Arisa had to look away. She balled her fists, longing to surrender to her anger. Anger at the unnecessary violence that had brought Hyando here. Anger that an innocent boy had been targeted for his harmless beliefs. Anger that she hadn't prevented it. She could barely contain the fury churning in her stomach.

She handed the father, who introduced himself as Cynfor, a fresh flannel to place on the boy's hot forehead. She hoped it would give him a distraction from pacing the floor and wringing his beaten hands. By the cot, Lina clutched Hyando's small hand in both of hers, as if willing him through touch alone to come back to her. Her red curls were wild and untamed, dark rings inscribed under her hazel eyes.

Arisa scrutinised the boy's ghostly face. It was strangely serene. Erun had given him a herbal sedative to help with the pain, and Hyando had slipped in and out of consciousness throughout the night.

He was a handsome boy, with perfect rosebud lips. Lips that suddenly contorted with pain.

'Kom iko koelt non. Onmy musi iko,' Lina whispered. *I'm here, little one. Mama is here.*

'He's moving. It's a good sign, isn't it?' Cynfor gave Arisa a hopeful look.

She glanced over to Erun, appealing to him for an answer, but he was preoccupied compounding more medicine. 'Let me speak to my guardian.'

Erun was surrounded by hundreds of vials of colourful liquids, creating an eerie glow around him. His brow was furrowed in concentration. Arisa dropped her voice to a whisper as she approached.

'Please say you can do something.'

Erun turned to meet her gaze. His harried expression said it all.

'There must be something.'

Erun shook his head slowly. 'He has ruptured several vital organs. They're beyond repair. All we can do now is help him with the pain.'

'Surely *you* of all people can fix him? You're a Scholar. This is what you trained to do.'

Erun took off his eyeglasses and rubbed the nape of his neck. 'There is nothing more I can do. It's beyond my powers and learning. The boy's father asked me earlier to send for the Shaman, in case.'

Arisa let out a strangled gasp. 'A Shaman? Are you sure it's come to that?'

'It has. I sent word during the night. The boy's parents will take comfort from the Shaman's ritual. Hyando will be at peace then.'

'But it's not right.' Arisa clenched her fists. 'It's not fair.'

'It may not be fair, but it is the reality.'

She slumped into a chair by the fireside and looked over at Hyando again. His father was earnestly patting his forehead. The futility of it engulfed her, a great fire stoked in her belly. Her fingernails dug into her palms.

'I will not have it, Erun. I will not have it.'

Erun came to sit beside her. 'You'll not have what, exactly?'

Arisa was about to say she would have justice for Hyando, but a small voice cried out from the other side of the room.

'Mama,' Hyando croaked. 'Papa.' His head thrashed from side to side, as if he were having a bad dream. Erun and Arisa raced to his side.

'Hyando!' Lina reached out to touch her son's brow.

Cynfor leant over the boy. 'We're right here.'

Hyando's eyes flung open. And that was when Arisa realised the boy's fate had been decided long before this night.

She stood frozen as she stared into Hyando's eyes. It wasn't the look of the sick and dying that struck her; she had seen that look many times before. It was something she hadn't noticed in the darkness – but now, with the arriving dawn, it was unmistakable.

Hyando's eyes were silver, like a shard of mirrored glass.

Arisa hadn't seen anyone with that eye colour since Rea. It brought a flood of emotions back to her. Emotions she'd tried hard to forget.

It didn't matter what happened here today. Hyando hadn't stood a chance in Lamore. Like Rea, he could never have escaped persecution. His eyes would always have betrayed his identity. Even if he could dress, speak and act like a Lamorian, it was useless if he bore the mark that only a Kengian with forbidden magic could possess. Arisa felt suddenly ashamed. Ashamed of the city she lived in, ashamed of her own relatively privileged and protected life. A level of shame she hadn't felt since Rea.

'Where am I?' Hyando asked.

Lina patted her son's hand. 'At a friend's.'

The boy's eyes sought out Arisa. His silver gaze locked on her amber one, but she had to look away.

Instead she watched Erun as he examined the boy. She looked up briefly to give his parents a half-smile. A smile that gave no false hope or promises. A smile that said: *Savour this. Savour this small moment in time, while you have your son back.*

Erun gave Lina a small nod and squeezed Cynfor's shoulder, then he and Arisa stepped away, back to the fireside.

'I'm cold, Mama,' Hyando squeaked.

'Here you go.' Lina pulled the blanket up over her son's shoulders, her face wet with tears. Hyando winced at her touch. 'Does it hurt a lot?'

'Not so much,' came the brave response. Lina patted his hand gently. 'Mama, tell me a story, please.'

'What would you like to hear?'

'A story about Kengia.'

'Which story?'

'The prophecy, of course.'

'No. Not that one.' She gave a pained smile. 'Not today.'

'Yes,' the boy insisted. 'That one, please.'

Like Hyando's mother, Arisa wasn't sure she wanted to hear it. The prophecy had been the trigger for last night's accident – but something about this family made her want to listen, to be part of their closeness somehow, even if she didn't believe in the story they were sharing.

Finally, Lina took a deep breath and began. She spoke in her native tongue, haltingly at first, but soon slipping into the lyrical cadence the Kengian language was known for. Even in her sadness, her storytelling had a musical tone. Hyando nestled into the cot, clearly soothed by his mother's voice.

'A long time ago – about two hundred years ago, in fact – King Alfred ruled the kingdom of Lamore. It was a golden age. Lamore's neighbour was the much larger kingdom of Kengia, our homeland. The two kingdoms were, of course, separated by the Nymoi Alps.

'In King Alfred's time, access between the kingdoms was possible via a narrow, winding mountain path. And despite their vast differences, the two nations lived in peace. Trade occurred between them, with Kengia supplementing Lamore's few natural resources. A formal alliance between the nations was cemented when King Alfred married the Kengian King's first-born child, Mary.'

Hyando's eyes lit up. 'And she had magic powers.'

Lina smiled. 'As the eldest royal child, Mary possessed an unusual power over nature. Stronger powers than any Kengian, even the silver-eyes like you. She was able to control the air and wind. While most Lamorians were scared of magic, Mary gave them no reason to fear her. They came to love their queen, as well as King Alfred's ability to bring peace and prosperity to their kingdom. It wasn't an empire, back then. King Alfred didn't rule over other lands or kingdoms. But not everyone revelled in Lamore's peaceful existence. Alfred's brother Emberto—'

'The Conqueror?'

Lina's brow furrowed. 'Yes, that is what the Lamorians call him. Emberto resented Lamore being reliant on the good nature of the Kengians, and was scared of Mary's powers. He urged Alfred to invade Ivane and Ette, across the Kyprian Sea, as they too were rich in natural resources. King Alfred didn't agree, which made Emberto look for a reason to turn on his brother. And he found a reason – in the prophecy.

'Emberto remembered hearing it as a boy. The prophecy foretold that someone of Kengia's firstborn line would cause the demise of the Lamorian regime. The prophecy said there would be a child who could—'

'Catch water.' Hyando's voice rose with excitement.

Lina laughed. 'You know this story too well.'

'Please go on, Mama.'

'Since Queen Mary possessed magical powers over nature, Emberto paid great heed to the prophecy. Alfred knew nothing of his brother's fears, which only grew with the appearance of a blood moon – the first sign the prophecy foretold. King Alfred and Queen Mary's son was born shortly after, and the child's birth was celebrated with a great display of lights in the sky.'

'Firesky!'

Lina nodded. 'The prophecy's second sign. It was all Emberto needed to be convinced the prophecy was coming to pass. He overthrew his brother, and imprisoned the King and his family, though Mary and her son were able to escape back to Kengia. Sadly, the child was not the Water Catcher, and Emberto soon invaded Ette and Ivane.

'He even imprisoned the last Firemaster, trying to force her to make great new weapons for him. Emberto may not have got his weapons, but through great determination he took Ette and Ivane as his own. It started one hundred and eighty years of Lamorian occupation, and what became the Kyprian Empire. The empire held until twenty years ago, when King Delrik's father lost Ette and Ivane.'

'But King Delrik took Ette back,' Hyando said quietly.

'Yes, he did.'

'And will he want Ivane back from King Laskar too?'

'He probably will.'

'And Kengia?'

Lina shook her head decidedly. 'No one will ever be able to take Kengia. Not while the Kengian King continues to use his magic over the coastal and mountain borders.'

'King Leo will protect Kengia until the Water Catcher comes and saves us all,' Hyando said.

'Yes. When the Water Catcher comes, everyone will live in peace, and we will return home again. Until then, Kengia will remain shut off from the rest of the world.' Lina paused. 'I'm sorry there isn't a happier ending.'

'It's alright, Mama.' Hyando smiled up at his mother. 'There will be a happy ending. The Water Catcher will come.' He nodded to himself.

Arisa wished she could share the boy's confidence. But she knew there would never be a Water Catcher.

She swallowed the lump in her throat, and tried to distract herself by twirling the silver chain and medallion that hung around her neck. Focusing on the coldness of the chain in her hands, she traced the medallion's intricate pattern, determined to stop the tears from forming. She caught Erun's eye, and he was by her side in a moment. His arm went around her shoulders.

'Everything will be alright.'

'It will not be alright.' She glanced over at Hyando and his family. 'Nothing's alright about this.'

'Arisa…' She could see a question forming on Erun's lips. 'You said something earlier. Tell me what you meant by it.'

'Sorry?'

'You said you "will not have it". What did you mean?'

Arisa dropped her chain abruptly and clenched her jaw. She met her guardian's gaze with a defiant look. 'I meant that I will not have this grievous act and many more like it go unpunished. The King and his advisers must suffer for what they have done to their people. They are hateful. They must be stopped.'

Erun rubbed his neck before speaking in a deliberately even tone. 'Arisa, you shouldn't speak in such terms.'

'In what terms?'

'In terms of hate. Hate only leads to violence.'

'Maybe violence is the only way.'

'Nobody wins from violence. It only leads to further pain.'

'The Lamorian regime needs to hurt. Hurt like they have hurt others,' she spat. 'How can you *not* hate them for what they've done? How can *you*, of all people, forget so easily?'

Erun flinched. 'I have not forgotten, but it doesn't mean I'm full of hate. I don't advocate violence against anyone, and you shouldn't either. I thought you wanted to protect and *help* people, not hurt them. Isn't that why you wish to be a surgeon? It's the reason I'm a healer. It's the best way we can help, at least until…' His voice trailed off.

'Until what? Until a Water Catcher turns up? We both know it will never happen. It's impossible. There can never be a Water Catcher.'

Erun shook his head emphatically. 'You must have hope. You must believe.'

'I believe. But I believe in justice, not ancient prophecies.'

'Who exactly do you speak of justice for?'

'I told you. Hyando. Hyando's family. My family.'

'And…'

'*And* Rea.' Arisa's voice broke as she said the name out loud, her eyes awash with tears. 'There should be justice for her.'

Erun gave her a swift look and tilted his head toward the rear door of the shop. She knew she couldn't cry in front of Hyando and his parents.

She ran outside into the garden. At least now she didn't have to meet the eyes of the boy she had failed – the boy they had all failed. Among the rows of herbs and medicinal plants, Arisa could be alone and cry.

She stood by the evergreen Kengian silverleaf tree. Erun said it reminded him of the sacred yew in Lochlen, the capital of his homeland: the source of all Kengian magic. There, under its silver boughs, she could shed tears for all the Kengians, for her fellow Lamorians, for her parents, and for Rea. The tears ran freely down her cheeks now as she sobbed.

At times like these, the wonder of Kengian magic seemed so far away. Every Kengian was born with some magic in their veins, and with the right training and dedication, they could become one with nature. Over time, the silver-eyes like Rea and Hyando could learn to communicate on a higher level with all the natural elements – hearing the crackling voice in a fire, the mumbling of a stone. The firstborn line of the Kengian royal family had those silver eyes, but were also gifted with elemental magic. They had the power to manipulate nature, bend it to their will, like the Water Catcher was prophesied to do…If the firstborn line existed at all. But it was lost – lost like the Firemasters, who could not only master the elements but also transform into different creatures. Now all that was left were Kengian Scholars like Erun, who learnt science and spells to harness the lifeforce known as *kira*; and the Shamans, who were the bridge between this world and the next, who could see through the eyes of those in the past, be it person or animal, and gain glimpses of possible futures.

Arisa wept. Because despite all of this magic existing in the world, none of it could save Hyando.

In her grief, she didn't notice the approach of the woman in the hooded cloak.

'Hush, child. It can't be all that bad.'

The woman appeared in front of her, as if she had materialised out of thin air. Arisa stepped backwards, seeking refuge in the shadows cast by the building's eaves. She tried to mask her face, but her gaze was drawn to the strikingly beautiful stranger.

The woman pushed back her hood to reveal a perfectly proportioned face, and long black hair that fell in waves midway to her waist. Her skin shimmered as if covered in silver dust. 'You must be Erun's ward.'

Arisa nodded, avoiding the woman's eyes.

'I came as soon as I got the message. I'm—'

'You're the Kengian Shaman.'

'I am.'

'You have taken a great risk coming to the city. Shamans are feared as much as silver-eyes.'

'We all take risks when we must.'

'But risk for what? The boy can't be saved.' Arisa kept her eyes downcast, but could feel the Shaman's gaze boring into her.

'I'm not here to save the boy, in the sense that you think. I'm here to guide his soul and help it transition into the next realm, into his next existence. There, he will be at peace.'

She snorted. 'Is that all there is to be hopeful for? That his soul will be at peace? Why can't he live? Why can't his family's life be easier in *this* world? Why can't we all be saved from this forsaken place?'

'Is that what you believe? That we can't be saved?'

'We can't. None of us can be spared from the hopelessness of this kingdom.'

Before Arisa realised it, the Shaman was standing directly before her again. She reached out and lifted Arisa's chin.

Arisa tried to resist, but was overcome by the strange energy and warmth emanating from the woman's hands.

The Shaman stared right at her. She was so close that Arisa saw her pupils dilate for a split second. The Shaman continued looking into her eyes for what felt like an eternity, before smiling and releasing her chin.

'You don't believe what you're saying. You know, as well as I do, that there is hope. The blood moon has come and the Water Catcher will follow.'

'I'm well past hoping and believing in an impossible prophecy,' Arisa scoffed. 'It isn't enough.'

'You're right. It isn't enough to just hope and believe. You must *know* it. You must know with every inch of your being: better times are on the way.'

Arisa made to argue, but the Shaman put up a hand to silence her. 'Hope and believe for now, and when you're ready, you will know.'

'Know what?'

'You will know when you know.' The Shaman gave a knowing smile and one last piercing look before disappearing into the house.

Arisa was left to puzzle over the cryptic words. What did she mean, Arisa 'must *know*'? The only thing she knew was that there must be justice. It wasn't enough to try to protect others. There must be justice for Hyando, for Rea, for everyone. The hateful Lamorian regime must suffer – suffer as much as she was suffering right now.

She may not know how and when, but Arisa would make it happen.

'They will be punished,' she pledged to herself, wiping the rust-coloured tears from her cheeks. Out here, her real self was exposed for the world to see.

Arisa raised her eyes to the sky – her Kengian eyes, as silver as the sun above. 'And I shall be the one who punishes them.'

4

———————

Theodora might have been the daughter of one of the most powerful men in Lamore – if not *the* most powerful man – but she was seen as nothing more than an ornament, or a pawn in Chancellor Horace's schemes. The latest of which was to try to capture the Prince's heart, and further cement their family's position at court.

While Theodora didn't object to the prospect of being the future Queen of Lamore, and the Prince was handsome enough, she hated that she had no say in any of her father's plans or scheming. She was far from stupid and a thousand times smarter than her twin brother, Guthrie – a buffoon currently being applauded for doing nothing in a faraway Lamorian territory. It frustrated her beyond belief that her father couldn't see that. But while the Chancellor's full attention was on the news from across the Kyprian Sea – that Ette had been invaded by a fearsome army from a far-flung nation in the north – Theodora had been sent to shop for gowns capable of snaring a Prince.

Her mother, Countess Datanya, had brought her to Obira's marketplace to visit an exclusive merchant who had the finest furs, silks and lace. While the Countess was giddily choosing materials for her own gowns, Theodora's eyes were on the marketplace outside. For a while she saw nothing but bustling crowds of filth – then a familiar figure caught her attention.

Her father. Disguised in a heavy cloak, without any guards. The only person with him was a huntsman Theodora recognised from one of their properties.

Without a second thought, she slipped from the shop and followed her father to a nearby tavern.

The Lion's Den was Obira's most disreputable establishment, frequented by drunks, criminals and the types of women who regularly associated themselves with those kinds of men. Theodora would never frequent such a place, but now she was here, she was determined to find out what secret business her father had.

She screwed her nose up at her surroundings. Pulling up her cloak further around her face, she found a table near enough to hear her father and positioned herself so a wooden pole stood in the line of sight between them.

'It was a baaaad omen, I tell you,' a man nearby slurred, wagging his finger knowingly.

The man's drinking companion sloshed his ale across the table. 'Bad for Ette, I hear, but in Lamore we are alive and well.'

'Bad for aaaallll of Lamore.'

Theodora watched as her father tapped his fingers on the table impatiently. Soon, a burly man plonked himself down on the bench opposite the Chancellor. His gold jewellery rattled as he moved. Even from this distance Theodora could smell sweat, rum and tobacco on the man, who she guessed by his appearance was a pirate – a vile one at that. She leant in closer to hear their conversation.

'The seat is taken,' Horace told the man gruffly.

'Yes, it is taken.' The man thumped his chest with his fist. 'By me.'

Horace shook his head in annoyance. 'You need to leave.'

'Well, that wouldn't exactly be in your best interests, now

would it…Chancellor?' The pirate leant in toward him, his trunk-like arms resting on the table. 'Especially since I have something for you.'

'You were the one who sent the message?'

The pirate beckoned to someone across the room. Theodora followed his gaze to see her brother, Guthrie, being shoved toward their father. He wore a torn and blood-stained army uniform.

'You're alive,' Theodora's father said, with a relief that she herself didn't feel.

'Sit down, my yellow-bellied friend,' the pirate barked, and his henchman shoved Guthrie onto the bench beside him.

'What are you doing here?' Horace asked. 'Why aren't you with your men? What happened in Ette?'

Guthrie hung his head and shrugged.

'It pains me to inform you, Chancellor, that your son is nothing short of a coward.'

Horace spun toward the pirate. 'I warn you not to speak of Lord Guthrie in such a manner.'

The man gave a cockeyed smile. 'Even if it's true?'

'Speak,' Horace ordered his son. 'Tell me what happened.'

Guthrie looked up at their father. Even from this distance, Theodora could see his eyes were swimming with fear.

'There were so many of them. So, so many of them.' He shook his head disbelievingly. 'Northemers. Great mountains of men. And bloodthirsty. They came at us like men possessed.'

'But you fought them?'

'We tried, but Sir Marcus and I were left without our full forces.'

'But where was Lakeford?'

'The Duke and Sar had gone to the Ivanian borderlands to settle a local uprising. There had been some skirmishes there, and talk of them joining forces with Ivane. They took both of their units with them. We were pitifully outnumbered. By the time Lakeford and his men were back, it was too late. We couldn't prevail.'

'So you surrendered?'

Guthrie gave a small shake of his head.

'Your son and Sir Marcus ran.' The pirate offered a gold-toothed grin. 'They ran from the battle like beaten puppies, their tails between their legs.'

'You *ran!*' Horace hissed.

Of course he did, Theodora thought.

'What were we supposed to do?'

'Fight. Fight with your men.' Theodora could practically see her father resisting the urge to stand up and shake his son.

'Father, you've never seen the likes of them.'

'Your son is right, at least in that respect,' the pirate put in. 'Giants of men. They snuck into the capital's port in hundreds of sleek-looking boats, the night of the blood moon. They reached the city gate before an alarm could be raised.'

'What do you know of these *Northemers*?' Horace demanded.

'They are a formidable enemy. I've never been to their lands, but I have met some who have spent time in their capital, Arykyl. I know until now Northem consisted of fractured provincial societies. Their arable land is sparse; most of the country is made of ice and rock. But after decades of famine and disease and internal squabbling, the country recently united under a new leader. They call him Malu.'

'So these Northemers seek new lands for resources – settlement, even?'

'I expect that is their primary objective. And with ships capable of crossing the open sea that can just as easily manoeuvre through shallow and narrow rivers, they are unstoppable.'

'Unstoppable! That is a rather grand statement to make.'

The pirate shrugged. 'I wasn't sticking around too long to see for myself. Your son and Sir Marcus arrived at my boat as I was leaving port. We'd been lying low in the city until we could make it safely back to our ship to escape. Your boy and the Governor were lucky to find me when they did.'

Horace shot a scathing look at his son. 'I'm not sure he should be feeling too lucky right now.'

'I suppose you'd prefer me dead?' Guthrie cried, with an irritating sense of indignation.

Yes, I would, Theodora thought.

'You may be better off dead by the time the King is finished with you. So what of Lakeford and Sar? What of the remainder of the King's forces?'

Guthrie looked down at the table, leaving it to the pirate to answer.

'The King's fleet was all but obliterated, from what I saw. Every ship in port was set alight soon after we left. My guess is your forces couldn't have lasted for more than a day or so. If they were able to retreat without being captured, what's left of your army will probably be trying to make their way home now.'

Horace leant back and scrutinised the pirate for a moment. 'I suppose I should thank you for bringing my son back.'

'Oh, you *will* thank me.'

'Don't toy with me, pirate. What do you want?'

'Now, hang on there. The name's Goldman and I'm no pirate. I'm the captain of a respectable trading vessel.'

'Don't insult me. What do you want?'

Goldman stroked his beard. 'Ten thousand pieces.'

'Ten thousand pieces of silver! That's daylight robbery.'

'Of gold.' The pirate smiled slyly, his gold teeth glinting. 'I want ten thousand pieces of gold.'

Horace laughed out loud. 'You can keep my son for that.'

Exactly, Theodora thought. *He's not worth even one piece.*

'And a further ten thousand pieces for Sir Marcus.'

'Where is Sir Marcus now?'

'Somewhere safe, I can assure you. You can see him when I see my gold.'

'I will have to discuss the matter with the King.'

'As I'd expect – and I will keep your fallen Governor as surety in the meantime.'

'Where shall I send word?'

'Here, of course.' Goldman waved his hands theatrically around at the tavern. 'My second home.'

'I'll leave you to your homecoming, then,' Horace hissed as he stood up, and motioned for Guthrie to follow him. It appeared that the Chancellor couldn't get out of the tavern fast enough. His huntsman fell in behind them as they left.

At a distance, Theodora followed to watch the beratement she knew would come and wasn't about to miss. Once they were out in the daylight, she fell back behind a market stall, and Horace spun on his son.

'The King will never forgive this, you stupid boy.'

'Father, surely you can convince him to be merciful. I am his kin and you are his most trusted adviser.'

'Perhaps I don't want to appeal to him,' Horace spat.

Guthrie's eyes widened and his mouth formed a scowl – tell-tale signs his infamous temper was about to flare. People were already looking at the soldier in his bloody uniform.

'Wait here,' Horace ordered. 'I need to get something for you to wear over your uniform, or you'll be dead before we can reach the castle.' He turned to the huntsman. 'Don't let him out of your sight.'

Theodora slipped away, pleased with the information she had learnt. So Ette had been lost to mysterious Northem invaders, and her cowardly brother had abandoned his post.

If there were ever a time for her to play a bigger role in her father's plans, it had to be now.

5

———

The Schoolmaster ran his fingers through his thinning grey hair. He had been sitting silently across from Arisa for an eternity. He was trying his best to look officious and serious – which was hard, given his reputation for being kind and fair rather than fearsome, and the fact that most of the older students towered over him. This didn't mean he wasn't respected by the students, though. He was, which was why Arisa dreaded these talks with him.

Finally, the Schoolmaster spoke. 'Your tutor has made a serious accusation.'

She didn't respond.

'Do you know what you're accused of?'

She shrugged, preferring to feign ignorance.

The Schoolmaster sighed. 'You're accused of hitting a fellow student.'

'Yes.'

He sighed again. 'It wasn't just any student, but a nephew of the Baron of Iveness.'

Arisa nodded.

'Would you mind telling me why you did such a thing?'

'He provoked me.'

'How?'

'He called me a pathetic Kengian sympathiser.'

'And that was reason enough to hit him?'

Another shrug.

'Arisa, I know things have been difficult the last few days. I heard what happened to the young Kengian boy.'

She winced, not wishing to be reminded of Hyando's death.

'But you can't bring your frustrations about the regime to school. You shouldn't speak of them anywhere in Obira. Tensions are already high since the blood moon. There has been talk of uprisings from displaced farmers, and there is greater uncertainty for everyone with the fall of Ette.'

Arisa looked away, wanting to discourage further conversation.

'You're a clever girl. I need not counsel you on why it's unwise to act in such a manner. But I feel I must remind you: you are only at this school by your guardian's good grace. I will be forever indebted to Erun for the care he gave to my dear wife in her last days. Despite that, I can't continue to tolerate outbursts like this.' The Schoolmaster's eyes went to the boy's clothes she wore. 'As well as...other oddities.' He appeared to be waiting for a response, but received none. 'You must know the danger you put yourself in.'

'My personal safety isn't important in the greater scheme of things. What's important is that people have enough to eat. That Kengians aren't persecuted. That silver-eyes don't die at the hands of a cruel King.' Her voice rose with each statement.

'Hush.' The Schoolmaster looked around the empty room. 'That may be true, but what you say borders on treason and could send us both to Lamore's dungeons, or worse.' He softened his tone. 'Wouldn't it be easier to try to fall in with the other students? In private, have what beliefs you want, but when you're at school, keep your head down. Don't draw attention to yourself.'

'Blend in,' Arisa responded in singsong, having heard the

same advice a hundred times before. It was an impossible task when she clearly wasn't like other people her age. She'd grown up in an adult world, surrounded by pain and death. She'd been forced to act beyond her years. Never able to be herself; too many secrets to hide. Yet she was expected to *blend in.*

'Just do your best to avoid confrontations. You may even gain admittance to the College of Surgeons, but not if news of incidents like this reaches the castle.'

'So I'm supposed to just let the other students insult me and my guardian, and treat every suspected Kengian and their supporters like scum?'

'Yes. For now, you must ignore it as best you can, and prepare yourself for more.'

She raised a quizzical brow.

'Surely you know there has been talk for many years that Erun is a Kengian. We know he is a talented physician and apothecary, but he is also rumoured to have *special* talents.' He paused before continuing in a lowered voice. 'Some say he may even be a Scholar.'

The Schoolmaster searched Arisa's face questioningly, as if trying to gauge whether his assumption was correct.

She pursed her lips. The Schoolmaster was a good man, but Arisa wasn't entirely sure she could trust him with Erun's secrets, or her own.

'Alright, Arisa. I understand why you don't want to tell me anything, but if you need someone who…' He seemed to be searching for the right words. 'Someone who sympathises with certain causes, you can come to me.'

'What, so you can *help* me, just like you helped Rea?'

The Schoolmaster's face screwed up in pain. 'You know I tried to do everything I could to help her, but—' His words came out strangled, and she immediately regretted bringing up Rea. It was really herself she was angry with, after all.

Arisa held her hands up in surrender. 'I shall heed my words and actions more carefully, but I can't promise I won't draw attention to myself. I am one of the only girls at this school, and I'm lowborn, as well as being the ward of a suspected Kengian. So, as you say, people's eyes will always be on me. That being said, I will do my best.'

'That is all I can ask.'

'May I be dismissed?'

The Schoolmaster gave a small nod, and she left him at speed before he had a chance to lecture her about anything else.

Exiting the school grounds, Arisa headed for home, following a path straight into the thick of the city and avoiding the city gates. She didn't need any reminders of the horrifying incident that had claimed Hyando's life. She walked swiftly, her cap pulled down well over her ears, determined to stay out of trouble.

Soon she reached the city's marketplace and passed the Lion's Den, averting her eyes from the sparsely dressed women and drunken customers spilling out of the doorway. Arisa looked up into the cloudless sky instead, admiring the purity of it, a stark contrast to Obira and its murkiness. It was as if the blood moon had never been.

Then she saw it. At first, it was just a tiny speck. Arisa rubbed her eyes and refocused until the dot slowly took shape: a lone starling, flying overhead. She stood still to admire the bird's iridescent feathers, a flutter of sapphire, emerald, violet, bronze and gold.

'A message,' she whispered to herself. With the Nymoi Alps protected by the Kengian King, the only way to send messages between the two nations was via starlings. But with such risk of being intercepted, the birds were only used for missives of the greatest importance.

'Look. A Kengian starling.'

The voice came from nearby. Arisa turned to see a thickset young soldier in an army uniform. There was something vaguely familiar about him. He was pointing the bird out to his companion: a huntsman, she judged by his clothing and the bow and quiver slung over his shoulder.

The soldier reached out and grabbed the huntsman's bow, as well as an arrow from his quiver, and aimed at the starling. He drew back the string and was about to fire—

Arisa mustered herself up to her full height and ran full force at him.

Somehow she managed to knock the soldier off balance, and the arrow went astray, rebounding off the wall of a stone townhouse. Arisa breathed a sigh of relief as the starling continued overhead and disappeared out of sight.

The soldier was glaring at her. 'What are you playing at, you little weasel?'

'Saving an innocent bird.' Her glib response may not have been a wise choice, given the sheer bulk of the man.

The soldier advanced menacingly on Arisa but she stood her ground.

'It's not so innocent,' he spat. 'That bird is carrying secret messages from Kengia. Our sworn enemy.'

'Kengia's not my enemy.'

'You little upstart. I'll teach you—'

Before she knew it, the soldier's fist was coming straight at her face.

Arisa turned to the side to try to avoid the blow, but his fist connected with her cheek and mouth. She fell backwards onto the ground, where she lay in shock, aware of nothing but the metallic taste of blood in her mouth and the throbbing in her face. She thought she could hear muffled voices, but they seemed to be coming from a long way away.

The soldier bent down and peered at her. Seemingly satisfied with his work, he turned and started to walk away.

Arisa told herself she should stay where she was. She should remain still, wait until he was well gone, until it was safe enough for her to get up and run away, but something inside her urged otherwise. She had the sense she was about to do something stupid, but she didn't care. This was her chance to get some of the justice she had pledged to fight for.

Arisa got to her feet, making a deliberate show of removing her satchel and placing it on the ground. She squared her shoulders and closed her fists tightly, trying to ignore the shaking in her hands.

'Fight!' an onlooker cried.

The soldier spun back toward her. She noticed the huntsman disappearing into the shadows as a crowd began to form. People poured out from the tavern onto the street, no doubt curious about the burly soldier and what looked like a strange stick of a boy about to fight.

Arisa glared at her opponent, staring straight into his black, lifeless eyes. 'Surely you can do better than that.' The crowd jeered and laughed at her recklessness.

The soldier took a step closer to her.

'Hey, I recognise him,' she heard one of the onlookers say. 'It's Lord Guthrie, the Chancellor's son.'

'What's he doing here? Isn't he supposed to be in Ette?'

'Ran from the fight, I just heard.'

The soldier glowered at the crowd. *Guthrie.* Arisa should have recognised him. Those eyes, the colour of death, were branded on her soul. Her promise to the Schoolmaster was fresh in her mind, but this was the boy responsible for taking Rea away. For trying to take *her.* She wasn't surprised that he didn't appear to remember her. He was a heartless oaf.

'So, what do you suppose the King will do with a coward?' she said, unable to resist the urge to torment him. They began to circle each other.

'It's no business of yours, weasel,' Guthrie snarled.

'The hangman's noose is what they reserve for cowards,' said another voice. Arisa spotted its owner from the corner of her eye. He was a bear of a man, with a pointy beard, shiny gold teeth and a hoop earring to match. From his seafaring clothes, she guessed he was a pirate. He stepped back into the shadows again before Guthrie could spot him.

Guthrie spun around angrily and addressed the whole crowd. 'How dare you insult someone so high above your standing? Show your face, *now*.'

No one made a move.

Arisa laughed.

Guthrie turned back toward her, his black eyes bulging. 'And what do you find so funny?'

'You may be higher-born than any of us, but you're still a bully and a coward.'

'I warn you, boy, to shut your face or I'll beat you to a pulp.'

She sized him up. Guthrie was at least two feet taller than her and probably twice as heavy. She knew he was more than capable of doing what he said, but she would not surrender to him.

'Maybe you can beat me to a pulp…but maybe you can't.' Her teasing inspired more laughter and jeers from the crowd.

Guthrie threw a filthy look at the onlookers before fixing his attention on her again. His eyes narrowed; his nostrils flared. Arisa could feel the hate oozing from him.

With a growl, Guthrie launched himself at her, aiming a right hook at her jaw. She managed to leap out of his range, narrowly avoiding the blow.

Guthrie grunted and stumbled as he missed. The crowd cheered as he tried to recover himself.

Arisa gave the crowd a victorious smile and a wave.

Guthrie scowled before charging headlong at her. This time she wasn't quick enough. He wrapped his arms around her torso, throwing her to the ground.

She fell with a thud. There was a stabbing pain in her chest as her rib cracked under Guthrie's weight. Her cap was thrown from her head by the force of the fall, and a wave of gasps rolled through the crowd.

'It's a girl,' someone cried, and Guthrie's face froze momentarily with shock.

'Guthrie's fighting a girl!' was the next cry, followed by a stream of laughter.

Guthrie's lip curled up in disgust. 'Not like any girl I've ever seen.' He stood over her and spat in her face.

Putrid spittle rolled down her cheek, but Arisa could do nothing to retaliate in her struggle to breathe. Her lungs screamed out for air as she clawed at her throat. Oxygen came to her only in short bursts and gasps.

Guthrie smirked as he landed his boot heavily on her stomach.

'You, and everyone here,' he roared at the crowd, 'will think again before provoking me. You shall remember to respect the King's kin.'

Arisa clutched her stomach, willing herself to find breath through the dirt and blood in her mouth.

'Long live King Delrik!' Guthrie cried.

Finally Arisa summoned the strength to wipe away the spit and force herself up onto all fours. Rising to her knees, she pushed her hair back from her face, raised her head and met Guthrie's victorious gaze.

'There is only one King.' She could only manage a whisper. 'And that is the Kengian King.'

'What are you muttering about, pig filth?'

'I said' – she spoke a little louder – 'the Kengian King is the only true king.'

'So you're one of *them*.' Guthrie sneered the last word. 'Trust me when I say you and your Kengian friends are on borrowed time. You should remember what happens to Kengians and their sympathisers when they defy Lamore's rule.'

Arisa shook her head and forced herself to her feet. She pushed her shoulders back, not wanting to show Guthrie the extent of her pain. 'I may be one of *them*, as you say, but at least I'm not a yellow-bellied coward.'

The crowd hushed. Guthrie's face flushed bright red.

He clenched his fists and charged at her again.

Despite facing the afternoon sun, Arisa was alert enough to predict Guthrie's move. She used her smaller size and speed to her advantage and sidestepped out of his way. He fell heavily to the ground.

Guthrie pulled himself back to his feet and was about to charge again, but this time *he* was looking toward the sun. He squinted as the light momentarily dazzled him. Seeing her chance, Arisa leapt forward and thrust the heel of her hand up into the bottom of his nose. She felt a bone crunch under her hand, and pain spread through her palm.

The crowd laughed uproariously as Guthrie held a hand to his bloody nose. 'You broke my nose, you whoreson!'

Nursing her hand, Arisa started to feel panic for the first time. She might have landed a lucky blow against Guthrie, but she was sure he would prevail overall. He stomped toward her, murder in his gaze. She closed her eyes in anticipation of the blow – but before it fell, a booming voice cut through the crowd.

'Halt! Halt this instant!'

Arisa opened her eyes to see a man in a black cloak standing before Guthrie. She couldn't see his face properly under his hood, but he spoke with such authority that Guthrie froze and the crowd hushed.

'Make your way home.' The man's thundering voice reverberated through the crowd. 'All of you! Guthrie, come with me at once.'

Guthrie shot a withering look at Arisa and looked back at the man in the cloak, before kicking the ground in frustration. He pointed a finger at her. 'I haven't forgotten the insults you paid me today, wench. I shall have the last victory. That I promise you.' After a final filthy look, he marched off, nursing his bloody nose.

Once she was sure he was gone, Arisa picked up her cap with shaking hands and tucked her hair back under it. She retrieved her satchel and took a few wary steps, trying to ignore the throbbing in her lip and hand, as well as the stabbing pain in her ribs. A few onlookers slapped her on the back, congratulating her on her nerve. She gave a shy smile before turning in the direction of home.

How would she explain her injuries to Erun? She knew he would be angry with her, yet couldn't help but smile to herself at the injuries she'd inflicted on Guthrie. She had wounded not just his nose, but his pride. It was a little bit of justice for Rea, and for the rest of Lamore. And she felt safe in the knowledge that Guthrie would return to his life at the castle. There was no reason Arisa would ever have to see him again, and she was glad of it.

6

———

*E*run sat hunched over the table, quill poised over the notes from his experiment. He scratched his head as he reread them. It was dark in the back room of his shop, particularly at this time of day. Embers from the kitchen fire cast an eerie glow on his face and intensified the wildness of his wiry hair.

When he wasn't compounding medicines, Erun conducted scientific experiments using the knowledge and skills he had learnt as a Kengian Scholar. He was intent on mastering his craft and discovering new ways to heal people. Putting his quill back in the inkwell, he looked down at the contraption on the table.

Erun screwed his nose up at the dead mouse splayed before him. He didn't like experimenting on animals, and was thankful he had found this particular subject shortly after it had fallen into a pot of water and drowned. He attached metal discs to two wire leads coming from either end of the device. Picking up the leads, he took a deep breath, then touched the two discs tentatively to the mouse leg.

There was a bright spark of light and the leg jerked in response.

Erun jumped back in his chair, wondering if his eyes had deceived him. He flung a hand to his mouth, before reaching for his quill and writing furiously. Then, just as abruptly, he stopped writing. There was a churning feeling in the pit of his stomach.

Something didn't feel right.

Looking up from his notes, he caught a familiar sight from the corner of his eye. The metallic sheen of coloured feathers flashed through the gaps in the shutters. It was a Kengian starling.

The bird sat on Erun's windowsill and cooed. A master of imitation, it sounded like a Lamorian pigeon, but he also heard its words: *An urgent message.*

Erun opened the shutters and quickly ushered the starling inside. He removed the message carefully from its leg. His hands began to shake as he unravelled the paper and recognised his mother's handwriting.

Queen Mira had written in code. He translated it easily in his head:

It pains me, son, to give you the news we have long feared was coming. Your father, the King, is dead. He fell suddenly ill with the coming of the blood moon. Nothing could be done. None of our medicine or powers could save him. I am devastated, as much as I'm sure you are, but there is no time to properly mourn our loss. It's inevitable the Lamorian King will soon discover the protection over all routes into Kengia died with my dearest Leo.

Many of our people are fearful and have long lost any hope and belief in the prophecy. The Mountain Chief and his people have holed themselves up in their villages and are preparing to fight. The tribes are already patrolling our shores for the arrival of potential enemies. They are deter-mined to be ready for Lamore and the Northemers – whichever comes first. They even speak of launching a pre-emptive strike against King Delrik.

I have begged the council to take a moment to consider, and reminded them this is not the Kengian way. I have asked them to maintain faith in the prophecy as the King has always done. They say the time for faith is over. They believe any hope of the prophecy being fulfilled died with Prince Alik, and as you know, I am unable to contradict them.

Erun stood up from the table and rubbed his neck anxiously before reading on.

I fear the appetite for war will lead us away from everything that makes us Kengian. I grieve for Kengia as much as I grieve the loss of the King.

I think the tribes are right in one respect. We must act now. We need assurances that our faith has not been misplaced. You must do what you can to bring our hopes to reality. Kengia's future relies on it.

Erun stared into the fire, lost in its hissing flames, thinking of the last time he had seen his father. They had parted on bad terms, and Erun had done nothing but disappoint him ever since. At least, that was how he felt.

He had left Kengia nearly eighteen years ago, promising to find and save his brother. Back then Erun had been known as the Kengian Prince, Amund. His elder brother, Prince Alik, had been staying in Lamore as a guest of King Delrik, but had suddenly disappeared. There were grave fears for Alik's safety and Erun had begged his father to let him go in search of his brother.

He remembered the conversation as if it happened yesterday.

'This is my fault,' the King had said. 'I should have stopped your brother. I knew nothing good could come of trying to make peace with the Lamorians.'

'Alik did what he thought was right. He was serving Ivane and their wish for an alliance with Lamore.'

'It shouldn't have been Kengia's problem.'

'How can you speak in such a way, Father? The Ivanians have always been our allies. After everything they have suffered at the hands of Lamore, there was no one else they could turn to or trust to manage the negotiations.'

'They were right to be suspicious of Lamore. As we speak, Delrik is planning to invade Ivane, despite the promises he has made to his young wife and her father.'

'We weren't to know King Delrik would be as ruthless as his father before him.'

'But I should have sent another envoy. Not our firstborn – not the key to the prophecy. It was too risky.'

Erun had bowed his head, wishing he had gone to Lamore in his brother's place. Yet Alik was the only one who could have made the journey. His powers over wind and air meant it was he, and he alone, who could open and close the mountain passage between Lamore and Kengia.

'We have all been deceived by the King and his Chancellor. Now Alik is missing, and the passageway to Kengia lies dangerously open.' The King had sighed in resignation. 'I have no choice but to permanently close off the mountain passage.'

'But there are so many of our kinsmen still there,' Erun protested. They had gone with his brother as a sign of good faith, to help the Lamorians cultivate their land. 'We can't abandon them. We can't abandon Alik!'

'I fear your brother is already dead. Why else would the passageway be open?'

'There could be a thousand reasons. Perhaps he is just ill, or…I don't know, but he may still be alive. Let me go in secret to Lamore. Let me try to find him and bring him home.'

The King shook his head adamantly. 'I can't risk the life of another son.'

'But what if he is alive? Then we must try to find him. It is the only hope for protecting the prophecy.'

The King looked at Erun with a pained expression on his face before nodding slowly. 'So be it.'

So Erun had gone to Lamore – only to discover that the Chancellor had already mobilised forces to attack Kengia. With no time to waste, King Leo had summoned a great earthquake, permanently closing the mountain pass between the two nations and creating a protective field around Kengia's borders. But this had left Erun stranded in Lamore, separated from what was left of his family, and others dear to him.

He never found Alik. But despite the loss of his brother, he still had hope that the prophecy would one day be fulfilled.

Belief, though, provided little comfort in the present circumstances.

As Erun sat staring into the fire with a heavy heart, he wasn't sure he could give his mother the assurances she needed. How could he be sure when the prophecy would come to being, and whether it would be in time to prevent all-out war? No answer materialised in the flames before him. But Erun reminded himself that there was one thing he did know for sure.

The blood moon had been the first sign. There was hope in the prophecy. Even if there was nothing he could do to hasten its realisation.

7

____

With Chancellor Horace away on something he described as 'urgent business', Takai finally got his meeting with the King.

It was odd spending time with his father, who might as well be a stranger to him. The King had gone to great effort to make him feel welcome, offering him wine and declaring that a great celebration would be held to celebrate Takai's upcoming eighteenth birthday, and the twentieth year of his own reign. He was in surprisingly good spirits, considering his initial reaction to the blood moon and the Northemer invasion in Ette. He'd taken himself to bed for a day, declaring it the end of the world. Apparently, he'd listened to no one other than the Chancellor, who had needed to employ his best persuasive skills to convince the King that the blood moon meant nothing, and that Ette would be his again soon enough.

It was hard to reconcile that man with the one who stood in front of Takai now, describing his grandiose celebration plans in almost delirious detail. Takai's father was known to be erratic at times, but seeing it play out in person strengthened the Prince's determination to be more involved in the running of the kingdom.

The King was about to show Takai a roll of parchment on his desk when Horace strode into the privy chamber unannounced. The Chancellor appeared to do a double take when he saw Takai was there, but quickly regained his composure and nodded his acknowledgement.

Takai's father stood up at Horace's arrival, grabbing the Chancellor companionably by the shoulders.

'Horace, my old friend. Your timing is fortuitous. I have some news to share.'

'As do I, Your Majesty.' Horace nodded toward Takai. 'News best shared privately.'

The King waved his heavily bejewelled fingers. 'Not now.'

'With all due respect, Your Majesty, you must hear what I have to say.'

The King's eyes narrowed as he frowned at being told what he 'must' do. But just as quickly, a courtier's smile spread across his face. 'Horace, whatever it is, I am sure you can handle it. I can't be distracted right now. I am entirely focused on one thing, and that is the great celebrations.'

'Your Majesty, I thought you would wish to discuss Ette and what its loss means to Lamore.'

'You have recalled all of my councillors to court to discuss strategy, have you not?'

'Yes. I expect your full council will be ready to meet in a few days.'

'What about Lakeford – any word?' Takai asked.

Horace bristled. 'We don't know what has become of the Duke or the remainder of the King's forces.'

A hard lump formed in Takai's throat. He cared for the man who had been a father figure to him – and his best friend, Sar, would have been by the Duke's side.

The King shrugged. 'Well, I expect you will do just as well in leading my council and developing a plan for Ette.'

Horace nodded, a smile twitching at the side of his mouth.

'In the meantime, I would like to speak about my celebrations.'

Takai frowned. His father's unpredictable nature aside, his focus right now on such trivial matters was odd.

'Your Majesty, I'm told there are safety concerns for the celebrations,' Horace said.

'What do you mean?'

'Sire, you have indicated a wish for a public tournament and a progress to the counties. Both would expose you to danger from your people.'

'Bah! There have always been threats against me.'

'Yes, but with the increase in taxes and now the loss of Ette, the mood is worse.'

'I don't suppose enclosing your lands helped either.' The King's sharp eyes rested on Horace.

A muscle in one of Horace's cheeks twitched. 'There was a minor disturbance on one of my properties – a small group of displaced farmers led by my former reeve, Sergei. But it was quickly quashed.'

Takai's ears pricked up. Displaced farmers? Minor disturbances? They didn't bode well for celebration events or a progress – or the running of the kingdom, for that matter. Law and order were imperative.

'So I have nothing to fear from this Sergei?' the King asked.

'No, sire, I will see to that. But I'm not sure the timing is right for a public tournament and a progress. Not while Lamore's future is so uncertain.'

The King shook his head angrily. 'I will have these celebrations, and my people must be there to show their adoration.'

'Father,' Takai offered, 'if you're so determined, may I suggest one thing?'

The King gave a small nod.

'Ask the Queen to attend the celebrations with you. My mother is still quite beloved by the people, is she not?' Not that Takai knew why, having no relationship with his mother to speak of and the fact it was an open secret that his parents had separate lives. But he wanted an opportunity to prove his worth to his father.

'Yes, she is still beloved.' The King sighed. 'You're right. I must have the Queen by my side for the tournament and progress. Goodness knows how I will convince her, but it must be done. If that's not enough to inspire fealty among my subjects, I will have to achieve the same by other means.'

'Sire,' Horace pressed, 'I really must now speak to you of Ette.'

The King sat again and put his feet up on the table, resting his hands behind his head. 'How do you suppose I retake it? How will I defeat these great Northern invaders? And how do you think I can strike fear in every Lamorian who refuses to bend the knee to their King?'

Horace appeared taken aback for a moment, as if the King expected him to provide immediate solutions to the questions he posed, but the smug look on King Delrik's face suggested he already had his own ideas. He sprang back to a regular seated position and jabbed a finger at a piece of parchment rolled out on his desk. 'The answer to everything is here, my friend.'

Horace and Takai edged closer. Takai soon saw the parchment was actually a painting. From the discolouration around the edges, he could tell it was old, but the colours were still vivid enough to show it depicted a great celebration. The words under the painting read: *The Commemoration of the Birth of His Royal Highness, Prince James, son of King Alfred and Queen Mary.*

'You know,' the King mused, 'for my own celebrations, I have been quite determined to create a spectacle like no other. It must be the greatest celebration this kingdom has ever seen.'

Horace nodded slowly. Takai's brow crinkled, unsure where the King's thoughts were going.

'Well, the blood moon got me thinking about the prophecy—'

'Your Majesty,' Horace interrupted, 'you know as well as I do the prophecy is no threat. We have seen to that.'

'Yes, yes. But it was something else mentioned in the prophecy that interested me. Here, look.' The King pointed excitedly at the painting.

Takai took a closer look. It was a typical celebration scene at the castle, showing a tournament in full swing at the tiltyard. There were brightly coloured stalls and tents, knights and their destriers, and finely dressed nobles. He cast his eyes upwards to the top of the painting. It was night. *Strange,* Takai thought. Tournaments didn't take place at night.

He looked closer still, but that part of the painting was faded, and parts of the sky appeared to be missing. No – not missing: simply a patchwork of different colours. He examined the shapes in the sky again. There was a large circle, dull orange in colour. The blood moon, he realised. But beside it were star-bursts of light. A shower of red, yellow, white and orange sparks—

'Firesky,' he whispered.

The King clapped his hands together and grinned.

'Sire, you want *firesky* for your celebrations?' Horace asked.

'I do. Or perhaps we launch it when we start our progress.'

'But sire – the secrets to firesky were lost with Kengia's last Firemaster, as far back as Emberto the Conqueror's time.'

'Horace, there are plenty of Kengians still in this kingdom. One of them must know something of firesky. Goodness knows, we also have enough books and manuscripts in this castle that one of them must hold clues to how it's done.'

The Chancellor took a deep breath. 'Your Majesty, not even Emberto could recreate firesky, and he had the last Firemaster as his prisoner.'

The King pressed his lips tightly together. 'Am I not as great a King as Emberto?'

'You are greater, sire.'

'Well, it's settled. You will give me firesky.'

Horace clasped his hands together tightly. 'Even if it's possible, wouldn't I be better occupied planning your strategy for Ette?'

The King gave a great laugh. 'Don't you see, my dear friend? If I have firesky, I have everything I need to defeat my enemies.'

Takai tried to follow the King's train of thought. *Firesky.* He let the image roll over in his mind. From his knowledge, firesky was created by lighting and propelling something into the sky that resulted in great noises and colourful light. How exactly it was done was unknown. And he was entirely certain that Horace could not produce something even the great King Emberto had failed at. Despite this, he must be prepared to entertain his father's idea.

'I suppose if it is possible to create thunder and lightning in the sky...' he conjectured aloud.

Horace nodded. 'It may be possible to make—'

'Weapons!' The King rubbed his hands together.

'Yes,' the Chancellor agreed. 'The same device that carries the substance into the sky could be launched at an army. Perhaps the power could be harnessed to launch projectiles... Like trebuchets, but much more powerful. Powerful enough, perhaps, to wipe out hundreds in one swoop.'

'Exactly!'

'It would be capable of bringing down the fortified walls of Ette.' Horace seemed to be getting wrapped up in the King's enthusiasm for this harebrained scheme.

'And Ivane,' the King added.

Horace stroked his chin thoughtfully. 'Perhaps even Kengia.'

'Not Kengia,' Takai said. 'Even if we had a navy – which we don't, after Ette – the last time you mounted an attack on Kengia, your fleet was destroyed by a tidal wave of the sorcerer king's making.'

Horace cast an annoyed look at Takai. 'I think our ships will be safe this time. We could pass over the mountains once the winter snow is gone,' Horace said.

But the King shook his head emphatically. 'Every attempt we've made at going over or tunnelling through the Nymoi Alps has brought King Leo's rockslides down upon our men.'

'That is what I have come to tell you.'

The King tilted his head at the Chancellor.

'I have just spoken to one of my huntsmen, who has come directly from Shizen Lake. He reports that the mountain range is eerily quiet.'

'Quiet? How so?'

'Sire, you recall the low hum that could always be heard in the area surrounding the Nymoi Alps?'

'Yes, the Kengian King's protection spell.'

'Over the last few days or so, there has been no sound. My man, curious at this, tried digging into the mountainside, and there was nothing. Not a single rockfall or rumble.'

The King's eyes lit up. 'You mean to say – the Kengian King may be dead?'

'That is my assumption, sire.'

'There it is!' The King clapped his hands together. 'With firesky, I can not only take back Ette and Ivane – I could have *Kengia*.'

'In theory, yes, you can, Your Majesty,' Horace allowed, 'but it would take time. Time we may not have if the Northemers come for us. And we must remember Kengia is likely to be ready for us. They will have a great army, and by all accounts we have none.'

'What do you suggest?' Takai said.

'I think we must rebuild our army and navy, but not to attack the Northemers. To invade Kengia first.'

'What if the Northem army comes for Lamore while we are occupied fighting Kengia?' Takai asked.

'I think we should offer an alliance with the Northem leader

– Malu, I hear is his name. We should offer to share the larger prize of Kengia with him.'

The King shook his head. 'I have no wish to share Kengia with anyone, and I must have Ette and Ivane back. It is my legacy.'

'I suggest we only make a temporary alliance. Long enough to get Malu's support to invade Kengia, and then when he least expects it, we will turn on him and take back what is ours.'

'But we know nothing of this Malu,' Takai protested.

Horace ignored him, addressing the King instead. 'It is our only chance. There is no way we can defeat them.'

'But what if we had firesky weapons?' the King asked.

'There won't be time enough for firesky, *even* if it were possible,' the Chancellor said, stressing the last part. 'Malu will make a move as soon as the weather warms. Spring at the earliest. We will not succeed against them.'

'How can you be so sure?'

Horace seemed to hesitate. 'I have had a firsthand account of these men.'

The King raised an eyebrow.

'I have spoken to Guthrie.'

'They are back? I thought you said the Duke—'

'No. It is only Guthrie, and apparently Sir Marcus.'

'What do you mean?'

'My son and the Governor escaped from the battle and found passage home with a pirate who is now demanding a ransom be paid.'

'But what of Lakeford and his men?' Takai demanded.

Horace clicked his jaw. 'I understand Lakeford and the rest of his men stayed.'

The King leapt from his chair. His face had turned a violent shade of red.

'What!' Takai cried.

'You mean to say your son and Sir Marcus ran from the battle?' the King roared.

Horace dropped his head shamefully. 'I'm afraid so, Your Majesty. All I can do is beg your forgiveness on behalf of my son. He has done much to offend you, and his performance at Ette will be an eternal embarrassment.'

The King clenched his fists. 'Your son and Sir Marcus must be dealt with.'

'Please, sire, let me deal with my son. Trust that I will ensure he atones for his wrongdoings. Allow me this.'

King Delrik exhaled heavily. 'I will allow you to deal with this matter. In fact, I may overlook your son's dishonour entirely, and let him take up his position on my council.'

'You would, sire?' Horace appeared confused.

'Of course I would do this for you. After all, no one can ever accuse me of not being merciful to those loyal to me.'

'Thank you. Your benevolence is overwhelming.' Horace gave a small bow.

'However, it is to be on one condition.'

'Sire?'

'You will deliver firesky to me for my celebrations – or the progress, whichever is first – and further determine how to weaponise it.'

Horace appeared to swallow nervously before he said, 'I will do my best.'

Good luck, Takai thought.

'You will have to do *more* than your best, Horace, if you wish to save your son from a traitor's death.'

A shiver ran down Takai's spine. He knew it was not an empty threat.

'Leave it with me, sire. I shall not fail you.'

'I knew you would take care of it, Horace.' The King clapped his hand on the Chancellor's back, a little harder than he needed to. 'I will think on the matter of an alliance with Malu. The rest of our strategy I will leave to you and my council. Right now I have some other business to attend to.'

Takai followed his father's gaze as a woman sauntered into

the room. He recognised her as the wife of the Baron of Iveness. Takai was shocked that he would so openly flaunt his latest mistress.

The Chancellor gave her a small nod of acknowledgement, before bidding the King farewell. 'Good day, Your Majesty.'

'Father,' Takai said, bowing his head and following Horace from the room. He felt a little sorry for the Chancellor, given such an impossible task. But even more, he felt concerned that the fate of the kingdom sat with an incompetent king, and a scheming adviser whose ambitions far exceeded his abilities.

8

———

*A*risa noticed the starling the moment she arrived home. She rushed forward excitedly. 'A message from Kengia?'

Erun stoked the fire and lit some candles before taking a seat at the kitchen table, not making eye contact with her. The starling sat in front of him, nibbling at crumbs of stale bread. 'Yes. A message,' he replied flatly.

'And...'

Erun sighed and looked up at where Arisa stood. His vision blurred with tears. 'My father, the King, is dead.'

Arisa's hand went to her mouth as she lowered herself into a chair. She reached out and cupped her hand over his. 'I'm so sorry, Erun.'

He managed a small nod. She embraced him as he tried to stifle his sobs.

'How will Kengia be protected now?' she asked softly.

'I don't know.' He shook his head miserably. Only then did he notice the marks on Arisa's face, the bloodstains on her tunic. 'What happened?'

'It's nothing. A few cuts and bruises.' She stood up and reached for her side with a grimace. 'Perhaps some cracked ribs as well.'

Erun sighed. He fetched a jar of poultice from his bag and tended to the wounds on Arisa's face and knuckles. She winced under his touch.

'Surprisingly, no breaks there.' He pressed her side gently, and she yelped in pain. 'I don't think you have any internal injuries. Take this.' He handed her a vial of foul-smelling liquid, which she dutifully swallowed. 'Tomorrow you will feel pretty sorry for yourself. No more than you deserve. It will help remind you of your own stupidity.'

'But you don't know what happened,' Arisa protested.

'I don't need to know. It's always the same. Your righteous quest for justice and belief you're always right, getting the better of you.'

'But I *was* right.'

Erun began pacing the room. 'Will you ever learn? Is there any hope?' he muttered to himself. Seeing the hurt in Arisa's face, he sat back down and tried a gentler tone. 'Tell me what happened.'

'Well, it started when I saw Guthrie.'

'The Chancellor's son? The one who…' He didn't need to say the words.

Arisa nodded. 'At first I didn't know it was him. I was just trying to stop him from killing a starling. *This* starling.'

'I see.'

'He didn't take too kindly to my interference. He punched me.'

'It appears as if you exchanged more than one punch with the boy.'

She shrugged.

'What did he say?'

'He made some reference to Kengians and the blood moon massacre.'

'That is no reason to fight.'

'And when I realised who he was?'

'That's still no reason to fight.'

Anger churned in Arisa's stomach. 'Someone has to be punished for what's being done to Kengians, to the silver-eyes. Someone has to stand up.'

'You have to accept that Kengians will be misunderstood here. We are too different. We will always be the first to feel Lamore's wrath.'

Arisa balled her fists. 'So it's alright to sit back while Guthrie, and many more like him, say and do such things.'

Erun rubbed the back of his neck. 'What was done to Rea, and many more like her, is unforgivable. But today it was only words. A few misinformed or senseless words from someone who probably doesn't know better.'

'But they're wrong!'

'That may be so, but you can't change everyone's beliefs. You can't challenge everyone who disagrees with you.'

'Why not? Someone has to. Someone has to change their minds.'

'People will see the truth when the time is right. That time hasn't arrived yet.'

'Maybe the time *has* arrived. I heard some farmers have rioted in the countryside, and more plan to rise up against their masters and the nobles. They want justice for what's been done to them, and I believe they will have it.'

'There are other ways to bring people to the truth and have justice.' Erun held up Arisa's fists. 'And it certainly isn't with these.'

'Don't you want to see the end of King Delrik's regime?'

'Of course I do, but fighting is a last resort. It's not the Kengian way.'

Arisa didn't reply. Erun sat and regarded her for a moment. Her fists were still clenched and her chin jutted out.

'Tell me what it was about Guthrie that made you angry enough to raise your fists.'

She paused. 'I suppose it's his ignorance and prejudice when it comes to Kengians and those lower-born than him.'

'You're right to find such intolerance wrong. However, you must look at yourself first to determine if you're so innocent of this crime.'

Arisa screwed up her face.

'Well?' Erun pressed. 'Are you tolerant and respectful of all?'

'Of course I am. As you have taught me,' she said defiantly.

'What of the nobles? What of those who live at the royal court? What of the tutors and the children of nobles at school? Are you tolerant of them, or are they to be tarred with the same brush as the King and Guthrie?'

'That's different.'

'Not really. We must be careful not to judge others so harshly, especially when we don't know their stories.'

Arisa crossed her arms. 'And is this why you won't teach me how to harness my powers? Because you don't think I can be trusted not to use them against the Lamorian regime?'

'As I have told you many times before,' Erun said slowly and deliberately, 'you have to learn to respect balance and harmony in all things. To connect with lifeforces, *kira*, and the responsibilities that come with it, means understanding there is light and darkness in all of us. You have to be ready to confront your darkness, and just as willing to accept there is some light in your enemies.'

'But you don't understand what it's like for me. I'm an outsider. If it isn't Guthrie, it's someone else mocking or challenging me. *They* bring out the darkness in me. You would understand if you knew what it's like to be so different, to not belong anywhere.'

'*I* don't understand?' Erun gestured at himself. He wore his usual ill-fitting tunic, which he had carelessly forgotten to belt. His frizzy hair stood on end and his beard was bedraggled.

Arisa sighed and managed a smile. 'What else did the Queen say in the message?'

'She says the Kengian tribes want to fight. Possibly make a

pre-emptive attack on Lamore. But she is calling on them to be patient and have faith in the prophecy.'

'Erun, there was a time I thought we could believe in the prophecy. But surely now, with both King Leo and Alik gone, there can't be any hope.'

'There may still be hope…We just need more *time*.' Erun muttered the last part as if to himself. He looked back to Arisa. 'I know it's hard to believe, but we must have faith.'

'How can anyone have faith in something when there is no evidence to support it?'

'You don't need evidence when you truly believe in something.'

Arisa raised a disbelieving brow.

Erun looked around the room. His eyes settled on the silver medallion hanging from Arisa's neck. 'Do you believe in true love?'

She rolled her eyes and groaned.

'Well, do you?'

'Yes.'

'Have you experienced it yourself?'

'No.'

'Do you have any proof it exists?'

'No. But it exists. It must.'

'How do you know?'

She crossed her arms. 'I just know.'

Erun smiled. 'Yes. Because you believe in it. You don't need proof it exists.'

'But you can't expect anyone to believe in the prophecy now. There have been three blood moons and still no Water Catcher. The Kengian tribes are right. They should prepare for war.'

Erun shook his head. 'There are no winners in war. Even if the regime were brought down, how long would Delrik's men stay repressed? We would have to fight again and again. We cannot rely on brute strength. It takes greater courage to seek peace than to fight.' His voice rose with each statement.

Arisa merely frowned.

'You have to understand this. There is a Water Catcher, and they will come. They must…' His voice trailed off.

Arisa stood up and rested a hand on his shoulder. 'You're right, Erun. There may still be a Water Catcher.' She didn't mean the words, but they were all she had to comfort him.

Erun dropped his head in his hands. 'We just need more time,' he muttered to himself once more.

9

The recalled councillors had arrived back at the castle. Takai had joined their meeting to determine the strategy for Ette, sitting at the long table among Lamore's most powerful noblemen. Leading the discussion was the Duke of Lakeford, who had arrived safely back in Lamore, Takai's friend Sar with him.

It was generally agreed that immediate retribution against the Northemers was required. Takai knew they were not aware of Horace's preference to seek an alliance with the invaders, but they would learn soon enough; the Chancellor had finally arrived.

He strode into the room, his head held high, the heavy gold chains of office gleaming around his neck. He took the King's place at the head of the table and eyeballed the two lines of councillors. A smile tugged at the corner of his mouth.

'Chancellor, you honour us with your presence.' Lakeford's voice was thick with sarcasm.

'Your Grace. It heartens me to see you returned to us in one piece.' Horace smirked as his gaze fell on the bloodied bandage wrapped around the Duke's head and ear. 'Or at least, *almost* in one piece.'

'Some of us stayed around long enough to see battle,' the Duke replied.

Undeterred by the thinly veiled reference to Guthrie's cowardice, Horace continued. 'My lords, shall we begin?'

'We have already begun. It is agreed that, as a priority, we will rebuild our naval fleet and army, and mount a direct attack on the Northemers before they dare to invade us.'

Horace met Lakeford's steady gaze. The Duke was a formidable-looking man, with steely grey eyes set in a strong, square face. Takai knew that, as Lord High Commander of the military and naval fleet, he held himself responsible for the defeat in Ette. But with only a few ships left – the rejected vessels that had been left behind in Lamore due to varying states of disrepair – and his battle-weary army only a tenth of its original size, Takai couldn't see how the Duke could prevail against the Northemers.

'What say you, Chancellor?' Lakeford demanded.

'*I* don't say anything,' Horace said calmly. 'Footing the expense of another war is a decision for the King and the King only.' He pressed on, ignoring the mumbling that had started around the table. 'And it is the King to whom I will refer your *request*.'

'And where is the King, I ask?' The Baron of Iveness appeared to have found his voice, seemingly oblivious to the fact that the King was at this very moment entertaining the Baron's own wife.

'The King is detained with more important matters.'

'What? Something more important than securing the future of the kingdom?' Lakeford demanded.

'The King has already decided a course of action.'

'Pray tell us what the *King* has decided.'

'The King is considering whether our attention would be better diverted to Kengia.'

The room broke out in uproar. Horace held up his hand for silence, but the Baron would not be quietened.

'You forget, Chancellor, that we have tried invading Kengia many times before, by both land and sea,' he rumbled. 'And it failed miserably every time.'

'I have reason to believe we will be able to invade Kengia virtually unchallenged.'

Lakeford raised an eyebrow in question.

'I believe the magic that has prevented access into Kengia has gone,' Horace went on. 'My spies in the counties report rumours that the Kengian King has died.'

A hush fell around the room.

'While this is interesting news, Chancellor,' the Duke said, 'we must divert all of our energies to tackling the Northemers head-on, before they move against us.' Takai had known Lakeford wouldn't be so easily deterred from his preferred course of action. Cries of 'Hear, hear' and the thumping of fists echoed around the room.

Horace shook his head emphatically. 'We need time to formulate a better strategy – one we have a chance of executing successfully. And fortunately we have time to do so. The Northemers will wish to consolidate their win in Ette before targeting another territory. Ivane will most likely be their first target due to its proximity, but the Northemers won't want to venture across the vast desert lands in the thick of winter when there is no food or supplies for their armies. Malu may send ships up the rivers into Ivane to scout, and possibly small raiding parties, but he will want to be well prepared when he attacks. As for us – he wouldn't dare risk a whole fleet to the winter storms at sea. Spring is the earliest he could make any move. I predict that Malu will bide his time and establish a stronghold in Ette.'

Lakeford thumped his fist on the table. 'Even more reason we need to move *now*.'

'What, with a decimated army and no naval fleet to speak of? And risk a sea-crossing in winter ourselves? Even if we made it to Ette, you expect to defeat the Northemers? You were there, Lakeford. Give us your honest assessment of these invaders.'

The Duke shifted uncomfortably in his chair. 'Their numbers are vast and the men are well equipped.'

'From the reports I've been given, these are giants of men who fight by no rules, who live to die on the battlefield. They appear to welcome blood and death, and their ships number in the hundreds, each capable of carrying several dozen men. They are vastly superior to us in number and equipment.' The Chancellor directed a hard look at Lakeford. 'And above all, they are as motivated as we are to find new lands – possibly more so. Would this be a fair assessment?'

'You seem to know a lot about these Northemers,' Lakeford sneered.

'It is my job to know.'

'I can only hazard a guess that some of your observations come from one who had the luxury of sitting back and watching the massacre in Ette from a safe distance, as the rest of us fought for our lives.'

Again, Horace ignored the barb clearly levelled at his son. 'So my assessment is true?'

'The Northemers are formidable and unlike anything I've ever seen before. But it's no reason to let them take territory we need for Lamore's future prosperity. Conceding the loss of Ette means losing access to major trade routes and resources we need to survive.'

'I agree. But I think, given some time to consider our options, we will be better equipped to deal with the threat.' Horace paused for a moment, no doubt wondering how to explain his ridiculous firesky plan. 'In fact, I am working on something for the King that will ensure we can take back not just Ette, but Ivane and Kengia as well.'

The room broke out in laughter.

'It's true,' he continued. 'By spring, I will have the means of bringing every one of our enemies to their knees.'

Lakeford held up his arms in mock surrender. 'Please

enlighten us, Chancellor. What is this mysterious project of yours?'

'The King has not authorised me to say.'

Takai raised a brow. Almost imperceptibly, Horace nodded at him.

Lakeford's eyes narrowed. 'You mean not to share this vital information with the King's own councillors.'

Horace gave a sly smile. 'On the contrary, I do have something to share with you. Soon I expect another to join us at council.' A curious murmur rolled around the table. 'His Majesty has agreed that Guthrie will soon take his place on the King's Council.'

The councillors rose to their feet as one, shouting in uproar. Takai was inclined to join them, having little trust in Guthrie's abilities, but this being his first council meeting, he chose to remain seated.

The Chancellor put his hand up to silence the room, and eventually, the councillors sat back down.

Lakeford's face had darkened. 'This must be a jest. The King would never honour Guthrie in such a matter. Not after Ette. The King himself has said the only acceptable punishment for such cowardice is death, and has sent Sir Marcus to the dungeons to await sentencing.'

'The King assures me that once my son proves himself, and I deliver on my task, Guthrie will take his place here. In the meantime, he will take up his responsibilities as Lord of Calliope.'

It was Lakeford's turn to smile. 'As he should. Calliope, I hear, will need a man of your son's…' He paused for effect. 'Ilk. Yes, ilk is the word I'm looking for. Guthrie's special talents will be needed at Calliope.'

'I don't pretend to understand your meaning.'

'I understand your plans to fully enclose Calliope's lands haven't been received well, particularly by your former reeve, Sergei. In fact, I hear he is reaching out to farmers across the countryside, urging them to rise up against the landholding lords.'

Since hearing the news of the uprising at one of the Chancellor's properties, Takai had sought more information. The property in question, Calliope, was far inferior to most of the other councillors' properties. It was difficult to produce profitable crops in the lowlands, so Horace had turned the common lands into pasture for wool production. It required far fewer farmers, and yielded a much higher profit margin. It was a pragmatic solution to the Chancellor's problem, but apparently his farmer reeve, Sergei, had not seen it the same way.

'Sergei is troublesome,' Horace began, 'but he won't be a threat for much longer. Guthrie will deal with him.'

'I'm sure he will – though perhaps he would do better to learn from my son, Willem. He has never had any trouble with the people at Talbot.'

Willem and Takai were good friends, having spent nearly every day of the last decade together. The Duke's son was a well-liked landowner, but he didn't have to manage the Chancellor's wife's inferior ancestral lands, which consisted mainly of boggy marsh. Takai suspected Horace wasn't the only one facing challenges, especially with the trading route to Ette now closed.

The Chancellor echoed his thoughts. 'I hardly think any of us are immune to the troubles brewing out there.'

There was a murmur of agreement around the table.

'You may be right, Chancellor,' the Duke said. 'For that reason, I too have taken precautions and asked Sar to help manage some of my lands.'

'Sar!' Horace exclaimed. 'A lowborn soldier?'

Takai shifted in his seat at the comment about his friend. He could think of no one more worthy than Sar of such an honour.

'Not for long,' the Duke said. 'Soon he will be a landowner in his own right; the King has agreed to knight him. Recognising, of course, that Sar is more deserving of such an honour than many of his peers.'

There was another murmur of agreement around the table as every eye went to the Chancellor.

Horace's expression was impassive. He sat up a little taller in his chair. 'Granted, I expect Sar will be a great comfort to you, since your own son is in such a sickly state.'

Takai gripped the table in front of him, resisting the urge to punch Horace in the face. 'I'm astounded...' he began, then faltered. It was the first time he'd spoken in the meeting, and he had everyone's attention. 'I'm astounded that any business gets done in the kingdom if most council meetings are like this — slinging matches of petty barbs and insults.'

Lakeford and the other councillors had the decency to drop their heads in shame, some offering apologies. Horace, however, did and said nothing for a moment. He held Takai's gaze, appraising him with narrowed eyes.

'My lords, this meeting is adjourned,' was all he said before stomping out of the chambers.

10

———

Takai gave his opponent a hard look. His sword glinted in the afternoon sun as he waited for the swordsman to strike. He didn't have to wait long – in an instant the man was upon him, wielding a series of strikes and thrusts.

The Prince parried and sidestepped, successfully avoiding each strike. The swordsman stepped back into position and removed his helmet to reveal a wide grin.

'Well played! You've been practising in my absence.'

Takai removed his own helmet and shot back an annoyed look. 'You take it too easy on me, Sar.'

Wiping the sweat from his face, he accepted a mug of water from a page. Takai slurped the water down greedily, taking a moment to catch his breath and admire his surroundings. It had been so long since he had been able to call the castle his home. He cast his eyes over the line of mature oak trees along one boundary of the garden; the castle peeked over the treetops in the distance. Behind him a crumbling granite wall gave way to a cliff edge and the Kyprian Sea. In the west, the sun slipped behind the Nymoi Alps.

He had missed this place. Somewhat.

Takai and Sar had been practising swordcraft in the castle's

81

abandoned south garden for hours. The Prince hadn't seen his friend for several months, and had been relieved beyond measure when he and the Duke had returned from Ette safely. On seeing how flat his usually carefree friend was following the defeat, Takai had found Sar after the morning's council meeting and suggested swordplay as a means of distraction.

Once they'd started, Takai's competitive streak had kicked in. He was determined to outplay his friend. While Takai was athletic and tall by any standards, Sar towered over him; his friend's muscular frame and time as a soldier provided a significant advantage over the Prince. This did nothing to intimidate Takai. Both of them had served the Duke of Lakeford as squires for many years, and trained together while living with the Duke and his family. So Takai could easily read Sar during swordplay – and anticipate his next move. He hoped it would give him an edge, for he was desperate to prove his worth as heir to the throne, to himself as much as anyone – not only by participating in matters of state, but by excelling as a warrior.

'Should we call it a day?' Sar asked.

Takai shook his head, not wishing to acknowledge the exhaustion he felt. The cool weather had done nothing to put him at ease, for he wore mail and armour on his chest and back. He was acutely aware of his saturated gambeson and clinging undershirt. The blunt-edged sword in his right hand felt as if it were made of lead, and was slippery in his grip. A wooden shield covered in leather hung heavily from his left arm.

Sar tilted his head and shrugged before they both put on their helmets and resumed their positions.

Remembering his training, Takai focused on keeping a balanced stance, his feet shoulder-width apart. He calculated the distance between himself and Sar, fixing his eyes on his friend through the slit in his visor as he waited for Sar's next move.

Sar matched his gaze before thrusting forward awkwardly. Takai easily parried, yet his face grew hot with anger. He knew Sar had feigned the clumsiness.

'Pathetic! You can't expect me to believe you're that uncoordinated.'

Takai could have sworn Sar winked at him from under his visor. 'It's more accurate to say I'm no match for your superior sword skills.'

'Save the flattery for a more appreciative audience, you silver-tongued rake.'

Sar responded with a jolly laugh. 'Well, you're in luck. I seem to have found a second wind.' He launched a combination of strikes back at the Prince.

Takai was forced to take several steps backwards to block each blow. He responded with an equally fast set of strikes and thrusts aimed at Sar's chest, belly and sides. Sar deflected each blow with his shield, but the force of Takai's attack threw him off balance and he fell heavily to the ground. Takai pulled off his helmet and grinned as he touched his sword tip to Sar's throat.

'You've got me, Your Highness. Well done.'

Takai dropped his sword to the ground, feeling only partially satisfied with his performance. 'You still took it easy on me. Anyone could have seen that that was a deliberate fall.' Sar took off his own helmet and shook his head earnestly, but Takai pressed on. 'I'm good, but I'm not *that* good, Sar.'

Takai nodded to the pages to come and help them remove their armour. His eyes went to Sar's bandaged forearm, stained with fresh blood.

'I think you underestimate yourself, Takai,' his friend said. 'You're an excellent swordsman. You beat me fair and square.'

'In that case, you better pick up your game, if you ever expect to lead my army.'

Sar bowed his head, kicking at the ground.

Takai turned to fully face Sar. 'Don't you want to succeed the Duke as Lord High Commander of the King's forces?'

Sar lifted his eyes. Their usual twinkle was gone. 'I'm not sure I could ever deserve such an honour.'

'Rubbish! There is no better warrior in the whole of Lamore.'

'A better warrior would have held off the Northemers.' Takai shook his head, but Sar went on. 'A better warrior would have done more than that. Would have defeated them soundly and sent them back to the forsaken land they came from.'

Takai reached out and rested his hand on Sar's shoulder. 'From what I heard, the Northemers were unstoppable.'

Sar's lips thinned. 'I've fought in skirmishes in Ette and against invading parties from Ivane, but nothing could have prepared me for the Northemers.'

'Were they as formidable as everyone says?'

'More so.'

'And their leader, Malu?'

'I saw many of my men fall before his axe. He fought like a wild animal, a man possessed. I don't think he is of this world.'

The tendons in Takai's arms tightened at his friend's account. This Malu did not sound like anyone Lamore should be seeking an alliance with. He released his grip on Sar's shoulder. 'As impressive as that?'

'I was lucky to leave with nothing more than this scratch.' Sar pointed to his injured arm. 'Many of our men suffered a far worse fate.'

'What of Malu's men?'

'Everyone was cut from the same cloth. I was told they appeared at dawn with the morning fog. They were already upon the capital's gates before an alarm could be raised. There were hundreds of them. Giants of men. And they were skilled with sword and axe.' Sar shook his head. 'They fought without fear or mercy. It was like they thirsted for blood. Up close, you could see it in their eyes – they almost welcomed death. Many of our men fled in their wake, only to be set alight by fire arrows. I would have stayed to the very end, had the Duke not ordered us to retreat.'

'As he should have done.'

Sar heaved a sigh. 'With all of our ships set alight we were lucky to flag down a passing fishing vessel to bring what was left of us home.'

A lump caught in Takai's throat at hearing how close he'd come to losing Sar. 'I'm glad to have you home.'

Sar nodded, his eyes downcast.

'The Duke believes we should rebuild our army and navy,' Takai said brightly, trying to make his friend feel better. 'That we must take back Ette immediately, before the Northemers try to take Ivane as well.' He was curious what Sar thought of Lakeford's plan, since the Duke was convinced the Chancellor's schemes were doomed to fail.

Sar shook his head helplessly. 'I'm not sure we can win against those men, Takai.' He lowered his voice. 'And I'm not sure that we should.'

'What do you mean?'

'Perhaps Ette and Ivane aren't ours to take.'

'Of course they are. They were our territories for near two hundred years. They are our – *my* – ancestral rights. We will rebuild our forces and take them back.'

'At what cost? You will have to levy more taxes your people can't afford. And you will have to conscript more Lamorians to fight an unwinnable war, all for lands I'm not sure we have a right to.'

Takai raised an eyebrow. 'You sound like one of *them*, Sar.'

'One of *them*? Like many of your people, you mean?'

Takai resisted the temptation to snap back at his friend. 'You know everything we do is for Lamore's benefit. We need those territories *for* the people, to provide the resources we all rely on. For that we must demand our people's support.'

Sar tilted his head and sighed.

'Let's not argue like this,' Takai said. 'I know we both want to do what's right, even if we can't agree on how it's done. But at least now you will have your own chance to see what it's like to rule.'

'Rule?'

'Yes – I hear the Duke is rewarding your bravery on the battlefield with a knighthood and some lands near Talbot.'

'I don't see it as an opportunity to rule. I'm determined to be fair in how I manage the land and its people. In any case, the Earl is ultimately in charge of Talbot. I am to learn from him.'

'Yes, you and my cousin, Willem, will be a fine pair, I expect. Both as soft-hearted as each other. I daresay you will both dispense of your responsibilities honourably. More than I can say for my other *distant* cousin.'

'What will happen to Guthrie?'

Takai grunted. 'My father is furious with him for his cowardice, but has struck some kind of deal with the Chancellor.'

'A deal?'

'Horace is planning on keeping Guthrie well out of sight. He'll be sent to Calliope to manage the lands Horace recently enclosed. The King says he will forgive Guthrie if Horace delivers on some promise.' He waved his hand dismissively, not seeing the point in entertaining the idea of firesky weapons. 'My father has agreed to make Guthrie one of his councillors if the Chancellor succeeds in his task.'

'What happens if Horace disappoints the King?'

'I don't venture to think what he will do to Guthrie in that case. Enough talk of Guthrie, though. It leaves a bad taste in my mouth.'

'Speaking of your *distant* cousin...' Sar was looking over Takai's shoulder. He turned to see Guthrie's twin sister, Theodora, and her companion, Selina, appearing through the oak trees. A famed beauty at King Delrik's court, Theodora was as sharp-minded as her brother was dim.

'Your Highness,' she purred as she waltzed toward them, Selina following dutifully behind. 'I'm most grieved to find you have finished your training.'

Takai gave Sar an amused look. Sar rolled his eyes in

response. Takai bowed with a mock flourish. 'To what do we owe the pleasure?'

'Selina and I had just been discussing who, out of you two, would win the tournament at the upcoming celebrations.'

'Really.' Takai couldn't help but grin.

'Unfortunately we couldn't agree on the matter. So I insisted we come down here and find out for ourselves.'

'And who do you favour, my lady?' Takai found himself admiring Theodora, even though he was fully aware of her father's scheme to match them. She wore a scarlet gown with a matching fur-trimmed cloak and hood.

Theodora twirled a ringlet of her raven-black hair flirtatiously around her finger. 'The tournament is made up of three contests, is it not?'

'Yes. Archery, swordfighting and a joust.'

'Clearly you are the superior archer, Your Highness.'

Takai shrugged indifferently. He was certain he was the finest archer in the kingdom.

'And Sar has a superior record in joust.'

Takai frowned, not liking the turn of the conversation.

'Which leaves swordfighting. While Selina was convinced you would be unbeaten in any contest, I wasn't so sure.'

Takai clenched his jaw. He wasn't accustomed to being insulted.

Theodora continued, oblivious to his annoyance. 'After all, Sar is said to be a true warrior, like his father.' She shot an appreciative look at Sar, whose face had coloured deeply. 'Your Highness, of course, is very clever...but...'

Takai gritted his teeth. 'It would be ungentlemanly of me to contradict a member of the fairer sex. However, I can assure you, Lady Theodora, that I can beat any man in the kingdom, regardless of the contest.'

Selina shot a look at Theodora that appeared to beg her to withdraw. Instead Theodora regrouped and dropped to the ground in a curtsey. 'Your Highness, please forgive my impertinence. Of course I know you're unbeatable, but I was so hoping to see a master swordsman like yourself in action. I thought to provoke you into proving yourself to us.' She lowered her catlike eyes. 'After all, I am nothing but a *silly* woman, and you know so many accomplished ladies.' She looked up at him through her eyelashes. 'I didn't know how best to attract your notice otherwise.'

Takai, somewhat placated, indicated she should rise. 'Well, who am I to disappoint a lady?' He summoned the nearest page. 'Get me my sword and shield. Sar, prepare yourself. You're about to find out who the real champion is.'

Sar shook his head to himself before picking up his own sword and shield.

The pages moved to fix Takai and Sar's gambesons and plate armour, but Takai waved them away. Theodora and Selina giggled. Takai and Sar wore only their linen undershirts and breeches. Takai wasn't concerned; this whole thing was only for show.

The two men circled each other before exchanging blows. They parried much the same as before, until Takai rushed at Sar. He landed a heavy blow on his friend's legs with the flat side of his sword. Sar thudded to the ground with a grunt.

Theodora, Selina and the pages clapped and cheered.

Takai wiped his wet brow and narrowed his eyes as Sar got back on his feet. 'Again! But this time show me what you can really do.'

'Takai, you have already bested me. Surely you don't wish me to be humiliated again.' Sar seemed intent on ending the performance.

'Again!'

Shaking his head, Sar drew back his shoulders. 'Very well.'

They resumed their positions, each waiting to see who would make the first move. Takai propelled forward with a combination of swift strikes. Sar sidestepped each one.

Takai persisted with several more strikes, only to be met by

Sar's sword each time. Suspecting Sar was unwilling to come at him with full force, Takai began to relax and apply some pageantry to his footwork.

He leapt over Sar's sword as if it were a jumping rope, to the glee of the onlookers. Quite lost in his display, he took a moment to turn and acknowledge Theodora and Selina with a theatrical wave of his hand and a bow.

At the same moment, Sar struck out at him.

Takai saw the look of horror on the girls' faces as he felt a sudden coldness and sharp pain in his left arm. The cut appeared superficial, but was bleeding heavily.

Sar's face paled and a hush fell over the group. 'Damn it. Get me something to bandage his arm,' Sar ordered the pages as he threw his own sword to the ground.

'I'm fine.' Takai waved him away, barely able to contain his frustration that he had been injured because of his own stupidity. He pointed his sword at his friend's face. 'Again. This fight is far from over.' He struck out at Sar, who jumped easily out of the way. 'Come on! I still have my sword arm.'

'You can't fight. Take a look at your arm.'

'It's just a scratch.' Takai waved his sword at his friend. 'Come on.'

Sar stood fixed to the spot. 'It's getting dark. Surely it's time to retire.'

'What, too scared to fight?' Takai spat. Sar looked at the ground, clearly unwilling to meet the Prince's eyes. 'What, no one here is brave enough to meet my sword? What cowards have we raised in this kingdom?'

Sar winced. 'I shall not fight you while you're injured, Your Highness.'

'But you shall, Sar. As my subject, you're ordered to fight me.'

Sar shook his head.

'It's an order!' Takai didn't really need or want to continue but he had an insatiable urge to prove he was worthy of his position as future King.

Sar took a deep breath before picking up his sword slowly. 'As you wish.'

A transformation had come over his face. Gone was his characteristic grin as a stillness took over him.

He charged at Takai with a set of powerful blows.

Takai blocked each strike with difficulty, forced to retreat several steps. Sar pressed on, and before long Takai had been pushed back against the boundary wall. Besides a dilapidated pile of rocks, there was nothing between him and the sea that raged far below.

Oblivious to the danger, Sar continued his attack.

Takai leapt up onto the wall to avoid his sword. 'Stop!' he cried, as the wall wobbled under his feet. Sar obeyed but it was too late – the wall crumbled beneath Takai.

Sar reached out, but Takai was already falling.

He saw the look of terror on Sar's face as he plummeted backwards. He tumbled down the cliff face, thrown around like a rag doll. He snatched glimpses of the black water below as the rocks tore into his skin. Blood filled his mouth as the waves rose to meet him.

Then everything went dark.

11

———————

heodora watched in horror as Sar dived over the cliff edge after the Prince. Takai had fallen dozens of feet down the sheer cliff face before plunging into the water below. Theodora hung over the edge of the wall, frantically willing a sign of life to appear. Selina was howling, the pages frozen in shock.

The fall itself could kill a man, let alone the jagged rocks lining the cliff face and jutting out from the sea. Then there was the water. It would be close to freezing, and a chill was setting in with the dusk. Theodora strained her eyes, looking for Takai or Sar in the swirling surface, but she could see nothing in the fading light.

She was convinced they were both lost when Sar's head emerged. He spun around desperately, then dived back under, again and again. But each time he came up with nothing.

A small voice in Theodora's head told her this was her fault. That she had goaded the Prince into proving his skills, and now he was probably dead. She dreaded her father's reaction when he discovered the part she had played in this ghastly scene. But her guilt suddenly turned to anger.

If Takai had been more forthcoming in his attentions, it would never have come to this.

Ever since he had returned to live at the castle, Theodora had tried every way she could to get the Prince to fall in love with her, all to no avail. Any other man at court would have thrown himself at her feet a thousand times over by now. Unfortunately, the Prince was the only one she wanted – or rather, the only one she'd been instructed to marry. But Takai had given no indication that he particularly favoured her. She often wondered if he had inherited his Ivanian mother's stubborn streak. The Queen didn't like Theodora, but once the Prince was captivated, Sofia's opinion mattered naught. Nothing would stand between Theodora and the crown. No one would dare to disapprove of her then.

She would have stopped to smile at the idea of being Queen if her plan hadn't been disintegrating rapidly before her eyes.

The inky water below seemed to go on forever. There were splashes as Sar continued his search, but nothing offered any hope. She scanned the surface again, squinting until she could make out Sar's outline – then, from the corner of her eye, she thought she could discern a small movement. A floating object.

She peered closer, and the shape took the form of a man, face down in the water.

'There! There!' she screamed, pointing.

Sar swung around and swam to where she indicated. He turned Takai's body over and started to drag him back toward the shore.

'Go get help!' Theodora ordered the nearest page, who still appeared frozen to the spot.

'Get Lore,' Sar yelled out from below. Lore was the Queen's personal physician and a traditional Ivanian healer. He lived at the castle, and while Theodora disliked the man, he could get to them faster than any of the King's physicians.

She shook the frightened page. 'You heard him – get Lore.' The page nodded and ran back toward the castle.

Selina had by now collapsed to her knees, and was crying out, 'He's dead! The Prince is dead!'

'Get up, you stupid girl,' Theodora barked. 'The Prince is not dead, and it's treason to say he is.' She pulled Selina to her feet, but the girl began sobbing hysterically. Theodora slapped her friend in the face. 'Pull yourself together. The Prince is going to be fine.'

Though still gripped by fear, Theodora knew it was up to her to take charge of the situation and maintain some sense of calm.

'You.' She pointed at the remaining page. 'We need rope. Anything to get them out of the water.' Sar had already dragged Takai toward the bottom of the cliff. 'Go, get rope!'

But the page remained standing still, his mouth agape. Theodora looked down the cliff face again to see that Sar had pulled himself from the water and was standing on a large, flat rock. In one swift movement, he scooped Takai over his shoulder and started to scale the rocky wall.

Theodora couldn't believe her eyes as she watched Sar take one shaky step after another, up the rocky incline. But not even he could make it the whole way up, especially with the added weight of the Prince on his shoulder. Sure enough, once Sar hit the vertical cliff face, he came to a standstill.

Theodora grabbed Selina by her shoulder and shook her. 'Take off your petticoat.' Selina's eyes widened. She stopped sobbing for long enough to shake her head. 'Just do it!' Theodora screamed.

She reached under her own skirts and took off her petticoat, then threw off her kid gloves. 'You!' She addressed the terrified page again. 'Help me make a rope.'

This time the boy nodded, and together they tore strips of linen, hastily tying them together to create a makeshift rope. She indicated for him to tie one end around a nearby stump.

Theodora threw the rope down to Sar, who wrapped it around the Prince and motioned for them to start pulling.

Theodora gripped the rope with all her might, and she and the page started to pull the Prince up the cliff, one painful heave at a time. Theodora felt as if her arms would pull right out of their sockets. The rope dug into her hands. She was about to cry out that she couldn't continue when Takai's body tumbled over the edge toward them.

Theodora threw the rope back down to Sar and fell back onto the ground, gasping for breath. As she took in gulps of cold air, her eyes scanned the Prince.

There was a gash on Takai's forehead. It was deep and bleeding profusely. He was covered in cuts and scratches from being hauled up the jagged cliff face. But what terrified her most was the colour of his skin. Even in the darkness, she could see it was a deathly blue. Theodora shuddered, resisting the urge to howl like Selina.

Sar appeared over the top of the cliff edge and scrambled toward his friend. 'Is he…?' He couldn't seem to say the word.

'I – I…don't know,' Theodora stammered. She felt a sudden urge to scream, to tell the world that the Prince had died and it was all her fault – but she registered a torchlight approaching them. It was the page she had sent earlier, now returned with Lore.

The physician ran to the Prince's side. Theodora was sure she saw him recoil momentarily as he took in Takai's lifeless body. He quickly recovered himself and told the page to hold the torch closer. Lore examined the cut on the Prince's head, then bent over and listened to his chest.

'He's alive, but barely,' he told the group.

Theodora took a deep breath of relief.

'What do we do?' Sar was shaking all over, his own lips turning blue, blood dripping from his hands and feet.

'Sar, sit down before you collapse in a heap. I don't need two patients on my hands,' Lore ordered. 'Roll the prince onto his side.' The page didn't seem to hear the order. Sar pushed him out of the way and attended to Takai himself.

Lore thumped Takai on the back and his body convulsed before a torrent of water gushed from his mouth. 'He needs to be warmed up.'

Theodora threw off her cloak and covered the Prince's body.

'We have to get him back to the castle.' Lore pointed to the page Sar had sidelined. 'Go and tell the King what's happened. Tell him to meet us at the Prince's rooms. Deliver the message directly to the King and no one else. Nobody is to know the Prince is gravely ill.' The page nodded frantically. '*No one,*' Lore emphasised as the page sprinted off.

Sar had already lifted Takai into his arms and was lumbering back to the castle. Theodora made to follow, but Lore reached out and grasped her elbow.

'Theodora, go directly to the Queen and inform her of what has happened.' He turned to the other page. 'Send for the Royal Physicians – we're going to need all the help we can get. Selina, please return to your rooms and act as if nothing has happened.'

Selina nodded obediently between hiccupping sobs.

'One word of this from any of you,' Lore finished, eyeballing each of them, 'and I will have your tongues.' He gave Theodora a final look of warning before running after Sar and the Prince.

Theodora followed the group, resenting the way the physician had ordered her about. She would tell the Queen about the accident, as Lore had bid her, but in her own time.

There was someone else who must be informed first. Someone far more important than the Queen.

THEODORA MARCHED past her father's guards in the presence chamber without so much as a nod of acknowledgement. She tapped her foot impatiently as the next set of guards came to life and swung open the doors to the Chancellor's private study.

She found her father in deep conversation with one of his secretaries. He dropped his voice at her arrival, so she only caught a few words – something about 'finding the right Kengian' and 'firesky'. Theodora had no idea what the significance of either was, but it must have been important.

Horace dismissed the secretary and looked over at her, his lips pressed firmly together. 'What is it?'

She baulked a little at his snappy tone, but stepped forward, wringing her hands. 'Father, the most terrible thing has happened.' Horace waved his hand for her to hurry. 'It's the Prince. He's had an accident.' Theodora paused, not wanting to say the words out loud. 'He's near death.'

'What!' Horace's face was pale. 'What happened?'

'He fell from a wall in the south garden.' Theodora bit her lip, deciding not to elaborate on the circumstances leading up to the accident – or her role in it.

'He fell onto the ground?'

She shook her head miserably. 'He fell down the cliff and into the sea. Sar dived in and saved him, but he was near drowned.'

Her father's eyes bulged. 'Where is the Prince now?'

'Lore had him taken to his rooms.'

'Is he going to live?'

Theodora shrugged.

'But he must.' Horace sat back heavily in his chair. 'The Prince must survive if we are to take the crown.' He rubbed his face a moment before continuing. 'How goes your seduction of the hapless boy?'

Theodora was taken aback at his change of subject. The Prince's welfare was the only thing on her mind right now. But then she remembered who her father was – and who she was: Lady Theodora, the future Queen of Lamore.

'As instructed, Father, I have taken great pains to recommend myself to Takai. And it's obvious he admires me.'

Horace waved his hand dismissively. 'It's not enough that he admires you. The Prince must ask for your hand. With the council against me, and your brother out of favour, I need to secure our position at court and our claim to the throne.'

'But what if the Prince…' Theodora's voice trailed off.

'If the Prince dies, the next in line is Lakeford, and his sickly son after him. They must perish before the crown comes to Guthrie through your mother's claim.'

Theodora rolled her eyes. She would prefer anyone to become King before her horrid brother. What particularly irked her was that she was the older twin, even if only by a few minutes. She should be in line before Guthrie – but that was how things were in Lamore; a woman had to find other means of securing power.

Her father continued outlining his schemes. 'While both the Duke and Willem may meet their demise in war or sickness, there's no guarantee of it happening soon enough to safeguard our position. In the meantime, we can't afford for Lakeford to get that close to the crown. No. The Prince must survive, and you must win him over.'

Theodora nodded obediently.

Horace stood up and walked toward the door. 'I must see the Prince for myself to determine where our future lies.'

'Wait, Father—'

He stopped. 'What is it?'

'Lore asked me to inform the Queen of the Prince's accident. Is that your wish?'

'Yes, you should inform her. Who better to hear this information from than a trusted friend such as you, my dear?' Horace gave a sardonic smile.

'Father, you know as well as I that the Queen has little time for me. She detests me.'

'Perhaps. But she is the Prince's mother. You have to be the first to speak to her of this.'

'As you wish.' Theodora curtsied and followed her father

from his rooms. He was right. She would have to play her cards well if she was to become the next Queen of Lamore.

THEODORA FOUND the Queen in her privy chamber, sitting in companionable silence with her chief lady-in-waiting, Gwyn. The Queen was gazing out the window across the Kyprian Sea. Gwyn was intent on the book in her hands. Neither noticed Theodora's approach. She sniffed in annoyance as the guard announced her arrival.

'The Lady Theodora seeks an immediate audience with Her Majesty.'

The Queen didn't bother to turn, instead directing her words to Gwyn. 'What could that treacherous minx want with me? I thought it was only my son she wanted. Send her away.'

Gwyn looked up and caught Theodora's eye. 'She is here already,' she said, completely without expression.

The Queen turned around with a sigh, seemingly unembarrassed by her indiscreet comments. She signalled to the guard to leave the room.

'Your Majesty.' Theodora gave a half-curtsey.

The Queen's dark eyes fell coldly on her. 'What do you want?'

'Your Majesty, there has been a terrible accident. Prince Takai—'

She didn't get a chance to finish her sentence before the Queen leapt from her chair. 'Is he alright? Where is he?'

'Lore is tending to the Prince now in his rooms.'

The Queen hurried from the chambers. Theodora made to follow, but Gwyn took hold of her arm.

'What happened to the Prince? Tell me everything you know.'

Theodora detested this upstart of a woman and the way she barked orders. She tried to wrench her arm away. 'I was told to inform the Queen of this matter, and the Queen only.'

Gwyn tightened her grip. She was deceptively strong. 'Tell me what you know!'

Theodora threw her head back defiantly. 'The Prince fell from the wall in the south garden and into the sea. Sar rescued him from the water, but there was little sign of life.' Gwyn nodded for her to continue. 'Lore had the Prince taken to his rooms for treatment, and word was sent to the King and the Royal Physicians.'

'Who else has been informed?'

'No one. We have been sworn to secrecy.'

'While it pains me to say this, your father, as Chancellor and keeper of the seal, needs to be told immediately.'

Theodora smiled triumphantly. 'My father has already been informed and is with the Prince as we speak.'

Gwyn squeezed Theodora's arm until she winced. 'And why is the Chancellor there already and not the Queen?'

Theodora gave her a wide-eyed look and shrugged.

Gwyn dropped her arm as if it were a hot coal. 'If it's as bad as you say, you'd better hope it's not too late for the Queen to see her son, or I will hold *you* personally responsible.'

And I will hold you *personally responsible for the humiliation you and the Queen continue to hand out to me,* Theodora thought as she rubbed her sore arm, following the two women to the Prince's apartments.

The air in the Prince's bedchambers was heavy with fear. Takai's lips and face were blue. His body was still completely lifeless. Theodora wouldn't have been surprised to learn the Prince was already dead.

Lore was by his side, recording observations in a small book. Sar stood next to Lore, staring intently at Takai. The King, eyes wide with bewilderment, was slumped in a chair on the other side of the Prince's bed. The Duke of Lakeford was deep in conversation with the Royal Physicians, their black garb matching the solemn expressions on their faces. And Theodora's father was there, of course, his hawk eyes taking in every detail.

The Queen and Gwyn approached Lore. In all the panic, no one seemed to have noticed Theodora's presence.

'How is my son?'

Lore held a hand to the Queen's arm. 'The Prince is breathing, but only just. I don't know what to try next. His injuries are beyond my abilities.' He glanced over at the Royal Physicians. 'As well as theirs, for what it's worth.'

'What do the physicians suggest?'

'They wish to bleed him, use leeches, cupping – but even they know it's hopeless. The Prince was underwater for too long. He took on a lot of fluid and the extent of his head injury is not fully known. I'm afraid he may already be—'

The Queen held her hand to her mouth, muffling a scream.

'Surely there is something that can be done,' Gwyn cried.

'It is beyond all Lamorian and Ivanian medicine.' Lore rubbed his temple vigorously, then froze.

'What is it?' Gwyn asked.

Lore appeared to dismiss his thought. 'No, it's nothing.'

'Whatever it is, it must be worth trying. What have we got to lose?'

Lore looked at the Queen and back to Gwyn.

'I have heard of a man. An apothecary in Obira. Some call him a healer.'

'Yes?' Gwyn prompted.

'It is said he has certain knowledge and abilities.' Theodora's eyes widened. Lore could only be describing someone who knew Kengian magic – perhaps even a Scholar. 'But the physicians would never agree to it.'

'Where is this man?' the Queen demanded.

'I don't know. As I said, I have only heard of him. His name is Erun.'

'My father can find him,' Theodora said with confidence.

Gwyn and the Queen rounded on her.

'Guard,' Gwyn called out. A guard appeared at once. 'Please escort the Lady Theodora to her room. She has undoubtedly had a stressful day and requires rest.' Theodora made to protest, but a sharp look from her father across the room silenced her. She caught one final glimpse of Takai's still form before the door slammed behind her.

12

---

*A*risa's nightmares no longer centred on Rea and the day Arisa had abandoned her. Now she dreamt of Hyando.

It was Hyando's accident repeating itself over and over again, but this time Guthrie was the guard who had knocked the boy to the ground. He loomed over Hyando, laughing, while Arisa stood fixed to the spot. She watched on helplessly as the light faded from Hyando's eyes and Guthrie spat on the boy, calling him a *dirty Kengian.* Then someone began calling her name.

'Arisa. Arisa…'

The calls echoed, as if coming from a long way away. Arisa winced as sudden movement jarred her ribs. It was as if someone were shaking her.

The call came again. 'Arisa…'

She stirred, one eye fluttering open.

'Arisa, wake up! I have something to tell you.'

'Huh?' she replied groggily. Her head was resting on an open schoolbook on the kitchen table. She must have fallen asleep studying again. She opened her other eye to find Erun gently rousing her. She grimaced at the pain still in her ribs; it was the only injury from Guthrie's beating that hadn't completely healed with Erun's potion.

Her guardian was looking at her intently. 'I have something to tell you.'

Arisa lifted her head and rubbed her eyes, taking a few moments to adjust to the darkness around her. She wondered what could be making Erun so excited. Her guardian had been in a daze since receiving the news from Kengia. He had taken to walking around the room in never-ending circles, talking to himself all the while. Understandably, he was grieving the loss of his father, but there had been something else on his mind. Arisa never quite caught exactly what he was saying, but she had been able to tell from his animated hand gestures that he was pondering a matter of great importance.

'We must leave,' he declared now.

'Is someone ill?' Arisa was used to being called out at night to assist Erun in his work.

Erun shook his head. 'No. I mean we must leave Obira.'

She sat bolt upright. 'Obira? But you have always said it's not safe for me to go beyond the city gates.'

'It's not,' he agreed. 'Lamore's not safe for any Kengians, especially silver-eyes. It's always been safer hiding in plain sight in Obira. It's where they least expect to find us. But now, with the threat of war on the doorstep, we must go to Kengia.'

'Kengia!' Arisa couldn't believe her ears. Her whole life, she had wished to escape Obira. For as long as she could remember, she had longed to visit her guardian's beloved kingdom – her father's homeland – but it had never been possible.

'Yes. Kengia. Although war may reach its shores, it is the safest place for us – for you. There we have allies. We have friends.'

'But how? Even with the King gone, the mountains are impassable in winter.'

'We will go by sea. I will find passage for us on a boat. A trading or fishing vessel. Anything.'

Arisa reached for her silver medallion, turning it repeatedly in her hands. She must still be dreaming. 'I dared not believe it was ever possible.'

'It will take a few days to organise, but I promise you, we're leaving.' Erun reached out and touched her arm. 'Arisa. We're going home.'

He started dancing around the room in fits of laughter. Arisa laughed with him, determined to share his joy, but part of her was torn. She was going to abandon the only home and people she had ever known. The people they had pledged to protect would be left to the mercy of the Lamorian regime, while she fled to safety. It would be like abandoning Rea again, a thousand times over. If the people of Obira City didn't die of starvation, many were sure to perish from sickness and injury that she and Erun would no longer be around to alleviate. The thought left a bitter taste in her mouth.

Erun stopped dancing and gave a great sigh. 'We have much to do in the meantime. You must start packing what you need. Just the most essential items. You should go to school as normal, as if nothing is happening. It is best that no one learns of our plans.'

'But who will take care of the sick in Obira?'

Erun rubbed the nape of his neck. 'Arisa, we can't take care of everyone. We never could. And right now, the only people we can take care of are ourselves.'

'But—'

'I will send word to the Kengian network. There will be another healer outside the city gates who may be happy to come to Obira and take over where we left off. I will leave my shop and garden to them. But…there are some things that can't stay here to be found by unfriendly eyes.' Erun pointed to a large pile of parchment scraps Arisa recognised as messages from Kengia, as well as forbidden Kengian books he owned. He exhaled loudly. 'It must be done.'

One by one, he picked up his precious belongings and examined each of them. He dropped every second item or so into the fire. Arisa winced at the hiss and fizzle as each piece caught alight and combusted. It was a gruesome task for a Scholar, but as Erun said, it needed to be done. She made to join him, but an insistent knock sounded at the shop door. Erun, absorbed in his task, didn't appear to hear it.

Late-night calls for medical assistance weren't unusual. Arisa crossed the room to the shopfront and unlatched the door, thinking that this could very well be the last time she went to someone's aid in Obira. She peered out into the darkness, only able to make out the outline of a man in a black cloak. There was something vaguely familiar about him. The man seemed momentarily taken aback at Arisa answering the door, but recovered quickly.

'Is this the home of Erun?' he demanded abruptly.

'It is. Who's asking?' She was more than a little suspicious of this man, who, judging by his fine cloak and the gold rings on his fingers, wasn't a resident of Obira.

'Erun is the one who has healing powers?' the stranger pressed.

Arisa didn't answer. Possession of powers was a dangerous claim to make in Lamore, but the stranger must have interpreted her silence as affirmation. He pushed past her and strode toward the back room.

Erun glanced up with a composed look on his face, but Arisa's keen eye noted his sleight of hand as he pushed the scraps of parchment under a large book. She wondered if the intruder had seen the same thing.

'What can I help you with?' Erun asked, standing up from his chair. It always surprised Arisa how calm her guardian managed to sound.

The man pushed back the hood on his cloak, revealing a long face ending in a prominent jaw that appeared off-centre. There was one person she knew of who fit this description – *but it can't be,* she thought. Not at their home. But what if it was him? Why had he come for Erun? Bile rose in her throat—

'I am Horace, the King's Chancellor, and I come on an urgent matter.'

Arisa shuddered. It *was* him! He was here for her. Guthrie must have discovered her identity and now she was to be punished.

Erun, though, appeared unrattled, as if the King's Chancellor visited their home every day. 'What can I do to serve you, my lord?'

'You and your special expertise are required at the castle.'

'My expertise?'

'I am told you are a man of, let's say, particular talents.'

'I'm not sure exactly what you're referring to, but I can attest to being a man of science and medicine.'

'Don't worry, I'm not here to arrest you.' The Chancellor smirked and looked meaningfully around the room. 'Though others might.'

Arisa took a step forward at his threat, but Erun shot her a warning look that stilled her in her tracks.

'My lord, don't you already have a talented physician at the castle? A man by the name of Lore, I recall.'

'He is the very one who recommended you.' Erun looked surprised at this, but the Chancellor pressed on. 'Enough. I don't have time for chitchat. You're required to come with me immediately.' He looked toward the doorway, where two Royal Guards had materialised.

Erun nodded, beginning to collect his cloak and medical bag.

Arisa ran to her guardian's side. 'You can't go with him.'

Erun patted her arm. 'There is nothing to fear. I'll be back soon. You know what to do if I don't return. Stick to the plan,' he added in a whisper as he was ushered out the door.

'No!' Arisa had every reason to believe Erun wouldn't return. She clutched at her guardian's arm, trying to pull him back, but it was hopeless. She directed herself to the Chancellor. 'You need me. I can help.'

'If you must come, young lady, so be it,' the Chancellor barked. 'But make haste!'

'No, Arisa. You can't,' Erun protested.

But the Chancellor called 'Guards!' and the front door flew open. The two Royal Guards frogmarched Arisa and Erun out into the darkened city, alongside the most dangerous man in Lamore.

WHAT COULD the King's Chancellor want with Erun? Do they know who he really is? Arisa wondered, as Horace led them wordlessly through the city's back alleys. She was acutely aware of the two guards following close behind. After a few minutes on foot, the Chancellor stopped in front of an unmarked carriage with a lone coachman at its helm.

So it wasn't official business. Arisa's feeling of discomfort grew.

The guards shoved Arisa and Erun inside the carriage, and it set off at a brisk pace to the south of the city.

This would be the first time Arisa had ever passed the city's walls. She had envisioned this moment a thousand times before. But never had she imagined she would be leaving to go to the place she dreaded more than anything – Lamore Castle.

'Will you tell me what it is you want with me?' Erun asked.

Horace merely raised his forefinger, as if to say, *'Wait'*. Arisa was surprised to see a film of sweat forming on the Chancellor's forehead, clearly visible even in the carriage's dull interior. It was strange, considering the winter weather and Horace's unflappable reputation. If the Chancellor was as nervous as Arisa felt, perhaps it wasn't Erun who was in grave danger, but someone else.

They travelled in silence, passing unchecked through the

city's south gates, then up the hilly headland toward the castle. Finally, they came to a stop outside the castle gatehouse.

Arisa shivered.

The coachman stopped to speak to a sentry, and Horace turned to Erun. 'His Royal Highness, Prince Takai, has injured himself.' The words fell tonelessly from his lips.

Erun blinked rapidly. 'How ill is he?'

'We are sure it's nothing, and the Prince will be returned to his usual good health by the morn.' The Chancellor waved his hands in a carefree manner that didn't invite question. 'But I'm sure you understand we can't take any chances in these matters. Lore suggested we obtain a second opinion.' He paused. 'Just to be sure.'

'Of course,' Erun said slowly.

Arisa suspected the truth was far from the words being spoken. The Prince must be very ill for the King and Queen to have sent for Erun.

They were on the move again, and soon they were whisked out of the carriage and into the castle. The guards ushered them through dark interiors, twisting and turning through a labyrinth of passageways and stairs. Arisa felt they were taking a peculiarly indirect way to their destination, as they didn't pass anyone other than a handful of stony-faced guards. Eventually, they stopped outside what were presumably the Prince's rooms. Horace led them through the first door and an anteroom with more guards before they reached the Prince's bedchambers.

Arisa's eyes went straight to the body in the bed, and even from a dozen feet away, she realised the gravity of the situation. Erun quickly cast his eyes around the room, his fingers tapping nervously on his bag.

An exceedingly tall man in Ivanian dress was changing a dressing on the Prince's head. A woman who, judging by her attire, was likely the Queen sat behind the Ivanian, a female attendant directly behind her in the shadows. On the other side of the bed was a huge young man wringing his bruised and bloodied hands. Three Royal Physicians in black robes whispered among themselves in a corner. A tall man in the dress of a high-ranking noble, with a penetrating stare and a bandaged head, stood guard-like next to a man Arisa recognised from his statues as the King. The King was slumped in a trance-like state in a chair, his eyes fixed on nothing.

The Ivanian paused to wipe his brow and looked up. His eyes locked on Erun and widened for a moment. The physician – Lore, Arisa recalled – regained his composure quickly and strode over to where Erun, Arisa and the Chancellor stood.

'Erun, I presume.' The Ivanian's tone seemed overly formal.

'Yes. And this is my…assistant, Arisa.'

'I am Lore, the Queen's personal physician. Thank you for coming.'

'I was given little choice.' Erun looked back at Horace, only to receive a blank gaze in response.

Lore dropped his voice. 'I'm not sure what you've been told, but the Prince has a severe head injury. He was without life for several minutes after falling into the sea. His breathing is slow and irregular and he hasn't regained consciousness since the accident. His heart is also extremely weak.'

Arisa processed the information with heaviness in her gut. Lore must know there was little Erun could do in these circumstances.

Reading the doubt in their faces, Lore attempted to offer some hope. 'The Prince's friend, Sar' – he indicated the young man Arisa had seen wringing his hands – 'pulled the Prince from the water reasonably quickly, so perhaps the damage isn't as…' He drifted off as Erun began to shake his head.

'Lore, even if the Prince can be brought back to us, his faculties may be——'

'I'm afraid a healthy and fully restored Prince is the only acceptable outcome,' Horace interjected. He waved Erun in the direction of the Prince.

Slowly, Erun walked over to the bed, Arisa following. They

were standing opposite the Queen, but her eyes were fixed on her son. The young man called Sar was having the worst of his wounds seen to by the Queen's attendant. She stepped out of the shadows as she fussed about him.

Erun appeared to freeze for a moment as the attendant's features became clear and her eyes met his. She tilted her head and scrutinised his face. Then her eyes fell on Arisa. She stared from one to the other, and for a moment looked as if she would approach them, but stopped herself.

'The Prince,' Arisa reminded her guardian.

Erun nodded and bent over Takai. He lifted up the Prince's limp arms and opened his eyelids to reveal vacant eyes. He put his head to Takai's chest, registering what Arisa knew would be his raspy breathing and the irregular beating of his heart. Finally, Erun waved his hands in small circular motions over Takai's whole body, reading the Prince's energy. He winced.

Arisa guessed that the Prince's lifeforce was barely detectable. Erun would have to move quickly.

Ignoring the suspicious looks he was receiving from the Royal Physicians, Erun leant over the Prince and pinched his nose before breathing four times into his mouth.

The room broke out with cries of protest. Lore shouted at everyone to stay back, but the King was suddenly alert, his eyes wild.

'Who are you?' he demanded. 'What are you doing to my son? Lakeford, do something!'

The noble standing next to him – Lakeford – called for the guards.

The door flew open and two guards entered, moving swiftly toward Erun. By now Sar had pushed Lore aside and restrained Erun in a powerful grip.

Erun addressed himself to the King. 'My name is Erun, Your Majesty. Lore asked me to come here and assist in your son's recovery.'

The King looked Erun up and down with a glassy-eyed stare. 'You're not one of my physicians.'

'I'm not a physician. I'm an apothecary and healer.'

'The best medical minds in the kingdom are already attending the Prince.'

'With all due respect, Your Majesty – the best medical minds have done all they can do, but have so far failed.' Erun's eyes went to the Prince's arms, which showed their futile attempts to bleed him. 'While I don't know if *I* can save the Prince, and I make no promises, I will do everything within my power to help him.'

Horace leant in to speak to the King. 'Sire, I'm told this man has special healing talents.'

Erun directed himself to the Queen now. He appeared oblivious to the penetrating gaze of her attendant. 'Your son has water in his lungs. No amount of bleeding, cupping or potions can fix that. For any chance of survival, you must let me do my work.'

The Queen looked at Erun, then to her son, and back again. Her eyes were alert, searching for truth in what he had said.

One of the physicians stepped forward. 'Your Majesty. Your son is phlegmatic. His body must be purged with use of hot tonics. It will put his humours back in balance.'

Erun shook his head. 'An outdated tonic will do nothing to get the water from his lungs.'

A change had come over the Queen's face. She drew back her shoulders and, with a steady gaze, nodded at Erun. 'You have my permission to do whatever it takes to save my son.'

Both Erun and Arisa looked toward the King, who also gave a slow nod.

Sar released Erun from his grip, and Erun resumed breathing into the Prince's mouth – one, two, three, four times. There was no response. He repeated the action another four times and waited. He was about to try again when Takai's whole body began to shake wildly and a gush of water burst from his mouth.

Erun turned the Prince to his side to be sure all the water was gone. The convulsions stopped, and as he turned Takai back over, Arisa noted the rhythmic rise and fall of the Prince's chest with relief. The Queen looked up with a hopeful smile and Sar visibly relaxed his defensive stance.

Erun bent over to listen again to the Prince's chest. He gave a small nod – a sign that the Prince was breathing a little easier – then stepped back from the bedside and spoke to Lore in a low tone. 'His breathing has improved, but I'm afraid there is still more water in the Prince's lungs. He's at risk of secondary drowning.'

Lore tugged his collar anxiously.

'What do you mean by secondary drowning?' The Queen had overheard them.

'It means any remaining water in the lungs builds up over time, eventually leading to…' Lore didn't need to finish the sentence.

Queen Sofia visibly stiffened, and her attendant reached out for her hand.

Erun hesitated.

Arisa knew why. If he intervened further, it would expose him to dangerous scrutiny. But she also knew her guardian and his commitment to do all that he could for those in his charge.

'There is something I can attempt,' he said after a moment. 'But it's not without danger.'

'Do it.' The Queen's face was wet with tears. 'Whatever it is, I bid you do it quickly.'

The King clenched his jaw and nodded.

Erun reached into his bag, removed a long piece of tube and bid Arisa to fetch a bowl. He fed the tube slowly down Takai's throat, clearly conscious that every pair of eyes was on him. He had to be precise. Arisa watched him take a deep breath, steady his hands, and inch the tube further and further down, listening all the time to the Prince's chest. It was painstakingly slow, but he had to get it just right.

Arisa could feel the physicians' threatening presence as they edged in closer. Erun nodded at her to place the bowl at the other end of the tube, and with one more movement, he slotted it into its final position. Almost immediately, a stream of fluid flowed from the tube into the bowl, eventually trickling away to nothing.

Erun bent over and listened again to the Prince's chest. He frowned. Arisa bent her own head to Takai's chest. The Prince's lungs sounded clear, but his heartbeat was still irregular.

'Did you do it?' The Queen looked at Erun with clasped hands.

'I'm satisfied all of the water has been expelled from the Prince's lungs,' he said, 'and he is now breathing evenly.'

The group gave a collective sigh of relief.

Erun directed himself to the Queen. 'I'm afraid, though, that the Prince is still in grave danger.'

The Queen looked to Lore, clearly confused.

He had listened to the Prince's chest as well. 'The Prince's lungs are better,' he explained, 'but his heart is still beating too fast and irregularly.'

'What does that mean?' the Queen pressed.

'If the Prince's heart continues like this for much longer, he will not be able to endure the strain and stress on his body. He will eventually...' Lore didn't finish the sentence.

'What's next?'

There was no response.

'What will you do next?' the Queen repeated, more desperately. She looked to Lore, who shook his head gravely. 'Is there nothing any of you can do?' she gasped, turning from Lore to the physicians and, finally, to Erun.

'There is,' Erun began slowly, '*one* more thing I could try.'

Arisa's throat constricted as the Queen's face brightened.

She suspected what her guardian was about to propose, and it was a bad idea – a *very* bad idea.

'I will require more supplies from my home to complete the treatment.'

One of the physicians stepped forward to address the King. 'Your Majesty, this man can't be trusted. Surely whatever he proposes next will be nothing short of witchcraft.'

Erun ignored the barb and waited for the Queen's verdict.

The physician tried again. 'See? He doesn't bother to deny it. He's nothing more than a Kengian witchdoctor. He must be taken into custody immediately and questioned.'

'Witchcraft…' The King spoke the word a little hesitantly. He looked from his son and back to Erun. It was well known how the King detested Kengians – or more accurately, feared them. 'Yes, he must be taken away.'

'Guards, take him,' Lakeford ordered.

Arisa froze. All of her worst nightmares were materialising.

The guards moved swiftly toward Erun as the Queen stood up to protest. 'Leave him be. He may be my son's only hope.'

The guards continued undeterred, but Sar stepped in front of them.

'If you want to take this man, you must go through me first.'

'Our son has a fighting chance now because of this man,' the Queen appealed to the King. 'Witchcraft or not, we must trust him to try to bring our Prince back to us.'

The King looked to be faltering at his wife's words when Horace spoke up.

'Your Majesty, perhaps leave the accusation of witchcraft with me to investigate once the Prince has recovered. I will personally see that we get to the truth of this man's practices. In the meantime, let's see if he can do as promised.'

The King nodded.

Arisa felt little relief. If Erun managed the impossible task of saving the Prince, he would still be at the Chancellor's mercy.

Nevertheless, her guardian reached for Lore's notebook and

scribbled out a list before tearing out the page and handing it to Arisa. 'My assistant will see that everything on this list is prepared.'

Arisa shook her head. She couldn't leave him here—

He put his hands firmly on her shoulders. 'You must do this. It is the Prince's only hope.'

Sar strode over to them. 'I will escort her.'

'Guthrie will go with you as well,' Horace declared.

Arisa's blood ran cold at the memory of her experience with the Chancellor's son, but there was nothing she could do about it. Both she and Erun were temporarily in the service of the Lamorian Court.

'Please, we must make haste,' Sar addressed her, urgently but not unkindly. Arisa followed him, Erun's list in her hand and a growing sense of terror in her heart.

Sar guided her through the castle at a cracking pace, only stopping every now and then to allow her to catch up. Arisa was thankful at least that she wore her usual boy's attire, and wasn't in danger of getting tangled up in a gown. They reached a courtyard, where Sar asked Arisa to wait while he got the horses.

'Boy! Get my horse,' a familiar voice sounded behind her.

Arisa spun around to face him. *Guthrie.* She allowed herself a small smile as she noted the crookedness of his broken nose and the yellow bruising on his cheeks. His eyes locked with hers and a flash of recognition washed over his face.

'You!' he barked. 'What are you doing here?'

'I am here at your father's request.'

He stepped menacingly toward her and grabbed her arm. 'Liar!'

But Sar had returned; he reached out and released Guthrie's hold on her. 'Unhand her. She is the healer's assistant.' He turned to Arisa, adding gently, 'Sorry, what's your name?'

'Arisa.'

'Arisa – we must make haste.'

She nodded, keeping one wary eye on Guthrie. She looked around for the carriage, but there were just three horses.

'The carriage?'

'It will be faster on horseback.'

'But I can't ride.'

'You can come with me on my horse.'

'Or you could come on mine,' Guthrie sneered.

Sar mounted his horse and held his hand out toward her. Arisa hesitated for a moment, looking back and forth between this giant of a man and his equally oversized horse.

'Don't worry, he doesn't bite.' Sar grinned as he gave the horse a pat on the neck.

'It's not the horse I'm worried about.' She glanced at Guthrie again as Sar pulled her up to sit behind him.

'Hold on.'

She gingerly placed her hands around Sar's torso, and with a clicking sound from him, they were on their way toward the city.

Back at Erun's shop, Arisa scanned the list he'd made.

Guthrie paced the room, examining vials, books and other items. He picked up a flask of what Arisa knew to be a dangerously strong acid and swirled it around recklessly.

She raced over and took it off him, replacing it gently on the shelf. 'Stop touching things. You don't know what you're doing.'

'Give me the list,' he snarled.

Arisa stood a little taller. 'As I'm the only one here who knows what these items are, I suggest you adjust your tone.'

Guthrie stepped closer to her. 'You will do as you're ordered.'

She remained unmoved and folded her arms across her chest.

Guthrie clenched his fists. 'I'm warning you.'

'No. It is *I* who am warning you. Do you know what all these potions and equipment are used for?' Arisa waved her arm around the room. 'You need me to get the correct items. It would be terrible if I let you select the wrong thing.'

'You wouldn't dare!' Guthrie spat, stepping toward her again.

Arisa stood up taller still. 'Wouldn't I?'

Guthrie was now so close she could feel his quickening breath on her face, but she wouldn't yield. 'I will have you sent to the gallows for such a threat.'

Sar, who had been waiting at the door, appeared with an extended forearm to block Guthrie from advancing further. 'I'm sure no one will need to be sent to the gallows,' he said firmly. He cast a kind gaze toward her. 'Arisa – please help my friend.'

Recognising she had little choice given Erun was being held at the castle, Arisa collected the items and packed them carefully into her satchel. Then, for the second time in one night, she willingly went back to the place she dreaded most.

13

'I've just heard the news.' Countess Datanya's cleavage heaved as she tried to catch her breath.

Theodora stood with her mother in the doorway of her father's private study. It had only been a few hours since the accident, and while everyone had been sworn to secrecy, it hadn't taken long for the gossipy Countess to discover what had happened. The Chancellor ushered his wife and daughter inside and dismissed his guards.

'How is the Prince, Father?' Theodora appeared deliberately composed. In truth, she was convinced Takai was dead, and all of her plans to be Queen were shattered.

Horace poured the Countess a glass of wine and indicated for them both to sit. Theodora saw him wince as her mother took several large gulps of her wine.

'The Prince fares better, but is far from well. The water has been expelled from his lungs but he has not regained consciousness. His heart is the main concern.'

The Countess flung a hand to her own chest and let out a high-pitched cry. Theodora resisted the urge to roll her eyes at her mother's melodrama. She sat silently, her back straight, her gaze fixed on her father. Other than the slightest twitch of her hands, she kept herself admirably poised. 'What do the Royal Physicians say?' she asked in an even tone.

'They are beyond useless. First they bled the Prince, then they argued over his humours, and then they declared there was no hope—'

'No hope?' Datanya squeaked from under the handkerchief she held to her nose.

'Lore suggested a healer in Obira City. I found the man' – a smug smile came over Theodora's face; it had been her idea to send her father to the city – 'and he has been solely responsible for the improvement in the Prince's condition.'

Datanya leaned forward in her chair. 'A healer?'

'Yes, a man of unusual abilities, from what I've seen so far. He claims he may be able to restore the Prince's heart to normal. He sent Sar to fetch more supplies from his home. Guthrie went with him.'

A short knock came at the door. As if on cue, Guthrie entered the room, his chest puffed up with importance.

'Father—' He baulked slightly as he registered the Countess and Theodora's presence. He gave a swift acknowledgement to his mother, but ignored his sister.

'What news?' Horace prompted.

'As requested, I looked around the healer's home. There were some strange-looking manuscripts and books in several languages I didn't completely recognise.'

Theodora snorted at her brother's ignorance; he shot her a dark look in response. Horace motioned for his son to continue.

'There were also many different potions and medicines. And these.'

Guthrie reached into his cloak and pulled out a stack of parchment scraps. Theodora leant forward to catch a look. The parchment pieces were covered in line after line of numbers. *Coded messages.*

'Was there anything else?' Horace asked.

'That was all I could do before the healer's annoying assistant stopped me.'

'You mean to say a presumably defenceless girl managed to distract you from the task I set you?' Horace's voice rose in annoyance.

Guthrie raised his head defiantly. 'Trust me, that girl is not defenceless. She's the same one who gave me this.' He pointed to his broken nose.

'I would very much like to meet this girl,' Theodora remarked.

'Hold your tongue, sister, or I will rip it from your pretty little mouth.'

'Enough, you two,' Horace interjected. 'I have to say, I'm very curious about this healer and his *assistant*. I'd like to get to know them both a little better.'

He stood up to leave, but the Countess grabbed his arm. 'But husband, what of our plans for the Prince?'

Horace smirked. 'Something tells me this healer may very well be the answer to several of our problems.'

'So Theodora *will* be the future Queen.' Theodora saw her mother's eyes sparkle at the thought – or from the wine; it was hard to say.

Guthrie snorted. 'Only if the Prince will have her.'

'He will, brother,' Theodora retorted. 'And you will rue the day. Because from that day, you will bend the knee to me – your Queen.'

14

Under the penetrating stares of the physicians, Erun rearranged the medicine and instruments on the table in front of him several times. Then he handed Arisa a list of instructions.

'We must prepare this.'

She recognised it as one of her guardian's experiments. It confirmed her worst fear: Erun was about to try something on the heir to Lamore that had never been practised on a human before.

She nodded gravely, and Erun started preparing the briny solution he needed. Arisa assembled the equipment she'd brought in her satchel, and was holding the main part aloft for Erun's inspection when Horace appeared at their side. The Chancellor's hawklike eyes were ablaze with curiosity as he followed every detail of the preparations.

'I expect the girl has brought everything you need?'

Arisa shot a fiery look at the Chancellor. 'The *girl* has a name, and it's Arisa.'

The Chancellor gave her a brief appraising glance in return. 'I too have a name, as you know perfectly well. I am the King's Chancellor, and you, *girl*, will not address me unless I give you permission to do so. Now, show me what you have in your hands.'

Arisa scrunched up her nose, then made a point of handing over the piece of equipment to Erun instead, leaving the Chancellor's hands outstretched and empty. For a moment she thought Horace would reach out and slap her, but he quickly composed himself and motioned for Erun to continue with his task.

A few minutes later, Erun and Arisa were ready.

'My lord.' Erun bowed to the Chancellor. 'Should I speak to the King for permission to begin?'

Horace glanced over at the King, slumped again in his chair; he appeared to be catatonic. 'Perhaps you should speak to the Queen.'

'As you wish, my lord.' Erun approached the Queen and her attendant, whose gaze had barely left them. 'Your Majesty?'

Queen Sofia ran her eyes over the equipment that was now set up next to the Prince's bed.

'I will not lie to you,' Erun continued. 'Your son remains in grave danger. There may be nothing I can do to help, and what I am going to attempt is incredibly risky, but I would like your permission to try.'

The Queen looked directly into Erun's eyes, back at the equipment and then at her son again, before nodding slowly.

There was no turning back now.

Arisa watched as Sar gripped Erun's arm. 'What can I do?' the Prince's friend asked. 'Please let me help.'

'I can see how much you care for the Prince, but the best thing you can do now is to get your own wounds tended to and get some rest.'

Sar shook his head. 'I will rest when the Prince is well again.'

Erun sighed, dropping his voice to a whisper. 'What I'm going to do next is something no one will have seen before. I'm going to use some unusual equipment on your friend. I have tested it many times, but never on a person.'

Sar's eyes widened with concern. 'How do you know it will work?'

'In truth, I don't know.' (Arisa knew that, to date, her guardian had only enjoyed partial success with a dead mouse.) 'But I do know it is the Prince's only hope.'

Sar released his grip. 'Alright. How can I help?'

'See these leads here?' Erun held up the wires to show Sar. 'When I apply the ends of these to the Prince, he will convulse, but it won't be as bad as it seems. I need you to trust me and keep everyone away.'

Sar nodded his agreement and moved across the room, placing himself strategically between the Prince's bed and the guards.

Arisa moved to stand beside Erun, squeezing his hand tightly. He took a deep breath and checked his equipment. It was set up the same way Arisa had always seen it for his experiments. There were layers of two different Kengian metals and brine-soaked cloth, fixed in a metal tower. If it worked as expected, energy would flow through the layers and out of the wires attached to the top and bottom of the tower.

'Theoretically, the energy created from the device can regulate Takai's heartbeat,' he said in a low voice – as much to himself as to her, Arisa thought. His calculations needed to be precise, or he risked killing the Prince.

She gave his hand one last squeeze. Then Erun connected the ends of the two wires together.

The effect was instantaneous. Arcs of blue and white light sparked out from the device. Gasps reverberated around the room, along with cries of *'Witchcraft!'* from the physicians. Satisfied the device was working, Erun ignored them, disconnected the wires from each other, and held each end to Takai's chest.

The Prince's body thrust upwards, before falling back down on the bed with a thud. Then – nothing.

Everyone in the room was silent, waiting for some sign of life. 'Come on,' Erun muttered to himself. 'Come on.'

Please work, Arisa begged silently. It didn't bear thinking what the punishment would be if it didn't.

'He has done it,' one of the physicians cried. 'He has killed the Prince!'

Erun winced. Arisa's stomach churned.

Then Takai's eyes flung open.

The Prince sat up, gasping. He looked about wildly before collapsing back onto the bed.

Erun put his head to Takai's chest, checking for a beat. He squeezed his eyes shut. Lore followed suit, then shook his head miserably.

Nothing.

The Queen appeared stoic except for a single tear rolling down her cheek. But an animalistic howl came from the King as he tried to get past Sar and reach Erun.

Horace called out to the guards, and they raced toward Arisa and her guardian. Arisa's legs started to give away underneath her. Everything they had tried was for nothing—

Then she heard it. A voice that came from miles away. At first it was a mumble, but it grew louder and clearer.

'What happened?'

Everyone turned in unison toward the voice.

'Someone tell me what happened.'

The Prince was sitting upright in his bed.

Cries of joy echoed around the room. Sar whooped and barrelled toward Takai's bed, embracing his friend in an affectionate headlock. Lore prodded Sar away gently to examine the confused-looking Prince. Then the Ivanian healer looked to the Queen with a broad smile.

'What...what is everyone doing here?' Takai croaked.

'There will be time for that later.' Lore tried to get the Prince to lie back down. 'Right now, you must rest.'

Arisa smiled up at Erun. 'You did it. I knew you would.'

But before Erun could reply, Horace motioned to him.

'Come with me.' Arisa froze as the Chancellor jabbed a finger at her, too. 'And you, *girl*. You come as well.'

Horace led them to his rooms. Arisa hoped he was going to thank them, perhaps pay them some coin for their services. Money they could use to get back to Kengia. And then he would send them on their way. Yes…that was what he would do. After all, Erun had done all that was asked of him.

They reached the Chancellor's study and Horace lowered himself into a throne-like seat. He nodded for Erun and Arisa to take two of the smaller seats, but Arisa's guardian remained stubbornly on his feet. He was surprisingly composed.

'On behalf of the King and all of Lamore,' Horace began, 'let me convey our sincere gratitude for bringing the Prince back to us.'

'I didn't realise you spoke on behalf of *all Lamorians*,' Arisa muttered under her breath. Erun shot her a warning look.

Horace either ignored the barb or hadn't heard it. He stood up and began to walk casually around the room. 'Yes, you seem to have performed quite the…What is the word I am looking for? Ah, yes. Quite the *miracle*.'

Erun didn't respond.

'No one would deny that the Prince was close to death, until you worked your…' Horace shook his head. 'I can't seem to find the words I want today.'

Erun still didn't react.

Horace stopped moving and narrowed his eyes. 'I suppose the word I'm looking for is *witchcraft*.' Arisa tensed, but Erun's face didn't betray so much as a twitch. 'Yes, witchcraft. That is exactly what I would call it. While you may have saved the Prince, you have used forbidden means. You used sorcery and untested equipment on the Prince, which could have caused him further harm, or even death. These acts can't go unpunished.'

Erun held steady as Arisa's heart hammered in her chest.

'We can't have our subjects ignoring the laws of the land. You have left me with little choice.'

Erun raised a brow at this comment. '"*Our* subjects", you say, as if you are the King himself.'

Horace's face flared red. 'Do you know the punishment for practising witchcraft?' he thundered.

Again, there was no response.

'It is death, healer! Death! Do you have anything to say to that?'

'How would you like me to respond?'

'I don't know. Shock. Anger. You could protest your innocence. Beg for mercy.'

'It is unlikely anything I say will detract you from whatever path you're determined to follow. So I will save my breath.'

Horace grunted. 'If you're not interested in preserving your *own* life, perhaps you're interested in what may become of your...' He waved his hand at Arisa. '*Assistant.*'

The corner of Erun's mouth twitched and he shifted his weight. Arisa felt sick that she was being used against her guardian.

'Yes.' Horace's eyes gleamed triumphantly. 'It's quite disturbing to think of what could happen to the girl, who I'm beginning to think is much more to you than a mere assistant... What would happen to her alone and with no one to protect her in these troublesome times? Just imagine the misfortune that could befall her.'

Erun's face hardened. 'What are you trying to get at?'

'Well, it may surprise you that on this occasion I have no wish to send you to the gallows. I must, though, think of some other way you can make amends for what you've done. You must provide a service of some kind to me – to the King.' Horace rubbed his chin for a few moments, as though he were trying to think of an appropriate task. 'I may have the very thing for you...You might have heard the King is planning a great celebration: a tournament in spring, and also a progress.'

Erun shrugged. Arisa couldn't think how he could assist with some ridiculous celebration events.

'The King is celebrating twenty years of his reign, as well as the Prince's eighteenth birthday. He wishes to mark the occasion with something spectacular. Something no one has seen before.'

'I can't imagine what that has to do with me.'

'I expect it will have a lot to do with you, for the King wishes to have a marvellous light display.' The Chancellor paused, presumably so they could gauge the full effect of what he was about to say. 'He wants firesky.'

Arisa's mouth fell open. A muscle in Erun's bearded jaw worked. There was silence while they waited for Horace to say he was jesting, but the Chancellor merely tapped his fingers together expectantly.

'Impossible,' Erun said finally. 'The secrets to firesky have been lost for centuries.'

'That may very well be the case, but the King has his heart set on it, so it must happen. And I am the one tasked with ensuring it does happen…with your help, Erun.'

Erun shook his head vigorously. 'I can't help you.'

'But I believe you can, and you will. I have never seen someone of your abilities before.'

'I'm just a simple apothecary with an interest in science.'

'Tut-tut, healer – you can't lie to me. What if I were to dig a little further into the life of Erun and his young…*assistant*? What exactly would I find?' Horace started pacing the room again. 'This is how you can atone for your crime. All you need to do is create firesky.'

'I told you – the secrets to firesky are long gone.'

'That is not known for sure. The King and I are convinced the key may lie somewhere in the hundreds of ancient texts and manuscripts we have here in the castle.'

Erun tilted his head, as if pondering whether he could in fact master firesky. 'Wouldn't a scribe suffice for that task?'

'There is no scribe in this kingdom who has your special

talents. Of course, if you refuse to help, I would have to rethink my position on your punishment, and what is to be done with your—'

'I'm his ward, if you must know.' Arisa jutted out her chin. 'And I don't appreciate your threats against my guardian.'

Horace spun around to face her. 'They aren't just threats, *ward*,' he hissed.

Arisa opened her mouth to make a retort, but before she could say anything, Erun said in a resigned voice, 'I will help you.'

Horace clapped his hands together. 'Splendid. Your duties begin immediately. Mind you, it is to be a secret task. Firesky is to be a great surprise at the celebrations. The King expects them at the tournament in spring or for the start of his progress, whichever comes first.'

'If it's a surprise, then what shall I say I am working on?'

Horace appeared to think on it for a moment. 'You have been tasked with documenting your great scientific discoveries for the benefit of the King and his physicians.'

'Erun, you can't work for the King…' she stabbed a finger at Horace, '…for *him*.' But Erun would not heed her protests, addressing the Chancellor instead.

'And how do you suggest I access your resources here at the castle to complete my *secret* task?'

Horace gave a sly smile. 'That won't be a problem, Erun. For you will be staying right here until the task is complete.'

Arisa reached for her guardian's hand and squeezed it tight.

'I need to work from my home,' he protested.

'You will be escorted home to gather anything you need, but you must return here later this morning.'

'What about Arisa?'

'I will personally see to her welfare. She will be my guest here at the castle.'

Arisa squeezed Erun's hand even tighter.

'But—'

Horace held up his hand to silence Erun. 'Guards.'

One of the guards came through the door.

'Take this man back to his home with his ward. They are to collect some items and return to the castle. And take my son, Lord Guthrie, with you.'

The guard grabbed Erun and the Arisa by the arms – her heart hammering – and led them from Horace's study.

Outside the room they ran into the Queen's attendant. The woman's brown eyes widened on seeing them. She opened her mouth as if to say something, but was interrupted by a guard announcing her presence.

'My lord, the Lady Gwyn.'

There was a lengthy pause before Horace said, 'Come?' – almost as if it were a question; as if he were surprised by her visit.

Gwyn nodded to them both, lifted her chin and strode into the Chancellor's study.

Arisa noticed a strange look on her guardian's face as he looked back in Gwyn's direction, but the door to Horace's study slammed and they were jerked away by the guard.

It was still dark when Arisa was ushered into a carriage. In a heart-stopping moment, Erun had been called back to receive final instructions from the Chancellor. She ran her palms up and down her thighs, hoping it was all a bad dream. That they would go back to their plan to leave Lamore. That the whole night had been in her imagination – but all of those hopes came to a grinding halt when Guthrie's bulky frame appeared on the seat across from her.

He smirked at Arisa and rubbed his chin thoughtfully, as if he were determining the best torture for her. She wasn't sure what he might have done if Erun hadn't arrived shortly after. She yearned to speak to her guardian and ask him about his conversation with Horace, but it would have to wait until they were by themselves, away from Guthrie and his disconcerting stare.

It was going on dawn when the carriage pulled up outside their home. Arisa leapt out, desperate to put some distance between her and Guthrie. Erun followed her more slowly.

She grasped his arm tightly as soon as they were safely back inside. 'We have to get out of here. There's no way we can go back to the castle.'

'You know we can't run. The guards are right outside to make sure we go back.'

'But we have to try!'

'We'll be fine. I *will not* let anything happen to you. Once the task is finished, everything will return to normal and we can leave Lamore as planned.'

'Surely the Chancellor's word can't be trusted. You know what he is capable of.'

Erun put his hand to her face gently. 'Yes, I know what he is capable of, and that is precisely why we *must* go.'

She bit back the tears that were threatening to fall.

'There is…something else,' Erun added haltingly.

'What else can there be?'

'The Chancellor called me back to say you have been invited to serve as a lady-in-waiting to the Queen.'

Arisa swallowed, trying to digest what Erun had said. 'A lady-in-waiting? I thought I would stay with you, and assist you.'

He shook his head.

'Please tell me you refused.'

Erun didn't respond. Of course he hadn't refused. Arisa knew he had been given no choice in that matter, but she wasn't going to surrender so easily.

'What about school? I'm only months off my final examinations, and then I apply to the College of Surgeons. What kind of study can I do if I have to serve the Queen?'

'I will insist that you're able to continue your studies at the castle. Perhaps we can send for the Schoolmaster to help you.'

'What of our work? What of all the people who need your help here in Obira?'

'I'm afraid they will need to look for help elsewhere. They would have had to find someone else anyway, if we went to Kengia.'

'You're sure we can really still leave this place when you're done?'

Erun nodded.

'You promise?'

'I promise.' Erun smiled, sending crinkles around his eyes.

Arisa wanted to believe more than anything that it was possible to leave Lamore. 'If donning a lady's gown and serving the Queen is the only way, then I will do it. But don't expect me to enjoy it.'

Erun gave a thin laugh. 'I would never expect such a thing. But I do expect you to be on your guard. Don't trust anyone.' He handed her a small silk pouch.

She pulled on the drawstrings to reveal a vial of amber liquid: the drops she used every day to disguise her silver eyes.

'We've been out all night. You should use some now,' Erun said. Arisa squeezed a drop into each eye, knowing it would immediately transform them from dull orange to bright amber. 'There is enough there to see you through several months.'

Arisa's face fell. '*Months?*'

'We have been given a deadline. Spring or earlier. Frankly, I don't know how long the whole thing will take.'

There was something in Erun's tone of voice that struck fear into Arisa's heart. 'Surely you don't mean to actually deliver firesky for Horace? I thought you'd pretend to try, buy us some time until we can escape. That you'd never willingly try and hand over Kengian magic.'

'To be honest, I believe the Chancellor wants much more than a pretty light display. And if my suspicions are right, those plans could be disastrous for all of Kypria.'

'Suspicions?'

'I'm probably overthinking it, being tired and the like. In any case, I must tread carefully…As you must.'

'Don't I always?' she teased.

He looked at her pointedly. 'Just avoid fistfights if you can. It's hardly becoming of a Queen's lady.'

Arisa snorted in a most unbecoming way and gave a forced smile. 'Trust no one. Tread carefully. And no fistfights. I think I've got it.'

In reality, she was wondering how much trouble she could cause before they made their escape – for there must be an escape before any Kengian magic was handed over – and how, in the meantime, she could use her new position at the castle to get the justice she had been waiting for.

15

'You can leave it there,' Theodora ordered the chambermaid. She gritted her teeth as she arranged the newly delivered tray of food on the Queen's table.

She despised the fact that she was not much more than a glorified servant to Sofia, despite being one of the highest-ranking ladies at court. The ladies-in-waiting took it in turns to arrange the Queen's morning meals. Every morning, soon after dawn, Sofia would break her fast. She was an early riser, unlike the rest of the court, who didn't surface until noon or well after. Most courtiers spent the night feasting and enjoying entertainment in the Great Hall, but not the sombre Queen.

Theodora supervised the laying out of food with heavy eyelids. She hadn't slept all night; thoughts of Takai's accident and how close he'd come to death had cycled ceaselessly through her mind. Stifling a yawn, she made a final adjustment to a lace-trimmed napkin as the Queen and Gwyn entered the room. Theodora gave a lazy curtsey and smiled to herself at the way the pair of women appeared to have aged ten years overnight.

'Your Majesty.'

The Queen swept past her without so much as a glance.

'Her Majesty won't be eating this morning. She needs to rest,' Gwyn stated matter-of-factly as she ushered Sofia into her bedchambers, and closed the door heavily in Theodora's face.

Theodora stuck out her tongue after them, sighing with annoyance that she had troubled herself with the meal. She looked around the room surreptitiously before sitting herself down in the Queen's high-backed chair at the head of the table.

Picking up a piece of crusty white bread, she bit off a chunk. Next she took a large gulp of spiced Ivanian tea. 'Blurgh!' She spat the tea back into the cup. 'How does she drink that swill?'

She moved on to the segments of mandarin imported from Ette. *Ha!* Theodora thought. *The Queen won't be getting her precious fruit anymore, now the Northemers have Ette.*

Theodora closed her eyes, imagining what delicacies she would have at her table when she was Queen. First of all, she wouldn't be dining at such an unrespectable hour. It went without saying that she would preside over every feast in the Great Hall. That way, every courtier could admire her beauty and declare their undying devotion to their Queen. Poems would be written about her beauty and balladeers would sing her praises. She savoured the vision in her mind, sure her days of serving this Queen were numbered.

Theodora opened her eyes reluctantly. Slipping a piece of cheese into her mouth, she made to leave the room, but the sound of voices coming from the bedchamber stopped her mid stride.

On any other day, she wouldn't have been interested in the Queen and Gwyn's conversation in the least – but the last day hadn't been like any other. If she hoped to influence or undermine the Queen, she would need to find out more about her. Theodora looked around the room to assure herself she was still alone, then tiptoed to the thick oak door of the bedchamber and pressed her ear to it.

She couldn't hear anything other than a jumble of whispered conversation. Theodora examined the door, looking for an opening she could listen through, but there was nothing other than a finger-wide gap between the bottom of the door and the floor. She shook her head as she got down on her hands and knees and pressed her ear to the gap, straining her ears until she caught their conversation.

'Before you sleep, there is something I must tell you.'

'Yes,' came the Queen's sleepy reply.

'Horace has appointed another lady-in-waiting.'

There was an unmistakable groan. 'I have enough silly girls and spies in my rooms already. Why would he do that?'

'I asked him to do it.'

'Oh. Who is it?'

'The girl is the ward of Erun.'

'Erun? The healer?'

How interesting, Theodora thought. She was looking forward to meeting the girl who had publicly humiliated her brother and broken his nose.

'Sofia, you mean to say you didn't recognise him?'

'Recognise him? Why would I—' The Queen paused. 'Goodness, you're right. It could be him. I suppose with everything going on I didn't notice. And it has been many years.'

'It has. And while he is older, it is undoubtedly him.'

'But why did Lore invite him here?'

'I expect he had only heard of Erun by reputation. He had never met him in person. Or at least, he didn't think he had. Had he known...' Gwyn trailed off.

'Erun's ward, you say?'

'Yes. Her name is Arisa. Horace insists that she stays here while Erun completes a task for him. I understand he is to record his medical knowledge for the King. To what real end, I know not. Erun and Arisa will remain in the castle until the task is complete.' Gwyn's voice dropped to a whisper. 'I fear for the safety of both while they are here.'

'They have my patronage and what little protection I can offer, but we must be careful. There is too much at stake.'

'You need not remind me.'

Gwyn's footsteps sounded from within; Theodora stood up quickly and backed away from the door.

So the healer wasn't exactly who he claimed to be. He had secrets – and whatever those secrets were, the Queen and Gwyn were privy to them.

She tiptoed back through the room and quietly exited into the presence chamber. 'The Queen is sleeping,' she said to the guards by way of explanation, before quickening her pace.

Theodora tried to suppress the smile on her face. She wasn't sure of the significance of what she had just heard, but she was sure it had all the hallmarks of leverage over the Queen and Gwyn.

16

———————

*A*risa looked out of the carriage window, feeling oddly curious and terrified at the same time. They had passed through Obira's southern gates and were riding back up the headland toward the castle. She caught a taste of salt in the air on the whistling breeze. Gazing down at the port below and the sea beyond, Arisa shivered at the memory of the last time she'd been there. She counted six ships – mostly trading vessels, she guessed – but the port was conspicuously quiet; there were dozens of empty berths where the naval fleet would normally be docked.

They travelled further up the hill, and Arisa had to suppress a gasp as the castle came into view in all its imposing glory. Up close and in the daylight, she couldn't help but feel in awe of its magnificence. Its grey stonework glinted as if it were silver.

The carriage passed through the main gate. It was made of wood and fortified with iron, set into a thick stone wall several stories high. The wall snaked off either side of the castle, finishing where the peninsula's cliffy ridges met the sea. There were four towers set into the wall, each dotted with narrow arrow slits and topped off with crenellations resembling crowns. Royal Guards patrolled the battlements.

The carriage approached the gatehouse along a pristine pebble roadway that branched off into what appeared to be a tiltyard and fields to the left and right. In the distance, rolling hills gave way to a woodland of oaks, elms, pine and silver birch. The castle grounds were vaster than Arisa had ever imagined.

They passed over a drawbridge and moat that surrounded the main castle before being stopped at another checkpoint. The castle was a busy hum of activity. Guards and servants moved in and out of small wooden buildings in the outer bailey. Farmers herded their livestock and chickens pecked at the ground. Everyone was going about the laborious task of serving the King and his court. None, though, were too busy to resist stopping and staring at the newcomers.

The carriage continued onwards until they reached the inner wall, passing under the portcullis that led to the main keep. The heavy iron gate and its pointy teeth hung ominously over their heads. Finally, they came to a stop in what appeared to be the main courtyard. From her side of the carriage, Arisa could see the stables and other work buildings.

A footman in the King's livery appeared, opening the door and helping Arisa out. Guthrie began barking instructions about what should be done with their belongings. Keen to distance herself from him, Arisa wandered around to the other side of the carriage, and there she found an altogether different view.

She was standing before a set of marble stairs set into a great stone breezeway that ran along the main building's perimeter. She was sure this wasn't the way she had been brought the previous night. Even in the dark she would have noticed the splendour of it. It ran the length of the western wing of the castle, joining the main keep and the older-looking southern keep.

Erun joined her as she peered up the steps, admiring the carved stone archways and marble columns. On the breezeway floor was a repeating pattern of tiles inlaid with heraldic designs. While all of this was amazing in itself, what caught her breath was the shiny gold fretwork adorning each arch along the breezeway. It dazzled in the silvery morning light.

'Everything that glitters is not gold,' Erun muttered in her ear.

'But I think it actually *is* gold,' she whispered incredulously.

Her guardian shot her a warning look that brought her immediately back to reality and their precarious situation. Here they were, a Kengian Prince and a half-Kengian girl – a silver-eyes – having to survive in the most dangerous place in Lamore. Here, their lives depended on whether they could keep their identities secret.

'There isn't enough gold in this entire world that could keep me here longer than we have to be,' she murmured.

Erun squeezed her shoulder. 'Nor me, my girl.'

The footman disappeared into the west wing with their baggage, leaving Arisa and Erun alone with Guthrie. He jutted out his chin and advanced on her. Erun stepped between them, but Arisa was determined not to let this bully get the better of her. She put both hands on her hips, and was about to challenge him, when they were interrupted by a booming voice.

'There you are!'

Sar was bounding down the stairs. He was dressed in the Royal Guard's uniform and his injured hands were bandaged. His hair was neat, his beard newly trimmed. With the exception of the dark rings under his eyes, he looked the picture of health, worlds apart from the grief-stricken man she had seen last night.

'If it isn't the famous healer, Erun, and his fine assistant, Arisa. A good morn to you both.' He gave an overly dramatic bow.

Arisa bristled at his condescending greeting. 'Do you mean to mock us?'

Sar's face fell. 'Of course not! I'm just so happy to see you both. When I heard you were to join us at the castle I insisted on coming to greet you. I would have been here sooner had my lady mother not insisted I make myself respectable-looking first.' He gave a lopsided grin.

Erun smiled gratefully. 'Thank you, Sar. We appreciate you meeting us.'

'No, it is I who must thank you for saving the Prince.' Sar scratched his head for a moment. 'Though I'm not entirely sure how you did it.'

'What you saw was science at work.'

Guthrie glared at Erun. 'By *science* you mean *magic*, don't you, witchdoctor?'

'Thank you, Guthrie,' Sar said dismissively. 'I can escort our guests from here.'

'*My lord*,' Guthrie corrected him, sneering.

'There's no need to call *me* your lord, Guthrie. I haven't been knighted yet.' Sar gave Arisa a wink.

Guthrie's face reddened.

'Was there anything else?' Sar asked innocently.

Guthrie gave a grunt before turning abruptly on his heel and disappearing into the castle.

'I can't believe he left so easily,' Arisa mused.

Sar's grin disappeared for a moment. 'He wouldn't dare challenge me so soon after Ette. He's lucky not to be locked up in the castle dungeons with Sir Marcus. Many lives were lost because of their cowardice.'

She felt an urge to reach out and comfort this giant of a man, who suddenly appeared so vulnerable. 'It must have been horrible for you,' she offered.

He looked down at her with a furrowed brow. 'It was horrible for all of my soldiers, but it is the Etteans I feel for most. They have gone from one oppressor to another in the Northemers.'

How curious. She hadn't expected one of the King's soldiers to demonstrate such empathy toward people who were essentially Lamore's conquered subjects. She would have pressed Sar further had he not changed the subject.

'Right. To the matters at hand. As of this moment, I'm making it my personal mission to protect you both as best I can while you're here.'

'I'm sure that's not necessary,' Erun ventured unconvincingly.

'Even if it wasn't, which I'm afraid it is, I'm on the Queen's orders to watch over you.'

Arisa smiled, believing in Sar's sincerity, but not so much his ability to deliver on his pledge. 'Thank you, Sar.'

He dropped his voice. 'I do mean it, though. You are both in the Chancellor's sights, as well as Guthrie's, from what I saw today. So I suggest you—'

'Keep our heads down,' she offered in singsong, but really she was pondering exactly how she could enact her revenge on the Chancellor – and Guthrie, for that matter.

Sar cocked his head to the side. 'That's exactly what I mean.'

A stern-looking guard armed with a halberd appeared by Sar's side.

'Klaus,' Sar addressed him, 'please take Erun to the Chancellor's rooms. He is expected there.'

'Do you mean for me to check on the Prince first?' Erun enquired.

Sar shook his head. 'He's currently resting, but Lore is with him. The orders are for you to be taken directly to the Chancellor.' He directed himself to Klaus again. 'Stay with Erun until he is safely settled in his rooms.'

Klaus nodded. He looked every bit as serious as Sar was not.

'You're in good hands with Klaus. He's one of my most trusted men.'

'And Arisa?' Erun asked.

'I'm going to escort Arisa to the Queen's rooms.'

Erun hugged her tightly. 'I will see you soon.'

She watched on with a sick feeling as her guardian followed Klaus into the castle. Her separation from Erun was a keen reminder to hold on to her darkness and hate. They were living among the enemy now. Arisa couldn't let any amount of glitter or gold make her forget that – or the fact that she had an important job to do.

Inside the castle, Arisa followed Sar into a brightly lit entranceway, at least three times the size of the house she and Erun lived in. The floors were covered in red-and-green mosaic tiles and the walls were panelled in rich, dark wood.

'That is the way to the Great Hall.' Sar pointed down a corridor to the right. 'It's also the way to the King's apartments, and the north-west tower, where I understand your guardian is to be housed.' He waved to the left. 'This way will take you to the Queen's apartments.'

Sar led her down a series of long corridors, the walls lined with tapestries and paintings of royals past. She screwed up her face as they passed a larger-than-life bronze statue depicting King Emberto.

Finally they came to a winding set of stone stairs. 'The Queen's apartments are on the third floor of the south-east tower,' Sar explained, as Arisa tried to get her bearings.

Sar strode up the stairs two at a time, with Arisa following as quickly as she could. They reached the top of the stairs and she stopped to catch her breath. She noticed all the wood panelling had disappeared; here there was nothing but bare stone walls. There were no tapestries or portraits, and glass was missing from many windows.

Arisa stopped to run her hands over a worn inscription on the wall. It was old, but she detected the semblance of a royal insignia. She traced the lines, squinting to examine the symbol more closely. It was a shield divided in four. In each quarter was a different animal: a koi, a lion, a phoenix and a bird – a starling. At the centre was a seed. She knew instinctively the seed came from the yew tree – a sacred tree in

Kengia. Below the shield were the remnants of Old Kengian words. She didn't need to see all of them to know what they were.

'*Oyuu whayl non ehwn ithyen,*' she said out loud, before she realised what she'd done.

'You can read that?' Sar raised an eyebrow. 'Do you know what it means?'

Arisa hesitated for a moment, remembering Erun's warning not to trust anyone, remembering that Sar was one of *them* – or was he?

'It says something like, "There is only harmony when every-thing is as one".'

'I like that. *Harmony when everything is as one.* You know, I've passed this spot a million times and never really noticed it before. It must be very old. Perhaps back to the time of Emberto the Conqueror.'

Arisa winced momentarily at the glorified title given to the Lamorian King from centuries before. 'It's the emblem of King Alfred and his wife Mary,' she explained. 'It represents the four elements that Kengians live in harmony with. The starling is for air, the koi for water, the phoenix for fire and the yew seed for earth.'

'And the lion was King Alfred's crest?'

She nodded, surprised at Sar's knowledge.

'So, the firstborn line of Kengia inherits powers over one of those elements.' Sar's eyes shone with curiosity.

'For the most part. There have been those who could control earth and air, but not the other elements.'

'Is the fire a reference to firesky?' Sar knew more than she had ever expected.

'Many Kengians believe it refers to the learned Firemasters. The last one died at the hands of King Emberto, and their secrets were lost forever. But many also believed one of the Kengian line would inherit the powers of fire one day.'

'That is, if the Kengian firstborn line had continued.' Sar's voice was tinged with unexpected sadness. 'Yet many people still believe a Water Catcher will come.'

'That is what the prophecy says.' Arisa didn't want to encourage conversation about the prophecy at the best of times, and certainly not here at the castle.

'And you – what do you believe?'

She looked into Sar's earnest face and sighed. 'I'm not sure what I believe.'

'I'm sorry to hear that. I find Kengian culture and magic fascinating.'

She froze, wondering whether Sar was genuinely interested, or if he was trying to get compromising information out of her.

He appeared oblivious to her discomfort and continued, 'So, all Kengians can hear or speak with nature, right?'

Arisa nodded hesitantly. 'That is my understanding.'

'But only silver-eyes have actual powers?'

She couldn't explain it, but she felt Sar chipping away at some of the darkness in her. Something about him made her want to open up. 'Silver-eyes are born with a gift to manipulate objects from the natural world, but their powers have to be nurtured – awakened through tutelage. Even then, their powers are not vast. They can perform simple tricks, really, nothing to harm a person.'

'I don't know – being able to *persuade* someone to do something is pretty powerful.'

She shook her head. 'That's different. The power of suggestion is a learned ability, reserved for a few elite Kengian Scholars. They study the connection between nature and science for years, perfecting a few simple spells and healing techniques. And persuasive power is only ever possible if the thing the Scholar is trying to suggest to a person is something they actually want to do, or that makes sense to them.'

Sar whistled. 'Still, that's pretty powerful stuff. It's a good thing we don't know any Scholars.'

Arisa gulped.

Sar didn't appear to have noticed her reaction. He looked back at the engraving on the wall. '*Harmony when everything is as one.* I like it.' He smiled broadly, his dimples taking over the space between his chiselled jawline and cheekbones. 'I wish my Kengian was as good as yours. I'm trying to learn the language myself.'

She raised a quizzical brow.

'I've been given some land by the Duke and I'm to learn from his son, Willem, about how to manage their lands at Talbot. Many of their farmers are Kengian, and I'm determined to be able to communicate with them in their language.'

Arisa was taken aback. 'But I thought you all hated Kengians.'

Sar cocked his head to the side. 'Not everyone.'

'What does the Duke think of this?'

'The Duke is the one who urged me to understand Kengian culture better. He has shown me how important it is to treat every tenant and worker with respect. And while he doesn't openly encourage some of the Kengian customs, he doesn't punish them for their practices, either. Silver-eyes — the few that are left — can live without fear on his lands, because he knows they will never use magic against him.'

'I find that hard to believe.'

'Well, I know it to be true.' Sar had lost his dimpled grin. 'After all, I lived at Talbot for nearly eight years, serving with the Prince as the Duke's squire.'

Arisa dropped her gaze, ashamed. 'I'm sorry, Sar. I believe you.' She was truly sorry to have offended someone who'd only shown her kindness.

Sar softened his tone again. 'Arisa, not everyone here at court is as bad as you think. In fact, many of us, including the Duke, wish to do good in Lamore, and yearn for peace.'

She raised an eyebrow. 'Peace? Isn't Lakeford one of the finest warriors of all time, and the King's great warmaker?'

'The Duke is the best warrior I've seen. I believe there was only one greater than him…' His voice trailed off for a moment. 'He is fiercely loyal to the crown, and as a soldier he will always recommend the best military action to protect the realm. But he doesn't advocate war for the sake of it. I know him to be a good man, and benevolent to those who work for him and the realm.'

Arisa believed what Sar was saying – or at least, that *he* believed it. But she found it hard to reconcile the fact that the King's man of war was also good and kind.

'I wish to become as great a man as the Duke,' Sar went on. 'That's why I'm trying my best to learn the Kengian ways and language, though I don't think I'm making much headway.'

'I don't know you very well, Sar, but something tells me you will be every bit as great as you hope.'

Sar gave her another face-splitting smile. How could she ever make good on her promise to make her enemies pay, when there was one among them so brilliantly capable of disarming her? Arisa was relieved that he didn't seem to notice the effect he had on bringing down her defences. He continued chatting away in his easy tone as he led her down a narrow corridor.

'I don't know what it is about you. Maybe it's because you seem so different from the other girls here at court, but I can tell we're going to be good friends.' He stopped abruptly and turned to her. 'That is, of course, if you want to be friends.'

'I could do with a friend.' She said it before thinking, but it was true: she wanted to be Sar's friend. 'I wasn't so sure when I first met you, though. I haven't had the best of experiences with the Royal Guards.'

Sar cocked his head in question, and she told him what had happened with Hyando. He reached out and put his great mitt of a hand on her shoulder. 'Unfortunately, those guards are not under my authority, so I can't get them the punishment they deserve. But I will speak to Lakeford and have them sent back to Calliope. And I will personally make sure they never set foot in the city again.'

'Thank you.' A lump had formed in Arisa's throat. She had never expected such kindness.

'Good. Come on, not much further.'

They continued, finally coming to a stop outside a set of heavy doors with two guards on either side.

'The Queen's presence chamber,' Sar announced.

The guards moved aside wordlessly and opened the doors to reveal a modestly decorated room, with a dais and throne set before the windows. The room was alive with music and chatter. There were women of all ages, all exquisitely dressed and dripping in jewels, as well as impressively dressed young noblemen. A young lady was in one corner of the room playing a harp, but at their arrival she stopped; her fingers froze above the strings as she stared at Arisa, her mouth agape.

Every eye in the room was on Arisa now, looking her up and down and taking in her battered boots and boy's tunic. She realised with a start how odd she must appear to them. She removed her cap and curtsied awkwardly to no one in particular.

The room erupted in laughter.

Stricken with anger, she shoved her cap back on her head and clenched her fists. Sar had been wrong. Everyone at the castle was the same. They were all judgemental fools. Arisa wanted to slap the smiles from their faces. She probably would have, had Sar not held out his arm in front of her and shot the courtiers a thunderous look.

It had an immediate effect. The laughter stopped. The harp player took up her music again, and everyone went back to their business, however unimportant it appeared to be. Other than a few sideways glances, no one showed Arisa any more interest.

'Come with me.' Sar gestured toward a door, and she followed him into another room with a long table and a dozen or so chairs at its centre. 'The Queen's privy chamber.'

There was a closed door off to one side and another pair of doors at the end of the room. A petite lady, her dark-brown hair flecked with grey, was asleep in a chair by the doors, a book abandoned in her lap. Arisa recognised her as Gwyn, the woman from the Prince's rooms. She hadn't left the Queen's side during the whole ordeal.

Sar bent down and picked up her book; Arisa recognised it as one Erun owned – a collection of ancient Kyprian tales. He gently roused Gwyn from her sleep.

'Sar,' came her sleepy voice as she opened her eyes.

'Lady Mother. I have brought you a visitor.'

Still half-asleep, the woman – Sar's mother – looked around confusedly, until her eyes locked on Arisa. Suddenly alert, she gave Arisa a warm smile.

'This is Arisa, the healer Erun's assistant. Arisa, this is my mother, Lady Gwyn.'

'It's a pleasure to meet you formally. You can call me Gwyn,' the woman said, taking Arisa's hands in her own and staring at her face intently. She tilted her head slightly, as if unsure of what she saw.

'Please forgive me, Mother, but I must leave,' Sar said.

Gwyn released Arisa's hands and directed her attention back to her son. 'What? You're not going to stay here and amuse an old lady?' she teased.

'If only you could point me in the direction of an old lady.' Sar made as if he were actually looking for one in the room.

'What did I do to deserve such a mischievous boy?' his mother cried mock-dramatically.

'Just lucky, I guess.'

Gwyn slapped him playfully on the arm. 'Begone with you.'

'Here.' Sar placed the book in his mother's hands. Gwyn clasped it tightly before putting it away in a pocket in her over-dress. 'Til next time, ladies.'

He bowed and left the room.

'I imagine everything must seem very strange to you here,' Gwyn said, once Sar was gone.

'You could say that.'

'Yes. I suppose that is a bit of an understatement. Are you tired?'

Until now, Arisa hadn't had a spare moment to consider this question, but on reflection she could admit she needed to sleep.

'Let me show you to your room. You will be staying in my suite, which you access via this privy chamber. The Queen's bedchambers are there.' Gwyn indicated the doors behind her. 'She is currently resting. Follow me.'

Gwyn led her through a smaller door to a neat chamber with two more doorways leading off it.

'These are my rooms. The other ladies-in-waiting share rooms down the hall from the presence chamber or reside in their family apartments. It's quite a full house at the moment, with most of the nobles here for a meeting of the King's Council. My room is here.' Gwyn indicated to the left. 'And this is yours.' She opened the door to the right.

The first thing that struck Arisa was the scent of fresh rushes and herbs laid on the floor, followed by the sight of a canopy bed that took up most of the room. Gwyn walked over to a tall arched window and pulled aside the drapes to reveal a garden view below and the blue-grey sea in the distance. There was a floral tapestry on one of the walls, a cupboard with a washbasin, and a small table and chair. Arisa bit her tongue, not wishing to admit she was in danger of being dazzled by her surroundings again.

'I hope it's suitable.'

Arisa nodded wordlessly.

'I took the liberty of having some of my older gowns brought here.' Gwyn gestured toward the bed. 'I hope I haven't overstepped.'

Arisa moved to the bed and ran her fingers indulgently over the gowns. She stroked the different fabrics, captivated by the unfamiliar feel of velvet, silk and satin. There were three gowns: one of scarlet, one of sapphire blue and one of gold, all richly embroidered and embellished with lace or pearls. There were also matching slippers and a gold cloak trimmed with fur. Everything was so different from the dull beige, orange and brown cloth she was accustomed to.

Arisa glanced down at her boots and tunic. She had never desired a gown before. She had always thought they were frivolous and hideously uncomfortable, but she had never been given the opportunity to wear something like this.

'Thank you,' she said begrudgingly, not wanting to let on her pleasure.

Gwyn's face fell a little, but she smiled kindly at Arisa. 'You must be exhausted. I will leave you to rest. Let me know if there is anything at all you require.' She opened her mouth as if to ask something, before changing her mind and leaving.

Arisa walked over to the looking glass above the basin and recoiled at her own reflection. She looked like a grubby street urchin. Dipping a cloth in the basin of water, she cleaned her face as best she could.

She wondered if she would ever fit in at this strange place, but immediately admonished herself for wanting to. She must do her best to get through this experience until they could make their escape. After that, they would both be free and on their way to Kengia. And while Arisa was stuck here, she must look for opportunities to cut down her enemies and get some of the justice she thirsted for…

But for the first time, she found herself questioning whether that was what she really wanted.

She shook her head, too tired to make sense of it all. She took her eye drops out of her pocket and hid them under a pillow on the chair before crawling gratefully into the oversized bed.

'Don't trust them. They're your enemy,' was the last thing Arisa said to herself before drifting off to sleep.

Arisa woke with a start. She sat up, trying to recall where she was. A swift glance around at the room and the gowns still lying on her bed reminded her she was at Lamore Castle. Beams of soft golden light streamed through the window. The drapes were still wide open, as they had been when she'd drifted off. Her stomach growled with hunger. How long had she been asleep? Someone was knocking at the door. The sound must have woken her.

The knock came again, more loudly.

Arisa scrambled out of bed to get her silk bag from under the chair cushion. She opened it and the vial it contained, and applied the drops quickly. She took a deep breath and readied herself.

'Come in.'

A harried-looking maid appeared in the open doorway and dropped to a curtsey. 'I'm sorry to disturb, milady, but you are required in the Prince's rooms.'

'Me? Are you sure?'

'I understand the healer was sent for, but the Chancellor refuses to let him leave his rooms.'

It was as Arisa had feared. Erun was being kept a prisoner. She would have to speak to Gwyn about seeing him.

'It was suggested you could assist,' the maid went on.

'I am sure the Royal Physicians can handle whatever it is.'

The maid wrung her hands. 'I'm afraid the Prince is quite insistent.'

'The Prince himself? He is fully awake and speaking?'

'That is my understanding, milady.'

'Very well. I'll just get dressed.' A quick glance at Gwyn's gowns and all of the associated contraptions a lady must wear confirmed that the task would take much longer than expected.

'I'm sorry, milady, but there is a guard waiting outside to take you straight away.'

Arisa shrugged. Her usual boys' attire and hastily tied-back hair would have to be good enough for the Prince.

ARISA FOUND Prince Takai sitting up in bed, deep in conversation with the Duke. His face was pale, but his eyes were clear and alert. She waited patiently in the corner of the room while they finished their discussion in hushed tones. Arisa didn't catch much, other than the mention of a strategy to deal with the Northemers and something about Horace's plans needing to be abandoned.

The Duke left and the guard announced her arrival. 'The healer's assistant.'

'Assistant!' the Prince spat. 'I asked for the healer who did this to me, not some useless boy.'

Arisa bristled at his reference to Erun's work – as if her guardian were responsible for the Prince's injury, when he had actually saved his life. She wasn't too happy about being called a *useless boy*, either.

She gritted her teeth. 'How may I assist you?' she asked, deliberately omitting any honorifics.

The Prince's eyes narrowed at the sound of her voice. 'You're not a boy.'

'I am not,' she said bluntly, 'but I am able to assist you.'

'I doubt that. I need a real physician's assistant.'

How dare he? Arisa clenched her fists at her side. 'I assure you that I can. I have been assisting my guardian for as long as I can remember, and I am studying to attend the College of Surgeons.'

The Prince made a scoffing sound. 'The college isn't open to girls.'

'Do you want my help or not?'

He shrugged. 'Yes. This blasted bandage on my arm stinks like a dead animal that's festered in the moat for a month.'

Arisa examined the dressing. There was a spot of blood on the top, but otherwise it looked clean. She carefully unravelled the bandage to reveal the wound.

The Prince scrunched up his nose. 'What is that?'

'It is a poultice, made from…herbs and the like.' Arisa had been going to specify *Kengian* herbs, but decided against it, given the audience. 'Your wound was deeper than expected and this poultice stopped the bleeding.'

'I don't care what it is. Get it off me.'

Arisa didn't care that the Prince had nearly died – it was no excuse for his rudeness. But she had promised Erun she would keep her head down.

'I can clean it off, since it has done its job, and I will apply a new dressing.'

He nodded. Arisa went to the other side of the Prince's bedchambers, where the Royal Physicians kept their supplies. She barely avoided being whacked by the door flying open at the hands of the King.

King Delrik waltzed into the room, dressed in full hunting gear, his face flushed. Arisa couldn't understand what kind of father would go hunting right after their only child had nearly died. She'd heard about the King and his wild mood swings, but this was something else.

'Ah, my son! You look quite fine.'

'I'm on the mend, Father, but have been ordered to stay put.'

'Rightly so.'

'But not you – you've been hunting?'

'Of sorts. As you may know, the Council won't let me visit any of my hunting grounds in the counties. Scared of that rebel, Sergei, and his rabble. Surely it can't be all that dangerous.'

'Lakeford is afraid it is. There have been riots in several villages over the latest tax increases, even though they're needed to fund the rebuilding of our forces.'

'Something must be done to get the people to bend to our rule and order. I will put Horace on the case.'

Arisa tightened her grip on the pair of scissors she was using to cut up a new bandage. For a moment, the darkness inside her spoke to her, and she pictured stabbing the King, all of their troubles washing away in a pool of his blood.

She shook her head and pushed the darkness to the back of her mind.

'Father, I'm not sure Horace—'

'Do not worry, son. Horace will do whatever I ask of him. He will help ensure the progress can still go ahead, despite these latest threats. But your mother must be by my side for it. She must.'

'I know not what my mother's plans are.' Arisa detected a tinge of sadness in the Prince's voice. 'But I'm sure if you speak to her and tell her how important it is to you—'

'Indeed!' The King patted his son on the shoulder, much too hard for someone in the Prince's condition. 'In the meantime, I must content myself with hunting in the castle grounds.'

'Much sport to be had?' Takai appeared to be feigning interest.

'Not usually. A few pheasants and the occasional fox, but

today I had my sights set on the Kengian wolf. Unfortunately I didn't succeed.'

A Kengian wolf in Lamore? It was unheard of and the King wanted to kill it. Arisa's breath quickened in anger.

'A Kengian snow wolf in these parts is not a good sign, especially since it appeared on the night of the blood moon,' the Prince mused. 'I fear it has something to do with Kengian magic. The creature must be dealt with.'

'Never fear. I won't rest until that wolf's snowy pelt dons my shoulders.'

Arisa couldn't wait to be gone from the Prince's rooms. He and his ridiculous father were nothing but close-minded fools. The sooner she and Erun could formulate an escape from this place, the better – but not before she had a chance to make the Lamorian regime hurt somehow.

LATER, she arrived back in her room to find Gwyn waiting for her with a tray of food.

'Lady Gwyn.'

'Good morning, Arisa.'

'Erun,' she said immediately. 'I need to see Erun. Can you please take me to my guardian?'

'He's alright. I've received word from Sar that he is fine and already working for the Chancellor. His rooms are in the north-west tower.'

Arisa collected her bearings. Erun's rooms were at the exact opposite end of the castle from where she was. 'I must see him.'

'Don't worry. You'll see him today. I'll take you there myself.'

'I need to go now.'

'You will see him soon. Unfortunately the Chancellor has placed limits on when you visit.' Gwyn looked at her kindly. 'You care for Erun very much, don't you?'

'Very much. He's all I have. Lady Gwyn—'

'Gwyn,' she corrected.

'Gwyn. What do you think will happen to Erun and me?'

She paused and took a deep breath. 'While Erun is in the Chancellor's service, you are both safe – that I can promise you. The Chancellor never discards anything or anyone while they are useful.'

'But what happens when something no longer has a use?'

Gwyn bit her lip. 'I'm sure it won't come to that. You both have all of the protection the Queen and I can give you.'

Arisa raised a sceptical brow.

'I promise,' Gwyn insisted. 'I won't let anything happen to either of you.'

Arisa nodded, though she wasn't entirely comforted by Gwyn's assurances, or her ability to deliver on such promises.

'Arisa, I was wondering if you could tell me a little about yourself.'

'What's there to say?'

'Well, how did you come to be Erun's ward?'

Arisa shrugged. 'I've been with Erun since I was a baby. My mother was a seamstress, not that I remember her. She died of childbed fever. Erun had tried to save her, but he couldn't.' She dropped her gaze. She hated that this was the only thing she knew about her mother.

'And your father?'

'He died in an accident shortly after my birth.' Arisa recited this part by rote. She couldn't share her real parentage with someone at the Lamorian court, or the fact that her father had died in the Kengian massacre. She couldn't tell anyone. 'Erun promised to take care of me after I lost them both.'

Gwyn nodded, as if she had expected such a tale. 'You must miss them.'

'I'm not sure if *miss* is the right word, because I never knew them. But I do think about them a lot.' She held up her silver medallion. 'I have this to remind me of them, at least.'

Gwyn reached out to try to take a closer look, but Arisa pulled the necklace back abruptly and tucked it under her tunic.

Gwyn seemed only momentarily taken aback. She changed the subject. 'So Erun has tutored you in medicine and science?'

'I'm his apprentice. I hope to be a great healer like him one day.'

'That is a worthy aspiration to have.'

There was something about the kindness in Gwyn's eyes that urged Arisa to share more with her. It was the same effect Sar had on her. Before she knew it she was rambling. 'Actually, I had hoped to train at the College of Surgeons.' She waited for the laughter, but it didn't come.

'You *had* hoped?'

Arisa hesitated. She wasn't about to tell Gwyn that she and Erun were actually planning on leaving Lamore. Instead she chose a convenient half-truth. 'I guess everyone thinks it's silly for a girl, and a lowborn one at that, to think she could become a trained surgeon.'

'I don't think it's silly at all,' Gwyn asserted. 'From the little I have seen of you in action, I'm certain you could do it.'

Arisa gave a small shrug and looked away, embarrassed. 'I would like to continue my studies while I'm here, but I would have to get permission for the Schoolmaster to visit with me.'

Gwyn's face brightened. 'Leave it with me. I will make the arrangements.'

Another knock came at the door, and at Gwyn's beckoning a maid entered, carrying a pile of garments. She curtsied and placed the garments on the chair, and before Arisa knew what was happening the girl had started tugging at her tunic. She winced as it caught against her still-tender ribs. 'What are you doing?' she squealed, as the maid pulled the tunic over her head.

'Helping you dress, milady.'

The maid persisted, but Arisa batted her hands away. 'Thank you, but I will dress myself.'

Undeterred, the maid bent down to remove Arisa's stockings.

'I said stop,' Arisa insisted. 'I have dressed myself without any assistance for as long as I can remember. I can assure you, I don't need your help.'

'But it is my duty to serve you, milady.'

Arisa swatted at her hands again. 'Stop it, I tell you! And don't call me *lady*.'

The maid gave Gwyn a pained look.

'It's fine,' Gwyn assured her. 'Perhaps you can prepare Arisa's clothes for her instead.'

The maid nodded and began laying out the garments onto the bed. Arisa picked up a fur rug and wrapped it self-consciously around herself as she peered curiously at each item. There were drawers and a chemise; a hoop skirt, underskirt and overskirt; a bodice, sleeves and stockings – actual silk stockings, not the coarse woollen ones she was used to. She realised she was well out of her depth with the clothes, but when the girl made to approach her again, Arisa shook her head violently.

Gwyn dismissed the maid with a smile and helped Arisa into each item, fastening all of the hooks and ribbons. It was a painstakingly slow process. Arisa managed a small 'thank you' when it was done. Gwyn bent down and eased each of her feet into the delicate-looking slippers, before taking a step back to admire her work.

She gasped. 'Arisa, you look beautiful!'

Arisa moved toward the looking glass, unable to believe what she saw.

Beautiful was not a word she would ever have used to describe herself, but today that was exactly how she felt. Yes, her nose was a little pointy, and sprinkled with freckles she hated; her face was also rounder than she would have liked, but she looked unusually becoming. The velvet-and-worsted-wool gown was a golden-amber colour that set off her eyes and olive complexion perfectly. The bodice was intricately embroidered with white-and-gold thread, and with its drawn-in shape, her boyish frame gained an hourglass appearance.

Gwyn reached for a brush and began untangling Arisa's

mousy brown mane. She brushed until Arisa's hair gleamed and fell in long waves around her face. Finally, she put her hand to Arisa's chin, scrutinising her with a sharp eye. Screwing up her mouth in concentration, she removed a golden silk scarf from her own neck and gently draped it over Arisa's shoulders. It matched the colour of her dress exactly.

'Perfect.' Gwyn beamed. 'Now, you should eat. I have already broken my fast.'

Arisa looked hungrily at the tray of food Gwyn had set down earlier, and didn't need to be told twice. She bit into a crusty piece of bread, washing it down with watered-down wine. Next she picked up a shiny-looking apple and rapidly chewed her way to the core. Finally, she popped a large piece of soft cheese into her mouth, letting out a sigh as she savoured the creamy texture.

Gwyn laughed. 'I'm glad to see you're enjoying it.'

Arisa nodded, stuffing her mouth with another chunk of cheese.

'Come now. We must be on our way,' Gwyn said. 'It's time to meet the Queen.'

THEY FOUND Queen Sofia sitting alone in her presence chamber, gazing out the window. She turned at their approach. Arisa felt suddenly dowdy. She had only seen the Queen once, in the Prince's rooms, and she hadn't been close enough then to appreciate the woman's beauty. Her dark eyes sat above high cheekbones. Her neck was long and slender. She looked as poised and as graceful as Arisa imagined a Queen should be. It was no wonder she, unlike her husband, was so beloved by the Lamorians.

'Your Majesty,' Gwyn said. 'May I introduce Arisa?'

Arisa curtsied clumsily.

Sofia's eyes brightened and she gave a warm smile. 'Of course. Arisa, you were with Erun when he attended my son.'

'Yes, Your Majesty. I'm his ward.'

'Which makes you a great friend of mine and my family's. You're very welcome here.'

'The honour is all mine.' Arisa was surprised to find that she genuinely meant it. For some inexplicable reason, she wanted to please the Queen. What was going on? She'd come to the castle expecting to hate everyone who crossed her path, but so far she had been met with friendship and kindness, at least from a few.

'I suppose you're eager to see your guardian,' the Queen said.

She nodded earnestly. 'I am.'

'Gwyn, you must take Arisa to see him this morning.'

'I shall, Your Majesty.'

'Tut-tut, Gwyn,' the Queen admonished her with a smile. 'There's no need for such formalities when it's just us in the room.'

Arisa was just starting to believe that her imprisonment at the castle could be bearable when the chamber doors flew open to admit a gaggle of visitors. She immediately recognised some of the group, remembering them from the Queen's rooms when she had first arrived. Yesterday they had been intimidating enough, but today had a different feeling all together.

At the head of the group was a dark-haired beauty with catlike eyes. She gave a haughty curtsey, barely dipping her head to the Queen. Then she took a moment to look Arisa up and down before moving on to take a seat at a card table. An older lady who bore a resemblance to the cat-eyed girl followed next.

'The one with the dark hair is Theodora, the Chancellor's daughter,' Gwyn murmured in her ear. Arisa realised the young woman must be Guthrie's sister — she should have guessed from her arrogant manner. 'Behind her is Theodora's mother, the Countess. By rank, the Countess should lead the ladies in. However, it seems that even she defers to Theodora.'

'And the other girl?' The harp player Arisa had seen the previous day was now curtseying to Sofia.

'Lady Selina. She's Theodora's companion. A silly but benign enough girl.'

The remainder of the ladies took turns addressing the Queen before taking their places around the room. Each of them chose a particular occupation – music, cards or sewing – leaving Arisa to ponder what she was to do.

'I suppose you sing and dance, like any young lady of your age?' the Queen asked her.

Arisa's face dropped. 'I have had little opportunity to learn either.'

'Of course. We're not much for singing or dancing ourselves,' Gwyn offered. 'Perhaps you sew?'

'Yes, I can sew.' She was relieved there was something she could do.

'Then you will be quite at home here,' Gwyn replied with enthusiasm. 'We have embroidered many of the tapestries you will see on the walls around the castle.'

Arisa dropped her head. 'I'm afraid I misunderstood your meaning. I can't do fine needlework. My experience of sewing is limited to mending shirts and tunics.'

Gwyn's face pinched at her misstep.

'Your skills won't go to waste, Arisa,' the Queen declared. 'Actually, I much prefer sewing something that is useful rather than just decorative. In fact, Gwyn and I spend a lot of time making clothing for the poor, and we could use another pair of hands.'

Arisa smiled brightly. 'Thank you, Your Majesty. I would be grateful to have something meaningful to do.'

'Meaningful!' Theodora had appeared beside her. 'You find making boring shirts meaningful? What a jest you make.'

'It's not a jest,' Arisa responded angrily. 'I much prefer to spend my time on useful occupations.'

'Pray tell me what you spend your time doing.'

'I have my studies, and assist my guardian in his work.'

Theodora's eyes widened. 'Your studies?'

'Of course. How else would I learn and make myself useful to others?'

'From my experience, being learned isn't an attractive attribute in a woman.' Theodora looked pointedly at Gwyn. 'Unless, of course, that woman prefers a life of spinsterhood.'

Arisa hadn't expected to be fond of Theodora, given her family members, but she hadn't anticipated that the girl would be completely insufferable. She couldn't believe how quick Theodora was to insult her – and Gwyn, for that matter. A part of her, though, was curious why Sar's mother was unmarried. But in any case, she wasn't going to sit by and play the polite courtier, pandering to the likes of Theodora.

It was time for her to draw on her darkness.

'What man worth having *wouldn't* want a learned wife?' she retorted. 'Someone who has her own opinions and can challenge a man's thinking?'

Theodora snorted derisively. 'What a man indeed! In our world, a gentleman desires a wife who is accomplished at dancing, music and singing, not one who is bent on lecturing him.'

'Well, I suppose I will not find a husband in your world.'

'Never mind. Even an old maid can somehow find a place here at court.' Theodora stared at Gwyn again, who returned her gaze with narrowed eyes.

'That is quite enough, Theodora!'

No one had noticed Sar's arrival, though from what he said next it was evident he had heard much of the exchange.

'What you forget is that a man also values humility and compassion in his wife.'

Theodora tossed her hair. 'I'm sure I don't need your advice on getting a husband. I'm quite well equipped to do it myself.'

'And that is exactly what I'm afraid of,' Sar grumbled.

Theodora shot him a dark look before sauntering back to her card table.

Sar shook his head to himself as Gwyn reached out and

touched his arm. 'Thank you for your support, but I can handle myself.'

'I know. But she makes me so mad. I hate to think what will happen if Takai succumbs to her *accomplishments*, as she puts it.'

So Theodora had her sights set on the Prince…

'As we all do,' offered the Queen.

'Your Majesty.' Sar bowed. 'I have it that the King is on his way to visit with you and your ladies.'

A shadow passed over the Queen's face, but all she said was, 'I am at His Majesty's service.'

'Your Majesty, I also have an update on the Prince's health.'

The Queen's eyes widened. 'What has happened? I only visited him last night and Lore assured me he was fine.'

Sar waved his hands frantically. 'No, no, he is fine. I have come only to report that he is truly on the mend. He has recovered enough to challenge me to another swordfight.'

The Queen exhaled. 'Thank you, Sar. You're a good friend to my son, and to our kingdom. I only wish he looked more to you than he does to others.'

Sar shuffled his feet awkwardly. 'I'm sure Takai will be a great king one day, Your Majesty. He is still young and, like all men of our age, still has much to learn.'

Arisa couldn't help but admire Sar's diplomatic response.

'Yes, but who is he to learn from? He stopped listening to his mother years ago,' the Queen lamented.

'Don't give up on him, Your Majesty. He needs your guidance now more than ever.' Sar looked meaningfully at Theodora.

The Queen nodded unconvincingly. 'Arisa, please come and sit with me, and prove that not every young girl at court is silly or scheming.' She seemed eager for conversation. 'I hear you hope to be a surgeon one day.'

'Yes, Your Majesty. I have trained as a healer since I was very young, and once I finish school, I hope to study at the College of Surgeons.'

'Trained surgeons usually only attend to nobles, do they not?'

'That is how it currently stands. The poorer folk in Obira, for example, must resort to barber surgeons. If the surgery itself doesn't kill them, infection probably will.'

'What do you propose?'

'I wish to tend to the people who need the help most.' Arisa hesitated for a moment, calculating how much of her greater ambitions she wanted to share. 'In fact, I wish to see a hospital built for the poor, where everyone can get the best treatment, regardless of birth or income.'

'It gladdens me to hear you speak so. I wish with all my heart that you succeed. I too had that kind of passion once.' A nostalgic smile spread across the Queen's face.

Although she hated everything about the Lamorian court, Arisa could appreciate how wonderful the Queen was. 'I know you did, Your Majesty. I understand it was you, as a young bride, who opened the school in Obira. That it was entirely your own idea.'

'Not entirely,' she said. 'You may not believe it, but the King was as passionate about it as I was. We both envisioned a school for everyone to attend, not only children of the rich or lesser nobles. But it wasn't quite as I wished in the end.'

'Well, not everyone who goes there is rich or a noble. I'm a student there.'

The Queen smiled wistfully. 'If only there were a thousand more of you.'

Arisa wanted to tell the Queen it wasn't too late. That she could still make a difference. That as Queen, and mother of the future King, she was in a unique position of power. But she feared her words would go unheeded. She saw that Queen Sofia had long since given up.

As if sensing the Queen's desolation, the King chose that moment to arrive.

'His Majesty, King Delrik, and Chancellor Horace,' a guard announced.

Arisa stood alert. Every lady in the room curtsied low to the ground, their eyes downcast. She did her best to mimic them, while allowing herself a brief peek at the King as he walked toward the Queen. He had changed out of his hunting attire, now dressed in puffed-up robes trimmed with fur and jewels, and wearing his crown. Horace was one step behind. She bristled at their confident approach, but as he neared his wife, the King appeared more uncertain. The Queen hadn't bothered to stand or acknowledge her husband in any way.

The King bent over to plant a hesitant kiss on her cheek. 'My dear wife,' he murmured, to no response. He persevered, not seeming to register, or care about, Arisa's presence. 'How are you this fine day?'

'As well as can be expected,' she replied flatly.

'You would be glad to hear the Prince is well.'

'Yes, I have heard.'

The King rubbed his hands together, looking unsure how to proceed. He was standing so close to Arisa that she thought she could see his carotid artery pulsating in his neck.

She clenched her fist, a plan beginning to take shape in her mind.

'Is there something else?' the Queen asked.

The King's cheeks flushed. 'There is another matter, *my dear wife*.' He stressed the last words. 'I have come to speak to you about the great celebrations. The Chancellor tells me you aren't meaning to attend the tournament or join me on the progress.'

'I have no interest in feigning any support for your reign or our sham of a marriage.'

The King's colour deepened. Those across the room appeared to be straining their ears to hear the exchange between husband and wife.

'So you intend on snubbing your own son's eighteenth birthday celebrations?'

The Queen merely stared back at him.

King Delrik's jaw clenched. Obviously he wasn't accustomed to such rudeness.

'You, *wife*,' he hissed, 'will preside over the celebrations. It is my command.'

The Queen appeared thoughtful for a moment. 'Well, if you were to grant me one request…'

'Yes?'

'I hear from my brother that Ivane is expecting an invasion from the Northemers. King Laskar believes Malu will mobilise his forces as soon as the warmer months set in.'

'That is a fair assumption.'

'I ask that you offer your support. That as soon as the navy and army are rebuilt, you help defend my homeland.'

Delrik's face contorted with anger. 'Nothing in this world could possibly induce me to help that man. He who claims to rule lands that are my ancestral rights. He whose father came to the aid of Ette and tried to take that from me as well. He who stands in the way of my birthright and has always sought to ruin my legacy.'

The Queen stood up. She was as tall as her husband. 'Ivane is my brother's birthright. And after Laskar and his family, it is *my* birthright. It is my *son's* birthright. It is not yours. It never belonged to Lamore and it never will.'

'That is where you're wrong, *wife*,' the King snarled. 'Ivane will be mine. That I promise you.'

'Surely you don't seek to take up arms against my homeland again?'

He stepped closer to the Queen so he was only inches from her face. 'I have big plans for Ivane and Ette, and even Kengia.'

Arisa's stomach dropped. Kengia was to be targeted?

'And how do you propose to succeed where you have previously failed?' the Queen sniped.

'That is a matter for me, your King – but what I will tell you is that I will *never* come to your brother's assistance.'

'You don't stand a chance against him. You have no forces to speak of, and you're dreadfully outmatched and outnumbered by the Northemers, Ivane and Kengia.'

'Don't worry your pretty little head about matters you could never understand. I have something that will send Malu running back to his land of ice. And it is only the beginning.'

Arisa shuddered. What could the King be speaking of with such confidence? What was capable of defeating all of his enemies?

The Queen, though, looked far from scared. She stood with her shoulders back, chin raised and gaze steady. She looked formidable. 'You speak of matters you say I don't understand, but there are plenty of things I comprehend more than you. Such as how we will never be husband and wife again.'

'You are my Queen!' the King protested.

'In name only. Your refusal to help my family proves I am nothing to you. If you won't go to Ivane's aid, then I call on your decency to let me return to my homeland, and do what I can to protect it.'

'What if I were to grant your first wish and send my army to the defence of your brother?' He dropped his voice, so that only those closest to the Queen could hear. 'Could I assume you would return willingly to my arms again? That we will be united once more?'

'How can I ever forgive you for what you have done to me and to Ivane? The only thing you can do for me is let me go.'

The King's nostrils flared and he raised his voice. 'You mean to say you wish to leave your son to join a land of usurpers!'

'The son you prevented me from seeing all of these years,' she shot back, as loudly as her husband.

The King threw his arms up in despair.

Horace approached him and placed a hand on his shoulder. 'Your Majesty, perhaps you should consider the Queen's request.'

'What?'

'What I mean, sire, is that there may be a way you could approve the Queen's request to be freed. Perhaps if she agrees to give you her full support – say, until spring. To be by your side at the tournament and progress, and until certain matters are resolved…'

The mention of spring caught in Arisa's mind. Spring was when Erun must deliver on his promise to Horace – the demands for firesky. Was it just a coincidence? She feared it wasn't.

'After that,' the Chancellor continued, 'she could be allowed to return to Ivane.'

The King stroked his chin thoughtfully. 'Until spring,' he said to himself.

But the Queen was adamant. 'I am no hypocrite. I will not support you.'

The King's hateful eyes gleamed. 'Oh, but I think you will. For if you don't, then I'm afraid there will be plenty of people you care about' – he looked pointedly at Gwyn, and turned to give Arisa an appraising look that made her shiver – 'who may suffer for your disobedience.'

'You wouldn't dare!'

'Just try me, *wife*.'

The Queen sat down heavily in her chair and fell silent. Finally, she spoke in a quiet voice.

'I will do what you ask.'

The King smiled broadly. 'Excellent. I wish you a good day.' He smirked as he and Horace turned and strode from the room.

Queen Sofia was frozen in her chair. Every courtier's eye was on her. Gwyn turned to the room.

'The Queen is unwell. You may leave us.'

The assembled group gave the impression that they were reluctant to go, but with a sharp clap of Gwyn's hands they filed out of the room. Arisa made to leave, too, but Gwyn held her back. Theodora shot a triumphant look at the Queen as Sar escorted her and the last of the courtiers out. He closed the door behind them.

'What have I done?' the Queen lamented.

'You can do it, Sofia. You can pretend to be reunited with the King. It won't be too difficult.'

She looked up at Gwyn with tears in her eyes. 'No. I mean agreeing to go back to Ivane without Takai. But the King has given me little choice. My homeland needs me, and it's more than I can do for Takai.'

'Don't punish yourself. As you said, it is the King who has kept you from your son for so long. It was he who never let you visit him at Talbot.'

'I only wish I could have been there to guide him. Help him become the great leader he can be, and see that his father's way isn't the right way. Then there may be some hope for this kingdom.'

Arisa wasn't convinced. She of all people knew there was little hope for Lamore. And if Prince Takai was anything like his heartless father – and she suspected from her short visit with him that he was – the country was doomed.

'There is hope for Takai,' Gwyn offered. 'As Sar said, it's not too late for him.'

'You may be right, but it is not I who can help him now. He has to find his true heart, and he certainly won't look to me for guidance.'

'But what if Takai can't change?' Arisa asked tentatively.

The Queen looked back out the window. 'Then Ivane, Ette, Lamore and Kengia are all lost.'

Sofia stood up and headed toward her bedchambers. Gwyn made to follow her, but the Queen waved her away.

'Please excuse me. I would like to be alone.'

Gwyn watched after her for a moment, before turning to Arisa with a strained smile. 'There's not much I can do to help the Queen, but at least I can help you.'

'Sorry?'

'I promised to take you to Erun. Come on.' She beckoned to Arisa with a thin smile, already halfway toward the door.

Arisa pulled up the bottom of her skirts and raced after her. Maybe Erun would know what the King and Horace were planning for spring. She needed to know exactly what she would be up against when she put her new plan into action.

Her plan to kill the King.

18

Theodora flashed a bright smile at her father as she followed him back to his study. She had been trying to get an audience with him ever since she'd overheard the conversation outside the Queen's bedchamber.

'Father, I have something to tell you.'

Horace picked up a quill and appeared to be pondering a message. He did not even look up at her. Theodora bristled, but pressed on. She would prove her worth to him.

'So you're *not* interested in a secret conversation I heard between Gwyn and the Queen.'

Horace put down his quill. 'You have my attention.'

Theodora gave a satisfied smile. 'Yesterday morning, I happened to overhear the two of them in the Queen's rooms. They were talking about the healer and his ward.'

'The healer?' Her father tilted his head. 'Go on.'

'They spoke as if they knew him. As if they had known him for a long time. They mentioned concerns for his safety and the ward's, as well as the need to protect some secrets.'

Horace sat back in his chair. 'How do you think Gwyn and the Queen know Erun? And why would they care about him and his ward so much?'

'I don't know…but I am sure I can find out.'

He stroked his chin pensively. 'Yes. You must befriend this ward. Get close to her. See what secrets you can discover about her and her guardian.'

She pouted. That wasn't what Theodora had been picturing when she'd offered to investigate further. 'Do I have to? She is dreadfully dull.'

Horace looked earnestly at his daughter. 'Theodora, it must be clear to you that you are my greatest hope for our family. While I would never admit it to your brother, it is you who has the nous and fortitude to rule this kingdom, not him.'

Theodora stood a little taller. 'Thank you.'

'You are unstoppable…Almost.'

She pursed her lips.

'You won't be completely unstoppable until you're prepared to do things you don't savour. You have to do things that are distasteful, but necessary. Getting close to the girl is one of these things. Become her confidante.'

He was right. It was a small price to pay for the power Theodora hoped to achieve. 'Yes, Father,' she said.

A commotion sounded outside the door, and a harried-looking guard entered the study.

'There is a…*gentleman*…demand— requesting admittance.'

The door flung wide open to reveal Goldman – the pirate Theodora had seen her father meet with at the Lion's Den. He wore an ill-fitting blue velvet jacket and breeches, and was dripping in gold chains and rings. A gaudy feather sat upright in his cap and his pointy beard had been groomed within an inch of its life. On top of that, he reeked of rum. He really was vile.

Goldman looked her up and down, and licked his lips. A shudder rippled through her body.

'Good day, my lady.' He bent down to kiss Theodora's hand.

'Good day,' she snipped, snatching her hand away.

'What are you—?' Horace hissed, before apparently remembering Theodora was still there.

He nodded to her. 'My daught— The lady was just leaving.'

Goldman gave a theatrical bow and tipped his cap at Theodora. 'My lady.' He shot Theodora one last hungry look as she left the room and the guard closed the door behind her.

Theodora was more than curious about why the pirate was there and what else he might have to say. She looked around the anteroom. There was only one guard nearby. She approached the man and gave him her most beguiling smile.

'Please, could you do me a favour? My father has asked for more wine to be delivered. For his guest. Would you mind?'

'S-sorry…my lady,' he stammered, 'but I can't leave my post. I'm sure one of the servants will be by soon.'

She dropped her bottom lip. 'I'm afraid my father cannot wait. Are you sure you can't help? There are two other guards right outside the main entry doors to these apartments.'

The guard bit his lip and, after a moment, nodded his agreement. 'I'll be back in a jiffy, my lady.'

As soon as he was out of sight, Theodora crept over to the study and pressed her ear to the door. She was in luck. Goldman had a naturally boisterous voice and her father had raised his.

'I already paid your ransom, and my son and Sir Marcus have been returned,' Horace barked. 'I can't see how we could possibly have anything further to discuss.'

'I have news I thought you may find of value. News of Malu.'

'Malu? The Northern leader? How can that be?'

'The Northerners sent a small scouting party up the coast of Ivane. Unfortunately, they came across a ship of…Well, let's just say a ship of my associates.'

'You mean they came across pirates.'

'*Associates.* Malu's ship was no match for my friends, and after a brief melee the Northerners surrendered.'

'I see.'

'It seems the leader among them was in fact a half-brother of Malu.'

'Where are these Northemers now?'

'They are my prisoners and are currently being kept on one of my ships, off Lamore's coast.'

'You must bring them to me. I must speak with them.'

'Then I'm afraid I'll have to disappoint you. Malu's brother is a valuable prisoner, and I expect to be paid a handsome sum for him.'

'You must let me speak to him first.'

Goldman tutted. 'If I were to let you speak directly to him, why would you need me, Chancellor? What would stop you from slitting my throat this instant, as you have desired to do from the moment we met?'

'You're a treacherous scoundrel,' Horace sneered. 'Why bother coming here and telling me any of this?'

'I thought that, in the process of handing over Malu's brother, I could take a message to the Northemers for you.'

There was a long pause. 'What message could I possibly have for them?'

'Chancellor, you're a smart man, as am I. And I'm certain you have no wish to tackle the Northemers head-on like the rest of the King's Council is rumoured to want.'

'Let's imagine for a moment that you know what the council and I think,' Horace ventured slowly. 'What strategy would you suggest?'

'An alliance, of course. Or at least making a show of an alliance with the Northemers.'

Theodora was a little taken aback by the pirate's comments. Was that what her father planned to do? Did he want to make an alliance with the famed invaders? It seemed preposterous.

'I doubt an alliance with us is an appealing option for the Northemers,' he said. 'We have nothing they need. They only need to bide their time, and wait through winter, and we will be at their mercy.'

'Which is why you will go to extreme lengths to find something to offer them…Or at least, that's what I would do.'

'Don't presume to understand what I would do.'

'So you don't have a message for Malu?'

'I will send one of my men with you to deliver a message.'

'No one, other than my own men, is allowed on my ships.'

Horace gave a great laugh. 'So you want me to give you a message…that you will undoubtedly read.'

'What? You don't trust the old captain with your plans?'

Horace sighed. 'I will send a message with you. What will it cost me?'

'Nothing, my lord, other than the honour of serving my beloved nation.'

Horace snorted.

'Of course, I wouldn't say no to a knighthood, or to governorship of Ette when you reclaim it.'

Horace laughed. Even Theodora had to admire the Goldman's unashamed confidence.

'Very well. When do you leave?'

'First light tomorrow.'

'I will send the message to you at the tavern tonight. And I never wish to see you here again.'

'As you wish.'

Theodora slipped away from the door and back out of her father's apartments. She was quite pleased with what she had learnt. She had no idea how she would use it to her benefit, but she did know that information was power…especially when it involved the fate of a nation.

19

———

*A*risa followed Gwyn from the Queen's apartments. She knew she should be concentrating on her bearings and remembering the route to Erun's rooms, but her focus was on the plan formulating in her mind. She'd wanted to find a way to undermine the Lamorian regime, but she'd never considered murder – that was, until she'd met the Queen and seen the extent of her husband's cruelty.

Initially her focus had been on the Chancellor. He was the one who'd refused to help Rea; he was the one who'd brought her and Erun here, and he was undoubtedly to blame for countless wrongs in the kingdom. But after the scene in the Queen's rooms, she had realised the King was just as ruthless, perhaps more so.

Being rid of him made sense. With the King dead, the Queen could rule the kingdom until Takai came of age. Sofia was formidable enough to sideline Horace, and was beloved by all of Lamore. Killing the King would deliver the justice Arisa hungered for, as well as destroying the Chancellor and his family in the process. To succeed, though, she would need to draw on every ounce of darkness she'd failed to conquer – and she would need to get to know her enemies better. It wouldn't be easy, because she'd have to take advantage of the few who had shown her kindness since she'd arrived at the castle.

'Gwyn, can I ask you something?'

'Of course,' Gwyn shot back over her shoulder.

'Do you think the King really has the means to defeat the Northemers?'

Gwyn continued walking. 'It's hard to say, but he was quite confident that matters would be decided soon.'

'Spring. He said spring, didn't he?'

Gwyn nodded. 'Yes, I think you're right. Spring.'

'The Chancellor must have something planned for then. Something that means he can take Ette, Ivane and…' She didn't continue, not wanting to give Gwyn any reason to question her heritage.

But Gwyn stopped and turned back toward her. 'And Kengia.'

'Yes, Kengia as well. Do you think that it's possible?'

Gwyn indicated a nearby bench for them to sit on. 'I don't see how Lamore could defeat Kengia. Even without the Kengian King's protection, they are strong. From what I know…' She paused. 'From what I've been told, the Kengians are great warriors. I expect they are already preparing for such a threat.'

'I suppose,' Arisa agreed hesitantly.

'There's also the promise of the Water Catcher.'

Arisa's jaw dropped in surprise. 'You believe in the prophecy?'

Gwyn looked intently at her for a moment, as if searching for something. Seemingly unsatisfied with what she'd seen, she sighed. 'Perhaps. In any case, Kengia will be safe for a while longer. The Chancellor will be quite distracted for some time, trying to manage the threat from the Northemers.'

'Yes, but how does he think he will defeat them?'

'It would be quite a useless pursuit to try to understand how and why Horace does anything, or what he will do next.'

'Do you know him so well?'

'I don't think anyone truly knows Horace, though there was a time when I did think I knew him.'

'You did?' Arisa thought she detected a hint of nostalgia in Gwyn's voice.

'I did. It seems a lifetime ago now.'

There was so much Arisa didn't know about the people at court. If she had any chance of succeeding in her plan, she needed to learn more about them all, and fast. 'Please, tell me.'

Gwyn took a deep breath. 'Alright. It was when I was living with the Queen and her family at Nadis Palace in Ivane.'

'You lived there? I've heard it's beautiful.'

Gwyn gave a girlish laugh. 'It's every bit as picturesque as they say and more. The palace is alive with every colour you can imagine. There are breezeways patterned in exquisite mosaics and glass tile. There are ponds and fountains and steaming open baths.'

'Open baths!' Arisa cried, not having to feign her interest or surprise.

'Yes.' Gwyn smiled. 'There are grand courtyards and terraced gardens leading into curtained rooms, blending the inside and outside. It was a beautiful place to grow up.'

Arisa was puzzled. Gwyn didn't share the same Ivanian looks as the Queen and Lore. She didn't have the unusual height or prominent cheekbones, and she had a fairer complexion. 'You're not Ivanian, are you?'

'No. I'm from Ette's borderlands adjoining Ivane. My father was the village chief. We were mainly farmers, and since we were far from Ette's capital, we had escaped most of the troubles with Lamore. That being said, we always knew one day our enemies would come for us as well. We asked the Ivanians to teach us their warrior ways, so we could defend ourselves.'

'You were a warrior?'

'Yes. Every man, woman and child was trained to be a warrior. Not that it did us much good, because King Delrik's father came one day with his great army. They razed our village, burning our houses and killing my father, and many in our village. I lost everyone in my family.'

Arisa reached out and touched Gwyn's arm, trying to lessen the guilt she felt pressing this kindly woman for information and abusing her trust.

'I was lucky, though, because the Ivanian King, Arlo, took me in. I was ten years old, the same age as his daughter, Sofia. I became her companion and friend.'

So this explained their closeness. 'What was the Queen like as a girl?'

'She was beautiful, as she still is now. But she was also light-hearted and one of the happiest children I had known.' Gwyn looked off into the distance. 'She was so fun-loving. Her laughter rang throughout every corner of the palace.'

Arisa found the description at odds with what she had seen of the Queen.

Gwyn seemed to read her mind. 'It's true. Sofia was romantic, clever and loyal – loyal to a fault. Her loyalty to her father and her country is what brought her to Lamore. As well as love.'

'Love?'

'Yes. When Sofia and I were around eighteen, her father the King rallied the Ivanians and what was left of the Ettean villages, to march on Ette's capital and take it back. You would probably know that they defeated Delrik's father, and Arlo gave the country back to its people.'

'And the Lamorian King died in battle.'

'He did. Soon after, Delrik was crowned King. He was young and had little appetite for war. Delrik reached out to King Arlo to broker peace with Ivane. He came to Nadis Palace to propose an alliance, and travelled there with another young man, Horace.'

Now Gwyn was getting to what Arisa really wanted to know. 'What were Delrik and Horace like?'

'Nothing like what you imagine. The King was exceedingly

handsome and charming. He fancied himself a romantic young knight. He was adept at poetry and sportsmanship, and was an avid scholar. He was more philosopher than statesman. From almost the moment he arrived, he was captivated with Sofia. He set about winning her affection, showering her with gifts, sonnets and love letters. Soon he wasn't only proposing peace; he was proposing marriage.'

Arisa shook her head disbelievingly. 'Surely she didn't return his affection?'

'She did. She knew it was good for her country, and while she never wanted to leave her homeland, she knew it was an important duty. She was also quite taken with Delrik's romantic ideals and his genuine commitment to peace.'

'I find that hard to believe.' Arisa didn't want to hear that the King had any redeeming features, even if they were in the past. She couldn't have any reason to question her plan.

'But it's true.'

'What about Horace?'

'Now, Horace. He too was handsome…in his own way.'

Arisa snorted. She couldn't imagine Horace ever being described as handsome.

'He was,' Gwyn insisted. 'As well as witty and intelligent. He was the statesman and the King's favourite. Like me, he had been a royal companion since childhood. While he was more reserved than Delrik, he was charming in his own unique way.'

'Charming!'

'At one time, yes.'

'But it was he who didn't want peace?'

'I think he actually did favour peace, at least initially. He saw it as the right strategic move. An alliance with Ivane brought a significant dowry, trade and resources that would secure Lamore's future, all without the waste of lives in battle.'

'Something must have changed for Horace…'

'A lot changed. An arrangement was made for Delrik and Horace to return to Lamore, and we would follow a few months later with a small contingent from the Ivanian court. The physician, Lore, and his wife came with us, and the famed Lamorian warrior, Elos, was our escort.'

Caught up in Gwyn's story, Arisa forgot her plan for a moment. 'Why didn't King Arlo come with you, to make sure all promises were kept?'

'He dared not. While Delrik was genuine in his wish for peace, he was still his father's son. King Arlo had to stay to protect his country.'

'Couldn't he send someone else?'

Gwyn shook her head. 'Every man was needed in case the negotiations fell through. They had to be ready for the worst. Prince Laskar, Sofia's brother, was just a boy at the time, so he couldn't come with us. Regardless, Sofia and I didn't believe we had anything to fear, and once we were in Lamore we had our own protector.'

'The Kengian Prince,' Arisa blurted. 'That is why he came to Lamore?'

Gwyn raised a curious brow at her mention of the Prince. Inwardly, Arisa chastised herself for making such an obvious slip. 'My guardian has schooled me in all Lamorian history, and on how the Prince died in the Kengian massacre.'

Gwyn nodded gravely. 'Prince Alik was a comfort to the Ivanians, but he was also a great friend to Delrik. They were kindred spirits. They spent much time together, talking of peace and philosophy. They were sure there could be a partnership between Lamore and Kengia as well. It was a truly magical time.'

'What changed the King's mind? What made him turn on the Prince and Ivane?'

'Jealousy. Fear. Greed. A bit of each, I suppose.'

'From the King?'

'No. Horace. He begrudged the friendship between Prince Alik and the King. And while he saw benefits of being at peace with Ivane and Ette, he didn't feel the same about Kengia, and had other reasons for disliking the country. He was determined to make Kengia a Lamorian territory. The last thing he wanted was to partner with them.'

'But from what you say, you were close to Horace. You could have convinced him to sway from his course.'

Gwyn shook her head emphatically. 'I could not. Any love he once had for me was long gone by then.' She smoothed out her skirt and stood up. 'I have delayed you for too long. I must take you to Erun as promised.'

Arisa didn't want to get up. She still had hundreds of questions about the King, Horace and Prince Alik, but Gwyn had already walked away. She rushed to catch up. There was one last question she must have an answer to. She had to know if the King had had any cause for pre-empting the Kengian massacre.

'You don't believe that Prince Alik tried to bewitch the King?'

'Of course not.' Gwyn kept walking as she spoke. 'The Prince had magical powers, but he would never have used them for anything other than good. Not that I knew him that well. I had little need to see or meet with him.'

Arisa's face fell in disappointment. She had hoped Gwyn could have told her more about Erun's brother. They had been here at the castle together, even if only for a few months.

Gwyn and Arisa walked down a few more corridors before stopping at the bottom of a set of stairs. 'This leads to the north-west tower.' Gwyn handed her a torch as they began their ascent into the dank air. 'Watch your step.'

The tower's damp stone walls absorbed all light, leaving barely a foot of visibility in front of them. Arisa began to fear the conditions Erun was being forced to stay in. She assured herself it would all be over soon. By spring she would have enacted her plan, and she and Erun would escape before being forced to hand over Kengian magic.

She had to succeed. Now, more than ever, she was certain Erun's firesky task was somehow linked to the King's plans for recapturing Ette, and beating Ivane and Kengia. The way the King had spoken, it seemed the whole known world would be at war and would soon fall under his control. It reminded her of the prophecy and its promises of destruction after the second sign: firesky…It was too coincidental.

Arisa took another cautious step in the dark stairwell, passing in front of an arrow slit. She faltered as a silver beam of sunlight shone directly into her eyes. It was bright, so bright, like the flames of a freshly stoked fire. A flame so hot it could engulf the whole city.

She stopped abruptly. 'Firesky,' she whispered.

'Pardon?' came Gwyn's voice ahead of her.

'Firesky! The reason Horace has brought Erun here. To deliver firesky before the celebration events in spring…He says he wants to launch it then or on the King's progress, but he really wants it for another reason. He wants to use it to defeat his enemies, as foretold in the prophecy. He wants to use it as a weapon – like King Emberto tried to get the last Firemaster to do, all those years ago.'

Gwyn's eyes widened. 'A weapon,' she said, almost to herself. 'Are you sure?'

'What else could be powerful enough for the King to set his ambitions so high?'

'Erun couldn't create firesky, could he?'

'I have no idea. Its secrets were lost hundreds of years ago when the last Firemaster was kept captive here. But if anyone can figure it out, Erun can. We have to stop him.'

They quickened their pace, exiting onto a landing with a door flanked by two guards.

'Halt!' one of the guards cried. 'Lady Gwyn, you're not permitted here.'

'But Erun's ward Arisa is permitted, and I am her chaperone. So you will give me access to the healer immediately.'

The guards looked unmoved.

'Or you can take it up with the Queen,' Gwyn threatened.

The guards looked at each other, then stepped aside. At the same moment, a loud bang sounded and smoke billowed out from under the door.

'Erun!' Arisa cried.

'Open the door,' Gwyn shouted.

One of the guards pulled a key from his belt and, after a few moments of fumbling, unlocked the door. Erun came running from the room, spluttering and coughing. His face and hands were covered in a black film.

'Erun!' Arisa raced to her guardian and put her arms around him. 'What have you done?'

He hugged her back with limp arms as he took in big gulps of air. 'Nothing of any use, I'm afraid. It's been a terrible failure.'

'You shouldn't be doing it at all,' she admonished.

Erun stood back and scrutinised her face. 'Not here.'

He looked back at the guards, who were now fanning out the room and opening the shutters. Soon enough, the worst of the smoke had been drawn out and the guards ushered them in.

Arisa stepped into a small anteroom, coughing as the last of the acrid smoke scratched her throat. As she moved into the main room, her eyes went to a long table laden with books on one end and tubes and flasks of bright-coloured liquid on the other. One flask had shattered, its remains covered in soot. An extinguished candle was knocked over beside it. The scene of Erun's failed experiment.

She shivered as a cold wind blew in through the open shutters. The fireplace looked like it hadn't been used in decades, and there wasn't a single tapestry or carpet to add warmth to the room.

Gwyn must have noted the same. 'This is unfathomable!' she cried. 'I will speak to the Queen and have this rectified. I can't believe even Horace would stoop as low as this.'

'Thank you. It would be much appreciated.' Erun turned to Arisa. 'How are you faring?'

She refused to meet her guardian's eyes, fearing he could guess her secret plan from one look at her face. 'I'm quite well.' She tried to sound as relaxed as possible. 'I mean, it hasn't been all great. I had to tend to that dreadful Prince this morning and change his dressing. Close-minded, arrogant—'

Erun frowned. 'What did we discuss about keeping your head down?'

'Well, as I said, I'm fine. Gwyn has taken particular care of me.'

'Thank you again.' Erun gave Gwyn a strained smile.

She returned a small nod of acknowledgement. Arisa wondered whether she was imagining it, or if Gwyn and Erun seemed uncomfortable in each other's company.

Erun stepped back and appraised her. 'Let me have a good look at you. I barely recognised you.' He smiled. 'A little different to your usual attire.'

'It's not very comfortable, but I suppose it will do,' she admitted grudgingly.

He laughed. 'Yes, I suppose it will.'

'More to the point,' Gwyn interrupted, 'how are you, Erun? And what were you doing to nearly get yourself killed just now?'

Erun rubbed the nape of his neck. 'Nothing. Just an experiment. It's all part of my task for the Chancellor.'

'Firesky?' Arisa asked. 'You can't do it.'

Gwyn's lips thinned. 'You have to stop now.'

Erun opened his mouth to say something, but closed it again just as quickly. He sighed. 'Horace has requested a light display for the great celebrations. It's nothing to worry about.'

'Nothing to worry about?' Gwyn cried. 'So you don't think that once Horace has the power of firesky, he will try to weaponise it? The King has alluded that they will, bragging that he will soon have the power to defeat the Northemers, Ivane *and* Kengia.'

Erun dropped his head.

'You can't do it, Erun,' Arisa begged. 'You have to stop these experiments at once. Use your suggestive p—' She bit her tongue, immediately realising she had said too much, but neither her guardian nor Gwyn showed any sign of noticing.

'That would never work on the Chancellor,' Erun said. 'He is set on having firesky.'

'Try to escape, then.'

'It's no good. The guards are Horace's men, and their fear of him is more powerful than anything I can do.'

'Then feign stupidity. Horace will give it up if he believes you don't possess the knowledge.'

'I'm afraid he won't give up until he has it. And if I don't do this for him…' He trailed off.

'What? He will hurt you?'

Erun sat down heavily. 'It's not so much that he'll hurt me.'

Gywn gasped and touched a hand to Arisa's arm. 'He will hurt *you*.'

She pushed back her shoulders. 'If it comes down to it, I'm prepared for that. My life is worth nothing compared to the many who will suffer if the King and Horace have firesky.'

Erun thumped his fists on the table. 'Your life is everything! I must do this. I don't know how, but I must. Everything depends on it.'

Gwyn nodded slowly. 'You're right. You will have to do what is asked of you, and we will help.'

'Have you both lost your minds?' Arisa protested.

They ignored her. 'Where do we start?' Gwyn asked.

As if responding to Gwyn's question, a wolf howl sounded from outside in the castle grounds.

Erun's head spun toward the window in surprise.

'I understand it's a Kengian snow wolf,' Gwyn explained. 'We heard it the first time the night of the blood moon.'

The wolf howled again.

'But a wolf hasn't been seen in Lamore for—' Erun began, rushing to the window. He closed his eyes, as if trying to understand the animal's cry.

'The book. The last Firemaster's book,' he mumbled, racing back toward them. 'It's here somewhere. Among these.' Erun pointed to the piles of dusty books and scrolls piled on the desk and floor. 'Horace had his scribes bring every book and manuscript dating back to the time the last Firemaster was here. Her legacy is here somewhere. I know it.'

'Her legacy?' Gwyn asked.

'All of her spells and learnings – her life's work,' Arisa explained.

'The last Firemaster spent many years here at the castle. Many of those were when she was a guest of King Alfred and Queen Mary – she was in fact Mary's governess,' Erun said, his eyes glinting. 'In all that time, she would have kept a record of her work, and we know that she produced firesky for the birth of the Lamorian prince. But after that, she was imprisoned by Emberto, who tried to force her to weaponise firesky. She gave her life to protect its secrets, but she wouldn't have completely destroyed them. She was the last Firemaster. Her duty was to preserve Kengian magic.'

'But surely in the two hundred years or so since she died, if there was such a record or book…it would have been found,' Gwyn said.

'No, it's here. I'm certain of it.'

Arisa watched in shock as the pair began sorting through the piles. How could they both be so willing to hand over firesky to Horace?

'There are so many here,' Gwyn sighed as she picked up a hardbound book, blowing a layer of dust from its cover.

'Stop it,' Arisa implored, to no avail. 'You can't do this. There's too much at stake.'

Erun glanced up at her, a sad look in his eyes. 'There's too much at stake if it's *not* done.'

What was he talking about? The potential threat against her life was nothing compared to the thousands of Ivanian, Ettean and Kengian lives that would be lost to a weaponised firesky.

'No!' She slammed her palms down on the table, knocking piles of books and scrolls to the ground in a cloud of dust.

Without commenting on Arisa's outburst, Gwyn got down on her hands and knees and began sorting everything into orderly piles.

Erun reached out, then, and took Arisa's hand in his. 'You have to understand that I will do everything in my power to make sure Horace doesn't weaponise firesky – assuming I can create it in the first place. But I *must* try to do this.'

'Why, if we're going to escape anyway?'

'You know why.'

Suddenly it occurred to her that Erun also saw firesky as key to the prophecy – and to the belief that the Water Catcher would come. A stupid, hopeless wish that could never come to pass. Why couldn't he see that?

'Don't worry,' he went on. 'I will protect any secrets I uncover with my own life. In the meantime, I must give the appearance of creating firesky in its purest form, which is the light display. The leap from that to weapons is a complicated one, which I will never help Horace make.'

'And I will make sure the Queen doesn't agree to a date for the progress, so we have time to plan your escape,' Gwyn added.

'So will you help me?' Erun asked Arisa.

She forced a smile, knowing her plan was more important now than ever but wanting to placate her guardian. 'Well, I suppose I *am* your assistant.'

'Good.' Erun pointed to the piles of books. 'Then get to work.'

Arisa sighed, then reached under the desk to retrieve a book. A rustling sound made her stop. She got on her hands and knees to try to locate the sound.

There were dozens and dozens of books piled up on the floor. A papery voice seemed to be calling to her – a rasping *'Here'*. Instinctively, her hand went to a particular book, which she took from the centre of a pile.

She felt, more than saw, the embossing on the cover. A warm energy buzzed through her hand. Arisa scrambled out from under the desk and examined the book closer in the light spilling through the shutters. She wiped away the layer of dust to reveal a red leather cover.

A gold embossed image slowly took shape: a phoenix rising from flames, almost leaping from the cover.

The emblem of the last Firemaster. Arisa remembered that the last Firemaster had died several hundred years ago and it was understood she could transform herself into a phoenix.

No. It couldn't be that simple. She couldn't have found it… Yet the tingling sensation that rippled through her body said otherwise.

She opened the hard cover, but the first page was blank. She turned the next page; it was the same. Then another, and another. They were all empty, each as blank as the last. She closed the cover heavily and dropped the book on the table.

'What's that?' Erun asked, adjusting his eyeglasses.

'A blank journal or something.'

Erun picked up the book and examined its cover. His smile spread to his eyes as he flicked through the blank pages and let out a small laugh. 'This is anything but blank.'

Arisa wondered whether Erun had begun to go mad in his confinement. She watched as he passed his palm over the first open page in a circular motion. He murmured some Kengian words, which she translated in her head:

Thoughts to words
Words to action
Reveal thy words
Speaketh your secrets.

A Kengian protection spell. She had heard Erun speak of such a thing only once before. Few Kengians possessed the ability to create such a spell. It made sense that a book as important as the last Firemaster's would have been protected – that was the only way it could have remained undiscovered all these years.

She listened in wonder as Erun repeated the words over and over, until his fingertips began to glow. The radiance spread slowly through his palm before forming a ball of blue light that hovered above the book.

Words began to materialise on the page.

Erun clapped his hands with glee. 'What does it say?' Gwyn and Arisa cried in unison.

'They are the words of the last Firemaster. This is her book.'

Arisa leant over and started reading the Old Kengian words. She recognised the familiar format of scientific notes.

'This is it,' Erun said again, grinning. 'I would bet my life this book contains the secrets to firesky.'

She gave him a dark look. Erun had a disturbing expression on his face, a look of wonder and anticipation Arisa had seen many times before. She realised the scientist in Erun wanted – no, *needed* – to create firesky. While she believed him when he said he wouldn't hand over the secrets to Horace, she knew he also desperately wanted to rise to this challenge. And now he had the means to do so.

'I still don't think it's a good idea,' she began, but they were interrupted by a noise outside the door, and the turning of the key in the latch.

'*Words begone*,' Erun murmured as he waved his palm across the book. The words disappeared as a serving boy entered with a tray of food.

Erun smiled maniacally at the serving boy as he placed the tray on the table and made a hasty exit.

Arisa tried again. 'Erun, you can't—'

'Arisa, this is it. Don't you see how exciting it is?' His eyes were shining.

'Not really. In fact, it terrifies me.'

'It is exciting,' Gwyn cried. 'It's the real beginning.'

'There has been a blood moon, and now there will be firesky.'

'And then there will be the Water Catcher,' Gwyn added with conviction.

No! Arisa wanted to scream at the pair. Firesky may come into being thanks to the book she'd found – how exactly had she found it? – but the Water Catcher wouldn't arrive to save any of them from its devastation. Arguing with Erun and Gwyn was useless, though. One look at them, glued to the book and its contents, told her they were already lost. Lost to the promise of firesky and a Water Catcher who would never come.

Arisa was the only one seeing sense now. Her plan was their only hope.

20

Takai attempted to get out of bed, but fell back with a grunt of pain. He had done the same yesterday, and the day before that. He slammed his fists down beside him in frustration. Another day stuck in bed, fighting pain and boredom.

His injuries remained a stark reminder of the foolishness that had brought him here. He had nearly died. He *would* have died if it hadn't been for Sar and the healer, or so he had been told. With so much time to kill, lying helpless in bed, Takai couldn't help but relive the accident over and over in his mind. He wondered if it was his own pride that had urged him to be so reckless, or if it was some entirely different reason all together. A reason called Theodora.

Takai admitted to himself that he had wanted to show off when the beauty had arrived to see him and Sar. He wasn't entirely sure why. He didn't think he loved her – he didn't even particularly like her – but he wasn't totally immune to her charms. Since his return to the castle, it had been made abundantly clear that Theodora meant to be his wife, and that the King supported the match. Takai was mostly ambivalent to the plans. He knew, as everyone did, that as heir to the throne he didn't have the luxury of choosing his own wife. He could do far worse, he supposed. Theodora was uncommonly pretty, and he knew he would be the envy of any man. Yet she was also untrustworthy and calculating; very like her father. Once Theodora set her mind to something, she wouldn't stop until she had it. This would make her a fiercely impressive Queen – someone he could benefit from having by his side.

The Lamorians clearly needed a firm hand and Takai intended to rule with one. Since the recent uprisings in the counties, he was more certain than ever that his future subjects could only be tamed by brute strength, by being shown who was in charge. With war on the horizon, the Lamorians needed to accept the wisdom of their rulers – those who knew what was best for them. Theodora would be the perfect partner in enforcing that.

Despite this, he needed to ensure that Theodora would bend to his will if required. Takai needed to prove he was the one who was in charge, that he was strong and not to be reckoned with. He had to have her respect. That was probably what had led to him nearly killing himself during the foolhardy fight with Sar.

The more he thought about it, the more Takai got used to the idea of marrying Theodora. The only small hesitation he had was what it would mean to his mother. A mother he barely knew but had never stopped wanting to please.

His last distinct memory of spending time with her went back to when he was eight years old, not long before he had been sent to serve the Duke at Talbot. Takai had won an archery competition. Won, not because he was the King's son and they had let him do so, but because he was the best on the day. Even at such a young age, he had been an accomplished marksman. He'd practised his longbow for hours every day, determined to impress his peers and gain the approval of his distant mother. And on that day, she had looked at him with such pride. She had given him one of her rare smiles, the ones that lit up her whole face, and embraced him. Even now, Takai could feel the warmth of her arms and smell the sweet perfume of rosewater on her skin.

'You remind me so much of him,' she had beamed. 'You will be a great warrior, just like my father.'

Takai had been furious, wrenching himself from his mother's arms. 'I'm not like the Ivanian usurper. The traitor who promised an alliance with Lamore but took up arms against my father.'

His mother had shaken her head adamantly. 'It isn't so, Takai. There was never an alliance. The King and Horace lied to my father.'

'It is you who tells wicked lies. You are no better than your traitor father.'

The Queen's face had screwed up in pain. 'One day, you'll understand. One day, you will know the truth about what really happened. In the meantime, you have to believe one thing: that I love you, more than anything.'

Takai had run back into his mother's arms and looked up into her dark eyes. 'More than anything? You love me more than anything?' he had asked with such seriousness.

His mother had laughed gaily. 'More than anything, and you must remember that every day you're at Talbot. You must never forget how much love I have for you.' Tears were forming in her eyes.

'Mother, you will come to see me at the Duke's, won't you?'

'Of course.' She had given a thin smile. 'Whenever the King can spare me.'

She never came, though, and with every passing day Takai had found it harder to believe his mother loved him. Over the last decade, he had only seen her at formal occasions, and since he'd been back at the castle they had barely spoken a word. He feared that if they did, he might discover that she had, in fact, stopped loving him.

Takai shook his head to clear the painful memory from his

mind. He was grateful to be distracted by raised voices outside his bedchamber door. A familiar female voice was talking over one of the guards.

'Don't you know who I am?' came the shrill voice.

'Yes, Lady Theodora, but your father ordered—'

'But *I* order you to let me see the Prince, and that is what you will do.'

'I'm sorry, my lady, but—'

'Selina, go immediately to my father's rooms and advise him that one of the guards is refusing to do my bidding.'

'Wait. That won't be necessary. You may enter.'

Takai couldn't help but smile at her confidence.

The heavy doors creaked open and an abashed-looking guard announced the two ladies.

'You may leave,' Theodora barked at the guard, who looked hesitant to do so.

'It's fine,' Takai assured him. 'I'm sure I'm perfectly safe with the Lady Theodora and Selina.'

'I sincerely doubt that,' the guard mumbled under his breath as he left.

Theodora shot a sharp look at the man's back, before directing a beguiling smile at Takai. 'My Prince.' Takai noticed she no longer bothered to curtsey to him.

'Your Highness.' Selina moved away discreetly to a corner of the room.

'Lady Theodora, what a pleasure,' Takai said. 'I was thinking of you only now.'

Theodora moved a chair to his bedside and leant in close. 'Only good thoughts, I hope,' she purred.

'Theodora, we know each other well enough to agree there is little *good* that comes to mind when thinking of you.'

'What have I done to deserve such an insult? I am all good-ness and respectability,' she cried with mock offence.

'Hmph.'

'What? Don't you think I have all the grace and loveliness of your lady mother, the Queen?'

There was something in her voice that made him think she was testing him. He chose not to acknowledge the mention of his mother. 'What brings you here, Theodora?' he asked.

'I had heard you were on the mend, but I had to see it for myself and put my mind at ease.' She sniffed. 'You know I have been inconsolable since the accident.'

'Let me assure you I am well enough.'

'Yes, I'm quite satisfied that you are.'

'Pray tell, what news do you have for me? I am beyond bored being stuck here.'

Theodora bit her lip and paused for a moment. 'Let me see,' she mused. 'Sar has been terribly odious to me. He *had* promised to take me out riding.'

'Riding? Why would you need Sar to take you riding?'

'Well, he is trying to tame the Kengian mare, Meteor, and I'm quite determined to be the first to properly ride it.'

'Surely you don't mean that? No one has ridden that horse in nearly twenty years.'

'Oh, I intend on riding it.'

Takai gave a short laugh that hurt his chest. She was fearless. 'I tell you, Theodora. Any woman who is capable of riding that beast is worthy of being my wife.'

Her eyes lit up eagerly – a little too eagerly for Takai's liking. He changed the subject. 'So, Sar's been busy?'

'Apparently he is quite occupied travelling to and from his lands in Talbot. When he is here at the castle he is preparing for his knighting, or entertaining the healer's ward.'

'The healer's ward?' The girl who had changed his dressing. Why would Sar – or anyone – be interested in her?

'Yes. She is serving as a new lady-in-waiting to the Queen, while her guardian completes some task for my father.'

How odd. Takai had met the healer's ward; she was nothing more than a street urchin, and he couldn't fathom why she'd be asked to stay at court. And what could Horace possibly want with the healer? He knew the man had been accused of witchcraft, and there were rumours he may be Kengian, but it hardly explained why the Chancellor would bring him into his employ. The only thing Horace would need someone like that for would be…

'*Firesky*,' he muttered aloud.

'Firesky?' Theodora asked. 'What a curious thing to say. Father mentioned it only the other day. Isn't it from a Kengian prophecy or something?'

'It is the second sign in the Water Catcher prophecy.'

She rolled her eyes. '*That* silly thing. Everyone knows there can never be a Water Catcher.'

'I agree. It's not the prophecy I'm worried about. It's—'

There was something in the way that Theodora suddenly sat up a little straighter, leaning in toward him, that made Takai stop. He had to assume anything he said would go straight back to the Chancellor.

'Tell me some more about the ward,' he said instead.

Theodora's shoulders slumped, but then she gave him another dazzling smile. 'Arisa is her name. She's a strange girl, to say the least. She doesn't dance, play an instrument or sing. She spends most of her time reading books and sewing shirts for the poor.' Theodora grimaced at the thought. 'Frightfully dull.'

'She must be handsome, then?' Takai teased.

'Not at all,' Theodora protested loudly. 'She was dressed as a boy the first night she came here. There is something odd about her, though I can't quite place my finger on what it is…I don't trust her.'

Takai suppressed a laugh that it was Theodora who didn't trust a poor lowborn girl. He felt a little sorry for the ward; without Theodora's approval, she would be eaten alive at court. 'How does the Queen find her?'

'The Queen and Gwyn are quite taken with the girl, but

they are equally as odd.' Theodora bit her lip. 'Your mother especially so.'

So Theodora had something she wished to say about his mother. 'Don't play your games with me, Theodora. If you have something to say, just come out with it.'

'Takai, I take no pleasure in what I'm about to say.' *A lie,* he thought. 'Something happened earlier today, between the King and your mother…'

He nodded for her to continue.

'The King had come to ask her to preside over the great celebrations and join him on progress.'

Takai groaned inwardly.

'Your mother said she would only do so if the King went to her brother's aid, and defended Ivane from the Northemers.'

'A preposterous request,' Takai declared. 'After all the trouble Laskar has been to the King…Time and time again he has tried to aid the Etteans in rebelling against us. I imagine my father refused.'

'Of course, but that wasn't all. Your mother asked the King to release her from her marriage vows so she could…' Theodora appeared to be looking for the right words. She caught Takai's eye before continuing. 'She asked to return to Ivane.'

Takai gritted his teeth. It was as he had always suspected. Ivane would always come first with his mother, and nothing else – no one else – mattered. 'I suppose she didn't indicate I should go with her.'

Theodora tilted her head, as if she were considering her response carefully. 'I can't remember her exact words, but she did acknowledge having had nothing to do with you for many years.'

Takai lay back against his pillows, absorbing the words. He knew Theodora would have exaggerated parts of the story, but there must be some truth in what had been said. 'What was decided?' he asked, his voice cold.

'The King has agreed to let the Queen go, as long as she

shows her public support for him at the celebrations and on progress.'

So his mother had made her choice. She had chosen a land of traitors over him. He turned away to hide the pain he knew was clear on his face.

'Takai.' Theodora shook his arm lightly.

Takai returned his attention to her. He was decided. His mother was truly lost to him. Her opinion of Theodora didn't matter and was no longer an impediment to him marrying her.

'Theodora, I have something to ask you.' The words didn't come as easily as he had imagined they would. She gave him an expectant smile. 'It's no secret that it's your father's wish, and the King's, that we marry.' He noticed Theodora's small intake of breath. 'Do you have any objections to such a plan?'

Her eyes were shining. 'I do not.'

Takai paused for a moment. Why was he still hesitating? 'Please ask your father to visit me. I have some important business to discuss with him.'

'Important business?' She raised a quizzical brow. He nodded. 'Of course.' Theodora smiled triumphantly before leaving the room with Selina in tow.

There was no turning back now. He would marry Theodora, one of the most beautiful women in the kingdom. So why didn't he feel happier at the prospect? Why was there a churning in his gut that hadn't been there before?

Takai felt suddenly exhausted. He closed his eyes, hoping sleep would bring him some relief. He was just drifting off when Sar bounded into the room.

'Wake up, lazy bones,' Sar bellowed good-naturedly, before dropping his voice to a whisper. 'Sorry. I didn't realise you were actually asleep.'

Takai opened his eyes and shot his friend a tired look. 'I'm not any longer.'

Sar became serious all of a sudden. 'I'm sorry. I'll leave. You need to rest.'

'No, please stay. Actually, if you're here, you might as well make yourself useful and help me out of this confounded bed.'

Sar scrunched up his nose. 'I'm not sure—'

'I'm not an invalid,' Takai snapped.

Sar frowned, but held out his arm to take Takai's weight as the Prince gingerly put one leg out of bed, then another.

Takai gritted his teeth at the pain in his chest and limbs as Sar helped him across the room. He poured himself a glass of wine, offering one to his friend as he steadied himself up against a high-backed chair.

Sar shook his head to the wine. 'I passed Theodora on the way in. She sure looked like the cat who got the cream.' He scratched his head. 'You know, she always has a certain look of being pleased with herself, but today she was positively glowing. Why do you think that is?'

Takai shrugged, not sure he wanted to share his news yet.

Sar laughed to himself. 'I thought for a moment you might have proposed.'

Takai took a large gulp of his wine. 'I practically have. I have sent for her father to discuss the matter.'

Sar's face fell. 'Takai, you can't marry her.'

'Why ever not?'

'Because she is cruel and spiteful. And don't forget selfish and scheming, as well as being Horace's daughter. What other reasons do you need?'

'You shouldn't speak of her in such a manner, because I *will* marry her.'

'Don't tell me you love her.'

'Whether I love her or not is of no consequence in a royal marriage.' The way Sar was speaking to Takai, presuming he could tell the Prince what to do, irked him. 'I don't expect you to understand such things.'

'What I understand is that the people need a Queen they can love. A Queen who loves them back.'

'A Queen like my mother, I suppose,' Takai spat.

'Yes, like Queen Sofia, who has always done what she can for Lamore.'

'And what would her beloved Lamorians think when they discover she wishes to abandon them? That she means to leave them and return to Ivane?' *Leave me*, was what he wished to add.

Sar hung his head.

'I see that what Theodora has told me about my mother is true.'

'But your mother—'

Takai put his hand up to silence his friend and sunk into a nearby chair. 'Sar, you have been a good friend over the years, and I have never needed to question your advice before. However, on this occasion I fear you are gravely mistaken. What this kingdom needs is a queen who will inspire loyalty out of fear, not charity. And that queen will be Theodora.'

'Takai, think about it for a moment. Maybe – just maybe – marrying Theodora is the right choice, but what harm could there be in waiting? Wait a short while until you have fully recovered. Wait until you are completely back to your usual self, to be sure you have made the right decision.'

There was some sense in what Sar said. 'Alright,' Takai conceded.

'So you will wait?'

'I will think about it. That is all I can promise for now.'

Sar nodded, seemingly happy with the compromise.

'At some time in the future, though,' Takai went on, 'I will have to fulfil my duties to the kingdom – however distasteful they are to you, or me.'

'You wanted to see me, Your Highness?' came a new voice. Horace had thrown open the doors and marched in, without waiting to be announced.

Takai thought quickly. He would have to find another valid reason for calling the Chancellor to him. He seized on the thought of his responsibilities to the crown, which was fresh on his mind.

'Chancellor, I would like to return to my position on the King's Council as soon as the physicians give me the all-clear.'

Horace tilted his head. 'Of course.'

'And while I'm confined to my rooms I expect to be regularly appraised of all council matters, including any news on the Northemers, and how plans go for any invasive or defensive action by us.'

'I will personally see to it.'

'Thank you.'

Horace's lips thinned. 'Was that all, Your Highness?'

'It is. You may go.'

The Chancellor bowed low. As he left, he shot a strained look at Sar, who grinned back at him. Takai gave an exhausted sigh and Sar jumped to help him back to his bed.

'The thing is, Sar…Even if I don't agree to marry Theodora, what makes you think the Chancellor would accept my refusal?'

'You're the future King, Takai, not Horace. He is of no concern.'

Takai sank back against the pillows, mouth set in a grim line. Sar obviously didn't know the Chancellor very well.

21

———————

'Tell me what you've found so far,' Arisa said, plonking herself down on a stool across from Erun. She noted with relief that a fire was well ablaze in his room, and that there were other comforts: a tray of fresh fruit, extra candles, tapestries for the walls.

Erun followed her gaze. 'Gwyn was as good as her word. Everything arrived shortly after your visit. On the Queen's orders.'

Arisa nodded, though she didn't understand why Gwyn and the Queen were going to such lengths to ensure Erun's comfort, or her own. What was more disconcerting was Gwyn's support for Erun's dangerous firesky quest. Every time Arisa thought about it, it reminded her how critical it was that she succeeded in her own endeavours before the firesky deadline. At least with no date set for the progress and spring a couple of months away, she had time to enact her own plan.

In the meantime, she couldn't deny her curiosity when it came to the big red book on the table. 'Well, what's in it?'

Erun murmured the spell and waved his hand over the pages to reveal the Old Kengian words. He flicked through a few pages. 'There.' He pointed triumphantly to a particular section.

Arisa started to read it out loud. 'Sulphur, one part, charcoal, two parts, and potassium nitrate, seven parts. Potassium nitrate?'

'Also known as saltpetre.'

'The food preservative?'

'Very good,' Erun said proudly. 'These are the exact ingredients and ratios for firesky. Of course, from what the book says, you can add many other things for colour and effect, but for the basic explosion of light, this is the Firemaster's recipe.'

'But it seems so simple.'

Erun shook his head. 'Almost everyone who has tried to make firesky over the years has used a variation of sulphur and charcoal, to disappointing effect. But saltpetre...No one thought to add that.'

'Saltpetre is extremely rare, is it not?'

Erun nodded. 'There are no known mines in Lamore, but there are other ways to procure it.' He flicked through a few more pages and pointed to another section.

Arisa read it to herself before turning up her nose. 'Dung! The recipe for saltpetre uses *manure*?'

'It does. It's quite a process to extract the saltpetre from said dung, but it's certainly our most accessible source.'

'Urgh!' After assisting Erun in his healing work for many years, not much was able to turn her stomach. But animal manure – that was downright revolting.

Erun didn't seem to notice her disgust. 'Now we know exactly how to create firesky,' he said, that disturbing gleam in his eyes again. The prospect of making firesky was all too attractive to her guardian's scientific mind.

'We will escape before you need to hand over any magic,' she reiterated.

'Arisa, you must understand – if we can't find a way to escape, I may have to produce firesky for the spring celebrations, or the progress if it happens sooner. But I will never let them get their hands on its secrets, or help them weaponise it.'

Arisa murmured her assent. 'So if the worst happens…'

'Which it won't,' Erun said. She gritted her teeth, feeling the pressure of her own task. 'We are all safe until spring.'

Unless the Queen is forced to go on progress sooner, now that she's agreed to join the King, Arisa thought. Just how long could the Queen hold out against her husband and the Chancellor?

'We will need to get a message to Kengia,' she said. 'Tell them we are here at the castle and warn them of the task you have been given, but assure them they are safe for now.'

'We need someone who can be trusted to help us contact Kengia. Someone who has a network of people beyond the city walls, and can find someone who can send a starling message.'

'What about the Schoolmaster? He is to visit with me soon, according to the Lady Gwyn.'

'The Schoolmaster? Do you believe he can be trusted?'

Arisa nodded. 'I believe he can.'

'I have heard he's a Kengian sympathiser, and we have an excuse to see him as part of your lessons,' Erun said thoughtfully. 'Yes, it may work. In the meantime, we must put on quite a show and create the pretence of working on this. There must be plenty of noise and action.'

'Not as much action as last time, I hope.' She recalled with a shudder the vision of Erun running out of the smoke-filled room.

'No, this time I know what I'm doing. We will maintain the illusion of trying and failing. In private, though, I will test the real recipe.'

Arisa frowned.

'Arisa, you know we need firesky as leverage, if nothing else goes to plan.'

If nothing else goes to plan. The words chilled Arisa to her core.

'Let's get started,' she proposed with forced enthusiasm.

22

'Father, you summoned me?' Theodora stood a little uncertainly at the entrance to Horace's study.

He waited a minute or so before speaking. Finally he sat forward in his chair and steepled his fingers. 'How go things with the Prince?'

'It's all going to plan,' Theodora replied with false confidence. Her father hadn't offered her a seat, which didn't bode well.

'It's hardly going to plan. The Prince hasn't asked me for your hand. Has he asked you?'

'He did everything but. I thought that was why he asked you to his rooms – to ask permission to marry me. I have been waiting for days to hear it from you.'

'I met with the Prince as you bid, but he wanted to discuss matters of the kingdom. Nothing else.'

Theodora bit her lip. 'He will ask. It's just a matter of time.'

'Time is one thing we don't have. We have until spring to shore up our position. The Prince must be mine to control by then.'

'*Ours* to control.'

Her father gave a small smile. 'Yes, ours to control. And for that to happen, you must be married to him.'

'I know, Father, but I'm at a loss as to why he won't propose. His mother may have been an obstacle before, but she should no longer be a problem. I've seen to that.'

'There must be another impediment. What is it you're overlooking?'

Theodora shrugged.

'Think, Theodora. Isn't it obvious? There is only one person now who has influence over the Prince.'

Theodora's eyes widened. 'Sar.'

'Exactly. His power over Takai can't be underestimated. You must make it your priority to win him over.'

'Believe me, I have tried, but Sar sees straight through me. I flirt with him. I massage his ego. I flatter him. Any other man would have been falling at my feet by now, but he keeps a distance.'

'You have to bring him to your side.'

'I barely see him these days. He is so preoccupied with Lakeford and the knighting ceremony. He has cancelled my riding plans to meet with the Duke on several occasions, and I hardly ever see him in the Queen's presence chamber.'

'I understand the Duke is sponsoring the whole event and feast. All for his lowborn prodigy,' Horace added bitterly.

Theodora suppressed a smile. The whole thing was an obvious snub to her brother, who had been practically banished to Calliope.

'I will think of some way to get to Sar. Perhaps through Arisa.'

'Arisa? The healer's ward?'

Theodora nodded. 'They seem fast friends. Goodness knows why. She is the most pathetic little creature.'

'Didn't I ask you to befriend her as well?'

Theodora rolled her eyes. 'Believe me, I have tried, despite it grating against the core of my very being. But she wants nothing to do with me.'

Horace looked down his nose at Theodora. 'And I suppose you haven't learnt anything of why the Queen and Gwyn are so interested in the ward and her guardian, or how they know him?'

Theodora shook her head miserably. 'I haven't a clue. They don't say a thing in front of me.'

'Even more reason for you to befriend the ward.'

Theodora groaned, unable to think of anything worse.

'Don't you see?' her father pressed. 'Arisa is the key. The key to influencing Sar, and the Prince through him. The key to uncovering her guardian's secrets and shoring up my plans to defeat our enemies. She is the key to our ultimate power.'

Theodora sighed in resignation. 'I'll do it...but it better be worth it.'

'Worth a crown on your head?'

Theodora could immediately picture it. Her in her grand royal apartments, perhaps her father's current chambers – rooms actually fit for a Queen.

'You're right, Father. I will befriend the ward and Sar. I will have them both eating out of the palm of my hand. I shall not fail.'

'Then get to it.' The Chancellor dismissed his daughter with a wave of his hand, but she remained. 'What is it?'

'Actually, I have some other matters you may be interested in.' This was her chance. Her chance to be brought into the fold. To be given tasks that were worthy of her ambitions and abilities. Tasks that didn't involve making friends with peasants.

Her father clicked his jaw, but nodded.

'I have heard that the Prince and the Duke have been discussing Lamore's military strategy, and petitioning the King to mount a surprise attack on the Northemers, as soon as possible.' She had in fact heard such a thing from the King's mistress, the gossipy Baroness.

'Ridiculous! We don't stand a chance against them. We have barely half a navy, and a quarter of our usual forces. Our best option is to—' Horace stopped, seemingly reluctant to share anything further in confidence with his daughter, but Theodora would not be deterred.

'Our best option is to make an alliance with the Northem leader, Malu.'

Horace's eyebrows shot up, but he appeared to recover himself quite quickly. 'What do you know of such things?'

'I know you have sent a message to Malu via an intermediary who knows a lot about these Northemers, and that he believes an alliance is the only way to avoid an unwinnable war. And together, Lamore and Northem can easily take Kengia and Ivane.'

Horace's mouth twitched at the corner. 'You are well informed.'

'And if you keep me *informed*, I may be able to help you with your plans. Who knows what else I may be able to discover?'

'Indeed.' Her father steepled his fingers again. 'What else would you like to know?'

A thousand questions threatened to burst from her. Theodora had to force herself to approach the opportunity slowly. 'What did you offer the Northemers in return for an alliance?'

Horace's fingers stilled. 'I have promised to share something with Malu. Something powerful that he couldn't resist.'

'Something more than those territories?'

'Something.'

Theodora's heart fell. So her father wasn't going to share anything important with her at all.

'Was there anything else?'

'No, Father.' *Not unless you really want to take me into your confidence*, she thought bitterly.

23

———

The days of bed rest were endless. Takai had never felt so useless. The frustration of not being able to do anything or go anywhere was tortuous. He had nothing but his thoughts to occupy him, and he badly needed a distraction from those. He wanted a break from thinking about the overwhelming troubles of the kingdom. And he most certainly wanted to forget the difficult matter of his marriage.

This morning he had woken determined to escape the four walls of his bedchambers. And escape it would have to be, as he knew there was no way anyone would consent to him breaking the bed rest order; not even Sar would help him on that front.

Yes, today would be his great escape, even if it were just for a few hours. And he knew exactly how to do it.

Just yesterday Takai had recalled something – a memory from when he was a small boy. He and Sar had discovered a secret passage out of his bedchamber. It must have been built as an escape route, but it had lain forgotten for centuries, until the two boys had found it. It led to a disused corridor and the north-west tower, and Takai and Sar had put it to good use many times, usually when hiding from an annoying tutor or nanny. But since Takai had spent nearly all of the last ten

years at Talbot, he'd had no reason to recall its existence –
until now.

The Prince hauled himself out of bed. Ignoring the dull
pain in his head and chest, he threw a cloak over his nightshirt
and shuffled to the side of his room. He tapped the wall's wood
panelling in several places, until he came across a familiar
hollow sound. Nudging the wall with his shoulder, he felt it shift
slightly. He shoved it again, harder this time, suppressing a
groan of pain. The panelling gave way to a pitch-black
passageway.

Takai lit a torch and stepped into the black void, pushing
cobwebs from his view. The torch showed nothing but darkness
ahead, but he instinctively remembered the path. Pulling the
wall panel closed behind him, he ventured forth.

He followed the passageway for a few minutes, coughing as
he inhaled the damp and musty air, thankful when the path
ended at another wood-panelled wall. He pushed the wall until
it swivelled, then stepped beyond it into a deserted corridor that
he knew led to the abandoned tower. It would be his perfect
refuge. No one would disturb him there.

Takai headed toward the spiral staircase that led to the top
of the tower. His goal was to make it to the very top and the
battlements, where he could enjoy the open air. He progressed
slowly, making it up three flights of stairs before he needed to
stop and wipe sweat from his brow. His head was beginning to
throb, and his chest was really aching now, but he pushed on.

He climbed another two flights before he needed to grip the
wall to maintain his balance. Realising he couldn't go any
further, Takai punched his fist against the wall in frustration,
and yelped in pain. Reluctantly, he turned back and began his
slow and careful descent, but he'd overdone it. Now his head
was spinning uncontrollably.

He reached out to the wall to steady himself, but his shaking
legs meant he was barely able to stay upright. Takai knew he
needed help – but there was no point calling out. No one would

hear him in this part of the castle. He had a terrible vision of himself stuck in the stairwell for days, before someone thought to come and find him there.

Taking a deep breath, he put one shaky foot in front of the other. He counted each step as he took it, trying with all his might to maintain his focus on the stairs. Everything began to go blurry. *Only a few more steps to go.* He was on the last flight of stairs and could sense the bottom landing was near. Takai lurched unsteadily toward it, but his feet didn't follow. His legs went to jelly underneath him. He put his hands out to stop himself from falling, but it was too late.

Takai tumbled the last few steps to the stone floor below. He landed with a heavy thud, his ankle twisting awkwardly underneath him. His torch tumbled down after him and extinguished, leaving Takai immobilised in the darkness.

'You fool!' he admonished himself. He was lucky he hadn't broken his neck. He made to stand up, but couldn't put any weight on his feet, and soon fell back to the ground. Takai felt his ankle, registering the swelling beneath his hands. For a moment he contemplated hobbling back to his chambers, but his light-headedness made that prospect seem impossible.

Takai shuffled over to prop himself up against the wall of the stairwell. He would have to settle in for an excruciating wait—

A noise sounded from above. A door opened and closed, and footsteps started coming down the stairwell.

Takai didn't know whether to be relieved or concerned that someone was approaching him from the deserted tower. He forced himself to his feet. Hiding in the shadows at the bottom of the stairway, he weighed up his options, knowing he really only had one. He would have to ask the person for help.

After a deep breath, Takai limped out into the path of the figure that was now directly above him.

The figure gasped. In the darkness, Takai could just make

out the silhouette of a slight girl as she made to run back up the stairs.

'No, wait,' he cried, and started toward her, before falling back to the ground with a moan. The girl stopped and turned back toward him. Her features were obscured by the torch she carried. 'Please. I've injured myself. I can't walk.'

'I'll go get some help.' She sounded surprisingly calm as she began to make her way back up the stairs. Goodness knew where she was heading. But Takai didn't want to risk anyone else knowing about his escape.

'No, please,' he implored her. 'Can *you* help me?'

The girl turned back and walked toward him hesitantly, stopping a couple of feet away. As she stepped forward, a stream of light from an arrow slit in the tower wall fell upon her. From the shadows, Takai was able to scrutinise her face. He took in her long, bronze hair, framing a round face and a small, pointy nose.

It was the healer's ward, Arisa. But she looked nothing like he recalled. Nothing. What struck him the most were her eyes. They were the colour of glowing embers. She was ethereal-looking in this strange light.

Takai was suddenly thankful for the shadows, as he realised he was staring at her.

'How are you hurt?' Arisa asked matter-of-factly.

He stood silent, still lost in her strange eyes.

'Where does it hurt?' she repeated.

'My ankle.'

Arisa put her torch in a wall bracket behind her and bent down, gently examining his ankle. 'It's not a break, just a sprain,' she concluded. Without any sign of embarrassment, she tore a strip of material from the bottom of her undergown and expertly bound his ankle. 'I need to get you some help.' Again, she made to leave.

'No,' Takai protested loudly. He would tell the physicians he had hurt his ankle falling from his bed. He just needed help to get back to his secret passageway. 'Please, don't leave. I think I can make it, if I could lean on you.'

She glanced around nervously, as if she wasn't sure what to do next. It was as if she were suddenly aware of the impropriety of being here in the dark with a strange man. Arisa looked back at Takai. She appeared to be trying to read his face, but she didn't have the advantage of the beam of light that shone on hers, and hadn't recognised him.

'Very well,' she said eventually. He saw her glance at the torch and back at him, realising she couldn't carry it and help him at the same time. 'We'll have to make the rest of the way in the dark.'

'It's alright. We're going to exit at this floor anyway.'

Arisa shrugged, and put Takai's arm around her shoulder. He was considerably bigger than her, and he thought he felt her stiffen slightly when he put his whole weight on her. 'Are you hurt as well?'

'It's nothing,' she replied dismissively as she led him through the doorway and back into the deserted corridor.

'So, what are you doing in this part of the castle?'

'I've been visiting my guardian.'

'Ah, you're the healer's ward?' He wasn't going to let on that they had already met – not yet. He wanted to get to know her a little.

Arisa nodded, her gaze intent on the path ahead.

Takai was quite curious about this healer. 'Is it true he saved the Prince with witchcraft?'

He felt her shoulders go tense.

'Erun is a respected apothecary and healer.'

'Yes, but from what I hear he also used tricks and magic on the Prince.'

'I didn't know consulting science and medicine was considered tricks and magic.'

'If it were only science and medicine he dabbled in, your guardian wouldn't be the subject of witchcraft rumours and made to work in the Chancellor's employ.' *Made to conjure firesky,* he nearly added.

'As I said, Erun is a highly respected healer in Obira – at least among real Lamorians who don't live a privileged and sheltered life like you all do here,' she sniped.

Takai was taken aback. Theodora had led him to believe the healer's ward was frightfully dull. Arisa was nothing of the sort. From what he'd seen so far, she was plucky and opinionated.

'The respect of *real* Lamorians, you say? An undisciplined and uneducated rabble, who fill their days pillaging, rioting and planning uprisings against their betters? I'm not sure I care too much for what *real* Lamorians think or say.'

'I'm one of those Lamorians you refer to. Do you think I do such things? Isn't what I think or say important?' she spat in rapid fire, still not looking at him.

'I don't know you, nor what you do when you're not here at the castle. You could be a rebel spy for all I know.'

'If that is the way you and your kind see Lamore's people, no wonder they despise the King and his whole court. No wonder they find reason to rise up against you all.'

It was Takai's turn to take offence now. He had never been spoken to – or rather, spoken *at* – in such a manner. 'The King doesn't require the love of his subjects. He requires them to respect his authority. It is necessary for him to rule in their best interests.'

'From my observations, the King only cares for what is best for him – or what the Chancellor tells him is best for him.'

Takai flushed with anger. 'If you're in the mood for uninvited observations, I have one for you. You, my lady, may be dressed as a noblewoman, but you are no more a lady than I'm a dirty Kengian.'

Arisa stopped abruptly and flung his arm from her shoulder. They were standing before a wider window now, and as she spun around to look at him, he saw her fiery eyes widen in recognition. Takai waited for a bumbling apology or an attempt at a curtsey, but none came. Instead, she pursed her lips and put his arm back around her shoulder. They resumed walking in silence.

Good, he thought. If he never spoke again to the sharp-tongued girl with those disconcerting eyes, it would be too soon.

Then, seemingly just to further spite him, Arisa spoke. Her voice was wound tight. 'You shouldn't be out of your bed. It's foolhardy and dangerous in your condition.'

She had reprimanded him as if he were a child. 'Do you always speak to royal princes in this manner?' Takai demanded.

'Only when they are as reckless as you.'

He stopped and took his arm from her shoulders. They had reached the concealed entrance to the secret passage. Arisa was glaring at him.

'You may leave me here.' She opened her mouth, as if she were about to lecture him further. Takai cut her off. 'That will be all.'

She spun on her heels and marched off.

Good riddance, he thought, shaking his head. He had never encountered such rudeness – but what could be expected from a lowborn Lamorian, the ward of a suspected witchdoctor and Kengian?

Takai looked around him to be sure there was no one else in sight. He swivelled the wall panel and slipped into the passage back to his rooms, welcoming the darkness. The further he hobbled on, the easier it was to forget the hate and anger he had seen in the strange girl's eyes, and the way it bothered him more than he cared to admit.

24

<hr />

*A*risa stormed through the castle on her way back to the Queen's rooms. She couldn't get away from the Prince quick enough. He was just as arrogant and detestable as she had imagined. What hope did the kingdom have when it would be left in his hands? Perhaps the Queen was justified in her concerns that it may be too late for the Prince to change. He was insufferable. And Arisa had let him get to her.

She hadn't wanted *anyone* at the castle to get the better of her. She didn't want to play into their beliefs that most Lamorians were violent thugs or 'filthy Kengians'. Losing her temper as she had wouldn't further her cause, either. But the most frustrating thing was that she had been alone, in an abandoned part of the castle, with an injured and vulnerable Prince – the opportunity to undermine the regime had been handed to her on a platter, and she had done nothing. It would have been so easy to dispose of the distasteful young man, and make it look like an accident; instead she had helped him. *Helped* him! Arisa was shocked to realise that despite the significant depths of her hate, she lacked the stomach to hurt someone, let alone kill them.

She had to rethink her plan.

Erun was already on the path to delivering firesky because

of the Chancellor's threats against her. Arisa couldn't have that on her conscience. She had to do something. She had to get out of this hateful place, take herself out of the equation, so there could be no firesky. She and Erun had to escape, and she needed the Queen and Gwyn to help.

Arriving at the Queen's presence chamber, Arisa marched straight past a small group of ladies occupied with needlework. She strode past Sar, who was playing cards with Theodora, Selina and another young lady. Sar caught her eye and gave a friendly smile, but she ignored him and made a beeline for Gwyn and Queen Sofia.

'Your Majesty. Gwyn,' she began urgently.

Gwyn dropped her sewing in her lap. 'Arisa, what is it?' Her brow was lined with concern. 'Are you alright?'

She was about to blurt out her demand to leave the castle, but hesitated. Every eye in the room was on her. She dropped her voice. 'I must speak to you and the Queen.' Arisa cast her gaze back over her shoulder. 'Alone.'

The Queen stood up abruptly and walked swiftly toward her bedchamber, indicating that Gwyn and Arisa should follow.

'What has happened?' the Queen enquired gently, once they were alone.

'I can't stay here. Erun can't stay here. I beg you to help us leave.'

'Absolutely out of the question,' Gwyn responded, with unexpected swiftness.

'But you promised to protect us, and to help us in any way you could.' Arisa wasn't sure how much the Queen knew of Erun's work, so she continued cautiously. 'The work Erun is doing could spell disaster for many, and he only does it to protect me. If it weren't for the threats against me, he would try to leave.'

'From what Gwyn tells me, the Chancellor is quite set on Erun delivering this…task.' So the Queen did know, but was just as careful not to mention firesky. 'He is under heavy guard by

Horace's men, so I'm not sure he could escape, even with our help.'

Arisa had been afraid this would be the response. 'Then help me escape. Without me, Horace has no leverage over Erun.'

'If you were to leave, Horace would find other means of forcing Erun's hand,' the Queen said.

'He would give his life before doing what is asked of him.'

'And you're comfortable with that possibility?' Gwyn asked her. 'You're alright with potentially handing Erun a death sentence?'

Arisa's eyes welled up. She bit her tongue, willing herself not to cry. She knew what she was suggesting would put Erun at risk, but it was better than her being responsible for thousands of deaths. 'Of course I'm not comfortable with it. But you could help me escape first, and then we can find a way to save Erun. You must know ways out of here.'

'Even if we did, think of the danger you put us in,' Gwyn implored.

'So you refuse to help me?' Arisa's voice rose angrily. 'I thought you were my friend. That you cared for me.'

Gwyn winced, as if Arisa had struck her in the face.

The Queen put a hand over Arisa's, before speaking in a softened tone. 'If it were as simple as getting you and Erun out of the castle, believe me, we would happily accept the risk to ourselves. But there is nowhere safe in the kingdom you could go. Horace has spies everywhere.'

'We could go to Kengia.'

The Queen shook her head. 'You'd never make it that far. I think the best course of action is for Erun to give the impression of complying with Horace's orders. It will buy us time to formulate more precise plans. And while it may not seem like it, Erun currently holds all of the cards. Right now, Horace needs him, and while that remains true, you're both completely safe.'

'What happens when Erun has to deliver…his work?'

'We will never let Horace get his hands on it, or the means

of weaponising it. None of us will allow it. We just need time to come up with a plan.'

'So in the meantime, I have to stay a prisoner here?'

'Arisa, I know it's hard for you at court, but you must give it a chance. And while it pains you to do so, it's important to show you are content at court. Play the part of a typical young girl, grateful for the excitement and opportunities we have here. Horace should have no reason to suspect you're so unhappy that you may try to leave.'

'I have no time for the frivolities and cruelty of this place,' Arisa burst out. 'It's stifling and torturous. I don't belong here.'

'I understand. I truly do,' the Queen murmured. 'But right now, it's your only choice.'

Arisa looked appealingly to Gwyn.

'I'm sorry, but the Queen is right,' Gwyn said softly. 'You need to make the most of your situation here.'

Arisa swallowed back the bile rising in her throat. Could she rely on the Queen and Gwyn to come up with a plan in time, or would she have to enact her original idea. The thought sickened her.

'Let's see what we can do to make your stay better,' the Queen said.

Arisa allowed Sofia to escort her back to the presence chamber. Sar approached them immediately.

'Arisa, are you well?' His voice was thick with concern.

'Quite, thank you.'

Her own voice was strained, but Sar didn't seem to notice. His dimpled grin returned. 'Good.'

The Queen gave her a kind smile and Gwyn squeezed her hand before they left her in Sar's company. She looked around the room, determined not to reveal the anxiety she felt.

Theodora caught her eye. Arisa looked away swiftly. That was the last person she wanted to see. Undeterred, Theodora stood up from her card game and walked directly toward her.

'Arisa.' Theodora reached out and touched her arm lightly. 'So delighted to see you again.'

Arisa tried to hide her confusion at the uncharacteristically kind gesture. Sar raised a curious brow.

Theodora carried on. 'I've been extremely remiss. As daughter of the Chancellor, it's my duty and wish to extend my friendship to you, our newest guest at court.'

She turned around, expecting to see some other person Theodora could be referring to, but Theodora's gaze was fixed on her.

'I should have extended such an offer on your first day, but I haven't been myself. You see, the recent scare for our Prince has been quite frightening. For *me*, especially.'

What was Theodora playing at? To her horror, the girl linked her arm through Arisa's.

'I would be honoured if we could become friends. The best of friends. There are so many things we must do together, and much excitement to be had. Sar, would you mind terribly if Arisa joined us next time we go riding?'

Arisa shot Sar a look, wordlessly begging him to say that, yes, he did mind.

Sar gave her a cheeky grin. 'Of course not. The more the merrier.'

'Splendid. Right now, you must join us for a game of cards.' Theodora led her toward the card table. Arisa looked to Gwyn across the room, but she only gave a small shrug.

'Selina, make room for Arisa.' Theodora motioned for her friend to vacate her seat so Arisa could take her place.

'But we have enough players for this game,' Selina protested.

'Well, you'll have to join another game, won't you?' Theodora sniped.

Selina gave Arisa a sharp look before moving sulkily away from the table.

If this was how Theodora treated her friends, Arisa was sure she didn't want to be one of them. However, with the Queen's words fresh in her mind, she decided to pretend to enjoy herself – at least until she knew how to proceed with her deadly plan.

Sar leant in toward her, close enough to whisper in her ear. 'Worry naught. I shall show you how to resist Lady Theodora and her wicked charms. I'm quite adept at it.'

Arisa couldn't help but smile. Somehow, Sar always managed to put her at ease.

'Now, Arisa, I have to warn you: I take no pity on women. There's no such thing as knight's chivalry when it comes to cards,' he teased. 'It's every person for themselves.'

Arisa scowled at him, and he gave her a wink. Perhaps maintaining this charade wouldn't be as difficult and hideous as she had thought, especially with a friend by her side.

25

Nearly a week later, Arisa made her way to the stables. It was to be her first riding outing with Sar and Theodora. In fact, it was to be her first riding outing ever. She had never had the opportunity, or need, to ride a horse in Obira. She pulled nervously at the riding habit she had borrowed from Gwyn, and rubbed her ribs, assuring herself they were healed enough.

It had been several days of firsts for her. Ever since Theodora had declared that she and Arisa would be friends, she had sought Arisa out at every opportunity. Theodora had included her in every game, taught her every dance, sat next to her at needlework. All the while, she asked Arisa questions about her life, and about Erun. The questions often went beyond polite curiosity. Instinctively, Arisa knew every answer would be reported back to the Chancellor, so she always responded carefully.

She didn't trust or like Theodora, but having her show of friendship was at least making life at court more bearable. With Theodora's endorsement, she no longer had to endure rude stares and whispers from the other ladies – with the exception of Selina, who had not responded well to being sidelined.

Arisa arrived at the stables much earlier than she needed to, hoping she could catch Sar. There was something she'd been wanting to ask him. She looked around her, but the long building appeared deserted. Eventually, she came across a stable boy mucking out the stalls.

'Have you seen Sar?'

The boy shrugged indifferently and continued his work.

Arisa wandered through the stables. She passed stall after stall, peering in at each occupant. Even her untrained eye recognised how magnificent the horses were. There were chargers, destriers, carthorses and ponies, in every shade of black, white, grey and brown. Some stomped at the ground impatiently, and others whinnied when she passed, as if to say *hello*. She stopped at one stall to get a closer look at a bay filly – it gave her something almost resembling a smile. Arisa scratched its nose and the horse nuzzled her hand, looking for a treat. Next time, she wouldn't come empty-handed. Perhaps riding one of these horses wouldn't be too hard.

Her relief was short-lived as a commotion broke out in the next stall. Arisa rushed over to see a huge horse rearing up in the stall and kicking out violently with its back legs.

The stable boy stood in front of the horse, a broom raised above his head. 'Get back, I tells ya,' he yelled, waving the broom at the animal.

The horse reared again and kicked out in front, its ears pinned back in fright. The boy struck out with the broom, thudding it hard against the side of the stall. The horse snorted, standing up on its rear legs before bringing its front hooves down on the stable boy. The boy yelped and fell to the ground, clutching his arm in pain.

'Are you alright?' Arisa called out as the boy got back to his feet.

He scurried out the stable door, securing it swiftly behind him. 'Ach. I'll be fine. Just clipped me arm, it did. Not much more than a scratch this time. I'd be better, though, if I didn't have to tend to that beast. She's more trouble than she's worth.'

He stomped away, all the while shaking his head and cursing to himself.

Arisa moved hesitantly toward the offending horse. The name 'Meteor' was written in rough hand on the front of the stall. Peering into the darkness, she saw a caramel-coloured mare, almost twice her height. Meteor snorted, nostrils flared and tail up high in the air. Her ears were turned back and she was stamping her hooves. Arisa should have been terrified but, strangely, she wasn't. In fact, she was intensely curious about this amazing-looking creature.

Opening the stall door slowly, she approached the horse. 'It's alright.' She reached out with one hand. 'I'm not here to hurt you.'

Meteor cocked her head to one side, her ears twitching.

Arisa stood calmly, her hand outstretched. Surprisingly, the horse slowly calmed, and after a few moments stepped hesitantly out of the shadows.

Arisa gasped. Meteor wasn't just tall; she was muscular, with a high rump and long neck. Her coat shimmered like liquid gold. She lifted her head and looked at Arisa with an inquisitive eye. She wasn't a young horse, but she was beautiful. Arisa had never seen anything like her.

Slowly, she extended her hand until it was on Meteor's neck, then patted her gently. 'There you go, my friend. I told you I wouldn't hurt you.'

Meteor's ears slowly moved to a forward position, her tail lowering. She let out a low whinny that sounded like a sigh of relief.

'Funny. That's exactly how I feel.' Arisa smiled and rested her cheek against the horse's neck. 'It seems we're both misfits around these parts.'

She closed her eyes, feeling oddly at peace in this creature's company. It was as if the horse knew her, and trusted her. Reluctantly, she opened her eyes.

'Meteor, I have to go now, but I'll be back to visit you soon. I promise.'

Meteor whinnied, as if she completely understood Arisa's words. Arisa gave the horse one last pat before leaving to continue her search for Sar.

She walked the length of the building, checking in every stall, until she came to the very last one. There wasn't a horse in it, but on closer inspection she spied Sar sitting in the far corner. A stream of light through the shutters in the back wall showed him hunched over a book, rubbing his temples.

'Good afternoon,' Arisa said.

Sar jumped up in surprise, flinging the book into the air. 'Blast!' He scrambled to retrieve it from the dirty floor.

'Is that how you greet a lady?'

Sar gave her a wide grin. 'My deepest apologies, my *lady*. I wasn't expecting you yet. I thought I had a bit of time to spare.'

'My fault. I'm early. What were you so engrossed in, anyway?'

'*Engrossed* is probably not the right word for it.' Arisa raised an eyebrow, and he continued. 'Do you remember, on the day you arrived, that I told you I was trying to learn Kengian?'

'Yes, so you could better communicate with the tenant farmers at Talbot.'

'That's right. But it's not the only reason. It's also because… Well…' Sar hung his head bashfully. 'I'm to be knighted.'

'I heard, but what's that got to do with learning Kengian?'

'As part of the knighting ceremony, I need to repeat a series of oaths and recite the Knight's Code.'

Arisa nodded, not sure where Sar was going with this.

'Everything is spoken in Old Kengian.'

'It is?'

Sar handed the book to her. She ran her eyes over the words

and realised he was right. It was all in Old Kengian. The words felt oddly familiar to her.

'The knighting ceremony dates back to before Emberto's time,' Sar said. 'It was a Kengian tradition adopted by King Alfred. It's actually based on—'

'The Kengian warrior code,' Arisa interjected enthusiastically.

'Exactly.'

'So you need to memorise this?'

'Yes. But I would like to do more than that. I'd like to understand these words and what they stand for. I wish to honour them and live up to their intent.'

Arisa was struck by how earnestly Sar had spoken. Every day, he managed to surprise her, and scratch away a little at the hate she was determined to hold on to. Sar made her believe there were people at court who were kind and just.

He also reminded her she could take advantage of that kindness to enact her plan.

'So you need to do some more study,' she said.

Sar looked down at his feet. 'There lies the problem. I have been making some headway with learning Modern Kengian, but I can't seem to make heads or tails of this older dialect.'

'That settles it, then.' She sat down cross-legged on the floor.

'What's settled?'

'I had been wondering how to repay you for your kindness, so here I am. I shall be your tutor.'

'Arisa, I'm a hopeless case.'

'As my guardian tells me, there is always hope.'

She didn't add that she didn't agree with Erun, and that she'd learnt how dangerous it was to rely on hope. For a moment the thought made her forget her real motive for seeking Sar out. But there was something else she needed from him.

'Sar, there is something I'd like to ask you.'

'Anything, for my new teacher.'

'In Ette…Did you ever come across any of the silver-eyes? In Sir Marcus's household?'

Sar winced. 'There aren't many of them left. From what I understand, many of them have escaped over the years and joined the Ettean tribes.'

'That's what I had heard, too.'

He reached out and touched her arm. 'Was there someone in particular you wanted to know about?'

'A girl. A few years younger than me. Her name was…' Arisa took a deep breath. 'Rea. Her name was Rea.'

Sar's face brightened. 'I remember Rea. She was the adopted daughter of a farmer from Talbot. I remember how furious the Duke was that Sir Marcus had taken her. He sent word to Ette as soon as he heard. It turns out she managed to escape, almost as soon as the ship docked.'

Arisa's heart raced and she felt a shadow of something she suspected may be hope, but Sar's downturned mouth quickly destroyed it.

'The Duke and her parents went to Ette looking for her, but found no sign anywhere,' he went on. 'I believe her parents stayed in Ette, hoping one day to find her, but have never succeeded. I'm sorry I couldn't give you better news.'

'It's alright. At least she got away.'

'She probably went to the Ettean tribes like the others.'

'Probably.' Arisa's voice was overly bright, but the darkness in her had awakened. She had to focus on the now. She had to focus on her plan. She owed that much to Rea. 'Sar, there's one other thing.'

He flashed one of his devastating dimpled grins. 'As I said. You can ask anything of me.'

'I'd like you to teach me to fight.'

His smile fell away. 'Fight?'

'Not fight. Defend myself.' She had to approach this carefully if she wanted Sar's help. 'I'm not sure if you know, but

Obira can be a dangerous place, especially at night when I have to go out to help Erun with his work.'

Sar furrowed his brow, his eyes brimming with concern. 'I don't suppose I'd thought about that before.' He scratched his head. 'I could show you a few things.'

Arisa reached out and touched his arm. He was key to her having any chance of taking out the King. 'Would you?'

'Alright, but just for self-defence.'

'Of course.' She gave her most dazzling smile, hating herself for deceiving him. 'So, how about I hold up my side of the bargain?' She pointed to the book.

Sar gave a resigned sigh. 'If we must.'

'We must.'

She started guiding Sar through the passages he needed to learn. It was painstakingly slow, but Arisa didn't mind. Sar was an enthusiastic learner, if not a fast one. They soon became so engrossed in the lesson that they didn't hear footsteps approaching.

'Well, what do we have here?' came a purring voice outside the stall. 'A lover's tryst, perhaps?'

Sar jumped up as Theodora and Selina popped their heads over the stall door. He seemed to be stumbling for an explanation. 'Arisa and I were just…'

Arisa stood up calmly and wiped down her skirt. 'Sar was showing me an interesting book he was reading.'

'Reading? Is that what they call it these days?' Theodora teased. Selina burst into a fit of giggles and the pair entered the stall.

Arisa gritted her teeth. Sar looked down and shuffled his feet awkwardly.

'I'm ready to start our riding lesson,' Theodora said as she linked her arm in Arisa's.

'Riding lesson?' Arisa was confused. She was sure Theodora was already an accomplished rider.

Theodora gave her a bright smile. 'I can already ride, of

course. But I wish to learn to ride a particular horse, and that requires some instruction.' She turned to the stable boy Arisa had spoken to earlier. 'Saddle up Meteor.'

The boy shook his head, his eyes bright with fear.

'You may try to approach Meteor in her stall, but you dare not attempt riding her,' Sar ordered, his arms folded. 'Not even I have tried that yet.'

Theodora's cat eyes narrowed. 'I will ride Meteor today.'

Sar shook his head adamantly. 'It's not safe.'

Theodora dropped her arm and glared at him. 'Well, it is my order that you allow me to ride Meteor, and as the Countess and Chancellor's daughter, I expect to have my orders followed.'

After a moment, Sar sighed resignedly and approached Meteor with the terrified stable boy.

Theodora and Arisa wandered up to Meteor's stall and watched as Sar tried to saddle her. Selina stood back at what she clearly deemed a safer distance.

'She's so beautiful.' Arisa couldn't help but praise the creature when she saw her up close again.

'It's a Kengian horse – left behind by some visiting dignitary, apparently,' Theodora said. 'It's been here for nearly twenty years.'

Arisa felt the hairs stand up on her arms. Based on the timing, this horse had probably belonged to a Kengian who had perished in the blood moon massacre.

'I believe the intention was to breed it,' Theodora continued, 'but no Lamorian horse has been able to get within a foot of the beast.'

'So, who rides her?' Arisa asked.

'No one. Or at least, no one has succeeded. Since coming back from Ette, Sar has been trying to break the horse in.'

'But you think you will ride her?'

'I do, and today will be the day.'

'Why so determined?'

Theodora gave her a secretive smile, but it was Selina who spoke up.

'Prince Takai said any woman who could ride her would be worthy of becoming his wife.'

'You want to marry the Prince?' Arisa asked Theodora incredulously, one eye on the great struggle playing out in Meteor's stall.

'Of course,' Theodora replied, as if it were the most natural thing in the world.

Arisa shrugged. 'Each to their own, I suppose. Personally, I can't see the attraction. I found him quite odious.'

Theodora's mood suddenly turned. 'You've met the Prince?' she snapped.

'Briefly. I tended to him when he was ill,' Arisa answered haltingly. 'And we ran into each other a few days ago.'

Theodora began tapping her riding crop in her hand. 'I thought the Prince was confined to his rooms.'

Arisa searched her mind for a suitable explanation. For some strange reason, she felt she shouldn't betray the fact that the Prince had left his rooms of his own accord. 'It was a meeting of chance.'

'And in your *meeting*, the Prince wasn't to your liking?'

'He was not,' she replied truthfully.

Theodora seemed somewhat placated, and Arisa went back to watching Meteor as the mare was wrangled out of her stall.

There were now three grooms helping Sar and the stable boy to get her to the mounting block outside the stables. Meteor was kicking and rearing, but after much effort, they managed to coerce her through the stable building. Theodora, Selina and Arisa followed cautiously as Meteor was manoeuvred to the block. Sar and his helpers kept hold of Meteor with ropes as Theodora marched up beside the rearing horse.

'Down!' she commanded, to no effect. 'Down, I say!' Theodora struck Meteor's neck with her riding crop.

The horse reared more wildly in response.

'You shall submit to me!' Theodora continued whipping Meteor until the whites of the horse's eyes showed.

'Stop it!' Sar and Arisa shouted in unison.

Theodora gave Arisa a sharp look and whipped the animal again.

Meteor reared up, pulling loose from the ropes, and Theodora blanched as the horse's hooves rose high above her head. Arisa raced to the horse's side, pushing Theodora away before placing a hand on Meteor's neck.

The effect was immediate. Meteor lowered her front hooves and leant into Arisa's touch as she rubbed her hands soothingly over the tender skin on the horse's neck. 'It's alright, Meteor,' she whispered, and the horse calmed further. 'I'm here. I won't let anyone hurt you.'

Satisfied Meteor was no longer a danger, Arisa looked to Theodora, who was being helped up from the ground by Sar. 'That horse nearly killed me!' Theodora shrieked indignantly.

Sar shook his head. 'I told you she wasn't ready yet.'

'She's a menace. She has to be put down.'

'It wasn't the horse's fault. You were the one who whipped her,' Arisa admonished, showing her rising anger. 'Perhaps you're the one who should be put down.'

Theodora gave her a furious look. 'I suppose you think you can do better?'

Arisa met her gaze defiantly.

'From what I saw, the lassie has quite a way with the beast,' the stable boy spoke up.

'Does she, now?' Theodora crossed her arms. 'So full of secrets, aren't you? The ward of a rumoured witchdoctor who has magical powers. Mysterious meetings with the Prince. And now you can tame wild beasts…Arisa, you must show us what you can do with that *thing*.' Theodora pointed distastefully at Meteor, the corner of her mouth lifting into a smirk. She suddenly bore an uncanny resemblance to her father. 'Really, you have to show us. *You* shall ride Meteor today.'

'No, Theodora. That's not happening,' Sar declared.

Arisa would normally have seen the sense in refusing such a challenge, but she couldn't stand Theodora's smugness, or her farcical attempts at friendship.

'It's fine, Sar,' she said. 'I would be honoured to ride Meteor.'

Sar grabbed her by the arm. 'Arisa, you told me yourself – you have never ridden. I beg you not to do this.'

'It's fine,' Arisa assured him. She wouldn't be swayed.

Theodora merely gave a serene smile.

Arisa walked up to the block. She was resolved not to show any fear.

Sar grabbed her arm again. 'You don't need to do this.'

'But I do. And there is no point arguing with me. I'm quite determined.'

'This isn't about being determined. This is about being stupid.'

'Call me stupid, then. But I shall ride Meteor.'

Theodora clearly hadn't expected Arisa to call her bluff. 'Perhaps Sar is right,' she said offhandedly. 'It's too dangerous… for *you*.'

Arisa ignored her and moved in closer to Meteor. The horse's ears were still turned back. She reached out to rub Meteor's face, the horse's hot breath on her hand. Leaning in close, she whispered, 'Meteor. You're in charge, my friend, and I trust you.'

Meteor went still and relaxed her ears, as if she had understood Arisa's words. Arisa steeled herself and stepped up onto the mounting block. Then, with one swift movement, she threw her leg over the horse's back and slipped into the saddle. She wasn't sure what to do next, but it didn't matter.

Meteor was away.

'Arisa, wait!' she heard Sar yelling as the horse thundered out of the yard.

Within seconds they had exited through the main gatehouse,

narrowly avoiding a collision with a water carrier's cart. Meteor pointed her nose to the woodland in the outer castle grounds, and left the main path at a gallop. Arisa clung onto the reins for dear life. Meteor was in full control – yet Arisa felt at one with the horse, and trusted her implicitly. Her hair flew around her face and the wind bit hard into her cheeks as she moved up and down in the saddle, matching the rhythm of the horse's movements.

Meteor galloped over a series of hills with ease, until they reached the woodland's edge. The horse pulled up. Her ears began to twitch and she let out a low whinny.

Arisa patted her neck. 'What is it, Meteor?'

Meteor pawed at the ground, as if she were unsure whether to go forward or backward. A strange feeling came across Arisa, like someone was watching them. She looked back over her shoulder; Sar was riding toward them, Theodora and Selina trailing in the distance.

Meteor continued to stamp her front hooves. Arisa cast her eyes back toward the woodland, but could see nothing amiss. She looked again, more closely, sure there must be something to see—

A shape slowly emerged from the shadows.

It was large, though not as large as a man. Arisa tightened her grip on the reins as it moved toward them. Meteor gave the same low whinny.

Arisa's breath quickened. Her head was telling her to guide Meteor away, but she was drawn to the shape in the shadows. The figure was almost at the edge of the woodland now, only a few feet from them. It crept out from the trees until it was fully visible.

It was the Kengian snow wolf.

The wolf raised its white head and nodded in acknowledgement. Its eyes were startlingly green. Arisa didn't know much about wolves, but she was sure they weren't supposed to have eyes like that.

Still, she allowed herself to be drawn by the wolf's gaze. Its green eyes pulled her in, and a flash came to her suddenly – a memory, a dream; she wasn't sure what, exactly. She saw a tall, muscular man with silver hair and matching silver eyes, dressed in brightly coloured armour, astride a horse. Not just any horse – the man was on Meteor. And there was a waterfall, set in a mountain range. Arisa could feel the mist spray on her cheek, hear the roar of the water, breathe in the icy air.

Then, as suddenly as it appeared, the vision left her.

Her head was a whirl of confusion. *What had just happened?* She would speak to Erun about it. Perhaps he would know who the man was, and why she'd seen him. Was this her silver-eyes power manifesting? The power Erun had refused to help her harness?

Should she tell him at all?

'That was the stupidest thing you could have done!' Sar cried as he pulled up next to her. 'Reckless, stupid and—'

'Shh.' Arisa put a finger to her lips and pointed back toward the wolf, but the animal turned on its heel and bound back into the woodland.

'The snow wolf?' Sar said, staring after it.

Arisa nodded. 'What do you suppose it's doing here?'

'I'm not sure, but I don't expect it to be here long.'

'Don't tell me the King is still trying to hunt it?'

Sar shrugged. 'The woodland doesn't produce much in the way of sport. The wolf is a great diversion.'

'Hasn't the King enclosed enough woodland and forest in the counties for his hunting?'

'He isn't able to visit his hunting grounds at the moment. It's not safe for him.'

'I know. Apparently he's scared of his subjects,' she sniped.

'Arisa, you shouldn't speak so of the King. At least not publicly.'

'I can't believe they would hunt such a beautiful creature.'

'I agree. It's a cruel and unnecessary sport. Taking any life, human or animal, isn't a matter to be treated lightly.'

A film of sweat formed at Arisa's brow. She wondered whether Sar suspected her and her plan. But one look at his face, contorted in pain, confirmed his thoughts were elsewhere.

She berated herself for her selfishness. Sar must be recalling the atrocities he had seen in Ette — and those he had inflicted. Arisa reached out and squeezed his arm, watching as he came back to the present.

He smiled gratefully at her. 'In any case, the wolf's days are numbered. It's made quite a nuisance of itself, taking livestock from the castle yards. I expect they will put a trap out for it next.'

'Something tells me the wolf can take care of itself.'

Sar gave a great belly laugh. 'Just like you, I suppose.' His voice thickened with concern. 'I really wish you hadn't ridden off like you did. You really scared me.'

'I'm sorry, Sar. But somehow I knew it would be alright. I knew Meteor would look after me.'

His face broke into a wide grin. 'I guess it was worth it, just to see the look on Theodora's face when you galloped away.'

Arisa grinned back. 'I wish I could have seen it too.'

'Looks like you soon will.' He glanced back as Theodora and Selina caught up to them, sour looks on both of their faces.

'I see you actually *can* ride,' Theodora sneered.

'It appears so,' Arisa retorted.

'Well, Sar, the work you have done with Meteor seems to have paid off.'

'Thank you, Theodora, though the skill is all Arisa's. I expect you would like to ride Meteor next week?'

Theodora looked troubled by the thought. 'Oh, no. I couldn't deprive Arisa. She seems to have developed such a bond with the creature.'

Arisa noticed Meteor's ears pointing toward Theodora. A nervous energy came over the horse whenever she was near.

Rubbing Meteor's neck, she leant in to whisper, 'Come on. Let's show her what you can really do.'

Meteor seemed to understand. She started off again at a fast gallop, heading further north-west across the castle grounds, her nose firmly pointed at the Nymoi Alps.

Soon enough, Sar caught up again, and Arisa slowed Meteor to a canter.

'Arisa, you need to stop doing that.'

'What? Riding away, or upsetting Theodora?'

'Both. You shouldn't—' Sar stopped mid-sentence. 'What is that?' he asked, pointing at her neck.

Arisa looked down, reaching for her silver chain. She realised with a start that her medallion had flown open. 'It's nothing,' she said quickly, closing it.

'It didn't look like nothing.'

Arisa stopped Meteor next to a small stream, allowing her to take a drink. Sar led his horse up next to her. She questioned whether she should say anything more to him. But something made her want to share with someone. Someone she didn't have to hide every secret from. Sar could be that person; she was sure of it.

She looked back to ensure they were alone, and was relieved to see that Theodora and Selina had given up pursuing them. It looked as if they were returning to the stables.

'Here.' Arisa opened the medallion and held it aloft, so Sar could see its contents.

'Whoa!'

Sar reached out and ran his fingers across the finely engraved silver coin inside the medallion. It was decorated with a koi. Arisa took the coin out and turned it over, showing the letter 'A' on the reverse.

'It's like the fish that's part of King Alfred's emblem,' Sar said. She nodded. 'Is it from a good fortune bracelet?'

'Yes.' Again, Arisa was surprised by Sar's knowledge of Kengian culture. 'Originally it would have been part of a bracelet with a coin for each of the elements – water, air, earth and fire.'

'Where would you get such a thing?'

'It was a gift, left by my father.' She paused. 'He gave it to my mother before he died.'

'Your father?' Sar's eyes widened. 'So your father was Kengian?'

'Yes.' It was powerful, the relief she felt in sharing her secret with someone. 'Yes, he was,' she repeated proudly.

'Wow! I mean, I'm sure people have suspected it around here, what with the rumours about your guardian, but to have it confirmed…Horace would want to know this.'

Arisa shrunk back from Sar, slamming the medallion shut.

'No!' He waved his hands wildly. 'I only meant – you have to be careful that Horace never finds out. Your secret is safe with me. And now that I know it, I will do everything in my power to ensure no one discovers it.'

'Thank you,' she mumbled.

'Do you have powers, though? Like – can you speak to nature?'

Arisa grimaced. 'I haven't been taught how to harness them.' She didn't mention her encounter with the wolf or the strange vision she'd just had, or even how she seemed to be able to communicate with Meteor. Those things were all startlingly new to her.

Sar looked disappointed. 'What happened to your father? I mean, if that's alright to ask.'

'He died in the blood moon massacre.'

'I'm sorry to hear that. My father died at the same time.'

She baulked. 'Please tell me your father wasn't one of the men sent to kill the Kengians?'

'No.' Sar shook his head emphatically. 'I mean, yes…'

'Yes or no, Sar?'

'From what I understand, he was sent to round up the Kengians, but Mother – Gwyn – told me he actually went to find someone – that he was trying to help one Kengian in particular. But he never returned.'

'You think your father really went to help?' she asked disbelievingly.

'Of course. Everyone you meet will tell you that unjust violence was never in my father's nature. Elos was a great warrior, but he lived by the Knight's Code.'

Arisa felt a little placated, given how earnest Sar was – and if his father had been anything like him, what he said could be true. 'Were your father and Gwyn...'

'Together?' He grinned. 'No, just good friends. My mother died in childbirth. I came into Gwyn's care after my father died.'

'I'm truly sorry to hear that.'

Sar gave her a thin smile. 'And your mother?'

'Died of fever, a few days after the massacre. Erun tried to save her but couldn't.'

'And that's how you came to be his ward?'

'It is.'

'It seems we have quite a bit in common, then.' He paused, a cheeky grin spreading across his face. 'Despite you being a Kengian and all.'

Arisa shot him a warning look.

'I know, I know. It's the last time I'll ever mention it. I promise. Come on, it's time I got you back safely to the castle.'

She tugged on Meteor's reins and pointed the horse's nose homeward. 'Don't you mean it's time I beat you back?'

Arisa laughed as Meteor pulled forward, leaving Sar to chase her for the third time that day.

26

―――――

Takai had finally been given the all-clear to leave his rooms. The wounds on his head and arm were healing well. His dizziness was all but gone. He only had a small limp, which he'd managed to convince the physicians had been caused by a fall from bed. The true circumstances of his fall bothered him, though. He hadn't been able to stop thinking about the healer's ward – Arisa. Her views of him and of his father's regime had hurt much more than Takai liked to admit. Was there some truth in what she had said? Was he prejudiced against Lamore's subjects?

Takai's thoughts circled each other as he took a turn around the Queen's Garden. After his first lap, it began to get dark, so he started his laborious journey back to the castle. Takai gritted his teeth as he limped across the moat bridge and through the inner south gate. He paused for a moment to catch his breath, stopping at the breezeway leading back to the main keep.

Theodora was in the courtyard, barking orders at a poor stable boy. She spat a few more insults before marching over toward the castle, Selina following in her wake. Theodora was so preoccupied she nearly ran straight into Takai.

'Oh!' She flung a hand to her chest in surprise, her filthy mood seemingly evaporating as she noticed the Prince. 'How wonderful to see you.'

Takai smiled as he took in her smart-looking riding habit. 'Been for a ride?'

'It was lovely, thank you.' She looked up at him through her thick lashes. 'You really must join us one day.'

Takai was about to respond that he might do just that, when his attention was caught by a group of groomsmen and stable hands assembled in the courtyard, whooping and clapping. He squinted to discern what or who they were looking at. It was an approaching rider—

Someone riding Meteor?

Takai rubbed his eyes. It *was* Meteor, though from this distance, he couldn't quite tell who the rider was. It wasn't Sar, that much he knew; the rider had a significantly slighter build.

'I see the great Meteor has been mastered at last,' he said in awe.

Theodora looked back toward the horse with narrowed eyes. And now, Takai could see the rider more clearly.

It was Arisa.

'What in the world…?'

'Enough of that boring girl already.' Theodora tugged at his arm. 'Let's get you back to the comfort of your room, so you can rest.'

Takai disentangled himself from Theodora's grip. He had to find out for himself how Arisa had managed to ride a horse that no one else had been able to tame in nearly twenty years.

He hobbled out into the stable yard, coming up beside Meteor as a groomsman helped Arisa down. She gave a mock bow to the cheering group, and spun toward him, laughing—

Her amber eyes widened in surprise. At the same moment, she lost her footing and fell forward into his arms.

'It seems I'm the one doing the rescuing today,' Takai said

drily, as he lifted Arisa back to her feet. He couldn't drag his eyes away from her.

She stepped away from him and composed herself. 'Thank you,' she said formally, giving a half-hearted curtsey.

Takai knew he should say something. He needed to stop staring – but the words wouldn't come. It was as if she'd put a spell on him.

'Pray tell, what do you find so detestable about me?' Arisa shot at him.

'Detestable?' He gave a start, then shook his head. 'Nothing detestable at all.'

'That's not the impression you give as you stare at me. In fact, you made it pretty clear last time we spoke how distasteful you find all of your Lamorian subjects, me included.'

So this was how it was to be. She was determined to judge him poorly.

Maybe he had seen nothing in those eyes that warranted his interest.

'Takai!' Sar bounded toward them. 'Look at you, out and about!'

Takai merely nodded.

Sar grabbed him and Arisa by their arms, linking elbows and leading them back to the castle. 'Takai, you must join us for a celebration. Arisa has tamed the mighty Meteor.'

'I'm not sure the Prince would like to keep company with the lowborn likes of me,' Arisa sniped.

Takai's jaw clenched involuntarily. She was impossible. 'I suppose not,' he shot back. 'Good day.' He gave a crisp bow and hobbled off at a dangerously swift pace, leaving Sar to call futilely after him.

Takai reached the refuge of the breezeway to find Theodora waiting for him, wearing a triumphant smile. 'Not now, Theodora,' he snapped, walking right past her.

What was it about Arisa that needled him so? She was wilful, rude and righteous, so sure of her misguided beliefs. But for some inexplicable reason, he actually cared about what she thought. He had never met anyone like her, and while part of his brain said she wasn't worthy of his interest, Takai was intrigued.

He must get to know her. If only she'd let him.

27

Arisa took her role as Sar's teacher seriously. While she was well equipped to help him with the basics of Kengian language, there were some nuances and differences between the old and new dialects she needed to familiarise herself with. On hearing what she needed, Gwyn had shown Arisa to the castle's library.

She was enchanted by what she found there. Floor-to-ceiling timber shelves, rows and rows of them, staircases to a second and third floor, and ladders to reach the highest volumes. The musky smell of ink and parchment permeating the air was intoxicating.

A scribe pointed out a section on the Kengian language, and Arisa grabbed a pile of books and set herself up at a table by the only window. She was deep in the rules of Kengian grammar when an unexpected voice brought her back to the room.

'Oh. Hello there.'

She looked up to see the Prince – a tentative smile on his face, but most definitely a smile.

'Hello…Your Highness,' she said, packing up her books. The Prince was the last person she felt like talking to.

'Takai. Please call me Takai.'

She nodded begrudgingly.

'So, what are you reading?'

Arisa barely managed to resist rolling her eyes at his annoying attempts at polite conversation. 'I'm reading up on Kengian language. And before you go accusing me of being a Kengian, please know I'm helping Sar learn his knight's oath.'

Takai held his hands up in surrender. 'No accusations here. I'm glad you're helping him. He deserves the honour more than anyone I know.'

'He does,' she agreed, letting her hackles settle somewhat. 'What are you doing here?'

'Well, now that I'm back at the castle, I've become a lot more involved in the business of running the kingdom. The council is trying to determine the best strategy to manage the Northemers and I thought there may be something to learn in past military journals, from previous battles.'

'That makes sense.' It occurred to Arisa that she could use this opportunity to find out more about Horace's great plans. 'I understood that the Chancellor already had a strategy in mind.'

Takai compressed his lips. 'He does, but let's just say that he doesn't exactly have the council's support, and personally I have little faith in his ability to deliver on his particular strategy.'

'Firesky. That is his strategy.' She was taking a risk, spelling it out to the Prince – but it was a calculated risk, based on the fact that he did not support Horace's plans.

Takai's eyebrows shot up. 'Yes, that is a key part of his plan. And something I understand he has tasked your guardian with delivering.'

'It is.'

'An impossible task. The secrets to firesky have been lost for centuries. No matter how clever your guardian is, we can't rely on firesky to save us or something as elusive as a Water Catcher.'

'I agree.'

He snort-laughed at that. 'That's a first.'

Arisa realised she liked the way the Prince's whole face and demeanour changed when he laughed. It was like all of his walls made of pride and privilege were down. Like he was someone she could even grow to like. But his smile was gone all too soon.

'The worrying thing is I'm not sure I can convince my father of an alternative strategy, even if it's the best thing for Lamore.'

If there was a brief moment when Arisa had hope that firesky wouldn't have to be delivered, it vanished in that instant, and only strengthened her resolve to forge ahead with her own plan.

'Speaking of my father...I must go to see him,' Takai said before bidding her farewell and leaving.

As Arisa watched him go she had a strange niggling feeling that something wasn't right. It might have been guilt over planning to kill Takai's father, or perhaps a realisation that the Prince wasn't a complete ogre. Either way, she didn't want to think about it, and went back to studying the books for Sar.

28

The King looked up at his son's arrival with a delirious smile. Takai had only been out of his rooms for a couple of days, but he had much to discuss with his father. He had to get him to see sense when it came to ruling the kingdom.

'So glad to see you, son. You have to see this.' The King pointed to lists of names and sketches of emblems scattered on a table. 'I have had a coat of arms designed for you to wear at the celebratory tournament. It's going to look splendid.'

Takai took a closer look. It appeared to be the King's insignia, a peregrine falcon, but this one was different. It was surrounded by flames.

The King followed his gaze. 'It's to represent firesky.'

'Of course,' Takai said hesitantly, not wishing to dampen his father's enthusiasm. 'Father, I wonder if we should in fact proceed with the Duke's plans, just in case firesky doesn't eventuate.'

'Horace assures me he's on track to deliver it by spring – or sooner, if we go on progress.'

'Do you trust him, Father? I mean, the Chancellor has done nothing to quell the uprisings in the counties, and his former reeve Sergei is gathering more supporters by the day.'

The King's brow furrowed. 'Yes, I have heard the reports of another riot – the rebels broke into a grain store and stole much of its contents.'

'It was on the Chancellor's lands at Calliope. The Duke says several of your knights were injured. One of them was killed.'

The King wrung his hands. 'The loss of life is regrettable, but I have it on good authority that it could have been much worse, had Guthrie not been there to quell it.'

'Had he not been there to instigate it!' Takai protested. 'I have looked into the matter, and Guthrie, in his infinite wisdom, was hoarding grain.'

'Horace explained to me that since our trade routes with Ette have been cut, there has been a need to manage what scarce resources we have.'

'Doesn't that mean rations? Not hoarding. The Duke believes that Horace was holding onto the grain to create a further shortage, and inflate profits later for when he sold it.'

The King waved a dismissive hand. 'Horace says it was just a few disgruntled peasants. Nothing out of the ordinary until that troublemaker Sergei arrived and stirred everything up.'

Takai believed his father was only right on one front – Sergei was a problem. Word had reached the castle of 'criers' in Obira urging all Lamorians, as well as Kengians and their supporters, to rise up in support of Sergei. Lamorians and Kengians united was an unlikely match, but it appeared they all agreed on one thing: with war on the horizon, they couldn't afford to sit around waiting for a Water Catcher who may or may not arrive. They had determined to take matters into their own hands. Many Kengians were already fleeing in fishing boats back to their homeland to join the forces there. The Kengians who were unable to leave Lamore believed Sergei was their best hope of protecting their future.

'You know this Sergei is calling for a great uprising against us – against me!' the King cried. 'They even propose an attack on the castle.' He scoffed. 'He and the Kengian criers must be dealt with. And publicly. We must send a strong message that I will not have my rule questioned.'

'I agree, Father.'

'I will ask Horace to get me one of these criers, and Sergei. I will have them executed as a clear message not to defy my rule.'

'Executed?' Takai hadn't been prepared for that. Was this what was required to be the King?

His father sat back in his chair. 'While we're at it, I will finally relieve Sir Marcus of his head. He's a living reminder of the loss in Ette. He must wear the blame for putting us in this wretched position in the first place.'

'Father, would you like to discuss it with the council first?'

'That won't be necessary. I am quite decided; this is what must be done. I want your mother to be there, at the execution, to show her support.'

'The Queen?' Despite her earlier promises, Takai's mother had evaded committing herself to a date for the progress with the King. He couldn't imagine her willingly attending an execution.

'Yes, the Queen and all of her ladies must be there. Everyone must see her by my side. They must know that their beloved Queen supports me in all things.'

'Father, I'm not sure the Queen—'

'I want it to happen as soon as possible. A week from today,' the King declared.

'A week...Isn't that the day of Sar's knighting?'

'I suppose it is.'

Had his father lost his mind? Takai tried to protest, but it was hopeless. The King appeared set on the idea.

'A good execution and a knighting is double the reason to celebrate. It will be an entire day and night of celebrations. I will leave it to you to speak to your mother about this. And when you do, get her to give a date for the progress.'

'Father. I must insist—'

But the doors to the King's privy chamber flung open to

reveal the Baroness, and the King was on his feet, leaving Takai to absorb the gruesome task ahead.

A COLD SWEAT had formed on the back of Takai's neck. While it was bad enough that his father was having him confront his mother, he also had to hurt Sar in the process. It was an altogether distasteful business – another unwelcome responsibility that came with his position.

Takai gritted his teeth as he strode through the Queen's empty presence chamber and pushed open the doors to the privy chamber. No one noticed his arrival; any noise was drowned out by the thwacking sounds of wooden sticks hitting together. Takai was taken aback at the sight of Gwyn and Arisa attacking each other with long wooden staffs. It was the last thing he had expected to see.

The pair wore loose-fitting tunics and tights in the Ivanian style, their wide sleeves flapping loudly as they moved. Gwyn advanced on Arisa with a rapid series of strikes. Arisa managed to block each one, but was forced to concede ground. The Queen shouted out her encouragement, while Sar issued instructions to Arisa.

'Hold your ground,' he cried. 'Parry!'

Arisa grimaced as Gwyn struck her hard on the arm, but she didn't surrender. She parried back, but Gwyn was unexpectedly adept, and with one sweeping movement brought her staff down on Arisa's hand, sending Arisa's stick clattering to the ground.

Arisa bit her lip, clearly suppressing a cry. Sar ran to her side and picked up her hands, checking her bloodied knuckles. Their closeness sent a strange sensation searing through Takai's chest. He stumbled back into the shadows, not wanting anyone to see his reaction.

Sar frowned. 'This is why I said no to swords. I think that's enough for today.'

'I'm fine.' Arisa picked up her staff and nodded to Gwyn. 'Again.'

'I think Sar's right,' Gwyn said. 'That's enough.'

The firm set of Arisa's mouth indicated she didn't agree. 'I'm not good enough yet. I have to keep going.'

Takai couldn't imagine what use Arisa had for fighting and why she needed to be any good at it.

Sar sighed. 'Fine. I know you well enough now to know it's pointless arguing with you, but if you're going to continue, you need to direct your focus.'

Arisa rolled her head from side to side. 'I'm focused.'

'You're not. When you're fighting, all you're seeing is Gwyn. You have to see past Gwyn, and see your enemy instead. Imagine, for instance, that Gwyn is Guthrie.'

'I don't think that's a good idea,' Arisa said. 'I might end up breaking her nose.'

'What?' Sar cried. '*You're* the one who broke Guthrie's nose?'

Arisa flashed a wicked grin, and Sar, Gwyn and the Queen burst out laughing. Takai had to bite his tongue to resist doing the same. Arisa was a never-ending parade of surprises. But what really captured Takai's interest was his mother's laugh. It was a musical tinkle he hadn't heard for years – or perhaps ever. Her face was alive with joy. He couldn't recall a time he had seen her so at ease. Takai longed to join the happy scene, but he feared his mother wouldn't welcome his presence.

'Alright, then.' Gwyn wiped a tear of laughter from her eye. 'Imagine I'm Theodora.'

Arisa shrugged. 'I don't know. I mean, I have wanted to punch her in the face a few times.' More laughter. 'Even so, I'm not sure I want to…' Her voice trailed off.

'The Chancellor,' the Queen suggested.

'Yes,' Gwyn cried. 'I can be the Chancellor.' She steepled her fingers on the top of her staff and smirked in a scarily accurate impression of Horace.

Arisa giggled. 'Not bad. The Chancellor it is.'

Arisa and Gwyn advanced on each other again, but Takai saw what Sar had seen – Arisa lacked focus and was quickly beaten, her staff sent flying across the room.

Wordlessly, Arisa stomped over and picked up the staff. She jutted out her jaw and resumed her fighting stance. 'This time I have someone else in mind.'

Gwyn nodded and, as before, the pair attacked each other in a flurry of flying tunics and spinning sticks. But this time it was different. Arisa blocked every one of Gwyn's strikes without giving any ground. Instead, she pushed Gwyn further and further back with a series of ear-splitting strikes. Her amber eyes flashed with grim determination, until Gwyn was pinned against the wall – but even then she didn't stop. Arisa held her staff against Gwyn's neck, and a shiver ran up Takai's spine. Even at this distance, he recognised the change in her. It was something he'd only seen in hardened soldiers.

A readiness to take another person's life.

'Arisa!' Sar and the Queen cried in unison.

Arisa gasped and dropped her staff as she returned from whatever dark place she had gone to.

'I'm so sorry,' she cried.

'It's alright.' Gwyn stilled Arisa's shaking hands. 'I'm fine.'

Sar exhaled loudly. 'Well, I guess I asked for focus. Just… who were you picturing when you did that?'

'The King,' came Arisa's pinched voice.

Takai's mother pursed her lips. 'I can understand that.'

Understand what? Takai thought, anger surging inside him. *Understand that the King should die?* What he'd just witnessed was akin to treason.

He stepped out of the shadows, clearing his throat loudly.

They all turned to look at him, in varying states of embarrassment – all except Arisa, who met his gaze with a scowl.

'My son.' The Queen approached him and fell into a low curtsey. Gwyn also curtsied, and eventually Arisa followed suit, albeit half-heartedly.

Sar strode toward him, his arms outstretched. 'Takai, you just missed—'

'I didn't miss anything, including the part where Arisa imagined Gwyn was my father when she nearly killed her.'

Arisa maintained a defiant stare, while Gwyn and the Queen exchanged an anxious look.

'It was just a training technique,' Sar insisted, his hands outstretched. 'It means nothing.'

'It may mean nothing to you, Sar,' Takai said, glaring at Arisa, 'but I couldn't say the same for her.'

The Queen followed Takai's gaze. 'So you two have met?'

'Several times,' he offered flatly. (*'Several times too many,'* he thought he heard Arisa mumble.) 'I have come to confirm a date for the progress,' he went on bluntly.

The Queen nodded. 'I have told the King I will comply.'

'But you must agree to a date.'

'I will discuss it with the King.'

Takai frowned, having failed in part of his task already. 'There is one other matter.'

The Queen nodded.

'There is to be an execution.'

Arisa and Gwyn gasped simultaneously.

'Who?' Takai's mother enquired in a low voice.

'Sir Marcus.'

The Queen's expression didn't change. 'I'm sure we expected as much.'

Takai knew there was no love lost between his mother and Sir Marcus, who had launched several failed invasion attempts against Ivane. 'The King also plans on executing the rebel leader, Sergei,' he continued. 'And at least one other. A Kengian.'

'What?' the Queen cried.

'What is their crime?' Arisa demanded.

'I understand it will be one of the Kengians who has been

publicly speaking out against the regime, and inciting support for the rebels.'

'Since when has speaking in support of justice been a crime?' Arisa cried.

'I suggest you hold your tongue on matters beyond your understanding and position,' Takai retorted.

'Takai,' his mother admonished.

'Enough, Mother. I will not have anyone, and I mean anyone' – he cast a cold gaze toward Arisa – 'threaten my father's regime, and my future rule.'

The Queen bowed her head. 'As you wish, my son.'

'And on the matter of the execution, you're required to attend with all of your ladies. You must show your support publicly. It must be clear you don't condone any such behaviour among our subjects.'

The Queen made to protest, but Takai spoke over her.

'I, your son, demand this of you!'

She dropped her eyes. 'When is the execution?'

Takai hesitated. This was what he had been dreading most. 'A week from today.'

'But Takai—' Sar cried.

'Yes, it's the day of your knighting. I'm sorry for that, my friend, truly sorry, but the date was not of my choosing.'

'No, I suspected as much,' Sar said miserably.

'If it's any consolation, the King believes it will further amplify the celebratory nature of the day. The court loves a good execution, he says.' Takai immediately regretted his words. He hadn't meant to sound so flippant.

'And that speaks to the truth of what is said about the cruelty of your father and his regime,' Arisa declared.

Takai compressed his lips. He refused to be baited further by the healer's ward. She wasn't worthy of his attention – not today, not ever.

'Good day,' he spat, and turned on his heel, exiting the room without looking back.

29

———

'Are you sure Erun knows what he's doing?' the Schoolmaster queried as he shovelled a fresh pile of manure into the bag Arisa was holding.

She screwed up her nose at the smell wafting up, but managed a nod in response.

'I'm not sure, Arisa. I know Erun is a talented scientist. One of the most talented men I know. But can he really do what he says he can?'

'He can,' she replied with certainty.

Erun had confided in the Schoolmaster about firesky. It had been necessary to get his help in delivering messages to Kengia. The Schoolmaster had proved his worth, and tracked down the Kengian Shaman who had her own starling messengers.

'As you say.' The Schoolmaster shovelled another load into the hessian bag. He stopped and looked around the stables; they were alone – Arisa had made sure of it. 'But surely it's too risky. If Horace were to harness firesky's powers, the whole known world would be in danger. I don't understand why Erun doesn't just refuse the task.'

She bit her tongue, knowing she was the reason Erun wouldn't refuse. She also wasn't about to tell the Schoolmaster

255

that firesky would never happen, because she had every intention of disposing of the King first – it just may not be done the way she'd originally planned. She had been kidding herself when she had thought a few lessons from Sar would give her the skills needed to overpower the Royal Guards and kill the King. But this realisation had only led her to identify a subtler solution. In the meantime, she had to stick to the script.

'There is nothing to worry about. While Horace believes he will get firesky as promised, Erun will not reveal its secrets. It can never be weaponised.'

The Schoolmaster pointed at the bag. 'Is that enough?'

'It will be, for today.' She twisted the top closed.

'I'm not sure the Chancellor will let Erun off so lightly,' the Schoolmaster went on. 'Not with the latest threats.'

'What threats?'

'You haven't heard? Sergei and his rebels are planning an attack on the castle. And this time they have support from many Kengians.'

'I had heard some Kengian farmers had joined with him, and there were criers speaking out in his support.'

She recalled the scene with the Prince when he'd told her that one of those criers was destined to be executed. The thought sent a fresh surge of anger through her.

'He doesn't just have the support of farmers, but many other Kengians. The general consensus is that it's too dangerous to wait for a prophesied Water Catcher. Even if the Water Catcher comes into being, it will be too late for Kengia, and probably Lamore. Many Kengians are trying to flee back to their homeland, braving the winter seas in leaky boats. And those who remain in Lamore are preparing to attack the castle with Sergei.'

Fear shot through Arisa like a lightning bolt. What if the rebels did make it to the castle? What would that mean for the good and kind people she'd met at court? People who didn't deserve to be lumped in with a cruel regime. People who didn't deserve to die in a violent attack.

'It's madness,' she assured herself aloud. 'They would never be able to get through the castle's defences and the King's forces.'

'I agree, but Sergei is not easily intimidated. He says it's time enough they took control of their own destinies.'

'It's a terrible plan. They will die needlessly.'

'Yes, but they believe it's better to die on their own terms than wait for the King's army to come after them.'

Arisa shook her head. 'They would be better served preparing to protect their homes and families when the Northemers arrive, because I fear it's inevitable.'

'It's too late. The King has learnt of Sergei's plans, and word has it he is prepared to send an army to stop them.' The Schoolmaster's brow furrowed. 'Some say he would send his army to defeat his own people before the Northemers.'

Arisa had heard the same thing from Sar. It hadn't surprised her, as Horace was hoping he would have firesky before spring, and wouldn't need the army to defeat the Northemers. But she had to find a way to stop Sergei from attacking. Too many people she cared about could get hurt.

'What if we were to send word the moment there were any specific plans to mobilise the army against Sergei or his supporters?' she suggested. 'I have good friends here, who are among the Duke's men. I will know the moment anything is planned.'

The Schoolmaster shook his head. 'It doesn't address the matter of firesky. Have you considered that if Horace gets hold of it, he may use it against the rebels?'

She gasped. 'You have told the rebels about firesky?'

'No. Only the Shaman and I know of it, but it's a heavy burden to carry.'

'Erun knows what he's doing.'

'But what if he doesn't, Arisa?' the Schoolmaster cried. 'How will we know if he has failed to protect firesky's secrets?

We will need to be informed, and informed quickly, if the rebels have any hope of defending themselves.'

'Don't you mean so they can launch their attack?'

He shrugged. 'What should I tell them?'

'Tell Sergei and his supporters we shall send word of any plans to send the army after them.' She paused, choosing her next words carefully. 'And if there is any reason they need to act more urgently—'

'You mean if firesky becomes a threat?' he pressed.

She frowned, knowing the Schoolmaster wanted some kind of alert system. Some warning that could reach Sergei quickly.

There was only one option.

'If it becomes a threat, we will send a signal. An unmistakable signal for everyone to see.'

'What kind of signal?'

Arisa gritted her teeth, conscious of the magnitude of what she was about to say. 'Erun will launch firesky himself.'

The Schoolmaster's eyes widened. 'He can't!'

'He has told me it is no more than pretty coloured lights in the sky, and that is all he'll ever produce. Weaponising it is another matter. That takes more time, and Erun will give his life before seeing it happen.'

'So, you're saying there will be time to mount a pre-emptive attack on the castle if needed, before Horace has a chance to do anything with firesky.'

'Yes, but no such signal will be needed.' She was sure of it.

'I will convey your message to the rebels, and hope they agree to stand down for now.'

'You have to do more than hope,' Arisa implored him. 'You need to convince Sergei not to attack the castle.'

The Schoolmaster wrung his hands.

'You have to convince them,' she said again. 'You have to.'

He gave a tight smile. 'I'll do my best.'

'Thank you. And thank you for helping with this today.' She pointed to the hessian bag.

'You're welcome. Though, when I agreed to come and give you lessons here, I didn't expect to be shovelling manure and smuggling secret messages.'

'Neither did I,' Arisa moaned as she lifted up the sack.

'Are you alright with that?'

She screwed up her nose at the stench. 'As alright as I can be.'

'Until our next lesson?'

'Yes, until then.'

The Schoolmaster picked up his satchel of books, and left her to carry the bag of manure back up to the north-west tower.

Arisa made her way through the castle to Erun's rooms. The guard unlocked the door and ushered her in quickly. They had long since given up examining the contents of the foul-smelling bags she brought regularly to Erun.

She stepped into the small anteroom and dumped the contents of the bag into a sealed barrel in the corner. Thankfully the smell dissipated when she secured the lid. Arisa reached out to open the door to the main room, but stopped on hearing two people speaking in hushed tones. One voice was female, and the other was Erun's.

She opened the door a small crack and listened. She could only catch a few words.

'So, it is what I suspect?' It was Gwyn's voice, Arisa realised.

'It is,' came Erun's reply.

'You've hidden the secret well.'

'I have taken every measure.'

'But why didn't you get word to me? Why wouldn't you tell me?'

'It wasn't worth the risk.'

'The risk!'

'There was no way I could be sure to get a message to you without the chance of one of Horace's spies intercepting it.'

'Do you know the pain you have caused?'

'It's the price we have to pay to protect our secrets.'

Arisa was puzzled. She had thought Erun confided in her about everything. But he had never told her anything about Gwyn. What secrets were they hiding that Erun didn't trust Arisa enough to tell her?

'We may now be paying that price.'

No response came. Arisa stepped in closer to hear better, but her skirt rustled loudly, giving away her presence. She pushed the door open and made a show of her arrival.

'Arisa,' Gwyn cried.

Erun looked at her intently, as if he were trying to determine how much she had heard.

'Gwyn?' she remarked innocently.

'Actually, I was looking for you,' Gwyn said. 'The Queen is making plans for the progress – of course, there isn't a date yet, but when we do go, she would like you to join us.'

'Oh…' Arisa wasn't sure how to respond. The idea of travelling with the Lamorian Court, as if she were one of them, didn't sit well with her.

'It will be an opportunity to see some of the wonderful countryside. I believe we will go as far as Shizen Lake and Falls.'

Shizen Lake. Right at the base of the Nymoi Alps. The trip was starting to sound more appealing, though in Arisa's mind, the progress would never go ahead. Not after she was done. She looked to Erun, who gave her an encouraging smile.

'Thank you,' she said eventually. 'I would be honoured.'

Gwyn gave Arisa a fond smile. 'Splendid. Good day to you both,' she said and left them.

Arisa gave Erun a piercing look, but he smiled back at her blankly.

'What were you and Gwyn talking about?'

He rubbed the nape of his neck. 'Nothing of importance. Did you get more—'

'Dung for the saltpetre. It's in the barrel. I recruited the Schoolmaster to help me.'

Erun laughed heartily. Arisa didn't join in. She was angry

that he wasn't going to tell her the truth of his conversation with Gwyn. Then she remembered she had her own secrets, and a job to do while she was in Erun's rooms.

'How is it going?' She gestured at the flasks of potions and the bubbling beaker set over a flame on the table.

'My real firesky experiment is on track. I have successfully extracted saltpetre from the manure and conducted some small tests.'

'It's quite an impressive display you have here.' Arisa made a show of peering at the labels of vials lined up on shelves along the wall. *Strychnine.* She needed to find strychnine.

'Most of what you see is for Horace's benefit,' Erun continued. 'That being said, I will need to fully test firesky out in the open at some point.'

'Is that a good idea?' *Strychnine.* There it was.

'We need to know if it works.'

She nodded, hoping Erun wouldn't notice as she slipped the vial of clear liquid into her pocket. 'I had to assure the Schoolmaster that firesky's secrets will be kept safe and away from Horace.'

'Good.'

'He wasn't convinced. He fears Horace could use it against the rebels.'

'He probably would if given the opportunity. Which he won't be.' Erun stressed the last words.

'In any case, Sergei has the support of many Kengians, and together they are planning to attack the castle.'

'Madness!'

'That's what I said. I told the Schoolmaster he must keep the rebels at bay for now, and we would send word of any plan to mobilise the King's army against them. I told him that if we thought for a moment Horace could get his hands on firesky, you would launch the light display yourself. That it would act as an immediate warning.'

Erun took off his eyeglasses and rubbed his eyes. 'I suppose it's the best option. Hopefully, we won't need to use it.' He put his glasses back on, turning to her with a tired smile. 'So, what have you been up to?'

It had been several days since she had seen her guardian. Horace had reduced the number of visits she could make, saying Erun could have no distractions. The Schoolmaster had taken over all of her lessons.

'Not much. Just the usual life of a courtier. Dancing, sewing, cards, riding.' She didn't add stick-fighting to the list, and was careful to curl her hand back inside her sleeve, where Erun couldn't see her bruised and bloody knuckles.

'Riding!'

'Sar says I'm a natural, but I put my success down to the horse.'

'It must be an exceptional horse?'

'It is. She is the most beautiful creature. The colour of liquid gold.'

Erun pushed his glasses back up his nose. 'Liquid gold, you say?'

'Yes. Apparently she has been here for years. She belonged to a Kengian, and Horace kept her.'

Erun stood up and walked toward the window, his hands clasped behind his back. 'But you say no one has been able to ride her?'

'Sar has been trying to tame her, but no one else can get near her. Except me, that is,' Arisa said proudly.

Erun wandered back toward her. 'You rode this horse?'

'I did. Her name is Meteor and she is magnificent.'

'There was nothing else, say, *strange* about this animal?'

Arisa hesitated. She had been planning on telling Erun about the vision she'd had when riding Meteor. About the strange silver-haired man she had seen. She had intended on telling him about the wolf, too, and about how she'd found the Firemaster's book, hoping he could explain what had happened and whether it had anything to do with her developing powers.

She would have told him about the arrogant Prince and his order for her to attend the executions as well – but then she remembered the secrets Erun and Gwyn were hiding.

'No.' She shook her head. 'Nothing.'

Erun scrutinised her face closely. 'You've got nothing else to tell me?'

'Not a thing,' she assured him with a bright smile.

He appeared as if he were going to ask her something, but changed his mind. Arisa suppressed a sigh of relief, and slipped her hand into her pocket, assuring herself the vial of strychnine was still there.

She just had to keep her plan to herself for a few more days. Then everything could go back to normal. She and Erun could go back to how they had been before, and there wouldn't need to be any more secrets between them.

30

———————

akai's ornamental robes made his skin itch. His physical unease was only made worse by the cold and wintry fog hanging over the castle grounds. It was late morning, but the grey, gloomy mist refused to budge. It was a stark reminder that today was execution day.

The ornate throne Takai sat on was hard and unforgiving. He shifted uncomfortably and looked around the balcony. He noted his father's disturbingly jubilant face as the King smiled and waved to the assembled crowd on the ground below. Every noble of note was in attendance, with the exception of Guthrie, who was still banished at Calliope. There was also a contingent from Obira – town officials and the like. They would make suitable witnesses without posing any threat of danger to the court.

'Long live King Delrik,' a few members of the crowd cried out, followed by 'Long live Prince Takai.' Takai winced. It didn't seem right to be cheering at what was a solemn and, in his view, distasteful occasion. Yet the crowd was in a celebratory mood. The executioner in his black hood stood on the gallows, urging the crowd to clap him on. There were stalls selling ale, pies and sweets. And all were dressed in their finery.

There was one person in particular, though, who had

surprised Takai by their lack of enthusiasm. Horace was standing behind the King, stony-faced and silent. Takai had heard that despite the Chancellor's redoubled efforts, he'd been unable to capture Sergei. This had left Sir Marcus and a Kengian woman as the only people to be executed.

Sar stood behind Takai in his Royal Guard uniform. His jaw set firmly, he appeared to be as uncomfortable as Takai was. Takai couldn't say for sure how Sar felt, because he had avoided his friend since the confrontation in the Queen's rooms. In fact, he had avoided everyone. Partly out of the shame he felt for his part in the encounter, but also out of anger that Sar and the others had been so disrespectful of his father. He had particularly been avoiding places he may run into Arisa. He was torn by the conflicting feelings he had around her. Today, though, there would be no escaping her. The Queen and her ladies were expected at any moment.

'Your Highness,' came a voice beside him. He turned to see his cousin Willem, the Earl of Talbot, bowing awkwardly before him.

'Cousin!' Takai jumped up to embrace him. 'Don't call me Your Highness. I'm just Takai to you.'

'Of course. *Your Highness.*' Willem grinned.

'It's so good to see you. It seems a lifetime since I was at Talbot. I have missed your company.'

'And it is grand to see you too. I just wish it were in more agreeable circumstances.' Willem cast his gaze toward the scene below.

'You're right. At least there will be reason to celebrate tonight.'

Willem's eyes lit up. 'Can you believe they're going to knight that big oaf?' He jerked his head in Sar's direction.

Takai thought he saw Sar's jaw twitch, ever so slightly. 'There'll be plenty of time to mess with our friend's mind later. He's on duty now.'

Willem grinned again, before glancing behind Takai and bowing.

The Queen had arrived. Behind her was Willem's mother, the Duchess of Lakeford, then Horace's wife, Countess Datanya, followed by Theodora, Gwyn and Arisa. The Duchess, Gwyn and Arisa were dressed head to toe in black, while the Countess and Theodora wore matching scarlet gowns. On any other day, Takai would have admired how becoming Theodora looked, but today the sight of her made him grimace.

His gaze went to Arisa. Her face was drawn and pinched. His heart lurched, but he reminded himself that she wouldn't appreciate his sympathy. She had made it abundantly clear she hated him.

'Lady Mother,' he addressed the Queen, as she took her throne next to the King. His father gave her a broad smile and grabbed her hand possessively. His mother's face was unreadable.

'It looks like it's going to begin.' Willem nodded below as Sir Marcus was led to the side of the gallows. 'We will talk properly later.' He stepped back to take his place next to the Duke, who had also just arrived.

Takai looked down. He barely recognised the former Governor of Ette. Sir Marcus was known to be a vain man, always dressed in the finest and latest fashions. Today, he wore a dirt-stained shirt and breeches, and his feet were bare, his face grubby. His beard had grown long and unruly.

Next came the Kengian woman. She was slight of figure, wearing a cap and a torn tunic. She looked around wildly as the crowd taunted her with cries of 'Kengian witch' or 'sorceress'. It was to be expected; most Lamorians feared Kengians, whether they had powers or not.

'No! No!' The woman struggled against the guards holding her. She shook her head so violently that her cap flew off, releasing a mane of frizzy red curls.

Then came a great yelp of pain, but it wasn't from the prisoner. It came from the far end of the balcony.

Takai swung around to see Arisa speaking frantically to Gwyn. She was pointing down to the scene below and shaking her head vigorously. Gwyn was patting her hand, trying to comfort her, but it appeared hopeless. Arisa gave a loud sob, which this time attracted stares from the crowd below, and an angry glare from the King.

'What is that commotion?' he demanded. 'Horace, deal with it.'

Horace beckoned to Theodora, who sauntered over and curtsied to the King and Takai. 'Your Majesty. Your Highness. Father.'

Horace pointed to Arisa. 'What is going on over there?'

Theodora rolled her eyes dramatically. 'Apparently, Arisa knows the Kengian woman. Doesn't surprise me that she would mix with such unsavoury types.'

'Horace, have the girl thrown out,' the King ordered.

The Chancellor gave one of his unsettling smirks and made to approach Arisa.

The words fell from Takai's mouth before he knew what he was saying. 'Father, let me see to…the ward. I will ensure she is managed.'

The King motioned for him to go ahead.

Takai found Gwyn pleading with Arisa to calm down, but to no avail. 'I'm sorry to intrude,' he ventured softly.

Arisa looked up at him, her amber eyes impossibly large.

His heart lurched again. No matter how strange or frustrating she was, or how much she disliked him, he somehow couldn't bear to see her in so much pain.

'Gwyn is right,' he urged. 'You must calm down. I fear you're upsetting the King.'

She stopped sobbing momentarily to give him a sharp look. 'I don't give a damn about upsetting anyone.'

Takai bent down and dropped his voice. 'I only mean to say

that I don't want to see any harm come to you.' From the glare she maintained, he guessed Arisa was unconvinced. 'Tell me what ails you,' he went on.

'Besides the fact that we're here to celebrate the murder of two people?'

Takai winced.

'What *ails* me is that I know that woman.' She pointed at the red-haired prisoner. 'Her name is Lina, and she doesn't deserve to die. She is no more a criminal than you or I.'

'Our laws say differently.' The words sounded weak, even to him.

'Anything she is accused of saying or doing has been born of grief. She lost her only child, her son, Hyando, on the night of the blood moon. Lost in a terrible accident caused by Royal Guards. I was there, and I can tell you if it weren't for the callous and reckless behaviour of those men, Lina's son would still be here today. The only thing she is guilty of is being a Kengian, and a grieving mother.'

Takai gulped. He wanted to believe everything Arisa said. He wanted to provide some comfort to her but he didn't have the power to do so. 'I'm sorry to hear that. But I'm afraid there is nothing to be done. The King ordered that anyone caught inciting violence against the regime, and supporting the rebellion, is guilty of treason. The punishment being death.'

Arisa looked at him with her strange amber eyes, her brow deeply furrowed. 'Let her be spared. Surely there's another prisoner, a real criminal in the dungeons who can take her place.'

'Arisa,' Gwyn implored. 'It's not for us to decide who should and shouldn't die.'

Arisa looked over to the King. 'No, but it is up to him. He can decide whether to save or kill an innocent woman.'

'Unfortunately, she isn't innocent in the eyes of the law,' Takai said. 'The King is quite decided.'

'I'm afraid my son is right.' The Queen had appeared at

their side. 'The King believes he must send a message to the people.'

'Couldn't that message be that he is a kind king? That he has brought Lina here today as warning to others, but as a merciful king, he will spare her life?' Arisa looked back to Takai. 'Can't you say that to him? Can't you convince him?'

Takai shook his head miserably.

Arisa turned back toward the gallows. The guards were leading the woman up onto the scaffold. 'Please do something,' she begged.

'I can't,' Takai said. 'The King must have his execution. It would only make him look weak to pardon her now.'

His mother nodded solemnly in agreement. 'The King's pride is at stake. He must have his execution.'

Takai's gaze shot to his mother. That was it. The King did value his pride, but he valued one thing even above that.

'Unless…There isn't exactly much in the way of precedence, at least not in our time…but it may work,' he said. 'I think it's an Ivanian custom. Something you told me of as a child, Mother.'

Realisation dawned on the Queen and Gwyn's faces. 'Yes. It could work,' the Queen said.

'What is it?' Arisa cried.

'The Queen could ask for the prisoners' lives to be spared,' Takai explained.

Arisa's eyes grew wider. 'She could?'

'Yes, the Queen could call upon the King to show mercy, out of his love for her,' Gwyn added excitedly.

'And I know there is one thing my father values above his own pride, and that's the idea of his own gallantry,' Takai said. 'He yearns to play the part of the chivalrous knight.'

'I think it's our best option, Arisa. Our only hope,' Gwyn said.

'Then please,' Arisa appealed desperately to the Queen, 'please do it.'

'I must hurry.' The Queen lifted up the bottom of her skirts and raced down the balcony stairs.

Takai watched on as the executioner placed a noose around the shaking woman's neck, and the crowd began to cheer. He looked back at his father, whose gaze was fixed on the scene below. Theodora caught his eye and raised a suspicious brow. She scanned the balcony, clearly looking for something amiss – and then she leant over to speak to her father. Takai was about to run over to her and do anything to buy his mother more time, when he heard the Countess shriek.

'The Queen! The Queen! What is she doing?'

Queen Sofia was standing in front of the crowd, just below the scaffold, looking directly up at the King.

The crowd hushed. The Queen curtsied down low and bent forward, her arms outstretched until her chest was on the ground.

The King's eyes narrowed.

Everyone waited silently for one of them to speak.

Eventually, the Queen raised her head and sat back on her knees. 'My lord King and husband.' Her voice rang out across the grounds, true and clear. 'I thank thee for allowing me to be by your side today. You have been so gracious to forgive all my sins against you, and to have welcomed me back into your arms.'

The King lifted his chin, ever so slightly.

'I am here today, among your people, to show them I am your servant. I am here to show them I am obedient to you and your cause. I have come to show them I am your greatest supporter, and that I am your true wife.'

The crowd was silent, as transfixed by the Queen's speech as Takai was. Her words appeared carefully chosen and deliberate. When she said she was the King's 'true wife', she was publicly declaring an end to their separation.

'Today, I see my husband only has the best interests of his people at heart. He is not cruel, as some say. My husband is the kindest of men, the greatest of benefactors and the most merciful of kings.'

The King was smiling broadly now.

The Queen stood up, unconcerned with the dirt all over her front. 'Which is why I ask this of you now.'

There was a long pause before the King's strong voice rang out. 'What do you ask of me, wife?'

'I ask that you spare the lives of these two people. That this be a warning of what will come to anyone who threatens the crown in the future. But it can also show that you are merciful.'

A great mumbling started in the crowd, as well as some boos and cries of protest.

Takai could almost see his father turning the proposition over in his mind.

'Please, grant me this one wish, out of your love for your people, and your love for your *one true wife*.' The Queen emphasised the last three words perfectly.

Takai sat down next to his father and leant in toward him. 'Father, I think what my mother says holds merit.'

The King gave a small nod, though his eyes never left the Queen.

'You can't do what she asks,' Horace interjected. 'The people expect an execution. You can't disappoint them. It would be a sign of weakness.'

The King tilted his head and frowned. It appeared as if he was wavering toward Horace's argument.

Frantically, Takai wondered what he could do. There must be some compromise that the King would agree to…Takai looked down at the prisoners, his gaze falling on Sir Marcus. He took a deep breath…It was the only other option. 'Perhaps one of the prisoners could be spared,' he suggested. 'That way, there would still be an execution.'

The King turned to him and smiled. Then he stood and looked down at the Queen. 'It is true, my Queen. Above all, I am a merciful king.'

The Queen beamed up at him and the mumbling in the crowd started again.

The King raised his hand to silence them. 'But I cannot disappoint my people who came here for an execution, and I cannot let all crimes go unpunished.'

Queen Sofia's smile froze.

'I also believe that a *true wife* should be granted favours from her loving husband, especially since my wife has so graciously agreed to a date for our progress…It is to be later this very week.' A murmur of excitement went around the crowd. The King narrowed his gaze at his wife, and she gave a small nod. 'So today, I will spare the life of one of these criminals.'

There was a mixture of cheers and boos. The King put up his hand and the crowd quieted down again.

'And you, my wife, shall make the choice.' He sat down with a satisfied smile on his face.

'Your Majesty, you must order the Queen to spare Sir Marcus,' Horace urged. 'He can still be valuable to us.'

'It is for the Queen to decide,' the King reiterated.

Takai watched as his mother sat still, as if absorbing the gravity of what she was about to do. She stood up slowly and walked over to Sir Marcus. He dropped to his knees before her.

'Your Majesty, please spare my life. I will be forever in your debt and your service.'

'Sir Marcus.' The Queen's voice rang out across the yard once more. 'I do not wish the death of any person in this world, and I would never have asked for this responsibility. But here we are, and I must decide.'

'I have been a good servant to His Majesty,' he clutched his hands to his chest, 'and I have done nothing but what was asked of me.'

'Quite. You were asked to invade my homeland, and you tried to do so on more than one occasion. I suppose my family and I should thank you for your ineptness, but I do not thank you for your attempts, and my husband does not thank you for your failures. On top of this, you kidnapped innocent citizens and forced them into your service. Countless people have suffered because of your deficiencies and cruelty.'

The Queen paused and appeared to take a deep breath.

'And that is why today, Sir Marcus, you will give your life.'

Sir Marcus grabbed at her skirts. 'No, Your Majesty—'

'That is the price you must pay for your actions. It is the legacy you leave and will be etched on your soul. You must come to peace with it in your next life. But remember this. It was you, and your actions alone, that put the noose around your neck.'

The Queen turned abruptly and made her way back up to the balcony.

'Your Majesty,' Sir Marcus cried out after her.

'My wife has spoken. Release the woman,' the King ordered.

'Sire—' Horace's protest was shut down by a thunderous look from the King.

The hangman removed the noose from the Kengian woman's neck. She fell heavily to the ground and was carried away. Sir Marcus was dragged up in her place, and the crowd began to cheer.

Takai had been right. Any death would do for them. Today a man would give his life for their entertainment. It didn't make a difference that Sir Marcus wasn't the best of men. No one deserved to die in such a manner. It sickened Takai – particularly the part he had played.

He averted his eyes from the gruesome scene and looked over at Arisa. She mouthed the words *thank you*. He gave a small nod.

Their eyes were still locked when he heard the snap of the scaffold floor dropping away, and the crack of Sir Marcus's neck breaking. It was over.

Yet something else had just begun.

31

————

The guard banged the tray down heavily on the table in front of Erun, spilling broth everywhere. His usual serving boy must be occupied at the Great Hall for Sar's knighting ceremony and feast, an event Arisa was to attend – but first she had to speak to her guardian.

Saving Lina had had one critical consequence. Now a date had been set for the progress. A date only a few days away. Arisa figured the King hadn't wanted to risk the Queen changing her mind. While the court made panicked preparations, Arisa tried to digest the implications for herself and Erun.

Her guardian was quite determined to deliver firesky for the progress, but she would not have it. She would finally have to enact her own plans. She would have to kill the King, and soon. Her stomach clenched at the thought of going through with it. With an actual deadline, it felt suddenly more real. Somehow she would have to find the strength to do it. It was the only way to stop firesky getting into the wrong hands.

Erun ignored his meal and paced the room frantically, mumbling to himself about firesky. He had experienced little success so far, with most of his experiments ending in a pathetic little fizzle or a burst of flames.

'You can't do it. There isn't enough time now,' Arisa reasoned.

'But I must do it. I have to protect you.'

'Don't worry about me. Everything is going to be fine. Just promise me—'

Erun stopped in his tracks. 'What do you mean, everything is going to be fine? What are you hiding from me?'

A lump stuck in her throat. Erun was like a bloodhound with things like this. When he caught a whiff of something, he wouldn't let go. She had to distract him somehow.

Arisa wandered over to his worktable and started reading his notes, cross-referencing them with the open Firemaster's book beside them. She couldn't spot any obvious mistakes. She ran her finger down the page that bore the handwriting of the last Firemaster—

A burst of energy rushed up her arm, and a vision came to her.

She was in the same room, but Erun wasn't there. Instead, there was a woman with dark hair tied up in a bun, wearing traditional Kengian dress. The woman sat bent over the table, scribbling away with her quill. Arisa leant over to read her notes. Her writing was identical to the last Firemaster's. She was writing so furiously she hadn't noticed she had smudged the last part of one word. A letter that began as a 'u' now looked like an 'a'. That one letter made a huge difference in Old Kengian. It changed a particular number by a factor of one hundred.

'That's it,' Arisa whispered to herself. 'It's not "erada", it's "eradu".'

'What did you say?' Erun cried, jolting Arisa back to the present.

'Nothing, just a—' She fumbled for an explanation to put Erun off the scent, but he had caught her meaning.

'Of course,' he cried, staring at the Firemaster's book. He began to rapidly write recalculations.

'No, Erun—' she tried to protest, but was interrupted by the arrival of a guard. It was Klaus, Sar's man, who had escorted Erun to the Chancellor on his first day at the castle. He wasn't one of Erun's usual guards, who were always Horace's men.

'Klaus, what are you doing here?' Erun asked.

'The Chancellor has ordered that his guards be given the opportunity to attend the celebrations and that I be deprived of such festivities. I guess that's what I get for being so closely aligned with Sar and not Horace's son.'

'The celebrations, Arisa,' Erun said. 'You must go.'

'But…' They hadn't finished their conversation. Arisa had to convince him to give up on firesky…but she knew it was impossible. To change his mind, she'd have to tell her guardian the truth, which she wasn't about to do. He couldn't know her real plans – plans she hoped to put in place that very night.

A GASP ESCAPED Arisa's throat as she entered the Great Hall with Gwyn.

'The Lady Gwyn and Maid Arisa,' the herald announced as they arrived for Sar's knighting ceremony.

The day had started so darkly with the execution. Arisa had thought she'd never recover from the shock of seeing Lina on the scaffold. She had been trying to reconcile in her mind why the Prince had intervened to save the Kengian woman. And while she wouldn't lose any sleep over Sir Marcus's death, she hadn't forgotten how close the King had come to executing Lina. It strengthened her resolve to go ahead with her mission.

Arisa tucked her hand inside the pocket of her gown. She felt the coldness of the glass vial there and closed her eyes, going through the steps of the plan in her mind.

She was intimately familiar with strychnine. Erun prescribed it sometimes, in the smallest amounts, to aid digestion or increase energy levels. In larger doses, it was a deadly poison; within minutes of consumption it led to extreme muscle spasms, before resulting in death by asphyxiation. Arisa had been waiting for an opportunity to get close enough to the King to use the poison – tonight would have to be that opportunity, even if it meant wrecking Sar's night. With this many people in one place and distracted with the celebrations, it would be impossible to know for sure who the assassin was. It had to happen tonight. In the meantime, she had to play the part of an excited girl attending her first royal celebration.

She discovered almost immediately how easy it was to slip into that role. Gwyn linked her arm in Arisa's, and Arisa could feel the joy emanating from her. Gwyn's enthusiasm was only amplified by the magnificence of the Great Hall.

Other than seeing the hall in passing, Arisa had never had occasion to visit it. She had taken all of her meals in the Queen's rooms or her own, so she had no point of comparison for how the hall normally looked. She could only assume it didn't shine as brightly as it did tonight.

The hall's proportions were ridiculously grand. The intricate wood carvings and gold-painted beams drew the eye upwards to the high loft ceiling, pressed with gold metal tiles. A group of musicians was playing in the gallery above.

Everything Arisa's eyes were drawn to took her breath away. There were tapestries and banners displaying coats of arms from each noble house, all hanging from richly panelled walls. Two rows of trestle tables and benches ran the length of the room, and a dais with a single long table sat at the far end. Each table was dressed with crisp white cloth trimmed with gold thread, and decorated with overflowing vases of flowers, greenery and fruit. Shining silver plates were laid out with matching cutlery. There was even a glint of gold plate from the table on the dais. And bringing the entire hall to life were rows of golden triple-tiered candelabras, holding long taper candles.

Then there were all the courtiers dressed in their finery. Arisa looked down at her own dress self-consciously. It was another borrowed gown from Gwyn, this time in green, white and silver. Gwyn had also loaned her an emerald brooch, which she wore at the centre of her neckline, and emerald slippers of the finest silk. Her hair hung loose, with a few curls pinned back with pearl pins. She looked the part, but couldn't help but feel completely out of place. She grabbed the silver medallion around her neck and twisted it nervously with her free hand.

'You look beautiful,' Gwyn reassured her, with a squeeze of her arm.

'As do you.' Arisa wasn't exaggerating. Gwyn wore a black velvet gown embroidered with gold roses. Long strings of pearls hung from her neck. She was every part the proud mother.

'This way.' Gwyn led her to the front of the hall. 'The ceremony is beginning soon.'

They would have arrived sooner, had Gwyn not had to help Sar prepare. He had been nervous, despite all his practice, and was now waiting anxiously in an adjoining room.

They walked toward the dais, where the King, Queen and Prince were sitting. Horace was next to the Queen. His solemn black robes matched his sullen expression. Gwyn stopped as they reached the last table in the line to their left, directly adjacent to the dais. Already seated at its far end were the Duke of Lakeford and his wife, the Duchess, as well as the Countess and Theodora.

A young man Arisa recognised from the balcony earlier that day was sitting nearest to them, and waved enthusiastically. Gwyn acknowledged him with a nod. 'Willem, the Earl of Talbot,' she said to Arisa by way of explanation.

'Where are we to sit?' Arisa asked, conscious of Theodora's cat eyes on her.

'Right here, of course.'

'Here? I can't sit here. This table is for the highest-ranking nobles in Lamore.'

'Yes, everyone sits in precedence. Recognising, of course, that I am the equivalent of a princess in my own lands.'

'Gwyn, you mistake me. I understand why you're sitting here, but why me?'

'Because you're with me.'

'But—' Arisa had wanted to be in a far less conspicuous position.

Gwyn gave her arm another squeeze. 'It will be fine.'

The Duchess beckoned Gwyn to take a seat next to her, forcing the Countess to shuffle further along the bench. On the opposite side of the table, Willem was indicating a seat next to him. Arisa ignored the daggers Theodora was shooting at her and wandered back toward the friendly-looking earl.

Willem stood up to greet her, albeit a little awkwardly. So this was the Duke's supposedly sickly son. Arisa noted his sallow complexion and fine features, but his round hazel eyes were clear and friendly, and he seemed to wear a permanent lopsided grin on his face. She remembered how highly Sar spoke of the earl.

'Lady Arisa, I'm Willem, and I would be honoured if you sat with me.'

'Lord Talbot. It is I who is honoured.'

His crooked smile widened. 'Willem, please. I have to say I couldn't wait to meet you in person. I have heard so much about you.'

She shifted nervously in her seat. 'Only good things, I hope.'

'Of course. If I hadn't been asked by Gwyn to save a place for you, I would have done it of my own volition. I had to see for myself if what I'd been told was true.'

'Really, Sar shouldn't have talked me up so.'

Willem cocked his head to one side. 'Sar?'

'No? Then who?'

'Prince Takai, of course.'

What was this trickery? Arisa knew the disbelief she felt was clear on her face. Despite the kindness the Prince had shown earlier that day, she was sure he still hated her. What exactly had Takai been saying about her?

Their conversation was interrupted by a blast of trumpets

reverberating around the hall. The ceremony was about to begin.

'Nominating Sar for a knighthood is undoubtedly the best thing my father has ever done,' Willem said enthusiastically.

The King stood in front of the dais in his red-and-gold military regalia. He wore a crown of sparkling rubies, each the size of a large grape. Around his neck was an ermine-trimmed cape of red velvet, and there was a gold sword in his scabbard.

The Duke, dressed in his own military uniform, took his position next to the King. The trumpets finished and the entire hall fell silent.

'Sar, Captain of the Royal Guards, Lieutenant of the King's Army and son of Sir Elos, Knight of the Order of the King,' the herald announced. A flourish of horns and strings rang out around the hall.

Arisa turned back to the main doorway to see a flushed-looking Sar make his entrance. He wore white ceremonial robes under a shiny silver chestplate. His flowing red cape touched the floor. She felt a flutter of pride as she watched him march slowly toward the dais.

Finally, he reached the end of the aisle and stopped before the King. Sar dropped to his knees and began reciting the words he and Arisa had practised together.

'My lord and King, I pledge my eternal fealty to you.' He held out his silver ceremonial sword and offered it to the King.

'Who sponsors this man in his quest to become a knight?'

Lakeford stepped forward. 'I, Your Majesty, the Duke of Lakeford.'

The King nodded and Lakeford stepped back. He indicated for Sar to stand. Sar got to his feet and sheathed his sword.

'I thank thee for your service to me, and your country, and accept your fealty and sword,' came the King's solemn voice.

'Thank you, Your Majesty.'

'You must now take the oath of a knight. Do you agree to take such an oath?'

'I do, gladly.'

'What is your pledge?'

Sar raised his voice and began reciting in perfect Old Kengian.

'Dalusami kichisya wlauro mamy.
Urtusa whayl naht. Rola yold. Reb bevar.
Fren venure koysou genash taprea.
Whayl raifiak akaty myten oppol.'

Arisa translated the oath in her head: *I pledge to always defend those who can't defend themselves. Speak only the truth. Be loyal to my nation. Be brave. Never avoid perilous paths out of fear. And only fight my opponent fairly.*

'I accept your pledge,' the King said. 'Kneel now, before me.'

Sar knelt.

The King brought forth his golden sword and lowered it to touch each of Sar's shoulders. 'I dub thee Sir Sar, Knight of the Order of the King.'

The hall broke out in thunderous applause.

Sar stood up and looked back at the room. His trademark dimpled grin was wider than Arisa had ever seen it. She noticed Gwyn wiping a tear from her cheek. The ceremony had gone perfectly.

'Let the feast begin!' the King declared.

A steward clapped his hands, and doors at the end of the hall opened to admit an endless stream of pages and servers carrying jugs of mulled wine and overflowing plates. The first dish was a whole stuffed peacock, seemingly intact, with all of its feathers on show. Then there was a full roasted pig, golden-skinned ducks, plump trout and geese. Arisa felt a pang of guilt at the extravagance of it all. She would be feasting tonight while many Lamorians would be starving. Sometimes, she wondered if she was turning into one of them – a courtier – but it was hard not to get caught up in the theatre of it all.

Each plate went first to the King's dais, where he, the Queen and Takai made their selections. The King would then send particular dishes to his favourites around the hall.

'I'm nearly full already,' Arisa said to Willem as she accepted a piece of carved venison covered in a richly spiced galantine sauce. After sampling several other dishes, she held her hand to her belly contentedly.

'You'll need to leave some more room. This is only the first couple of courses,' Willem explained between mouthfuls of food.

'Surely not!'

He laughed. 'There will be no fewer than thirteen courses. I remember one feast that went for seventeen.'

'You jest!'

'I do not. I think it was the King's celebrations to mark ten years of his reign. I was only a small boy, but I recall the feast went all night. Sar and I refused to go to bed and eventually we fell asleep under the table. I do remember that between each course there was dancing and mummery, and a fire breather.'

'Will there be the same tonight?'

Willem looked over to the centre aisle and, as if on cue, a group of jugglers, acrobats and jesters appeared and began performing.

'Sar acquitted himself quite well tonight,' Willem said.

'Yes, we have been practising the oath together.'

Willem raised a curious brow. 'So you're the reason his Kengian is so good.'

Arisa didn't respond, unsure whether it had been an innocent remark, or if he was fishing for information about her allegiances. She was always wary of anyone connecting her to Kengia. For all she knew, the Prince's instructions to Willem may have been to try to uncover her secrets.

'Please, tell me exactly what Takai said about me,' she said.

Willem grinned and touched the side of his nose. Arisa pursed her lips.

'Alright,' he relented. 'In the brief period we spoke, he didn't tell me much at all. Other than to say that you are ward to the healer who saved him.'

'And?' she prompted, knowing Takai wouldn't have minced his words.

'He said while you have quite fantastical views of the world—'

'Fantastical,' she snorted.

'I believe that was the word he used. He said while you held strong opinions about how the kingdom could be run better, he was grateful particularly for the friendship you had shown our brother, Sar.'

'That is hardly a glowing recommendation.'

'It's more what he didn't say.' He gave a cryptic smile.

'What do you mean?'

'You have to understand the Prince has never been one to hide his true opinions from anyone.'

'Now, that I believe,' Arisa scoffed.

'And when it comes to Sar and me, he tells us practically everything.'

'I don't see what that has to do with me.'

'Perhaps nothing to do with you,' there was that cryptic smile again, 'and more to do with someone else. You see, Takai has suddenly stopped speaking of another altogether.' He looked pointedly at Theodora. 'Yet yours was almost the first name he mentioned when we spoke today.'

'That hardly surprises me. He likes to talk about how distasteful he finds lowborn Lamorians like me.'

Willem frowned. 'I'm afraid you must have misunderstood the Prince. I have known him my whole life as nothing but a kind and generous person. Yes, he can be overly proud and arrogant at times, but no less than you would expect from a son of the King, and the future heir.'

'Well, I'm sure you will find him much changed since his return to the castle. For his opinions of his subjects are most unkind, and closer to the King's than what you describe.'

'From what I saw today, and his intervention at the execution, I found him wholly unchanged.'

Arisa raised a sceptical brow. 'What he did today was heartening, but it was his mother who saved the Kengian woman.'

Willem shook his head. 'I believe I know the Prince better than most, and the behaviour you saw from him today was typical of his character.'

She glanced over at Takai, sitting high in his throne, his jaw slightly lifted. Arisa didn't understand how he could inspire such loyalty and friendship from men like Sar and Willem.

Takai must have sensed her watching him and caught her eye. He stared at her for a moment before giving a half-smile. She looked away swiftly.

'Perhaps when the Prince's companions were just you and Sar at Talbot, then his character was as you described. But now he is back at the castle, and under the influence of others, don't you think he could have changed?'

Willem looked over at Takai, as if scrutinising his face for the answer. 'I think the responsibilities of the kingdom rest heavily on him, and he is finding his way in troubled times. He must navigate the sycophants at court, and the power-hungry advisers. He must also relearn his relationship with his parents and find where he belongs. Takai must reconcile his duties and his character. It is a burden none of us can imagine. I believe, though, that given time, he will choose the right path.'

Evidently Willem had given it much thought. 'What if he chooses the wrong path?' Arisa asked.

'I don't think he will, particularly if he has the right people by his side.'

Willem looked at her intently, which only served to confuse her more. She would have asked him to clarify his last statement if it hadn't been for Sar bounding toward them, Gwyn following closely behind.

'Willem!' Sar lifted his friend from the bench and enveloped him in a giant bear hug. Willem's feet dangled in midair.

'Sar,' Gwyn admonished.

'It's alright.' Willem grinned as Sar set him back to his feet, and he quickly rearranged his messed-up doublet. 'He's nowhere near as rough as he looks.' He slapped Sar on the back. 'Congratulations. I have never been so glad to see someone knighted.'

Sar flushed and shuffled his feet awkwardly.

'Now, don't think you can go lording it over me all of a sudden. Even if you are now a landowner, I'm still the Earl of Talbot.' Willem flung his head back in mock superiority.

'As you say, my lord.' Sar gave a theatrical bow. 'So, tell me news from Talbot.'

Gwyn rolled her eyes at Arisa. 'They'll be at this for ages. Come with me.' She led her to a quieter corner of the hall.

'Are you enjoying yourself?'

'Quite.' Arisa's eyes followed the serving boy tasked with topping up the King's goblet. It appeared the pitcher he held contained wine exclusively for the King. 'Sar did marvellously.'

'He did, rather. And Willem is good company.'

'He's a fine young man. How does the Queen?' Arisa asked a little hesitantly, conscious of Sofia's declarations to the King at the morning's execution. She looked at how tall and proud the Queen was sitting on her throne. The King had a tight grip on her hand and looked deliriously happy, clearly oblivious to the strained look on his wife's face.

Gwyn followed her gaze and frowned. 'The Queen will bear her duty with grace.'

'But she has made such a sacrifice today. It's wonderful that she did it, of course, but she publicly declared herself as Delrik's true wife. I'm so sorry it came to that...' She trailed off miserably.

'The Queen did what was right. In all honesty, it's been a long time since I have seen her so alive. She had all but given up the fight, but today she stood up for something important. And she succeeded. Sofia will not see this as sacrifice. I'm sure that now she has committed herself to this path, she will work the situation to her advantage somehow. Now she may be able to influence the King again and make a real difference to Lamore's people. If that's the case, being by the King's side is a small price to pay. And importantly, the Queen now has a better chance of protecting you and Erun…I assume your guardian has made no further progress on firesky?'

'Not that I know of,' Arisa lied.

'The Queen is sorry that the price of what she did today was setting a date for the progress. She couldn't have known the King would want to go so soon.'

Arisa shrugged and looked at the Queen again. She was talking animatedly with Takai, and they were both smiling, seemingly at ease in each other's company. A seed of doubt formed in Arisa's mind as she thought of her plan. Maybe Gwyn was right, and the Queen could use her power over the King for good.

Just as quickly, she dismissed the thought. It was too late. Someone had to pay for all the wrongs done to Lamore. To her father. To Rea. Arisa would have her justice.

'What are you two gossiping about?' Sar cried, as he and Willem joined them.

'Nothing of any importance at all,' Arisa said.

'Good, because it is time for you to do me the honour of dancing with me.' Sar offered her his hand.

'Me?' She shook her head wildly. 'No, absolutely not!'

Sar scratched his head. 'I've been rejected by women before, but not with so much passion.'

'It's not you, Sar. It's actually that I can't dance.'

'Of course you can. I've danced with you many times in the Queen's rooms,' Sar said.

'But I can't dance here. Not among everyone else.'

'Ah. But what if it's not among everyone else?'

She shot Willem a look, appealing for help. He merely shrugged and grinned.

'Good. Come on.' Sar linked his arm through Arisa's and led her toward the two lines of dancers showing off their fancy footwork at the centre of the hall.

'But I don't know that dance,' she protested, grasping desperately at any excuse not to join the group of accomplished dancers.

Sar did an about turn and led her to a quiet corner of the hall. 'We shall have our own dance.'

'Right here?'

'Exactly. How about a pavane?'

'Just the two of us?' She was thoroughly confused. The pavane was supposed to be a dance performed in lines.

'Come on,' he urged.

Together they paraded back and forth, their fingers touching lightly. Sar's steps, while not completely seamless, were precise and technically perfect.

Soon Arisa was uncaring about the strange looks they received, surprising herself by how much fun she was having. They even tried a slow bassadance and an almain. In all, Arisa thought they were quite good. She would have continued gladly had she not seen the King's wine server appear nearby.

'May we take a rest?'

'If you insist,' Sar sighed, 'but for the record, it was you who tired first, not me.' He led her back toward their table, but her eyes never left the serving boy as he topped up the King's wine. This time the King pointed to the Queen and Takai's goblets and the boy dutifully topped them up as well.

Damn, Arisa thought. She would have to reassess her plan.

She must have been watching the group on the dais quite intently, as she realised Takai was staring right back at her. She looked away quickly.

'I thought you said you couldn't dance,' Willem quipped, shifting in his seat with the smallest hint of a grimace. Sar had told Arisa that the Duke's son had been born with a physical condition that affected his limbs and movement – that some days he was in so much pain he couldn't leave his bed.

Arisa didn't want to intrude, especially since they had just met, but she liked the kind young man and wanted to help. 'Does it hurt much?'

'No more than I've always known,' Willem said matter-of-factly, offering her a bowl of rose pudding.

'I wonder if there is anything I could do to assist.' She dipped her spoon through a layer of nuts into the silky smooth pudding and took a mouthful. An explosion of rose-flavoured cream filled her senses.

'I don't suppose so. My father has had me seen by the finest physicians in the land.'

'Yes, but I wonder if they have tried other means?' she asked cautiously.

Willem narrowed his eyes. 'Kengian medicine, you mean?'

Arisa froze. She had the impression that he was testing her. Had she read Willem entirely wrong? Wasn't he as open-minded as she had thought?

Willem broke out in a broad smile. 'I tease you. At Talbot, our Kengian farmers have tried many of the traditional remedies. They did offer to bring a Shaman to me once, but father drew the line at that. I am resigned to the fact that there is no cure.'

'There may not be a cure…but something more could be done for the pain,' she said with certainty. 'My guardian has taught me many things, perhaps things that even your tenants don't know.'

'Yes,' Willem said slowly, 'he is rumoured to be a talented man.'

'Could I return the kindness you have shown me this evening, and prepare some medicine for you?'

'It is you who does the kindness of letting me share your company.' His smile extended all the way to his eyes. 'I do gratefully accept your offer, though, while being careful to manage my expectations all the same.'

'But I intend on exceeding your expectations.' She took another mouthful of pudding and gave Willem a satisfied smile.

'I have no doubt that you will, just as you've exceeded another's.'

Willem looked meaningfully over at Takai, leaving Arisa to further contemplate what the Prince really thought about her, and why she actually cared.

32

This was one thing Takai hadn't missed when he was at Talbot. Having to sit on show at great feasts and watch everyone around him enjoying themselves.

At an occasion such as this, custom dictated that Takai remain at the dais and wait for the King to dismiss him. With the Queen's encouragement, his father had spent most of the night listening to the Duke's plans to deal with the Northemers. Horace, who had been relegated to the seat beside the Queen, had been excluded from the conversations. When the Duke took the King to one side of the dais for a particular discussion, Takai turned to his mother.

The conversation between the two of them was surprisingly easy. She enquired after his archery and his time at Talbot. She laughed at the tales he told about Sar and Willem's antics. She expressed regret for not visiting him at Talbot, saying only that her separation from the King had resulted in many unintended consequences.

Noticing Takai's eyes on Arisa, his mother spoke fondly of the girl and her commitment to helping the poor. She spoke of Arisa's ambition to become a surgeon, saying Arisa reminded her of herself when she had first come to Lamore and opened the school in Obira. She expressed a wish to work with his father to do more to help the people. Takai didn't have the heart to tell her the King had little sympathy for his subjects these days – but then again, that may change now they were reconciled.

All the while, it hadn't escaped Takai's notice that Arisa had disappeared out of sight with Sar. He had caught glimpses of them dancing in the shadows, and it had awoken a strange feeling in him – a mix of curiosity, frustration and anger. Yet when he had seen Sar dance with Theodora, he had felt absolutely nothing. His gaze continually went to Arisa instead.

'My dearest Queen, would you do me the honour of dancing with me?' The King had finally finished speaking with the Duke.

The Queen gave the King a small smile and followed him onto the dance floor. Finally, Takai was allowed to leave the dais, and he wasted no time going in search of the swish of silver, green and white he'd been admiring all evening.

He found Arisa and his cousin in conversation at their table.

'Your Highness.' Willem stood up and bowed.

Arisa got up slowly from her seat and curtsied. 'Your Highness.' Her voice was wound tight.

Takai tried to catch her eye, but she refused to meet his gaze. 'I see you've been dancing.'

'If that's what you call it.' Theodora had magically appeared by his side.

'It looked quite splendid from where I was sitting.' Takai had been trying to compliment Arisa, but it was wasted on her as she still wouldn't look at him. Theodora, though, had read his meaning perfectly.

'I can hardly see how Arisa has any appetite for dancing after her performance today. Don't think your little outburst passed unnoticed. Father is furious the Kengian woman was released.'

Arisa glared at Theodora and jutted out her chin but maintained her silence.

'I hardly think the Chancellor should look to Arisa to blame,' Takai said. 'It was my mother who petitioned the King.'

Theodora pressed her lips together tightly. 'You're right. Exactly what did *you* make of what the Queen did? Lying face first in the dirt and making a fool out of herself? The whole thing was laughable, especially the part where she declared herself as the King's true wife.'

Takai clenched his jaw. He wasn't as comfortable as he'd been in the past with people insulting his mother. 'I thought she was absolutely magnificent. She proved she was more of a Queen than anyone else could ever be.' He looked pointedly at Theodora and thought he saw her jaw actually drop.

Arisa was now looking straight at Takai with those changeable amber eyes. She smiled at him, and he felt as if he were the only person in the room.

This was the opportunity he'd been waiting for.

'Arisa, would you dance with me?'

Her eyes didn't leave his but there was a moment of hesitation before she replied, 'I will.'

He led her toward the dance floor, conscious of Theodora's eyes on them, but more aware of the warmth he felt with Arisa at his side. She exuded a bright energy that spread to him and coursed through his body. It thoroughly confused him.

Before that day, perhaps even before that night, Takai hadn't been sure if he liked Arisa. And he believed the feeling was mutual. She had made that abundantly clear several times over. Yet here they were, arm-in-arm and about to dance together, and nothing felt more natural.

The dance was a cinque pas – a lively five-step number. He felt Arisa tense and wondered if it was because of his company, or because every courtier's eyes were on them. He took her other hand and squeezed it lightly as if to say, *It's fine. I'll look after you.*

Arisa smiled back at him weakly. She might have been nervous, but it didn't show once the dance started. She was confident and light on her feet. While she wasn't as accomplished a dancer as Theodora, she danced with abandonment, letting herself get lost in the movement. She laughed and closed her eyes, as if to feel the music better. Her enthusiasm was contagious. Every touch of her hand shot sparks through his body. At this moment, their differences didn't matter. The troubles of the kingdom were far away, and Takai could forget his responsibilities.

Neither of them spoke during the first dance. It was as if they didn't want to break the spell. Wordlessly, they agreed to stay on for the next dance. It was much slower, and Takai seized the chance to speak to her.

'Arisa, why did you agree to dance with me?'

'I'm not sure.' She crinkled her brow. 'Perhaps it was to spite Theodora.'

He laughed. 'Well, I think we both succeeded in that.'

'I think we're also spiting the Chancellor.'

Takai followed her gaze to see a stern-looking Horace sitting alone on the dais.

'I also wished to thank you for what you did today,' Arisa added.

'It was nothing. As I told Theodora, it was my mother who saved the woman's life.'

'Yes, as you said, the Queen was magnificent. She is every bit the warrior she was trained to be.'

'I suppose so.' It had never occurred to Takai to think of his mother as a warrior. For most of his life he had only seen a distant woman, pining for her homeland, but he was beginning to see her differently now.

'It's good now that she is by the King's side. Perhaps together they can make a difference to Lamore.'

Takai nodded. 'Maybe she can reach out to Sergei and his rebels and urge them to unite the kingdom.'

'Is that what you really wish for? A united kingdom?'

'Of course. What do you think will happen if we are at war between ourselves? We will be at the Northemers' mercy. Our people must stop *fighting* us, and *support* us instead.'

'I understand that Horace has plans for the Northemers?'

He wondered what exactly Arisa knew, and if she knew more than him.

'I'm sure he has. But while the King considers our strategy against Malu, our focus must be on being united in Lamore.'

'That is where we have common ground. Your people want to be united, but under leaders who are benevolent toward them. Leaders who understand them and help them.'

Takai gritted his teeth. 'I suppose they think they'd get that under Sergei's rule?'

She shrugged. 'He has the support of the people. In many ways he has already united the kingdom – Lamorians and Kengians alike.'

'But why do they all follow him?'

'Some follow him because they believe in him. Others follow him while waiting and hoping for something else.'

'What could they possibly be waiting for?'

Arisa paused. 'A Water Catcher.'

'I thought you didn't believe in a Water Catcher.'

She sighed. 'I've been taught to believe in something, to have hope in a better future, even if it seems impossible. But I don't subscribe to sitting around waiting for something, or someone, that may never come. There is time, though, to make amends with your people and unite them. You just have to stop treating them as if they are your enemies.'

Here she went again with her lectures. 'But they have made themselves our enemies by rising up against us,' Takai retorted.

'Surely when you were at Talbot you got to know some of these people and saw that they aren't all as you think?'

Takai tilted his head in thought. 'There *were* tenant farmers at Talbot who were good, hard-working people.'

'That describes the majority of your people.'

'Not from what I have seen in recent times. I've only seen ungrateful whiners, criminals and vagabonds.'

Arisa lifted her chin in challenge. 'You mean to say that in all the time you spent in the countryside, you never convinced any of them that you weren't their enemy?'

'Outside of the Duke's lands I was never accepted. Many hated me just for who I was, and where I was from.'

'Many of your people can relate,' she snapped straight back at him.

Takai's shoulders tensed. 'I was spat on, abused and had to be protected by guards at all times. Others kept a wide berth, never fully trusting me. Some Kengians threatened to put spells on me.'

Arisa stifled a laugh.

'I don't see how threatening to use magic against someone is funny.'

'I only think it's funny because Kengian magic doesn't work that way.'

'And what do you know of Kengian magic?' Takai had good reason to be suspicious of Arisa given who her guardian was and her understanding of the Kengian language.

'It's just something I've heard.' She sounded unconvincing.

'Yes, well, you have probably heard wrong. Kengians are dangerous. Remember, one of them tried to bewitch my father, and nearly succeeded in getting him under Kengia's control.'

Arisa's lips thinned. 'Is that why you seek to punish your subjects now? Because some farmers called you names, and a couple of Kengians said they'd use magic on you?'

'Punish them? I want to help them by bringing law and order back to the land. That is the only thing they seem to understand.'

Takai felt Arisa stiffen under his arms.

'I don't know how you can be so…so…' she blustered.

'So what? Heartless? Cruel? Cold? Isn't that what you truly

think of me?' He looked intently into her eyes. Why was she always challenging him? Why did she hate him so? And why did he care? 'Come on. Just say what you think of me!'

Arisa stopped dancing and dropped his hand as if it were a hot coal. 'In truth, I *think* nothing of you, Takai. You're nothing to me at all.'

Takai felt as if he had been slapped in the face. 'Yet you agreed to dance with me.'

'Yes, I thought for a moment you were the kind of man that Sar and Willem believe you to be. But it seems we have all been greatly deceived.'

Takai felt the colour rise to his cheeks. 'I am who I am, and if that isn't good enough for you, Arisa, and good enough for this forsaken kingdom, then so be it.'

Arisa's brow furrowed, as if she regretted some of the hurt she'd inflicted. She reached up as if to touch his face, but he pulled her hand away.

'I bid you goodnight, and rest assured I will not trespass upon your good nature, or force you to endure my distasteful company ever again.'

Takai bowed and turned abruptly, leaving Arisa standing alone on the dance floor.

He made a beeline for the closest door leading out of the hall. On the way, he passed Theodora, who gave him a seductive smile. He didn't stop. Takai wanted to get away from Arisa, from Theodora, as far away from everyone as possible. This would be the last time he would seek approval from Arisa – or from anyone else, for that matter.

33

Theodora stormed into her father's private study. The Chancellor had left the celebrations prematurely, and Theodora hadn't been far behind after the Prince and the peasant ward had humiliated her.

'Please tell me you are doing something about that horrible girl. I'll never be Queen while she's playing interference.'

Horace looked up from his desk and glared at her. 'What do you think I'm trying to do?'

'It looks to me that you're just staring at a bunch of parchment pieces...' She wandered closer to her father's desk to get a closer look. The pieces were covered in lines of numbers, a code of some sort. 'Are they from the guardian's house – the notes Guthrie found?'

Horace nodded. 'I believe they are, in fact, messages from Kengia. I've been staring at them for weeks, trying to decode them. I just know they contain something important about Erun. Something I can use to force him to deliver firesky.'

Finally she had confirmation of what the healer was working on. All the references to firesky suddenly made sense. Why hadn't he told her sooner? Maybe she could have helped.

'I need something to stop the King from coming after me and your brother.'

Theodora harrumphed, making it clear how she felt about Guthrie.

'Your brother aside, your future is just as tied up in this. I have to find something, soon. There are only a few days until the progress.'

'Can't you find someone who is good at…' She waved her hand at the parchment scraps.

'Deciphering code? I have some of the best codebreakers in the land in my employ, but none of them have managed to decrypt these messages. They aren't a typical kind of cipher. Our best guess is that there is a key of some sort. A reference key of words, such as a book or passage that corresponds to the numbers in each message. I have had the guardian's house turned upside down and every book checked, but we've found nothing. Whatever the key is, it must be something significant to Erun. Probably something he knows by heart. It would be something important to Kengians.'

Theodora sighed.

'I don't know much about Kengians, other than what Guthrie says about them…being filthy and the like. And the Prince…He still believes that Kengian Prince tried to bewitch his father. It's strange that he believes in their magic, but thinks that whole prophecy thing they believe in is ridiculous. If you ask me, it's all a load of—'

The Chancellor held his hand up to silence his daughter.

'*Prophecy*…The Water Catcher prophecy…That's it. That's the key!'

Theodora smiled, realising that she'd helped and that the prophecy may also be the key to being rid of Arisa once and for all.

34

$\mathcal{E}$run went over his reworked calculations for the hundredth time, not daring to believe that he actually had the answer to firesky in front of him. But each time he interrogated his notes, he became more convinced. Now all he had to do was test it. Test it before the progress.

He went to his window and opened the shutters. It was dark, and the fog that had been around all day was still hanging over the castle grounds. Right now the entire court was occupied with the celebrations in the Great Hall.

It was now or never.

He called Klaus into his rooms. 'I need to conduct a sort of experiment…outdoors…for the Chancellor.'

Klaus raised a sceptical brow.

'It is something quite important. Arisa's life depends on it. Many people's do.'

The guard tapped his hand along his sword hilt, as if considering the request. Finally he nodded. 'It's my duty to serve my Captain in everything he demands. I serve Sar as I served his father before him. And Sar has put you and your welfare in my charge, so I will help you.'

Erun sighed with relief. 'Good. Because I need to—'

Klaus cut him off with an impatient wave of the hand. 'I don't wish to know. In fact, I think it's better that I don't know exactly what you're up to. Plausible deniability, I believe they call it. As long as you don't pull a fast one on me and try to escape, and as long as neither of us is caught, my duty is fulfilled. Now, get to it.'

Erun pulled on his cloak and threw some items into an inside pocket. He grabbed a thick paper tube he had prepared in case this opportunity arose. He had filled it with charcoal, sulphur and saltpetre, in the exact ratios outlined in the Firemaster's book. A long rope wick poked out of one end.

'Is that it?' Klaus pointed to the tube.

'Yes.'

'Hmph.'

'I'm sorry for dragging you into this.'

'All I can say is, whatever it is you're doing, I hope it's worth the effort and risk.'

'It will be.' Confirming that firesky worked would be the insurance Erun needed to protect Arisa. And if he was completely honest with himself, he was bursting with excitement about the prospect of what he might have created.

Erun followed Klaus down the castle's deserted corridors until they reached the main courtyard. It was shrouded in fog. Music carried from the hall, making it hard to hear anything else. Erun began to believe they could succeed in this errand undetected.

They waited for a pair of guards to pass before running across the open area and merging into the shadows alongside the stables.

'Where to?' Klaus whispered.

Erun thought quickly. Should they go to the woodland? No – it was possible that firesky could break through the fog and be visible to the city. *The archery oval?* he wondered. No, it was still too visible. He needed somewhere hidden from the main castle that would give him plenty of cover overhead.

Then he had it. 'To the south garden,' he told Klaus. 'But I'm going to need some ropes.'

'Ropes?'

'Yes. Long ones.'

'They'll have some in the stables.' Klaus disappeared into the darkness of the long building, Erun following cautiously behind. The beacon of light from Klaus's torch got smaller and smaller.

Erun turned his ear to the sounds of the horses as they slept. It was a strange symphony of heavy breathing, with the occasional snort. A small whinny came from his right. Curious, Erun followed the sound until he came to a stall with a sign reading *Meteor*.

He raised the torch up to see the horse's face and she whinnied again. There she was. Older, of course, but unmistakably his brother's horse.

'Hello, old friend.' He let the mare nuzzle his hands. 'I never thought we would meet again.'

He put his forehead to Meteor's long nose. Together they shared a moment, remembering and mourning the brother and master they had lost.

'So you have met Arisa?'

Meteor whinnied again, much louder this time.

He bent over and whispered in the horse's ear. 'I have good news. Arisa and I will be gone from here soon. We will leave here, one way or another, and go back to Kengia. And you, my friend, will come too. We will return home together.'

This time Meteor let out a loud neigh and started pawing the ground with her front hoof.

Klaus came hurtling back toward him, ropes coiled over his shoulders. 'Keep it down,' he hissed. 'What were you thinking, stirring up that beast?'

'She's no beast. Goodbye for now, my friend,' he whispered again to Meteor, giving her a scratch behind the ear.

Klaus shook his head exasperatedly before leading Erun out of the stables and to the Queen's gardens, stopping only once for Erun to use his suggestive powers to get the guards at the south gate to let them pass. They were part of Sar's unit, and it had been easy to convince them that Klaus was acting on the Captain's orders. He also persuaded the guards to forget he and Klaus had ever been there.

They continued walking under the blanket of fog and night, until they reached the south garden. Here, Erun stopped abruptly. He felt as if someone were watching them. He looked out into the night – and then he saw it.

A flash of green eyes. Green eyes he had known from childhood.

So you have come, he thought.

I'm here to watch over you both, came the voice in his head.

Erun felt an overwhelming sense of comfort. *Thank you.*

'What is it?' Klaus stood beside him, peering into the darkness.

'Nothing. Just a squirrel, I expect.'

'So we're here. What next?'

'Over there.' Erun pointed toward the crumbling wall along the cliff edge.

'What! Are you crazy? That's where the Prince had his accident.'

'Precisely. I need to get down the cliff.'

Klaus shook his head vigorously. 'No. It's too dangerous.'

'But it must be there. It's the only place.'

Klaus continued shaking his head. Erun stood stubbornly fixed to the ground. It appeared they were at a standoff, until a howl broke through the fog.

Klaus swung around. 'This is a bad idea. We have to go back.'

'You will need to tell Sar you have failed him. You were to help me do my work.'

'Yes, but not help get us both killed.'

'We can be quick. You just need to lower me down the cliff face using the ropes and keep an eye out.'

'For the wolf, you mean?'

'Come on. A seasoned warrior like you, armed with a halberd, against one little wolf? I venture you'll be safe. But we must move quickly.'

Klaus looked from the cliff face to the castle and back again. 'I can't believe I'm going to help you do this,' he grumbled, as he wrapped one end of the rope securely around a tree stump. Erun tied the other end of the rope around himself, creating a kind of harness.

They moved to the edge. Erun looked down the cliff face, immediately regretting his decision. There was nothing but blackness and the ominous sound of waves crashing on the rocks far below. Carefully, he tucked the paper tube in his cloak.

'Good luck to you.' Klaus gave him an encouraging pat on the back. It nearly made Erun lose his balance.

Klaus walked back to the stump. Using it as a pivot point, he pulled the rope until it was completely taut. Erun turned his back on the water and stepped down onto a thin ledge jutting out from the cliff face. Klaus slowly started to release the rope inch by inch, as Erun stepped down toward the water, digging his heels into the jagged rockface. It was painstakingly slow and awkward. How Sar had managed to get up this, and carry the Prince part of the way, he'd never know.

After what felt like an age, Erun arrived at the bottom and landed on a flat rock clear of the water. He untied his harness and started removing the items from inside his cloak. First was the paper tube, which appeared to have made the precarious journey down the cliff unscathed. In the darkness, he managed to create a small platform out of rocks and propped the paper tube on it. Its long rope wick peeked out from underneath.

Now he needed a flame to light it. He looked up at Klaus, who was peering over the edge with his torch. He needed to somehow launch firesky without alerting Klaus. As Klaus himself had told Erun, the less he knew, the better.

Erun's green-eyed friend must have read his mind, because it let out a great howl at that very moment.

'Stay there,' Klaus ordered before disappearing in search of the wolf.

Wondering where Klaus thought he would go, Erun reached into his cloak pocket and produced two pieces of flint and a pile of parchment scraps. He bent down and placed the parchment at the end of the wick. Next he picked up the two pieces of stone and took a deep breath, before striking them together until they sparked. It only took two tries before the parchment caught flame, and Erun scrambled as far away from the paper tube as he could get.

There was an almighty bang and light whizzed up dozens of feet toward the sky, falling just short of the top of the cliff. Then the balls of light exploded into showers of yellow and white stars.

Erun pushed his eyeglasses up his nose. He couldn't believe what he was seeing. He had done it. He had created firesky. It was as spectacular as he had imagined. The lights sparkled and sizzled as if they were living, breathing creatures, dancing with the night sky. It was a perfect dialogue between the light and darkness – the core of Kengian magic – it was the Firemaster's legacy.

Seeing it in real life, even on such a small scale, terrified and exhilarated him at the same time. For he knew now just how devastating it would be if Horace got his hands on it. He knew now, without a doubt, that he could not deliver firesky for the progress. He would need to find another way to protect Arisa.

'What was that?' Klaus's head appeared over the cliff edge. He was a little out of breath. 'That bang sound?'

'It was nothing. All is well. In fact, I have finished.'

'Finished?'

Erun nodded. He gathered up his equipment and harnessed himself again with the rope. Looking up, he saw the fog clearing to reveal a bright full moon.

He smiled to himself. It reminded him of the first sign of the prophecy – the blood moon. Now there was firesky. It left only the third sign: the Water Catcher. The Water Catcher would come now, he was sure of it. And that made all the risks he had taken completely worth it.

LATER, Erun tossed and turned in bed. He couldn't put from his mind the thrill he had felt bringing firesky to life. He had done it. While it was never likely to see the light of day again, he couldn't help but feel elated that he had succeeded where so many before him had failed. It had also given him a renewed faith in the prophecy coming to being. The first two signs had appeared; surely this meant the Water Catcher would come soon, just as he had always hoped and believed. Now he just had to figure out how to keep Arisa safe.

Erun was pondering this when the door to his room swung open, and a smug-looking Horace stood before him. He felt a surge of panic. Had he been found out? Did Horace know that he had tested firesky?

Warily, he got out of bed, prepared for the worst.

'So, you think you can toy with me? Make a fool out of me before the King?'

Erun put on his eyeglasses slowly and deliberately, trying to buy himself some time. His legs shook underneath him.

'You will stop your games and deliver firesky as promised.'

Good. Horace didn't seem to know. So what had caused him to bluster into Erun's room at such an hour?

'I warn you, Erun,' the Chancellor went on, 'if you don't give me what I want – and soon – it won't be only you who will suffer.'

Erun had become used to the threats against him, but references to Arisa still made his stomach churn. 'Arisa has done nothing. Keep her out of this.'

'Ha!' Horace scoffed. 'This very night she made a fool out of herself in the Great Hall, throwing herself at the Prince. And earlier she manipulated the Queen into begging for a criminal's life. I think she has done quite a lot to undermine the balance of power at court.'

Erun raised an eyebrow. He had heard from Klaus about the Kengian woman Lina being saved, and Arisa's involvement, so that news didn't surprise him. But what he didn't understand was why Arisa was being associated with the Prince.

'What exactly did Arisa do at the hall?'

'She danced with the Prince.'

'I didn't realise that was a crime.'

'It is when the person you're dancing with is promised in marriage.'

'To whom?'

'My daughter.'

'The Prince and Theodora are engaged?'

Horace waved his hand dismissively. 'It is practically arranged.'

'Ahh. So the Prince is still a free man and, last time I checked, my ward was also free.'

Horace narrowed his eyes. 'Not for long. You will deliver firesky or I will see that your precious Arisa is imprisoned.'

Erun told himself it was an empty threat, and that Horace was only posturing because his own power and plans were being threatened. Klaus had also told him the Queen and King had reunited, which was another major blow to the Chancellor.

'The King will not agree,' he said. 'The Queen will speak for Arisa.'

'The Queen may temporarily have the King's ear, but it doesn't change the fact that the King wants firesky as much as I do,' Horace retorted. 'You will not fail me, because if you do, you will also be failing your precious ward.'

'But I'm doing my best. You have to understand that firesky can't be ready for the progress. It will take time.'

Horace shook his head vehemently. 'Time you don't have, especially now I've got what I need to convince the King that you and your ward can't be trusted. I have what's required to force your hand.'

Erun tilted his head to the side in question.

Horace held up a scrap of parchment in answer.

Erun's eyes grew wide as he recognised it as a coded message from the Kengian Queen.

'I see you recognise this. I have had this, and many more like it, in my possession for some time. But it wasn't until now that I figured out how to decode them.'

Again, Erun thought the Chancellor must be bluffing. The code was safe, he was sure of it.

'Admittedly, it had me baffled. I was about to give up. But the answer, in the end, was simple.' Horace paused, a smile tugging at one side of his mouth. 'The key is the prophecy.'

Erun couldn't help his small intake of breath. Horace had it. He had the key, and goodness knew how many secret messages from Kengia.

The Chancellor scrutinised his face carefully and smirked. 'So I was right!' he cried. 'It's now just a matter of time before I have all of your secrets, and I will have no trouble convincing the King that you're a danger to us. He will readily agree to have Arisa imprisoned. And who knows what treasures of information we will uncover about our Kengian enemy when we decode all of the notes?' Horace clicked his jaw. 'If firesky is not delivered in time for the progress, I can promise Arisa will be swapping her fine room in the Queen's apartments for a dungeon. Do I make myself clear?'

Erun swallowed hard. 'Perfectly.'

Horace turned and flung open the main door leading out to

the walkway. He addressed himself to the guard who had replaced Klaus. 'No one, other than myself and the serving boy, is to be allowed admittance – under any circumstances. Convey this to the rest of the sentries. Anyone who defies my orders will have their life end prematurely on the gallows.'

'Yes, Chancellor,' the guard replied earnestly, as Horace walked out the door and locked it.

Erun slumped onto his bed and rubbed his neck nervously. He had destroyed many of the messages from Kengia, but there were still probably some that alluded to his identity. Once Horace realised he was a Kengian Prince, his value as a prisoner would rise exponentially.

The taste of vomit filled his mouth. Horace could use him in negotiations when they invaded Kengia. There were also references in the most recent message about Kengia's strategy against the Lamorians. Erun's messages could be the cause of his beloved homeland's downfall.

But that wasn't the worst of it.

Many of the messages referred to other matters – secrets – that would be devastating if Horace got his hands on them. Erun had to resign himself to the fact that Horace had the leverage he needed to force him to release firesky. Unless he could get Arisa to safety first. If she was safe, Erun was prepared to sacrifice himself in order to protect firesky's secrets.

Somehow, he had to get a message to Arisa, telling her to escape before it was too late.

35

‘Are you ready?’ Gwyn looked eagerly at Arisa as she put on her travelling cloak and gloves, ready for the progress.

‘I think so. My trunk went with the carts yesterday.’

Winter was not an ideal time to travel, but the King would not waver. He was determined to go on his progress and show his *newly devoted* wife to the people. Their ultimate destination would be Talbot, not far from Shizen Lake, where the King and his court would enjoy some hunting and other leisure activities. On the way, they would stop at Iveness, but first they would visit the marketplace in Obira. The King wished to address the city's inhabitants with the Queen by his side.

He had told those at court that he had ‘quite a surprise’ prepared for the marketplace. Arisa didn't know what it was, but had been assured by the Queen that it wasn't firesky. This had come as a huge relief, since Arisa had failed to enact her plan, but she was riddled with concern for Erun.

Arisa had been refused access to her guardian, who, it appeared, was being punished by the Chancellor for not delivering firesky – and in turn, the Chancellor was out of favour with the King for his failure. The only saving grace was that

Erun would be safe while Horace was occupied on progress. The journey would also buy Arisa time, and hopefully opportunity, to see her plan through, once and for all.

She threw her satchel over her shoulder and patted her gown pocket, where she had put the vial of strychnine. It was still there, ready to do its worst. In the meantime, she would make the most out of this progress.

'I'm going to go down to the kitchens to see if they can spare any food for us to give out,' she told Gwyn.

'What a wonderful idea,' Gwyn replied. 'But you will have to hurry – the King won't wait for anyone.'

Arisa raced to the kitchen. After a brief negotiation with the cook, she managed to get a large crate filled with breads, pastries, cheeses and even sweet honey wafers. She was just arranging for the crate to be delivered to the carriages when a serving boy she recognised from Erun's rooms appeared in front of her.

The boy put his finger to his lips and indicated for her to follow him into a storeroom. He was holding a worn-looking piece of paper in his fist.

Once the door was closed behind them, he spoke. 'My lady, I have been meaning to give this message to you for days, but the Chancellor has had eyes on me. I tried to give it to one of the maids who works in the Queen's apartments, but she was too scared to take it.'

'It's alright,' Arisa assured him. 'You're giving it to me now.'

The boy nodded and handed it over before disappearing out of the room.

She unfolded the note and recognised Erun's writing straight away. He'd written in Old Kengian. She translated it in her head.

I have to be careful what I say, in case this note is intercepted, but I can say you're in grave danger.

Horace has discovered how to decode all of the messages.

He will use any information he discovers to force my compliance, and convince the King to act against you.

The Chancellor is intent on his path. And while I'll willingly put my own life on the line to stop him, I can't say the same of yours. Remember the woman who visited us the night of Hyando's accident? (Erun must mean the Shaman.) *She will help you. This is the only way to prevent Horace from becoming absolutely unstoppable.*

Arisa screwed the note up in her hands. It couldn't be as Erun said. *He must be exaggerating. He can't wish for me to escape without him.* She ran out of the storeroom and raced toward her guardian's rooms, taking the north-west tower stairs two at a time until she arrived, breathless, outside of Erun's door.

'I must see Erun,' she said to the guard on duty, between gasps for air.

'He's not having visitors,' came the gruff reply.

'But I must see him now.'

The guard shook his head. 'No one. On the Chancellor's orders – on pain of death.'

'Erun!' she screamed at the top of her lungs, hoping he could hear her.

'Enough.' The guard grabbed her arm and tried to drag her away.

Arisa kept screaming out for her guardian, until she heard a faint voice from the other side of the door.

'Arisa?'

She broke free of the guard's grip and ran back to the door. 'Yes, it's me.'

'Arisa, you know what you must do,' came Erun's muffled response.

'No, I'm not going to do it.'

'But you must.'

'No—'

'You must,' came Erun's voice, much louder.

'Get out of here before I send word to the Chancellor,' the guard grumbled.

'Erun!'

'Goodbye, little one.'

It was the last thing she heard Erun say as the guard dragged her back to the tower stairs.

'Begone with you!' The guard shoved her into the stairwell.

Arisa slumped onto the top step in shock. She couldn't leave Erun…but part of her knew she had to. She couldn't be responsible for Horace getting his hands on firesky. Even if she went through with her own plan, Horace would ensure the Lamorian regime knew the contents of the secret messages. Maybe she could speak to Gwyn, see if there was anything she could do. But Arisa knew what the answer would be. No one wanted Horace to have the power of firesky.

She gritted her teeth. If she couldn't manage to carry out her plans soon, she would have to make her escape. In any case, she had to go on the progress. She just hoped she could still make it.

She raced to the castle's main courtyard and was relieved to find two royal carriages still there. They were flanked by dozens of guards, all under Lakeford and Sar's watchful eyes. Most of the other nobles had gone ahead to secure safe passage in their domains, and ensure that only the King's loyal supporters came out to greet him along the road. Every sign of trouble would have been removed. Arisa had heard the dungeons below the castle were currently at capacity with anyone who had been identified as a potential troublemaker. Yet no one was confident that the progress, as carefully orchestrated as it was, would go as smoothly as the King hoped. They still had to make it safely through Obira. Arisa could almost taste the tension in the air.

The King strode out from the breezeway with Queen Sofia by his side, Horace and Gwyn following them. They were ushered into the first carriage. Arisa wasn't sure where she was supposed to go, but assumed she would be with Gwyn, so she dashed toward the first carriage.

'You.'

Someone yanked her arm, and she turned to see Guthrie scowling down at her.

'What are you doing here?' he demanded.

'What are *you* doing here?' she sniped back. 'I thought you'd been banished to Calliope.'

'I'm part of the security detail for the progress, if you must know. But you, guttersnipe, aren't welcome.'

'The Queen sees it a little differently, since it was she who invited me.' Arisa spoke with more confidence than she felt.

'Well, the Queen isn't here now.'

She looked around, hoping to catch Sar's attention, but he hadn't noticed her arrival, and the Queen and Gwyn were already out of sight. She had to be part of the progress – but the scathing look from Guthrie confirmed he wasn't budging from his position.

'Do you mean to defy the Queen's wishes?' came a voice from behind. Arisa spun around to see Takai.

Guthrie bowed. 'My apologies, Your Highness.'

'It is not me you should apologise to.' Takai looked meaningfully at Arisa.

'My apologies to you,' Guthrie hissed at her.

'You may leave us now,' Takai said. Guthrie grunted and stomped off.

'Thank you, Your Highness,' Arisa murmured. She was a little stunned that the Prince had intervened on her behalf.

Takai didn't look at her, but gave a curt nod in response and held out his arm. He guided Arisa to the nearest carriage, ushering her into the corner and sitting down opposite her. Theodora was already inside, and shuffled closer to Takai. She was dressed in a dark-blue gown and matching travelling cloak trimmed with fur. Her mother, the Countess, was sitting next to Arisa, suspicious eyes looking her up and down.

'Your Majesty,' they both simpered at the Prince, who gave another curt nod.

'Lady Theodora. Countess,' Arisa offered politely.

'What have you been doing?' Theodora demanded. 'Your face is covered in sweat. You look absolutely ghastly.'

Arisa wasn't about to tell her where she had been. 'Just excited, I expect. It's not every day a lowborn peasant girl would get to enjoy such an experience as this.'

The Countess nodded knowingly, oblivious to her sarcasm.

'How are we to know what you have and have not experienced?' Theodora said in a sickly sweet voice. 'We don't even know the *real* you, or your guardian. Of course, my father and I are determined to rectify that...and are already well on our way.'

Arisa's heart stuck in her throat. Theodora was referring to the coded messages; she must be. Takai's gaze bore into her like he could see every one of her secrets.

She forced a smile. 'I'm an open book. All I want is the best for this kingdom and all of Kypria.'

'As we all do,' the Prince said, not unkindly, his eyes never leaving her.

Theodora's cat eyes darted from one to the other, her cheeks reddening. 'Yes. Of course.'

The carriage jolted to a start. Arisa averted her gaze to the scenery outside and the cloud-filled sky. As they left the castle, she realised it might be the last time she would ever see it – and Erun. She felt sick at the prospect.

As they neared the city, she reached for her satchel and opened it to check the contents. It was filled with ointments, salves and linen bandages. While she was in Obira, she was determined to make some use of herself.

'What have you got there?' Theodora asked.

'Medicine for the poor.'

Theodora screwed up her nose. 'What? You're intending to touch those people?'

The Countess snorted. 'Goodness knows what you'll catch from the filth. They live like pigs.'

The carriage jostled through the city's gates and the familiar smells of Obira wafted in.

'What is that stench?' Theodora screeched, holding a handkerchief to her nose.

'It smells like death,' the Countess cried.

'That's because it is,' Arisa replied sharply. 'I'm surprised to see you ladies here, agreeing to come to the marketplace.'

Theodora arched a brow. 'Surprised?'

'Well, mixing with the filth, as you refer to them, can hardly be something you would enjoy.'

'We must all do our duties,' Theodora replied smugly, giving the Prince a beguiling smile. Takai didn't acknowledge he'd heard anything, his eyes intent on his view out the window. Arisa couldn't blame him. Listening to these women was torturous. But she couldn't let them off the hook so easily.

'*Duty* is not the only important virtue you can have.'

'What other virtues do you suggest we employ?' Theodora demanded.

Takai had turned toward Arisa now. He was scrutinising her face closely, as if he were looking for hidden meaning in what she had said.

'Compassion, empathy, respect, justice, fairness,' she listed. 'Shall I go on?'

'Please don't,' Theodora moaned, looking away.

Takai's eyes, however, were still firmly on Arisa. She shifted uncomfortably in her seat. She wanted to demand why he was looking at her so. She wanted to know why he had so cruelly left her on the dance floor. Why one moment he could show her such kindness, and the next return to his usual arrogant self. She would have said something if it weren't for a rumbling sound coming from outside the carriage.

Arisa looked out toward the noise to find they were approaching the marketplace. She poked her head further out the window, and saw the road ahead lined with what appeared to be well-wishers. 'Long live King Delrik! Hooray!' they shouted. She groaned inwardly, knowing Horace must have planted these actors.

Further ahead, she could see the usual busy marketplace. As they moved closer, the crowd started to surge toward the first carriage. Now their cries were mixed with boos and hisses, and a large portion of the sky had turned an ominous greenish-black colour.

The progression slowed as the drivers tried to negotiate their way through the throng of people. Masses of hands started pawing at the sides of the carriages. Outstretched arms reached through the windows. Theodora and the Countess batted the hands away, emitting high-pitched squeals.

Mothers held up babies and small children, some seeking blessings, others trying to snatch a look at the royals. The Countess huddled up against Arisa, shaking, and Theodora paled. Takai's face appeared to be frozen.

'It's alright,' she said. 'They're not trying to hurt you.'

Her companions looked unconvinced.

Soon both carriages were swamped. Arisa watched as the Duke and Sar rode into the crowd and urged the people to step back. Guthrie, though, was shoving people away. He didn't discriminate as he threw men, women and children to the ground. She saw him hit several men over the head with the hilt of his sword, and kick another in the stomach.

What had initially started out as inquisitive behaviour by the people was quickly turning to anger.

The carriages inched their way slowly toward the centre of the marketplace and finally came to a stop in front of a temporary stage. It appeared as if the whole city had turned out. Lakeford stood before the crowd, calling for quiet. Royal Guards now flanked the stage and the carriages, their sword hands at the ready.

Soon the noise fell to a low murmur, and everyone waited. Finally, King Delrik emerged from his carriage. He stood tall and proud, the diamonds from his crown sparkling like what could be seen of the glittering silver sun overhead, but his drawn face spoke to his nerves. He stepped up onto the stage and gestured for the Queen and Takai to join him.

Arisa leant out the window again to see the Queen disembark and walk up to the stage. The Prince took a deep breath and got out of their carriage. Sar was immediately by Takai's side, shadowing him to the stage.

Arisa leapt out after Takai. She had no fear. These were her people. The Countess reached over and closed the door firmly behind her. She and Theodora weren't moving from their sanctuary.

Arisa found Gwyn standing beside the first carriage, her brow furrowed with concern. She reached out and squeezed Gwyn's hand. Gwyn squeezed it back, her eyes not wavering from Queen Sofia.

The King began to speak. 'My loyal subjects,' he said shakily. 'We come in thanks.'

Thanks? What an odd thing to say. The crowd seemed just as perplexed as Arisa, and the mumbling started again.

'We know times have been…' King Delrik paused and wiped his brow. 'We know times have been trying, for all of us, in recent years.'

'Aye, real trying for fancy folk like you,' a stallholder heckled, and was met with a chorus of 'hear, hear's. The King gave the man a sharp look and Guthrie stepped closer to the crowds until they quieted down again.

'Yes, trying for us all,' the King continued gravely. 'Our great nation once again comes under threat. Our kingdom of Ette has been taken from us by the invaders from the north, and our rightful territory, Ivane, is next in their sights. But be assured: we will defend our territories and home with vigour.'

The crowd responded with a few grunts of assent.

'We are rebuilding our navy and forces, and preparing to take on our enemies.'

'Hear, hear!' came some more cries.

'We are doing everything we can to shore up your future. And once victorious, we will all have enough food to eat, clothing to wear and metal to forge, so no rationing or tax increases will be necessary ever again.'

'You mean *we*, the people, are doing everything *we* can,' an unseen man in the crowd cried out. 'It is *we* who will give our lives, conscripted into your army to fight unwinnable wars. It is *we*, your subjects, Lamorians and Kengians alike, who have had everything taken from us. It is *we* who have been thrown from our lands and stripped of our livelihoods. And it is *we* who are being forced to hand over every last coin and crumb, so the likes of you can live in luxury while we starve.'

There were great shouts of support for what the well-spoken man had said.

'Who is that?' Horace hissed. Guthrie set out in the direction of the voice.

King Delrik's brow crinkled. 'And for your support, I thank you.'

'Thanks! Is that what you call it when you abandon your people and throw anyone who challenges you into jail, or worse?' the unknown man responded.

'It's Sergei,' a voice cried. And the crowd cheered in recognition.

'Get him!' Horace pointed at the nearest guards, who pushed their way into the crowd.

But Sergei would not be silenced. 'Well, we are no longer at your bidding, for we are united. United against you. Your rule is on borrowed time, *King* Delrik.'

'I too wish for the kingdom to be united,' the King pressed on. 'Together we can defeat our enemies and, with your support, we can all live in prosperity once again.'

But his misplaced words were wasted. Sergei had vanished, disappearing into Obira's twisting roads and dark alleys.

Sure enough, Guthrie and the other guards held up their

arms in surrender. The King's biggest critic had eluded them once again, to shouts of support from the crowd.

Strangely, the King seemed unperturbed. He reached out beside him and grasped the Queen's stiffened hand. 'My Queen, the Prince and I truly thank you all for your support, and know the sacrifices you have made will help deliver all of us from these dark times. And before long, we will all have reason to celebrate.'

There were some dubious-sounding murmurs from the crowd.

'In the meantime, let me ease some of your pain.' He waved at a pair of groomsmen, who opened a chest on top of the King's carriage and began throwing handfuls of coins into the crowd.

So this was his surprise.

There was wild cheering and scrambling as people pushed and shoved each other to get to the coins. King Delrik held up the Queen and Takai's hands in triumph. The King smiled jubilantly, but the Queen's eyes were wide with horror. Evidently, she had had no prior knowledge of this theatrical display; if she had, she would surely have prevented it.

Arisa had lived long enough in this troubled city to predict what would happen next. There were hardly enough coins to go around the crowd. It was a terrible miscalculation, with dangerous consequences.

Within moments, the mood of the crowd turned again, and initial cries of surprise and glee transformed into shouts of pain and outrage as coins were snatched out of hands. Punches were thrown and children were crushed under the crowd. The stage on which the King, Queen and Prince stood began shifting violently, and the horses began to paw at the ground, their tails swishing hard and fast.

The realisation that the stunt had failed crept across King Delrik's face, as Guthrie and the other guards demanded order.

Lakeford and Sar moved in swiftly to escort the royals back

to the front carriage. The King and Takai were ushered in first, but the Queen stood fast on the spot, refusing to get in.

'Sofia!'

The King tried to appeal to his wife, to no avail. Lakeford begged for her to get in as well, but the Queen was unmoved. Horace shoved past her and leapt into the carriage, pulling the door securely shut behind him. Gwyn and Arisa raced to the Queen's side, imploring her to get into the carriage.

Queen Sofia was impassive. She had a strange mix of wonder and sadness on her face. The King screamed at his protectors until they let him away from the carriage. He stood between the Queen and the crowd, clutching his sword with the shakiest of grips.

Every guard was engaged in keeping the citizens from the carriages, the King and the Queen. Sar and Lakeford tried to fend off each attacker as they approached, but they were hopelessly outnumbered. The wooden chest had long been pulled from the carriage and now lay smashed on the ground.

A trio of men brandishing sticks advanced on the King, one of them striking the sword easily from his hand. They dragged him away, becoming lost in the fray.

Every nerve in Arisa's body was alive – on fire. The crowd surged toward her, the Queen and Gwyn. They glanced at each other, then to one of the coachmen, who was retrieving swords from the carriage's locked hold.

'We can't.' The Queen spoke for all of them. They couldn't take up arms against the Lamorians.

'Up there!' Arisa indicated the roof of the carriage. Above it, the entire sky was shrouded in a blanket of dense black clouds, the sun enveloped in darkness.

Gwyn helped the Queen to the top and Arisa was about to follow, but hesitated as she saw Takai being pulled out the window of his carriage. His head and chest were already through – and one man was approaching him with a knife.

She grabbed the remains of a halberd from the ground. Its

blade had been snapped off at the top, but it was a reasonably serviceable staff, similar to what she had used in training. She wondered if she could get to the Prince in time, but realised immediately that even if she could, she couldn't best the knife-wielding man, who was at least twice her size. She swept her gaze across the scene until she found Sar. He was dispatching the men who'd dragged the King away and were now attacking him.

She shouted his name, waving frantically toward Takai. Sar looked back and forth between his best friend and the King.

The King focused his swollen, bloodied eyes on his son. 'Go! Go!'

Sar nodded and leapt into position between the Prince and the approaching man, leaving the King to the mercy of a growing mob of attackers.

Arisa froze. She was stuck between her natural instinct to do something to help, even if she was dreadfully ill-equipped for the task, and remembering that she wanted the King to die, that it had been her mission all these months. She stood transfixed by the swarm of flying fists and makeshift weapons swallowing up the King. She was only roused when Guthrie shoved past her. He was advancing on a mountain of a man making to join the attack on the King.

Guthrie raised his broadsword above his head and was about to bring it down on the huge attacker's shoulder, but the man had spotted him, and with unexpected deftness, stepped out of reach. Guthrie grunted and raised his sword again, but this time his target shoved a small boy in front of him as a shield. The boy looked up, his eyes panicked.

His eyes were silver. The same as Hyando's. The same as Rea's.

Arisa saw a flash of the silver-haired man from her vision. He too was one of the silver-eyes. *Someone has to do something,* he was saying. *The darkness cannot win.*

She tightened her grip on the wooden staff, willing it to be up to the task. She felt the lifeforce of the tree from which the staff had been forged awaken deep within, sending pulses of energy through her palms and fingertips. It was as if everything slowed down around her, yet she was soaring as she raced toward the boy. She reached him and thrust the staff above his head, only an instant before Guthrie's blade made contact and bit hard into the wood.

The force of the blow reverberated through Arisa's arms, pushing her backwards. She steadied herself and heaved her weight forward, intuitively taking a front-fighting stance and wrapping her hands around the staff in a wide hold. The boy she'd saved scurried away to safety.

Guthrie's black eyes widened as he scanned the length of the staff for damage. It should have broken under his sword, but the only evidence of the blow was a shallow scratch-like mark. Arisa was as surprised as Guthrie. She thought back to Rea's powers, to how her friend had been able to move rocks with her mind – the silver-eyes magic had been uncommonly strong in her. Had Arisa somehow awoken her own abilities? She hadn't ever thought it was possible, but what other explanation was there for the lifeforce she had felt?

Guthrie shifted his attention to her, narrowing his eyes, as if to dissect her face for answers. A bitter cold shiver ran up her spine as she remembered how he had scrutinised her in a similar way, the day they had come for her and Rea. Arisa gripped her staff even tighter and jutted out her chin, unwilling to show Guthrie any fear.

His lip curled. 'I haven't forgotten that day in Obira. How you picked a fight with me over a stupid starling. And how you humiliated me in front of my father.'

'I haven't forgotten that day, either.' She forced a smile. 'And how satisfying it was to break your nose.'

Guthrie's face contorted. He struck out at her with his sword. She blocked the blow with her staff, but this time the force knocked the weapon from her hands and sent her sprawling onto the ground. She scrambled to retrieve her staff, reaching it at the same moment she felt the tip of Guthrie's sword press into the base of her throat.

He licked his lips. 'I could kill you right here. I could blame the crowd. No one would know any different.'

The voice rang in her ears again. *The darkness cannot win. Someone has to do something. You have to do something to help them.*

She should have felt scared. She knew Guthrie was right. That he could – and would, without hesitation – kill her right there. But she was no longer scared, not even as she felt the point of the sword break her skin and a trickle of blood run down to her chest.

She was angry. Angrier than she could ever remember being.

Her anger had always been there, bubbling away below the surface all these years. She'd learnt to control the worst of it; learnt, for the most part, not to let the darkness take over. But in this moment, with everything she valued in the world crumbling around her, Arisa released the anger from where it had been buried deep inside her. She let it consume her. She felt as if her stomach were filled with the same storm clouds as above; as if she would explode in a furious ball of fire.

She looked to the sky. She would release the rising darkness, and let it spew like lava from her.

Arisa opened her mouth and screamed, a piercing, animalistic sound that would have turned every head if there hadn't been another sound and sight to behold. The sky had cracked open with bolts of lightning and a cacophony of thunder. One all-consuming lightning bolt zigzagged toward the marketplace and struck the bronze statue of King Emberto. The fighting momentarily ceased, and Guthrie spun around to watch the show of ricocheting sparks coming from the statue. The clouds burst open, releasing torrential rain on them all.

Arisa seized the moment. She got to her feet and decided to make her escape. A better chance had never been given to her to make good on her promise to Erun to get to safety, and there was nothing more she could do to help the people.

The darkness had won.

She pushed through the crowd, but had only made it a few feet when she was confronted by the boy with silver-eyes. He stood alone in the rain, staring wordlessly at her.

'Get to safety,' she urged him. 'Find your family.'

The boy was unmoving. Around them, everyone had resumed fighting. The King lay in a puddle of bloody water on the ground, his hands futilely trying to protect his face as one man after another hit and kicked him. Takai and Sar were completely surrounded by attacking Lamorians.

'The darkness hasn't won. Not yet. You have to do something.' It was the boy speaking to her, but his voice was oddly the same as the silver-haired man's. What kind of magic was coming from this man in her visions? Should she do what he said?

If she did nothing, she could make her escape. The King would most likely die, and possibly all of Lamore's troubles with him. The other lives lost today would be collateral damage.

But that would be letting what Arisa knew now was the *real* darkness – hate – win. The silver-haired man and the boy were right. She had to stop this madness, for everyone's sake. She couldn't watch another innocent child or Lamorian die. If she were being honest with herself, she couldn't watch Takai die either. She had to push aside the hate and do what was right.

But what exactly could she do? The marketplace had erupted in a full-blown riot.

Arisa closed her eyes, trying to find the silver-haired man in her mind, hoping he would give her the answer, but all she could see was Takai's face. His dark eyes – intense, probing, then smiling, dancing, alive.

A great whooshing sound roared in her ears. She opened her eyes to see a wall of water barrelling through the marketplace, an inexplicable wave formed from all the water on the ground.

Arisa watched in horror as the wave rushed toward her and the silver-eyed boy. She held up her hands in a futile attempt to protect herself, but the moment of impact didn't come. Instead, the water parted around her, picking up Lamorians by the dozens, tossing them like they were ragdolls and carrying them down the cobblestone streets. Those not in the wave's path ran to higher ground.

Arisa silently thanked the silver-haired man, and with the silver-eyed boy at her side, ran toward Gwyn and the Queen, who had taken shelter on top of one of the carriages. Sar and Takai were with them, as well as the injured King.

Wherever Arisa and the boy went, they carved out a path in the water.

'This way,' she shouted through the rain, leading the group back through the marketplace. They stopped at the other carriage, where the Duke, Horace, Guthrie, Theodora and the Countess had hidden.

'We have to hurry!' Arisa urged the group as the water started receding.

'Where to?' Takai asked.

The boy pointed to the Lion's Den at the top of the market-place. It was on high ground. Arisa nodded and led the group to the tavern, leaving a sea of water behind them.

THE RAIN-SOAKED and battered royal court burst through the doors of the tavern to find the place empty, except for a greatly surprised tavernkeeper. Arisa surmised that his customers had all been drawn to the spectacle in the marketplace, and that the water had blocked their path from taking shelter there.

'Dunderhead, why did you bring them here?' the tavern-keeper admonished the boy.

'They needed help.'

'They don't need us, boy.' He cast a distasteful gaze at the group. 'They're rich enough to look after themselves.'

'Exactly!' the Chancellor snarled. 'And in the name of the King, we commandeer this place.'

The tavernkeeper's expression hardened, and his eyes went to a sword above his bar.

'Please.' The Queen approached him. 'We do not order you. We humbly request that you let us take shelter here. We have nowhere else to go.'

The keeper's face softened slightly at the Queen's earnest appeal. 'Aye. Do as you please, but mark me words – that mob will come for you, as soon as…' He waved his hands toward the window. 'As soon as whatever that is settles down out there.'

The Duke nodded to Sar and, with a handful of guards who'd made it to the tavern, they barricaded all the entrances to the Lion's Den.

Arisa went immediately into healer mode, visually assessing and prioritising the group's injuries. No one in the group had escaped some form of injury – except for Horace and his family – but most, herself included, only had minor cuts and abrasions. Takai, though, had a bloody gash on his arm. She suspected his original wound from his accident had reopened. Her first instinct was to go to him, but the Queen was already tending to her son.

Then Arisa's gaze fell on the King. His entire face was bloodied and bruised. He held a hand to his ribs and winced whenever he moved. Gwyn was already examining him.

'Bruised ribs, I think. Nothing broken,' she said.

Arisa did her own examination and confirmed Gwyn's assessment. She looked around for her satchel, but remembered it was still in the carriage.

'We need some clean linen and boiled water,' she told the silver-eyed boy, who immediately fetched what she requested. Then Arisa grabbed his arm and pulled him aside. 'Thank you for bringing us here, but you can't stay,' she whispered. 'Not after what happened out there. They will think it was silver-eyed magic – yours.'

'But it wasn't me, miss.'

'I know.' It had been the silver-haired man. 'But they don't know that.' Arisa nodded toward the Chancellor.

She took off the felt hat that had protected her own identity from being revealed in the rain and removed the pin from it. It was silver, set with three precious Ivanian stones. 'Take this and get out of Obira. Get yourself to safety.' The boy nodded and slipped out of sight.

Arisa split up the linen and water with Gwyn and the Queen and they got to work, with even Theodora lending a hand. It appeared she only objected to tending to poor people.

Arisa started to clean the King's wounds, but he clutched at her gown. 'Please, see to my son…It is no matter if I die…but not my son,' he gasped.

'Your Majesty, you are not dying. I expect a full recovery… assuming we get out of this place in one piece.'

His eyes widened in alarm. Her attempt to comfort him had only seemed to make him more anxious.

'It's alright.' The Queen's hand was on her shoulder. 'I'll see to the King, so you can help my son.'

Takai winced but said nothing as Arisa checked his arm. The wound wasn't as deep as she had feared, and the Queen's bandage had stemmed much of the bleeding.

'You got any more of that special poultice?' he joked.

'I didn't think you liked the smell of it.'

He winced again as she tightened the bandage. 'Some smelly gunk on my arm would be the least of my worries right now.' He glanced out the window, where the crowd had already reformed in the pouring rain, then dropped his voice to a whisper. 'What exactly happened out there? That storm – it was like it was from another world. And the wave, and the water parting around you and that boy? What kind of Kengian magic was it?'

'I don't know,' she said. It was the truth.

The Prince's jaw tightened. 'This kingdom will never be at peace while the threat of Kengian magic remains.'

'*Enough,*' Arisa murmured.

'What did you say?' he snapped at her.

She met his piercing gaze. 'I said *enough*. Enough of this ridiculous fear you have of Kengian magic.'

Takai sat up straighter and lifted his chin. 'I have good reason to fear it.'

She knew he was speaking of how the Kengian Prince was supposed to have bewitched his father. 'Your good reason is based on lies.'

He opened his mouth as if to protest, but his gaze went back to the window. The crowd outside was chanting.

'What are they saying?' the Prince asked.

Arisa trained her ears on the crowd. It was hard to hear over the rain, but after a while she recognised the Kengian words: *Mikret Tawreh elli tacusa.*

'The Water Catcher will come,' she translated.

'See! When they're not worshipping that troublemaker Sergei, they're waiting for some magical Kengian to turn up and save them. Someone who can never exist.'

Arisa would have agreed with him. She knew the Water Catcher would never come, but seeing the desperation among the crowd today, she had finally understood why so many believed.

'It doesn't matter if there isn't a Water Catcher,' she said, speaking mainly to herself. 'The Water Catcher is a symbol to them. A symbol of hope.' *It's what Hyando had. It was what Rea had.*

Hope, Takai mouthed, his gaze unwavering.

'Yes…That's it,' she realised excitedly. 'Give the people *hope*. Real hope that things are changing. That the King has changed. That everything is changing for the better. Give them that, and they won't need to look to Sergei or a prophecy to save them. They won't need saving.'

'Hope,' Takai repeated, like it was the first time he'd ever heard the word, and at that exact moment, the rain outside stopped.

The Prince smiled at Arisa and reached for her hand. She didn't recoil.

There was the sound of shattered glass and a sudden flash of light, and Takai was on his feet. It only took Arisa a second to realise the crowd was throwing torches through the tavern windows.

They intended to burn the nobles alive.

She ran to King Delrik as Sar, the Duke and the guards raced to extinguish the torches before the flames took hold. 'You can stop them. Talk to them,' she begged the wild-eyed King. 'Talk to your people.'

'The time for talk is over,' Horace barked. 'Send the Duke and his men out there to deal with them. No mercy.'

'That is exactly what you must show them – mercy,' Arisa said.

'Most of those outside are unarmed, sire, and are no match against our guards. The Duke and his men could hold the crowd long enough to get you to safety,' Horace argued.

'No!' The Queen turned to the King. 'You can't take up arms against your own people. Please, husband.'

'Sire, you will be safe, I promise you. Guthrie, find safe passage out of here for the King.'

Guthrie, though, stood fixed to the spot, dropping his gaze to the ground.

'It is a fool's mission.' The King gave a wry laugh at his own words. 'The Queen and Arisa are right. I need to speak to my people, but I fear it's too late. I will ask the Duke to see you are all taken to safety, and I will stay.' He got to his feet. 'I will give myself to the people and they can decide my fate.'

'No, Father—' Takai blocked the King's path. 'There must be another way. There must be...' Takai's gaze went to Arisa's, and as if they were one mind, they mouthed in unison: *hope*.

Before Arisa knew what she was doing, she and Takai were

removing the barricades from the door of the tavern. The crowd stilled when they appeared in the doorway. 'The Prince!' someone shouted, and the crowd surged toward them.

Sar and the Duke raced to Takai's defence and Arisa used the distraction to push her way into the marketplace. Clear of the crowd, she found an abandoned cart. She climbed to the top of it and took a deep breath.

Someone has to do something.

'Stop!' she shouted at the crowd. 'Stop, all of you!'

She kept shouting, louder, until the uproar slowly subsided. Fists froze in midair. Every eye in the marketplace was on her, waiting to see what someone stupid enough to throw themselves at the mercy of an angry mob was going to do next.

'What do you want, girlie?' The mountainous man Guthrie had tried to fight earlier glowered up at her.

Arisa looked around nervously. What *did* she want? If only Erun were here, he would know what to do. But Erun wasn't here, and she was a poor substitute. She was just one girl.

Guthrie's gaze found her and his usual sneer curved into a smile as he saw the precarious situation she was in. She wondered if she could get back down and explain that she was a prisoner of the court. The crowd might let her go. She could still escape. But what then? What would happen to the mob that had threatened and attacked the King and his court today? She knew the answer. Every single one of them would be hunted down. It would be a repeat of the Kengian massacre, and she couldn't have their blood on her hands. Not if there was something she could do.

She looked down and caught Takai's eye. His sword was at the ready. His eyes were locked on her, as if his sole purpose were to protect her. She drew strength from his gaze and willed her legs to steady. The marketplace was filled with expectant silence.

'You ask what I want. I want nothing except for you to listen to me for a few moments.'

'Why should we listen to you?' the huge man demanded.

'Because I'm one of you.'

She was met with guffaws and cries of disbelief.

'You don't look like one of us.'

'But I am. I was born in Obira. It is my home. I'm a Lamorian, just like you are, just like every man, woman and child here is. Just like the King and his family are.'

'We're not the same as them.' One man pointed toward the tavern and spat on the ground.

'The King and his men have done plenty wrong by us and deserve everythin' comin' at 'em,' another man cried. 'Sergei will see to it.'

She continued determinedly. 'You're right. Many wrongs have been done, but does it justify fighting each other like animals? It makes you no better than them.'

'Easy for you to say, dressed in your finery. You don't 'ave four starvin' babes to feed,' shouted a thin woman with a baby swaddled against her chest.

'You're right, I don't. But this isn't the way.' Arisa waved her hands before her. 'Together, we must show the King and his advisers that all we want is to live honest lives. That we respect ourselves and each other.'

'*We*, you say. You keep saying *we*. You don't speak for us. You're nothing like us.'

'But I am the same. You don't understand—'

'Bah! I've had enough of your talk. Let's show her *our* way.'

The crowd surged menacingly toward her, with the mountainous man at its head. Arisa had no way out. Before she could move, a pair of hands had wrapped around her ankle and was attempting to drag her to the ground. She kicked herself free.

'Fools!' cried a new voice. 'Don't you see?'

No one had seen the woman with the fiery hair push her way to the front of the crowd. She now stood between the angry mob and the cart Arisa was standing on. It was Lina, Hyando's mother – the Kengian woman the Queen had saved from execution.

'Don't you see it?' Lina shouted again.

'Keep out of this, or you'll get hurt too, woman.' The huge man held up his fist threateningly.

'She *is* like us. In fact, she is the best among us. She is Arisa, ward of Erun the healer.' There were murmurs throughout the crowd. 'You would attack the very person who has brought you cures for your ailments in the middle of the night? The one who has helped bring your babes safely into the world? The one who has tended to your wives, husbands and children when they lay in bed with fever, all with no regard for her own safety?'

The mob leader looked unconvinced.

'It is her. It *is* Arisa,' the woman with the baby shouted. 'She looks different, but it's her. Bless you, Arisa.'

'Bless you, Arisa,' came further cries.

'Arisa is right,' Lina continued. 'None of us are blameless. We have done some wrong, just as the King has done some right. The King has shown us he is capable of showing mercy, even to those who have spoken out against him. And I know this because I was to be executed, but the Queen begged for my life, and the King spared it.'

'Out of the way, wench,' the mountainous man growled. 'I don't care if *she*' – he pointed at Arisa – 'is the Queen herself. I won't stand for her do-good talking.' He moved a step closer. He was now within arm's reach of where she stood on top of the carriage, a knife in his hand.

Lina made to step between them. 'You make one move toward her, and you'll have me to deal with,' she said.

'And me.' Sar had appeared, and was standing in front of the cart.

'And me.' It was Takai's voice this time. He moved in to take his place by Sar, and guards fell in beside him.

The mountainous man stopped and stood for a long

moment, clenching his fist, before grunting and stomping away, cursing under his breath all the while.

The crowd was silent.

Sar helped Arisa down to the ground. Queen Sofia, who had ventured out of the tavern, approached Lina and embraced her.

'Thank you for your bravery,' she said.

Lina looked down in embarrassment. 'It is nothing, my Queen. Thank *you* for what you did for me.'

'You're welcome, but it is another you should thank for appealing to me.'

The Queen turned now to address the crowd.

'We all have to thank this remarkable girl you see today. She has shown us what is important, and that our differences are not so great. A girl who understands your pain and bridges our two worlds. A girl who wishes for nothing but peace and prosperity for all of you.'

Arisa hung her head, ashamed at the Queen's comments. If only she knew that Arisa had been planning to kill her husband.

The Queen turned back to her. 'Bless you, Arisa.'

'Bless you, Arisa,' came shouts from the crowd again.

'I humbly appear before you today to ask for your blessings as your Queen,' Sofia called. 'For I am your servant, and I am nothing without all of you!'

'Bless you, our Queen,' the crowd cried in unison.

The King hobbled over to the Queen's side. His adoring, albeit beaten, face shone as he watched his wife conquer the crowds.

'Your Majesty,' Horace called out from the safety of the tavern. 'It is time we left.'

But the King replied, 'Chancellor, I am here to help my people, and it is that duty I will perform.'

OVER THE NEXT HOUR, Arisa watched as the King and Queen went among the crowd and offered blessings. The King even asked to help hand out the food Arisa had collected from the castle kitchens. Arisa couldn't believe he was capable of such mercy and kindness, especially after being attacked by his own people – all because of his love for the Queen.

After Gwyn had distributed the last loaf of bread, a man with a nasty-looking burn on his arm asked for Arisa's assistance. She told him to wait while she fetched her satchel of supplies.

At the carriage she found Horace berating Theodora and the Countess. 'I command you to play your part,' he hissed. 'You're being shown up by the Queen and her pathetic offsiders.'

'The smell of them,' the Countess wailed, pinching her nose closed. 'I'm afraid I'll be sick.'

'You, daughter – do as I command.'

Theodora crossed her arms. 'So my brother can refuse to perform his duty to the King, but I must do as you command? I refuse to be your puppet anymore, *Father*.'

Horace clicked his jaw. 'Just hand out a couple of coins. Smile sweetly. You need not even take off your gloves.'

Theodora looked toward the Queen, who was kissing a baby's grubby face. Then her eyes fell on Arisa. 'Let her do it. They are *her* kind of people, after all.'

Arisa ignored the barb and grabbed her satchel from the carriage, turning around abruptly to head back to her patient. She was so intent on her task that she didn't notice Takai in her path. She ran headlong into the Prince, narrowly managing to catch a bottle of ointment from her satchel before it fell to the ground.

'Sorry,' she muttered.

'No, it was entirely my fault,' Takai stumbled. 'I'm afraid my attention was diverted elsewhere.' He cast a glance of distaste back at Theodora. Arisa wondered if he had heard the whole exchange with the Chancellor. Takai opened his mouth as if to say something else, but stopped short. He stared at her with a strange, questioning look on his face.

Disconcerted, she excused herself, but Takai remained fixed in her path.

'Is there something the matter?'

'No, why do you ask?'

'You're staring at me as if I have a pock on my face. Do I have a pock on my face?'

'Don't be ridiculous. Of course you don't.'

'May I speak freely?'

He raised a quizzical brow. 'If you haven't been speaking freely before now, what have you been doing?'

Arisa sighed, thinking that nothing she had said before now had seemed to have made a difference, but perhaps now, perhaps after today…'These are your people.' She waved a hand around her. 'These are the people you hope to unite. The people who will entrust their lives to you. They will fight in wars that mean nothing to them. Many will not return. They pay the taxes to keep you in your fine clothes and the expensive wine on your table, yet they can't afford to feed their own children.'

She saw Takai's jaw harden, but she wouldn't be silenced now.

'Many of them have faced significant obstacles, not of their choosing; yet strive only to make a fair and honest living. What little or great you can do to ease their burden will not be unfelt.'

Takai stood in silence, his proud chin lifted. He was infuriating.

'Frankly, if you can't show compassion, the least you can show them is respect. By their very survival, each one of them has proved they are more deserving of respect than…' She stopped, but looked up at Takai defiantly.

'More than me? They deserve respect more than me? Is that what you think?' His face was distorted with anger.

'Well, that's entirely up to you.'

Takai looked across at his mother. She was pushing coins

into an elderly woman's hands. 'But what can I do?' he asked softly.

Arisa knew the question spoke of things beyond the here and now. She felt a sudden urge to reassure him, to tell him there was much he could do. But she wasn't sure he was ready to change.

She shoved the satchel into his arms. 'Follow me,' she ordered.

In the time that followed, Arisa couldn't believe the transformation she saw in the Prince. He joined her, the Queen, Gwyn and the King in listening to the long line of people's requests and tending to their ailments. No amount of blood, filth or smell made Takai flinch. He was every bit the Prince she imagined he should be.

Eventually the line thinned, and with no supplies left, Arisa stepped back to take a rest. The silver sun was back, and the sky was clear and blue, as if the storm had never been. Takai appeared by her side but stood silently for a while.

Finally, he spoke. 'The people have all the hope they need now.'

She turned to face him. The Prince was standing with his arms folded, his eyes on the crowd. But then he turned and gave her a kind smile – his mother's smile – a smile that went all the way to his dark eyes.

'They have you,' he said. '*We* have you.'

Arisa was flustered by what she'd heard...or thought she heard. She would have asked Takai to repeat what he had said, but he was already walking away.

What if she had been wrong about everything? What if Takai was right? Could she do more good if she stayed in Lamore? Could the memory of her father, Rea and Hyando be better served by joining those she thought were her enemies? She wondered what would happen to the Lamorians, and Erun, if she left. She wondered what would happen to Takai, who continued to confound her. She felt there was a chance that he was on the verge of becoming a great leader. The leader his people needed.

With a start, Arisa realised that the very place she had always wanted to leave was the only place she belonged. It was the only place where she could make a difference. And perhaps no one needed to die to get the justice she demanded.

An unfamiliar warmth lit up inside her. Was this hope? She had long forgotten what it felt like. She had thought all hope had died with Rea, replaced by the darkness – yet there it was. A burning light inside her like the Firemaster's phoenix rising from the flames. But was she ready for it? Could she trust it?

There was only one way to find out.

It was decided. She would return to the castle. She would see Erun again, and maybe he would help her harness any abilities she may have. And the King could live…at least for now.

As for the threat of firesky – Arisa would have to find another way to protect its secrets. Right now, Lamore needed her. And, just maybe, the Prince needed her too.

EPILOGUE

Horace was late to the King's Council meeting, performing a double take when he realised the King was in his seat at the end of the table, flanked by the Queen and Takai. When the progress had been cancelled, the King had recalled all the nobles to the castle. While the trouble in Obira had now dissipated, Sergei was still on the loose, and there were no means of guaranteeing the King's safety – or anyone else's – in the counties.

In the meantime, the Queen had become a permanent fixture in the King's rooms. King Delrik had dismissed his mistress, sending her back to her own husband. He had also banned Horace from his privy chamber.

The King was now hearing all petitions himself, and managing his own correspondence, with only the Queen and Takai by his side. Horace had been given no official business to see to, other than the great celebration event at the start of spring. He had been officially demoted to a master of cere-monies and the title of Secretary.

Takai felt little sympathy for the man. He had wielded too much influence over the King all these years, and seemed intent on Lamore making a dangerous alliance with the Northemers.

'I'm so glad you could join us, Secretary,' the King sneered at Horace. His cold expression, coupled with the yellowing bruises on his face, was altogether unsettling.

'Your Majesty.' Horace bowed briskly and took the only vacant seat at the opposite end of the table.

The King turned back to his councillors. 'I think we have made great progress.'

'Progress?' Horace glanced around for an answer.

'We have decided that the best path forward is to negotiate terms with Malu,' the King replied.

'Malu will never agree to terms,' Horace scoffed. 'He holds every advantage.'

'But he may accept terms if the inducement is enough.'

'What? You don't propose *paying* him to leave Ette? With what money? The treasury is practically empty.'

'But Ivane's treasury is not. Lore will go to Ivane and, with the Queen's brother, he will arrange for formal negotiations to take place with the Northemers. We will form an alliance with Ivane and Ette.'

'Alliances, sire? Why would you partner with usurping countries that are your rightful territories?'

The Queen locked her eyes on Horace. 'Fighting for territories we have no claim over is not something we can afford, in lives or coin. As true allies, Ette and Ivane will ensure Lamore's prosperity.'

Horace turned to look at the councillors. 'Surely you haven't agreed to this madness?'

They all nodded.

'Lakeford?'

'It is agreed,' the Duke said. 'The navy and army will continue their preparations in case the negotiations fail. But I have no interest in taking my men to a war my King or Queen have no appetite for.'

'But—'

'Enough!' The King held his hands up. 'It is decided.'

'We do have one other matter to discuss,' Takai said. The King nodded and motioned for the door to be opened.

A confused-looking Arisa was ushered into the room. She curtsied, her eyes downcast. 'Your Majesties. Your Highness. Councillors.'

Takai watched Horace click his jaw as the King nodded his acknowledgement to Arisa.

'I bring you here to give thanks for what you did in Obira. Speaking as you did took real courage, and stopped what was sure to be a tragic outcome from occurring.'

Arisa looked up, and the Queen gave her an encouraging smile. Takai's eyes were glued to her. A beautiful whirlwind of fire, energy and bravery.

'To recognise this,' the King continued, 'I have decided to give you your own lands, adjoining the Duke of Lakeford's, and a discretionary title.'

It gave Takai pleasure to see Horace's cheeks redden on hearing that Arisa was to be elevated to the peerage and given prime lands. Lands much better than what his family had.

'From now on, you are to be known as Lady Arisa, Marchioness of—'

'I'm so sorry to interrupt, Your Majesty,' Arisa said, 'but I can't accept such an offer.'

The King's expression froze.

'I'm honoured, to be sure, but I don't believe this is the best way I can serve you or your people.'

The King cocked his head to one side. 'What do you suggest?'

The councillors all leaned forward in their seats. No one had ever refused such a generous offer, let alone someone of her standing.

'There is one thing I think I can do to help the most needy Lamorians. And that is to become a trained surgeon.'

The King let out a hearty laugh, followed by the rest of the councillors.

Arisa pursed her lips.

The Queen reached out and touched the King's hand. The laughter stopped immediately.

'Arisa, the College of Surgeons has only ever been for…' The King appeared to be struggling to find the right words. 'Surgeons are always…' He stopped and looked at her earnestly. 'Arisa, you're a girl,' he stated bluntly.

Her eyes flashed angrily. 'Yes, a *girl* who saved you from being killed by an angry mob.'

The King gave a small laugh. 'I suppose you're right. You're the match of any man. When do you wish to start at the College?'

Arisa raised her eyebrows in surprise. 'Well, I must pass the entrance examinations first.'

'No need.' The King waved his hands. 'You can start immediately.'

Immediately? But that would mean she would leave – leave the castle. Takai's breath caught in his throat. He wasn't ready to say goodbye to Arisa, not when they'd only just…just what? Had a moment?

It didn't matter. She couldn't go. Not yet.

Arisa shook her head. 'There *is* a need. I will earn my place.'

'Very well,' the King said, and Takai exhaled.

The Queen leant over toward her husband. 'I understand the examinations are in two months' time.'

The King nodded and turned to Arisa. 'So, you will stay with us until then?'

'Yes, Your Majesty.'

'Thank you again, Arisa, for your service.'

'Your Majesty.' Arisa curtsied and the King nodded to a guard to escort her from the room.

Just before she left, she turned in Takai's direction, a shadow of a smile on her face – a shadow of hope, but enough to send a ripple of excitement through him.

Once she was gone, the King clapped his hands together

and adjourned the meeting. He held his arm out to the Queen and Takai followed his parents from the room.

Horace raced to follow them. 'Your Majesty,' he called out. 'I beg for you to hear me.'

The King turned, giving him an impatient look before nodding. Horace looked nervously at the Queen and Takai.

The King seemed to read his meaning. 'Sofia, I will follow in a moment.'

Takai's mother didn't budge.

'I'll be right behind you, my love.'

The Queen left them, but not before shooting Horace a dark look.

'Be quick with it,' the King barked.

'Sire…' Horace looked in Takai's direction.

'Anything you have to say to me can be said to my son.'

'Very well,' Horace said hesitantly. 'I must insist that you don't proceed with this strategy. Ivane can't be trusted. The Queen's brother is against us. And I have already made overtures to Malu. Remember, forming an alliance with the Northemers means we can take back Ivane and Ette. You must stick to our plan.'

'Must! You dare to tell me what I *must* do?'

'Your Majesty, I only seek to give you the best advice, as I have always done.'

'I'm not so sure your advice has always been in my best interests. Rather, it has always been in yours. In fact, I'm not even sure I need your so-called *advice* anymore.'

'Your Majesty, if you insist on this strategy, you can't expect Malu to go away forever. He will come back again and again with his army of giants, with his hand out for more coin each time. There is a way, though, for you to be rid of the Northemers once and for all — and to have Kengia.'

Takai saw a flicker of interest in his father's eyes.

'It is all possible, Your Majesty. You will have Kengia and be the most powerful ruler in all of the lands — the most powerful ruler in history. Because you will have firesky…and I will not fail you now.'

The King stroked this chin. 'Horace, if you deliver firesky, as promised, by the time of the great celebrations, I will reconsider our strategy for Ette and Kengia. But I will never invade Ivane, or act in any way against my Queen's wishes. I lost her once, and for too long, because of your advice, and I will not lose her again. But…if you fail to give me firesky…' The King didn't finish his sentence. He didn't need to. Horace knew what was at stake if he failed.

'Sire, I won't disappoint you. I just need you to grant me one favour to ensure this.'

The King sighed. 'What is it?'

'The girl, Arisa. I must have her under my control. She is the only way I can guarantee Erun's compliance. She must be my prisoner.'

'Father! You cannot do anything to Arisa,' Takai interjected. 'Not after everything she has done for Lamore – for you.'

The King nodded his assent. 'You will have to find another way, Horace.'

Horace paused and licked his lips. 'What if Lamore was to learn their so-called heroine and her guardian weren't who they say they are?'

The King raised an eyebrow.

'I have proof of Erun receiving secret messages from Kengia. They appear to be messages of great importance.'

A hard lump had formed in Takai's throat. 'What do the messages say?'

'I'm in the process of deciphering them now.'

The King waved his hand. 'Until you can prove something of substance against Erun and his ward, you aren't to make a move against the girl.'

Takai stifled a sigh of relief. Arisa was safe…for now. But what was she hiding from them? From him?

It occurred to Takai that he and Horace had at least one

thing in common: they were each determined to uncover Arisa's secrets…albeit for very different reasons. Horace knew any hope of clawing back his power relied on deciphering the secret messages and controlling the healer through Arisa.

All Takai wanted was to understand the girl who was threatening to steal his heart.

CAN I ASK A FAVOUR?

Thank you for reading *The Firemaster's Legacy*. I hope you enjoyed it and would appreciate if you could take a moment to leave a review. Reviews are the lifeblood of independent authors and key to others learning about our books.

You can **share your review** via your favourite online bookstore or Goodreads.

Read on for a sneak peek of Book 2 in the Kyprian Prophecy Series – *The Water Catcher's Rise*.

THE WATER CATCHER'S RISE: THE KYPRIAN PROPHECY BOOK 2

Lamore is on the brink of war. Victory will depend on two things: who commands firesky and whether one silver-eyed girl can make the biggest leap of faith — believing in herself, believing in love and believing in the prophe-sied Water Catcher.

Read the first chapter of the *The Water Catcher's Rise* now!

THE WATER CATCHER'S RISE – THE KYPRIAN PROPHECY BOOK 2

AN EXCERPT

The Kengian snow wolf crept to the opening of her den. She was tucked away in a rocky outcrop at the edge of the castle grounds, as far from the humans as possible. When she had heard the noise, she'd wondered whether they had finally found her hideout. They seemed determined to hunt her down and talked of taking her thick white coat as a trophy.

She sniffed the salt air. Nothing came to her on the night breeze other than the musky earthiness of the nearby woodland with its undergrowth of fallen leaves, pine needles and damp soil. She pricked her ears, but there was no sound. If it hadn't been the humans, it may be a small animal in distress.

The young wolf licked her lips. She hadn't eaten for a few days, as her choices were limited at Lamore Castle. She was used to hunting with her pack in the Nymoi Alps, the mountain range bordering Lamore and her Kengian homeland. She and her brothers and sisters would take down a deer and bring it back to their family to share. While prey was scarce – especially in winter – at the high altitude where they lived, the animals that did cross their path didn't stand a chance against their pack. But here the wolf was alone. Stranded in Lamore without her family, and surrounded by people who wanted her dead.

She yearned to return to her pack in the mountains, far away from the grand stone castle nearby, but some strange power stopped her. It was the same power that had overtaken her body leading up to the night of the blood moon. Many things had changed around the time of the blood moon's appearance, at least in the human world. The Kengian King had fallen ill and later died – at least, that was what must have happened, for that was when the King's protection over the mountain border had disappeared, and she had made her journey across the Nymoi Alps.

Since she'd been a pup, the wolf had known she could never venture beyond the top of the Alps. She'd been told any animal or human who tried to cross the mountains dividing the two nations would be forced back by a great trembling of the earth – and that was merely a warning. If they persisted, monster-sized rocks would fall down on them. Chasms would open in the mountainside and gobble them up. She had never dared to see if it was true. That was, until the night the power found her.

That night, it was as if everything she did or saw was through the eyes of another. A force had come over her, reaching into her mind, asking for cooperation. She hadn't fought it. Somehow, she'd known the energy wasn't evil. The power had chosen her as its vessel and was sending her on a quest – an important one.

So she had left her pack and the warm comfort of their cave to cross the Alps. She had negotiated the wintry path, thick with several feet of snow, until she'd reached the summit. The power had told her not to fear any trembling of the earth, that it wouldn't come. And without hesitation, she had stepped over the other side and descended into Lamore. The power had led her through the Lamorian countryside and then to Obira City. She'd arrived at the castle the night of the blood moon and had remained at one with the power ever since.

For the most part, she lived as any wolf would. She ventured into the woodland and hunted for food, and she watched. She watched the castle's inhabitants and their comings and goings, always from a safe distance.

Sometimes the power would speak to her with a human voice. If she saw something unusual, or a particular person, she would sense the force guiding her. She wasn't sure what her quest was, exactly, but she accepted that it was important enough not to fight it. That was the way of the natural world in Kengia: humans and animals lived in harmony and balance. But it wasn't the way of Lamore. Here, she needed all her wits to survive.

The wolf trained her ears to the air, and the noise came to her again. A scratching. The sound of twigs being crushed underfoot in the woodland? Her ears twitched. No – it was the sound of gravel and small rocks scuffing along the ground, and it wasn't coming from the woods. It was coming from the jagged hillside that led up to the castle's north-east gate from Obira City.

Her curiosity urged her to edge further out from her den. She looked around and assured herself she was safe. There was a bright full moon in the cloudless sky, its light carving out the craggy outline of the Nymoi Alps in the distance. The wolf could see her path to the boundary wall was clear. She bounded out into the clearing and took a path that hugged the coastline, seeking refuge in the line of rocks running along the cliff's edge.

As she neared the castle wall, a new sound came to her on the wind, but this time from a different direction. She spun her head to the sea, and paused. She could hear waves. Waves slapping against something. Slapping – not crashing like they did on the rocks far below. And she heard human voices; only whispers, but they were definitely voices, carrying from the water. The wolf looked down the cliff face to the murky depths below, scanning the water, her eyes alert for any movement, but there was nothing. She stared out a little further, but saw only the black sky merging into the inky blanket that was the sea.

She was about to turn back when the moonlight caught on

something shiny. Her night vision confirmed it as the hilt of a sword glinting back at her. Now she knew where to look, the shape started to take form.

It was a long, low-set boat.

When the wolf had first arrived in Obira, the surrounding sea and harbour had been heaving with ships, but in recent days it had become a graveyard. The voice inside her mind had explained that all of Lamore's trade relied on resources from a place called Ette and its seaside capital – territory Lamore had since lost to invaders called Northemers. Only the occasional merchant ship that had found other far-flung ports to trade with visited Lamore now. So the appearance of this boat was unusual. More so because it was different to any vessel she'd seen before.

The boat was open to the elements and a dozen or more giants of men were rowing it. The oars slipped in and out of the water with barely a ripple. Each man had a shield strapped to his back, and swords or axes tucked behind him. At the boat's prow was a snarling sculpture of a water serpent.

The boat disappeared behind a rocky formation, a tiny island several hundred feet from shore. The wolf heard the splash of a stone anchor being thrown overboard. She was certain these men in their stealthy boat were not Lamorians. And they weren't Kengians. They could be none other than the Northemers. And they were waiting for something – but what?

The wolf's natural instinct was to return to her den, to avoid whatever complicated human business was afoot, but she felt the familiar force wash over her. Energy rushed through her veins, warming her limbs, reaching every muscle in her body, until her golden eyes transformed. She was no longer herself, not entirely. She was the other presence as well as the wolf. She knew her golden eyes had transformed to green. The voice in her mind told her she must turn her attention back to the noises coming from the other side of the wall.

She loped back toward the boundary wall, clinging to its

shadows. The north-east gate was a narrow passage, only wide enough for a single file of livestock to pass. There were only two guards on duty, and they seemed oblivious to the noises intensifying outside the gate. The wolf was certain now that the creatures making the noise were humans. And judging by their overpowering scent, they were close.

She listened as the intruders' feet crunched in the gravel on the slope below. She willed the guards to spot them despite their inferior sense of hearing and smell, but her hopes were in vain. The guards stood motionless in their gatehouse. Neither had noticed the approach of the snow wolf, either. She peered through a crack in the wooden gate, seeing an army of large granite slabs and boulders jutting out from the hillside like broken teeth.

At first the wolf could see nothing out of place, but then she registered the slightest movement from the corner of her eye. Two crouching shadows were fleeing from one rock shadow to the next. Cloaked in black, they were gargantuan-sized men who moved as sleekly as cats. Before she realised it, the pair of men had scaled the castle wall and leapt into the gatehouse.

The intruders were upon the guards before they had even a chance to scream.

The Lamorians' bodies slumped to the ground, blood running freely from gaping slits across their necks. One of the intruders let out a low whistle, and another four Northemers materialised like ghosts. One was carrying a wooden casket. The wolf slunk back into the shadows as the intruders opened the gate. There were too many of them for her to overpower. She contemplated howling to give a warning to the castle, but it would only draw the Northemers' attention, and they would be rid of her as quickly as they had seen to the guards. She would have only one chance to raise an alarm, and she would have to choose the exact right moment. She couldn't sacrifice her life. The voice told her that her protection was needed beyond this night.

She followed the Northemers as they set off on foot through the castle woodland. They kept a surprisingly swift pace. The wolf trailed them as close as she dared, past the tiltyard and through the castle's northern grounds. They came to a stop outside the outer gate and waited until the patrolling guards on the battlements were out of sight. The intruders silently dispatched four guards at the gatehouse, dragging their bodies inside. Then they did the same thing at the next castle gate.

The Northemers slipped into the inner courtyard, where they came across a hapless servant. The man's mouth opened as if to scream, but a flying axe to the chest distorted his cry into a gurgle of blood. A kitchen boy appeared from a side door of the castle, his eyes wide with horror. His mouth gaped as if he too would scream, but he was quickly stopped by the smallest of the intruders, a hooded figure who muzzled the boy with a tattooed hand – the tattoo an intricate red-and-yellow feather extending up the Northemer's wrist. The intruder then pressed a knife to the boy's throat.

'Do you want to live?'

The wolf stepped a little closer, intrigued. The Northemer's voice belonged to a girl – one who spoke perfect Lamorian.

The boy nodded vigorously.

There was a flash of white teeth, a grin, from under the Northem girl's hood.

'Good.' She removed her hand from the boy's mouth and put away her knife. She pointed to the casket one of the Northemers was still carrying. 'Do you see that?'

The boy nodded again, his chest heaving with muffled sobs.

'Deliver it to the man they call Horace.'

The casket was dropped at the boy's feet.

At that moment, another of the castle's inhabitants appeared at an open window along the west wing. The wolf's fur bristled.

It was *her*. The one she must protect.

Arisa looked like she was only passing through, heading

toward the main keep, but she stopped at the window and peered into the darkness, as if sensing the intruders' presence.

The Northem girl clamped her hand over the servant boy's mouth and stared at Arisa. She tilted her head curiously. One of her fellow Northemers raised a loaded bow and pointed it at Arisa. The wolf advanced to attack the man, knowing she had little chance of covering the distance in time, but she froze when the Northem girl held up her free hand and, with a flick of her wrist, stopped the arrow in mid-air.

The wolf pushed aside her curiosity about the magic she'd just witnessed to focus on Arisa's safety. *Go now,* she thought, planting the words in Arisa's mind. *Your guardian is waiting for you.*

Arisa appeared to hesitate. She stared intently for another moment, before giving a slight shrug and disappearing out of view.

The Northem girl released the servant boy. 'We're going now. Count to two hundred before you leave this spot. Do not raise an alarm, or we'll be back for you. Do you understand?'

The boy nodded frantically.

'A wise choice.' The razor-sharp edges to the girl's voice didn't invite defiance. She thrust a closed hand toward the arrow that was still suspended in the air and flicked open her fist. The arrow burst into flames and disintegrated.

The boy choked back sobs. His legs shook violently. His eyes fell to his feet, planted in the pool of blood spreading from the slain servant, but he didn't move. And as stealthily as they had arrived, the Northemers were gone.

Get Your Copy of The Water Catcher's Rise

You can find out more about and purchase any of Kylie's books via **www.kyliefennell.com** or the below QR code.

AUTHOR'S NOTE

I believe magic lives in every book. The written word has the ability to transport you to different times and places. You're drawn into new worlds – worlds created entirely in the imagination of the author. I don't think it gets any more magical than that!

Yet the magic doesn't happen because of the author alone. It takes a support crew like no other to bring a book into the world.

I would like to acknowledge and thank my magical crew for their unwavering support in bringing my words to life.

Thank you, Mum, for encouraging my love of reading and writing from such a young age. I treasure the memories of the frequent trips to the library and you setting me up in the back-yard with a picnic so I could read or write. In more recent years I've really appreciated the confidence you and Geoff have expressed in me and my writing.

To Nathan, Arty, Dad and the rest of my family members, thank you for your endless encouragement – it has meant a lot. Among my family I count Matey and my super fan, Hannah. Love you all a million squillion.

When it comes to the writing stuff, I "literally" couldn't have done it without my Write Club – a group of brilliantly talented authors in their own right. Alyssa, Anna, Jodie and Lane, it's hard to find the right words to express my gratitude for everything you have done. And by everything, I mean your valuable critique, your passion for my stories, your keen editing eyes and your pep talks. Every writer needs a cheer squad like you.

My editors, Claire Bradshaw and Aleesha Paz – you are absolute wizards with words. You have lifted my work to levels I could never have achieved alone. Thank you for your guidance and truly excellent editing skills.

Thank you to the other writers and early readers who have helped me immeasurably throughout my writing journey. There are too many to name but please know I am forever grateful for your support. That being said, I'd like to give a special mention to one of my earliest beta readers, Sally, who I haven't managed to scare off…yet.

A shout out must go to the Lighthouse and #AusWrites gangs, and the amazing crews at *The Long Way Home*, *Queensland Writers Centre*, *Australian Writers' Centre* and *Aussie Speculative Fiction*. Your organisations and the opportunities you provide keep the writing community (including writers like me) connected and strong.

Finally, I want to thank you, the reader. Giving your time to reading someone else's words and living in their world takes commitment, so I'm incredibly honoured you chose to spend time with me and my world.

ABOUT THE AUTHOR

Kylie Fennell has made a 25-year career out of wrangling words, working as a journalist, editor and content creator, and more recently an author of speculative fiction. If she wasn't a writer, she'd be a superhero librarian – conquering the Dewey Decimal System by day and saving the world one book at a time by night.

As an Australian writer of European and Aboriginal (Gumbayn-ggirr and Bundjalung) descent she likes to explore culture and identity through her writing, as well as magic…always magic!

Kylie lives in Brisbane (Yuggera and Turrbal Country) with her husband, son and too many pets.

To find out more or to purchase Kylie's books go to *www.kyliefennell.com*.

If you want to stay up-to-date with Kylie's writing **or be part of her book review team** you can sign up to her mailing list via her website. All subscribers receive a **free** book – *Seeds from the Story Tree* – a collection of award-winning speculative fiction stories and other short works, exclusive to Kylie's subscribers.

You can also connect with Kylie on social media.

facebook.com/kyliefennellauthor

twitter.com/kylie_fennell

instagram.com/kylie_fennell

bookbub.com/profile/kylie-fennell

goodreads.com/Kylie_Fennell

pinterest.com/kyliefennell

tiktok.com/@kyliefennellauthor

patreon.com/KylieFennell

BEGINNINGS: THE KYPRIAN PROPHECY – AN ORIGINS NOVELLA

Get it now for free!

No Email Address Required

"Only a fool can't understand that there cannot be light without the darkness, and that power lies in harnessing the very thing people are scared of."

As a silver-eyes Laha has an extraordinary ability to harness the power within nature. She is also a royal companion to the Kengian Princess Mary, and with all of Kypria finally at peace Laha should be content…but she is far from it.

Laha has lost her powers and a darkness claws away inside her. She doesn't fit in at the Lamorian court, nor does she want to. She yearns for a life of excitement and adventure, but most of all she yearns to regain her powers and understand her dark urges.

The answer arrives in the form of a mysterious fortune teller whose prophecy and presence threaten to destroy everyone Laha cares about including the Lamorian Prince Emberto. Despite this she is drawn to the fortune teller and the woman's offer to help her realise the full potential of her powers...if she's willing to embrace her darkness.

Laha's choices lead to discoveries about her own identity and her friends being caught up in a deadly showdown between the most powerful of all Kengians – the Firemasters.

Beginnings is a stand alone novella that also sets the scene for the Kyprian Prophecy series and Book 1 – ***The Firemaster's Legacy***.

Beginnings is **available for FREE** on all major online book retail sites including Amazon Kindle, Apple, Google Play, Kobo and Nook. No email address required!